Into His Keeping

GAIL FAULKNER

ELLORA'S CAVE
ROMANTICA PUBLISHING

An Ellora's Cave Romantica Publication

www.ellorascave.com

Into His Keeping

ISBN 9781419961199
ALL RIGHTS RESERVED.
Into His Keeping Copyright © 2007 Gail Faulkner
Edited by Mary Moran.
Cover art by Syneca.

Electronic book publication April 2007
Trade paperback publication 2010

With the exception of quotes used in reviews, this book may not be reproduced or used in whole or in part by any means existing without written permission from the publisher, Ellora's Cave Publishing, Inc.® 1056 Home Avenue, Akron OH 44310-3502.

Warning: The unauthorized reproduction or distribution of this copyrighted work is illegal. Criminal copyright infringement, including infringement without monetary gain, is investigated by the FBI and is punishable by up to 5 years in federal prison and a fine of $250,000.
(http://www.fbi.gov/ipr/)

This book is a work of fiction and any resemblance to persons, living or dead, or places, events or locales is purely coincidental. The characters are productions of the author's imagination and used fictitiously.

INTO HIS KEEPING
∽

Special Thanks To...

J. and C. Thank you both for the gift of your experience and insights. Your gift of honesty is stunning. To A., whose support and understanding are priceless gifts.

Trademarks Acknowledgement

⊛

The author acknowledges the trademarked status and trademark owners of the following wordmarks mentioned in this work of fiction:

BrainSUITE: BrainLAB AG Corporation

Corvette: General Motors Corporation

Dairy Queen: American Dairy Queen Corporation

Dodge: DaimlerChrysler Corporation

Fleet: Blain Pharmaceuticals

Ford: Ford Motor Company

GQ: Advance Magazine Publishers Inc.

Harvard: President and Fellows of Harvard College Corporation

Hemi: DaimlerChrysler Corporation

Mustang: Ford Motor Company

Navigator: Ford Motor Company

Presbyterian: Presbyterian Medical Services Corporation

Princess Diary 2: Disney Enterprises, Inc.

Q-tip: CONOPCO, Inc.

Star Wars: Lucasfilm Entertainment Company Ltd. Corporation
Super Bowl: National Football League Uninc. Association
Superman: DC Comics Warner Communications Inc.
Transformers: Hasbro, Inc.

Chapter One

Holdin pulled his pickup to a stop half a block away from the little white house with friendly green shutters. The diminutive home was bursting with life and he half smiled. That was how it should look. There were bright toddler toys scattered about the yard and a blue bicycle had been dropped in the grass next to the front steps.

In the back, the oppressive blaze of late summer sun was filtered through shade trees. Tall leafy guardians over the fun to be had on short slides and a turtle sandbox. Abruptly two children burst from the back door and added the raucous melody of a family to the scene.

Holdin forced his gaze to linger on the picture the family made. Pain tightened around his soul and he opened himself to it. This had to be over at some point.

Today he was going to lay her to rest. It was the reason he'd come here. The compulsion to look at this house was a bit like visiting her grave. This was the last place he'd seen her. For him, the future as he knew it had ended here. He needed to let it rest here.

He'd only had her for little more than a spring. She appeared in his world in late January, disappearing from it in early July. One golden spring when his life had been complete. In the arrogance of youth, they hadn't been aware the relationship consuming them was the rarest of gifts. A pure expression of a dominant and his woman. She'd created hungers in him that he'd planned on exploring for a lifetime. His perfect, precious Jill. Freely, she'd given him her soul and the price had only been his life. Then she was gone as abruptly as she'd arrived in his world.

The day after Fourth of July she hadn't answered her phone. The memory played before his eyes, obscuring the summer afternoon and wrapping his world in winter. He'd become a barren landscape of dead emotions and frozen future. That summer evening had removed the sun from his world and he'd never found a way to get it back.

When he pulled up to this house that evening, he could feel its emptiness even before he stepped out of the old pickup. Walking up the short path was a baffling pain he couldn't understand. The house was dark when there should have been lights smiling at him through the windows, not shadows that faded to blackness. Some part of him had known her soul was not here anymore. He hadn't knocked, just kicked the door in. He'd wanted to believe he was panicking because he sensed danger. Not because he sensed nothing at all.

There were bits of her and her father everywhere but empty closets were as final as a suicide with no note explaining why. Eventually he had to accept that they were gone and he didn't even have the closure of a "goodbye" to hang his grief on. He'd never known silence could be vicious.

The loss destroyed him and then it rebuilt him into a modern-day hero as he would never have imagined being.

So this was the day he had to give up Jill for good. Today was the first day of training camp and he wasn't there. He'd thought he'd given up football the day he'd announced his retirement after last season. It hadn't been that day. Today was the day he gave it up. Not being in training camp was the final step. He really was out of the public eye.

No more flickering hope that she would call, find him, show up at a game. No more thrusting himself in front of the cameras because he needed to be visible to as many people as possible so Jill would know where he was. His entire adult life had been a quest to make it easy for her to come back to him.

He'd shaped himself into the king of the gladiators as ruthlessly as any man who'd walked the blood-soaked dirt in the original Coliseum. Holdin had poured out his soul on a thousand fields of honor and still she'd not come back.

He couldn't convince himself that she was dead. Her spirit still walked this earth or he'd have felt her leave. Their connection was that strong. But it was time she was dead *to* him. He had to find the strength to let her go. For fifteen years he had battled this moment. Now that it was here, the pain filled him with a darkness he couldn't fight his way past.

Watching the children play, Holdin's big body shuddered as he let soul-wrenching sorrow wash through him. What would their children have looked like? He turned away from the thought as it sliced a new piece of his soul off into the abyss. His future was not her future. It never had been.

Damn you, Jill!

An aging Ford Taurus drove slowly past him and down the street. The rumble of the motor reminded him of the bull the vehicle had been named after. He watched it because he couldn't look at that house anymore. Time to go. He had one more stop to make in town. One more place to gouge out of his heart so he could finally get on with the rest of his life.

* * * * *

Jill slid into the old soda fountain booth, gazing around in amazement. It was exactly the same. The shine had faded but chrome and linoleum still seemed to coat every surface from the bight red booths to the black-and-white-checkered floor. Nothing had changed.

Closing her eyes, a little over fifteen years fell away and she was eighteen again. Every cell in her body was in a frenzy of hormonal euphoria as *he* slid in the booth beside her. Tall, terminally cute, *he* was Holdin Powell. His long arm folded around her shoulder, a large hand pulling her body into his hard, muscled side and his head dipped down to whisper in her ear, "Hey, sexy," as he bent to drag his tongue up her neck to her earlobe.

The move was a public display as several other guys slid into the booth across from them. He owned her and he'd been making sure every other male knew it since the moment they'd met. His open possessiveness never failed to turn her on. She tried to disguise it but didn't do it very well. She knew he knew. And he liked it, liked how she glowed for him.

She responded with a wild blush as her neck arched to accommodate him. "Behave, Holdin," Jill gasped as her body clenched. There was no controlling him or her. Heat sizzled deep in her womb like a low-burning fire that never quite went out. She smoldered and all he had to do was look at her for the embers to flash into full blaze.

His lips still nibbling on her neck, the arm around her shoulders bent so his hand glided possessively into the loose, modest neckline of her top. Long hard fingers grazed her collarbone and came to rest just brushing the top of her breast. Not actually groping her but making it clear he had a right if he wanted to. This possessive touch thrilled her. It always did. It was such an erotic expression of their relationship and his wanting her. Sexy and adult, he made her special in ways she hadn't known it was possible to be. Other guys looked at her and she saw it in their eyes. They wanted what Holdin had.

He saw it too. She knew he loved that in his casual, cool way. He showed her off as his woman. He was proud of her. Holdin acting as if she were the most beautiful woman on earth made it so. He was the fantasy, the embodiment of everything she'd ever dreamed of and he couldn't keep his hands off her. Life was perfect. Absolutely perfect.

"I can't behave, woman," he growled into her neck. "You drive me nuts."

Jill shuddered under the onslaught of sexual heat he always drove her to. He was the type of good-looking that wet girl's panties at twenty paces. He didn't walk. He prowled with all the controlled power of a lion who owned his world. He possessed the body of a young Greek god and the cool attitude of an alpha male who is master of his domain. Holdin was "it" in every possible way.

Before Holdin, she'd thought her slightly plump body was fat. Her full breasts had developed early, as had her hips. She was rounded with womanly curves that she'd despised until Holdin looked at her. His look had been heavy-lidded sensuality from the first, and he'd truly been there from the first moment she stepped into The Connersville Major Department Store.

She'd passed the required tests for running a register and was the newly hired early morning cashier. They'd been happy to get a girl who didn't have children to put on a school bus or other complications. The store was probably one of the last of its kind but still going strong. It included a grocery department, full home supplies, furniture, office supplies, clothing and a jewelry counter along with a soda fountain.

Shy and nervous, she'd picked up her timecard and work schedule from the personnel manager. Steeling herself with a deep breath to face walking into the staff room, Jill turned away from the manager's desk to see the unbelievably cute guy leaning against the door she needed to exit through.

"That's all right, Mr. Blain," he'd said casually. "I'll show her where to go." The busy manager nodded in relief and went back to the stack of papers on his desk, abandoning Jill.

As the door closed behind them, he'd grinned down at her from his studly height. "Hi, I'm Holdin. You're Jill, right?"

All Jill could do was nod as his hand landed gently on the small of her back. He didn't exactly have his arm around her, but almost. Suddenly Jill couldn't breathe as she glanced shyly up at him. He didn't seem to notice. Fighting back the embarrassing blush rushing up her neck, Jill managed to get out the doorway and partway down the hall without stumbling.

"Your first day is tomorrow?"

"Yes, I guess they needed an opener pretty bad."

They walked through the busy store to the back. "Lockers are in here." He took her into a relatively small room with a door leading out to the back parking lot. "This one is almost empty. You can share it with me." He offered as he stopped at a locker midway down the line and opened it to show her how the old latch worked. The lockers were the old-fashioned full-length ones. Big enough for a person to step in, Jill thought as she watched him.

"Um. Okay" was the only thing she could manage to say while she stared dumbly as his large hands. Giving herself a stern mental shake, Jill dredged up reason with great determination. "Are you sure? I mean…" But then he grinned at her and her thought processes snapped off again. He was just too beautiful to speak to.

His grin was intimate. "I'm sure." He abruptly stopped and a very concerned look crossed his perfect face. "You don't mind, do you? Sharing with me, I mean."

Jill knew her body was consenting like crazy and he probably recognized it. She shook her head and bit her lip. His intense gaze made her warm in places she was uncomfortably aware of.

His eyes remained on her face as his fingers came up to graze her flushed cheek. "Good."

Passing out would be just too embarrassing. Her eyelids fluttered down as she tried to breathe through the heat his touch ignited.

"Come on," he said softly, his big hand at her back again. He turned her and they moved to the time clock beside the door. He showed her how to line up her card on the old time clock and where to put it in the slots on the wall.

"I'll be here at six when you get in. I work the early shift too. If you have any problems, just ask me. It's a good place to work, but you have to be careful of some of the guys." His deep voice was sincere and Jill nodded. She couldn't think of a thing to say. What was she going to do? Argue that she didn't have to avoid the unknown "guys"?

The next day at her lunch break, he was in the crowded locker room talking with a group of men. Being the youngest of the group didn't seem to make him the "boy" in it. As soon as Jill came through the door, he excused himself and was at her side.

"Hey, how'd it go?" He took her uniform smock as she slipped out of it as if he'd been doing it forever and hung it up in the locker.

"Great" was all she could manage while what seemed like the entire staff population acknowledged Holdin and watched them as he deftly took charge of her. His touch had clamped a lock on her vocal cords and sent butterflies flitting around her lower belly in mind-boggling abandon.

He was very well liked, it seemed. The men clapped him on the back or called friendly, though slightly rough comments. Several of the women slid assessing glances at Jill and tried to joke suggestively with Holdin. He was polite but his attention always turned back to Jill. His complete command of both her schedule and her needs was baffling.

Jill glanced around nervously. She knew the signs. He was popular, obviously sought after by the entire female half of the staff regardless of the woman's age. She was a new girl and not skinny. Nothing about his attention made sense except the worst possible outcome for her.

As he was about to shut the locker with her bag lunch in his hand along with his, Jill frowned up at him before he could touch her again. "Why are you doing this?" she whispered urgently.

"What?" Holdin asked seriously and subtly moved so her back was to the locker, the tall open door concealed her on one side and his big body shielded her from anyone else's view. He'd managed to put the two of them in an intimate space, blocking out the chaos of the group going to lunch around them. Everyone who started at six had lunch now. Later shifts would have it after this crew got back on the floor or stockrooms.

"Why are you being to so…so nice to me?" Jill asked directly, her eyes searching his face. "You don't even know me."

Holdin studied her silently for a second. "Do you want me to back off?" he asked, ignoring her "why" question and asking one of his own.

"I don't know. I don't know *you*," Jill responded, confused.

"I know." He smiled slowly. It was the brain-scrambling grin again. "So let's get to know each other, Jilly-girl. Okay?"

Jill nodded again and clenched her legs together. The clench reaction was as new and shocking as everything else. His free hand let go of the locker door, allowing it swing open slightly. Holdin's hand slowly raised to Jill's face, his index finger bent so his knuckle gently rubbed her bottom lip, which she was biting again.

"Stop that," he crooned softly. "It's sexy as hell and you need to go easy on me, woman. I'm a helpless male, you know. Slave to my hormones. Try to be gentle with me, Jill."

She burst out laughing at his silly comments. They both knew who was in control and it wasn't her. He'd called her "woman". It was almost too much. Laughing up into his smiling face made her dizzy on a cotton candy type of high. His hand moved from her mouth to casually reach around her, pulling her up against his body so he could kick the locker door shut. It was done so fast and smoothly she hadn't even stopped chuckling before he released her and had a hand on her back again as they walked out of the locker room. She had no idea which direction they were going.

That was when she knew it didn't matter if this was some sort of joke. Being the center of Holdin's attention, even for a little while, was worth it. She'd worry about the crash and burn later.

He grabbed her hand. "Lunchtime, dollface." he announced as they strolled into the larger staff room.

Holding hands meant they were dating. It was the sign that said "Holdin's woman". Jill knew it but was to breathlessly shocked and then thrilled to question him. She ate lunch with Holdin and didn't mind at all as he made introductions. It was nice not to have to sit alone and watch people chat. Being the new hire could have been intimidating in this situation. It was late January and too cold to eat lunch outside. Everyone had to gather here. Holdin put her at ease as simply as that. Not only was she included at the center table, she was accepted as Holdin's woman.

There were questions and a few almost nasty comments from some of the other women. Holdin put an end to the nasty comments by acting as if the women had to be joking and then ignoring the subject. The older men around the table could have been more of a problem, Jill realized. Holdin took care of that too. At his side, no one bothered her more than once.

His attention hadn't been a joke. No, it was almost the most amazing thing that had ever happened to her. Holdin surrounded her, folding her into his world. She was his woman. His girl from the first day she'd stepped into The Connersville Major Department Store.

Holdin became the center of Jill's world in ways that were movie cool, right down to being the type of glossy yet rugged good-looking that graced the pages of *GQ*. Last year, as a senior in high school, he'd been the star quarterback of the football team, he'd lettered in both track and football. His easy personality made him popular no matter where he was and he made her the instant queen of his world.

She'd learned that Holdin was taking a year off school to work because his father thought he needed to know what it felt like before going to college. Besides, his dad had been a stock boy in this store before he went to college and considered it a building block to settle the boy down and show him the value of an education. Holdin said his dad was trying to scare him into taking his future seriously and understanding what he'd end up doing for the rest of his life if he didn't.

Privately, Jill was pretty sure Holdin didn't need the scare tactic, but she was glad he was there instead of in his first year of college somewhere. The reasons she was there were much more complicated. Not that she told him that. Her story was well rehearsed and he'd not pressed her on it. When they were alone together, they usually had other things to do.

She'd never know if she'd made the right choice. Not telling Holdin the truth about her life was probably what sentenced her to the last fifteen years of loneliness. At the time, it had seemed like the only choice. Experience had taught her there was seldom only one choice in anything. At the time, her father had been so paranoid, so protective. He had reason to be just that, but at eighteen, she really should have made some choices for herself. She'd thought she was protecting Holdin with her silence. Perhaps she had managed to give him the gift of safety. Look at what he'd become without her.

Again in that familiar booth, the past evaporated and Jill reluctantly let it go to focus on the present. She looked up to see the man-child striding back to her from the soda fountain counter. He was now the center of her world. He was the reason she was here on what could only be called a desperate mission. *So much like his father*, Jill mused as he slid the tall fountain glass of water in front of her. The boy naturally took charge where he could. Strong and tall, he would be the image of his father's genetic blueprint in a few years.

"Here's the ice water. Are you sure you don't want to sit in the corner booth? It's not so bright. Right here by the window is too much, Mom."

"No. This is fine. Really. I'm fine. A few minutes and we'll go get a motel room. If you go look in aisle four, I bet they still have an excellent selection of hot rod magazines. I'll be all right in a minute."

"I can sit with you. I'll look at the magazines later. It's no biggie, Mom."

"Right. How cool is that? Sitting with your mom. Go on."

His chuckle was too deep for a fourteen-year-old and his legs too long as he turned and strolled away in a rolling gate. Jill watched him go, partly to keep her head turned away from the afternoon sun streaming in the wide windowpane beside her and partly because she couldn't take her eyes off him.

Fear settled into the booth with her as he disappeared out of the little soda fountain that was still part of the old-fashioned department store. Hopelessness whispered around her, bringing the shadows that refused to recede. They were her constant companions and never seemed far away these days. These few short days that pressed down on her. Time was her enemy. Each hour that slipped away was a loss she couldn't recover.

Jill remained turned away from the window, shielding her sensitive eyes from the sun. She sat there a moment, looking down at the black-and-white-block linoleum when two large cowboy boots stopped beside her at the table. It took a moment to realize they had not continued moving on. Worn jeans loosely sheathed muscular legs and her eyes reached the knees before it dawned on her that looking higher might involve more drama than she needed right now. It was too soon and much too late. Fate couldn't be so cruel! But then, had she ever seen a smile from it that wasn't cruel?

"Hello, Jilly-girl," a deep baritone rumbled above her head. The rich tones were foreign and so familiar they grated over her bent head like clawed talons.

She'd been in town for twenty minutes! This had to be some kind of record for locating the person one is on a wild goose chase to find. Fear washed over her. In its wake resigned endurance settled in for the painful exchange.

She looked up cautiously. Up the long male legs and over the generous bulge she knew would be below his belt buckle. Up his flat abdomen that showed not even the slightest bulge after fifteen years. His chest was wider, she noted, his neck a bit thicker and then there was his face.

Looking down at her were those familiar piercing hazel eyes surrounded by seductive dark lashes. His jaw was firmer and the lips above it were not stretched in the mobile grin she remembered. There was a rougher texture to his face that she didn't remember. It was grim as he gazed down at her. Dark blond hair, still naturally wavy, was tousled on his head. The prince of Connersville still wore his crown. But now he was more like king of the world, she mused in slightly hysterical shock.

"Hello, Holdin." She managed to sound almost normal. An amazing feat of will considering how many ways her emotions were trying to fly around her body. She was surprised by the burst of joy stabbing her heart. She'd come here to find this man. Now looking at him shook her to the core.

"Mind if I have a seat?" he asked seriously.

"Please do," Jill responded while silently marveling at how civilized this was.

"You're a surprise. Visiting the past?" Holdin asked, his voice icily controlled as he slid into the booth across from her, his big body folding into it with practiced ease.

"Ah. Something like that," Jill hedged as she tried to work her way through this moment. She'd imagined it a million times in the last few days, came up with a million different outcomes and still it was starkly terrifying.

One thing she did know, this was a very public place and there was almost no way to stop the shock that was coming. "Actually, I wanted to talk to you, Holdin. I was planning on calling the ranch this evening…" she trailed off as the reality of sitting across from this man shivered through her again.

"That's very thoughtful of you. I've been expecting a call for around fifteen years. However, since we're both here, maybe we could chat now," he offered calmly. He sounded friendly, but it didn't disguise the tight set of wide shoulders and almost rigid immobility of his face. Jill knew those signs for what they were. He was clamping down control on his emotions. He had amazing control. He always had it while she felt like an idiot.

Jill nervously glanced at the department store part of the establishment. "Ah, perhaps it'd be better if we met up later." She stopped and realized there was no later. Right now was going to happen in full view of anyone who passed by.

"Later's not a good time for me. I have some…" Holdin started then stopped as his eyes followed hers and they both watched the lanky young man stroll up to the table.

Holdin stood slowly as the young man approached them, his eyes measured each stride, the crisp features of a face he couldn't help but recognize. On that young visage he could see matching hazel eyes, a nose that was Roman straight and lips that weren't exactly full but not thin. The boy's jawline was a firm, clean line that jutted out at the moment as he approached the booth.

"Mom, everything all right?"

"Ah. Yes, yes it is. Drifter, this is Holdin Powell. Holdin, my son Drifter."

Drifter's jaw clenched in a restrained show of emotion that was as powerful as it was controlled. He held out his hand. "Mr. Powell," he greeted the tall man before him, and attempted to take control of the situation by initiating the handshake.

Holdin took the boy's hand in a firm shake. His eyes sliced to Jill for a brief second charged with unspoken emotions that churned with the heat of molten lava between them. "Your mother didn't mention her married name, son. However, it's very nice to meet you, Drifter."

"That would be because she never married, sir," Drifter replied, his young eyes challenging yet defensive as he regarded the older set that studied him.

Holdin sucked in a deep breath and let it out slowly, his eyes never leaving the youthful face that so closely mirrored his own. "Jilly-girl, you have something to tell me," he murmured softly.

His silky tone rumbled with a thousand unsaid things that made Jill flinch.

Drifter withdrew his hand and spoke before Jill could. "We were planning to give you a call this evening after my mother had rested. She's not feeling well. No one intended to spring anything on you, sir. We just pulled into town and she wanted a cool drink."

"No one has exactly sprung anything yet. However, when I call you 'son', am I being literal?" Holdin asked tightly.

Jill knew the softer Holdin spoke, the more intense his response to whatever was happening. His amazing control again. He used to baffle her with it.

Drifter frowned and laid a hand on Jill's shoulder in a protective move years past his age. "We can be gone in the morning, Mr. Powell. No need to burst a vein over it after all this time. We're not here to ask you for anything."

Apparently Drifter recognized the intensity in Holdin. Briefly Jill speculated on genetic imprinting and such. Her son knew his father was either mad as hell or something equally explosive. Drifter was reacting to the underlying aggression instinctively.

"Wait a second there. Give me a minute to understand this before you two go pulling another disappearing act. Which your mother is very good at, by the way." Holdin's jaw clenched.

"Please, both of you! This doesn't have to be a pissing contest. Would you both sit down and let me explain? Sit! Now!" Jill barked at the two glaring males.

Drifter slid into the booth beside Jill, Holdin folded himself into the seat across from them.

"I had hoped to do this much more gracefully," Jill started tiredly, "but life is seldom that kind. I wanted to call you and have a quiet chat about what happened fifteen years ago, not ambush you with information like this. I realize it's totally unfair to expect you to deal with the reality of a fourteen-year-old son."

"Tell me now, Jill." Holdin glanced around the empty shop. There were several customers in the department store portion and the soda fountain clerk had gone to help one of them. They were relatively alone except for curious glances from people too far away to listen.

Drifter shifted and focused on his mother. "Mom, are you sure you're up to this? You need to lie down. We've done what we came here to do and I'm fine with it. You don't have to go on if you don't want to."

"I'm not exactly fine with anything, son. I'd like to hear an explanation," Holdin interjected firmly.

"Don't call me 'son'." Drifter's head snapped back to the man. "I've done the math. She was barely eighteen when she got pregnant." Drifter's face was a bitter, accusatory mask. "We came here because she wanted to, not me."

Jill laid a hand on Drifter's arm, squeezing in a mother's message to stop talking. "Drifter! Stop it. This isn't his fault. It never was. I can't believe you're being so rude."

"He's protecting you." Holdin shifted back, his big body relaxing with a slight smile on his face for the first time. "Don't worry about it. I understand the instinct. Now, can you please tell me what's going on? And why he thinks you can't handle this?"

Jill heaved a sigh. There was no easy way to do this. "Okay, here's the really short version of what happened back then. I'll start there because it directly affects the situation now.

"My father was a bad guy on the run from worse guys. That's why we moved around like we did. When I walked in the door after the Fourth of July fireworks show, he already had the car packed. We had to leave. I didn't want to but I was terrified. Nineteen exhausting hours later and two states away, we had an accident. The car flipped and burned with my father in it.

"By the time rescue people got there I was the only person to take to the hospital. I was in a coma for fourteen days. There was no identification on me, the car and everything in it had burned. The car's VIN number showed it was a stolen vehicle from New Orleans. No one had any way to figure out who I was. The only thing they had to go on was the necklace I was wearing with the name Jill spelled out in the charm. Also, I was pregnant." Jill's hand went to the neckline of her T-shirt and she smiled softly as her fingers traced the charm beneath the cloth.

Jill continued. "I woke with no memories. Everyone expected my memories to come back at some point but they didn't. I wanted to keep my baby so the kind people at the hospital made my approximate age eighteen and put me in a program the city had for inner-city pregnant teens. Since I had no previous identity, I had to get a GED in the months before Drifter was born and qualified for technical education. I became a dental hygienist, a success story for the program and its funding."

Holdin's jaw clenched and he drew in a deep breath. "I should have put my name on the damn necklace," he growled softly. He felt as if he were holding on to sanity by a thread. The shock of looking into her face today had nearly killed him for a moment. He'd gotten over the fear of that death as he watched a smaller version of himself stroll up to the booth. He'd been almost sure he was going to survive the afternoon but this abbreviated explanation was doing its damnedest to beat the life out of him.

At his center, each clipped sentence stabbed him. He recognized terrible pain behind the emotionless, unvarnished relating of facts. It was a common tactic used by victims to distance themselves from pain. That simple fact was almost too much for him to bear. Alone and abandoned, the beautiful girl had been forced into being a woman. Not just for herself, but to protect the child she didn't even know how she'd conceived. He should have been there. She was his woman and that had been his baby. Holdin clamped down on the vortex of emotions, afraid she'd try to disappear as the boy wanted if she saw it.

Jill's gentle, tired voice continued. "Two weeks ago I had an incident and minor head trauma. When I woke up, I remembered everything." Jill spread her hands in a shrug. "I couldn't just call you. I wanted to see this place and we needed to talk face-to-face. It seemed important to do this in person. You deserved to at least meet your son while I could manage it." Jill leaned back and shut her eyes for a brief second of rest from the emotional storm silently raging around the booth.

The afternoon sun glaring in on them was beginning to stab at her along with the stress of this little meeting. It was all wrong. She'd imagined telling him so many times in the last few days. None of those times had it been in a rush with these two males growling at each other.

Holdin turned his gaze on Drifter. "Why are you concerned that she's not up to this? What's wrong with her right now?" he asked quietly in a man-to-man tone.

He restrained the impulse to lunge across the table and gather her into his arms. It was almost overwhelming as she wilted back in her seat and closed her eyes. He forcibly reminded himself that he didn't have the right to shelter her, nor could he. The young man sitting beside her was doing his level best to be a man and that ripped a strip off Holdin too. He was proud as hell of the spirit he saw in his son and at the same time mourned this boy's need to answer that instinctive call to protect his mother.

Jill opened her eyes in surprise. She'd expected questions, accusations, anger, not the calm inquiry that she'd just heard.

"Her accident was more serious than it appeared," Drifter answered immediately. "A very small sliver of her skull bone is lodged against her brain. They think it's stable but they want to do surgery to remove it. They also think that's why she remembered everything. It's possible she'll forget again when it's removed. Or if it moves on its own, she could…well, they don't know for sure what will happen. The point is, she insisted on coming here before surgery."

Holdin sucked in a hissing breath as he jerked in renewed shock. "What!?" He glared at Jill in obvious anger for a second then ruthlessly shut it down. Remaining calm was vitally important. Both Jill and the boy appeared ready to flee at any moment and he couldn't allow that to happen. Perhaps it was that he didn't really believe she was here. Whatever, he shoved his instinctive responses behind the mask he'd worn so long. "You should be in the hospital? How did you get here?" He glanced out the big window at the car parked in front. "You drove in this condition? Isn't that dangerous?"

"Stop yelling at me!" Jill snapped. "We drove. We live an hour away now and I needed to do this for my son. What if I wake up blank again? No memories of him even? I had to give him an option, some resource. I couldn't make him do this alone, damn it. It's too hard."

Jill leaned forward across the red tabletop. "You're his only hope if I'm gone. I came here to beg you not to let the state take him. That's all. I couldn't let them cut into my brain before I knew he was safe!"

"I can remember just fine for both of us, Mom. We don't need to beg him for anything." Drifter slung an arm around her shoulders. "Come on, you need to lie down. We're done here. I've met him. He's seen us. It's enough."

"I agree, you need to rest, Jill. Come out to the ranch and we can get you back to the hospital in the chopper as soon as you can travel." Holdin ignored the aggressive half of Drifter's statement, stood and moved back, obviously waiting for them to join him.

Drifter frowned up at the tall, stern-faced man beside him. "You have a helicopter?"

"Yep. Much smoother ride and a lot quicker than a car." Holdin nodded.

"Wait a second. I'm not going out to the ranch. I had to drive here from Dallas, I felt pretty safe on paved roads but the dirt road out there is a bit risky. Besides, what about your family and everything? You've told us nothing and I understand it's none of our business, but I don't want to suddenly invade your home, Holdin. That's not why we came and I don't want to face that kind of stress at the moment. We'll be fine at the motel."

"My family is right here, Jill." Holdin tried to relax as he continued. "The road is paved all the way out there. It has been for several years. Things have changed. What if we need to get you back to the hospital fast? Coming out to the ranch is the safest option."

Holdin looked at Drifter and used the man-to-man talk again. "I know you want to take care of your mother. This is the safest option for her."

Drifter searched Holdin's face worriedly. "Are you okay with us?" he asked with more insight than a boy his age should have. "You can't hurt her anymore. I'll not let you."

Jill answered before Holdin could. "Of course he won't hurt me! I know I've only had a short time to tell you about your father but I thought you got him. He'd never hurt me. Never." Jill glanced up at Holdin worriedly. "We can talk about this in the room."

"Mom, you've been in pain over him since the moment you remembered. You haven't told me everything but I'm not an idiot. I can read between the lines. That and I can hear you crying at night. Every night, since you got home from the hospital."

"Oh geez, baby. No, not because…" Jill looked up at Holdin again. The man before her was so much more than the lover she'd known. He was a stranger. And yet, looking at that face, hearing his voice, all of it nearly cut her in half.

Her memories had been brand-new. Intellectually she'd been aware they were events from fifteen years ago, but that didn't do a thing to distance her from the pain of them. She hadn't really had fifteen years to get over them, to coat them with the protective cushion of time. Emotionally, she'd been ripped away from the love of her young life just two weeks ago. She'd lost her father at the same time.

Jill tried again as she turned back to her scowling son. "Try to understand. When I remembered everything, it was not fifteen years old for me." She took a shaky breath as both sets of eyes watched her intently. "I lost my father, who I loved very much, Drifter. I've never mourned him. But you're right, I also lost Holdin at the same time. For me, it all just happened and I was very much in love with your father. Then there was the urgency of everything. It's overwhelming. I'm so sorry." Jill's shaking hands covered her face a moment. "I'm sorry I worried you. So sorry, baby."

"Mom," Drifter started, but Holdin interrupted him.

"Jill, relax. It's going to be all right. This is a huge shock to all of us." He dropped to his haunches beside them, bringing his big body to her eye level. One large hand rested on the table, the other on the back of the bench seat where both Jill and Drifter sat. "But you did the right thing coming to me, coming here. We can get through this. Now come home so we don't have to do this in front of the whole town." Holdin moved his hand to place on top of Jill's, which were flat on the table.

The connection was warm and comforting. They hadn't touched yet. Jill's hands naturally turned over to grip his as she looked into his eyes and smiled a bit sadly.

"You're doing it."

"What?"

"Taking possession of me. You did it the first time I saw you." Jill chuckled softly as she looked around her son into the eyes of a man who wasn't quite a stranger but wasn't her Holdin either. "I'm not eighteen anymore. It doesn't work that way."

Holdin's head tilted to the side slightly, his grip tightened on her hand and his lips ticked up in a slight grin. "Yeah? Is that what I did?"

"You know it is. I was barely hired here and hadn't even stepped out of the store's office and you had an arm around me. Mr. Blain agreed you could show me the staff room, not take possession of me."

"I was showing you around. As I recall, I didn't get my arms around you for a week." Holdin's voice dropped as he looked into her eyes and remembered that first kiss. But she wouldn't let him enjoy it.

"Bullshit. You might as well have hung a sign around my neck that said *Holdin's girl*," Jill accused in soft tones that sounded of youthful embarrassment and shy pride. Her smile and voice were at odds with the words.

"Hey, hey, can we not scar me for life?" Drifter interrupted, glancing between them. "I'm not old enough to hear this crap. We've all got whatchamacallits. So can we just figure this out right now? I mean what we're gonna do in the next hour. Mom, you need to lie down somewhere."

Holdin chuckled in a deep rumble. His hazel eyes crinkled with new lines around them that Jill had never seen. She was fascinated. Lean cheeks had always creased with his grin, but the changes of time hadn't detracted a thing from his heart-stopping good looks. It'd just added to it.

"Whatchamacallits?" he asked Drifter.

"You know, that stuff talk-show people are always bleating about. Issues. Discussing those seems to take way too much time. Getting to what needs doing is more important.

The deal is, we came here to meet you. That looks to be done. The reasons for doin' it are on the table. Mom has to have the surgery and she's scared of forgetting again so now I know who you are and there's nothing wrong with my head. I'll remember. I'm taking her to the motel so she can rest. The damn issues will be the same when she wakes up. No need to sling them around now."

"Agreed, your mother needs some rest. The ranch is twenty minutes away." Holdin stood up. "And you can meet your grandparents while she naps."

"No." Drifter slid out of the booth and stood to face Holdin. Almost six feet already, Drifter still had to look up to his father. "She wants the motel. That's where she goes. In case you hadn't noticed, she's already stressed. Goin' out to your place will add to that."

Identical hazel eyes sized each other up. The younger set in a defensive face while the older one's bland expression was a mask. Jill almost held her breath. The unexpected confrontation between these two was a bit surprising. She'd known there would be tension, but the maturity of her son's arguments was unexpected.

Holdin nodded curtly and pulled a cell phone out of his pocket. Looking out the soda fountain window and down Main Street, he obviously dialed the motel's number off the huge sign clearly visible from there.

"Mrs. Parkman?" he said politely as someone answered. "This is Holdin Powell. Is the room on the end, farthest from the road available? Excellent. Does it have two beds? Good. Please open it and leave two keys on the dresser. I'll be up to fill out the paperwork. Yes I know. No, of course not, ma'am. I have a friend in town and she's feeling ill. It will be her and her son staying. Correct. Yes. See you then."

Drifter turned and held out a hand to help Jill out of the booth. "Let's go, Mom."

Jill scooted out. "You're still doing the 'take charge' thing, Holdin. I can rent my own room."

"Oh Lord, get over it, Mom. He compromised. Don't you know anything about guys?" Drifter asked in mild male disgust.

Holdin's brows went up and he grinned at Drifter. Jill snorted and turned to exit the soda fountain and stopped abruptly. There were at least eight people standing near the entrance watching them. Some of the faces she vaguely recognized and names flashed through her mind but mostly embarrassment washed over her.

"Geez," Drifter murmured beside her.

"Time to go." Holdin stepped up between them. He slid an arm around Jill's waist, his other hand rested on Drifter's shoulder as he stepped forward. They swept through the little throng with Holdin nodding and smiling as if it were nothing to see him walking out of the department store with a boy who matched him feature for feature and the woman who'd disappeared fifteen years ago.

The motel was a long strip of rooms that opened to the parking lot. The garish orange and teal paint was a bit more faded now and still begging for a new coat. When it was new, the hotel court was supposed to have a tropicana feel to it. But the planters had been dirt holders and nothing more for quite some time. It was exactly the same as Jill remembered.

Jill pulled her Taurus into the parking space in front of the last room. Holdin's big Dodge king cab had been on her bumper and he pulled in right beside her. He was at her car door before she could put her feet down on the cracked pavement. Her head was pounding and she smiled tightly as he took her elbow as if to steady her.

Drifter was already at the room door, opening it. They'd all heard Holdin instruct the motel owner to leave it open. "Any bags to bring in?" Holdin asked Drifter as he gently steered Jill to the bed along the far wall.

"Sure, I'll get them," Drifter answered automatically, unaware the man was directing them all.

Holdin flung the spread back and Jill sank down on the cool sheets. Her eyes closed immediately. "I'd have lain down without the strong-arm treatment, Holdin."

"Yeah, but I feel better now," he answered her mild protest as Drifter came back in with two small bags. "You guys weren't planning on staying long." Holdin accusingly eyed the bags.

Jill could hear it in his tone. "We don't have much time."

Neither male had flipped on the lights nor opened the drapes. As Drifter kicked the door shut, the room was suddenly plunged into a murky twilight. Jill opened her eyes a crack to find Holdin looming in the narrow space between the two double beds, hands on hips, frowning down at her.

"You just going to stand there?" she asked.

"Yeah, I think so." Holdin ran a hand through his hair and shut his eyes briefly in a squeezing motion then he was gazing down at her again. "If I take my eyes off you again, you might disappear. So I can't."

What he'd really been doing was resisting the urge to wrap his body around her in some useless effort to protect, shield, somehow take the weight he could feel her carrying. The emotions that this encounter had generated were all fierce. Anger was pushed to the bottom of the pile because he couldn't afford it right now. The two he was having trouble suppressing were possessiveness and protection. Those were the ones she'd always triggered in him. Not the gentle civilized versions that would have been acceptable either. These were primal responses to Jill. They always had been.

Drifter flopped down at the end of the other bed, his long legs dangling over the end as the huge yellow mums on the orange bedspread seemed to explode around him. Even in the dim light, the mums glowed. His hands stacked behind his head as he stared at the ceiling. "Are you two going to fight?" he asked in a deceptively disinterested tone.

Holdin sat down on the yellow and orange bed behind his knees and relaxed back in the same position. The two of them only fit on the thing because they were at right angles to each other. "No." Holdin sighed. "This isn't fighting. This is issues. Fears. All that junk."

"You have fears?" Drifter asked in the same bored tone.

"Yep. I was in love with your mother. One evening she was gone and I couldn't find her. It hurt me bad. Now she's back and I've met you. I guess I'm sorta terrified that if I let you guys out of my sight, I'll not be able to find you again. Does that make sense?" Holdin asked his son conversationally.

Drifter grunted a male sound then after a few minutes' silence asked, "So you minded that she left?"

"Big time," Holdin confirmed. "Hired a private detective once. All I found out was that whatever her real name was, I didn't know it. Made me mad as hell. But I always wanted to find her."

Jill listened in silence as Holdin exposed his soul to their son in fearless honesty. The abbreviated sentences and blunt expressions males used with each other were so stark. It was a nakedness women always wanted to dress up with explanations.

She suspected Holdin was doing it deliberately. Letting Drifter ask whatever he wanted was not only bonding with the boy but explaining to her as directly as he could. Covering ground it'd take the two of them hours to go over because she was not brave enough to ask.

"You're not pissed? At us showing up, I mean." Drifter sounded slightly amazed but he still managed to inject a tone of boredom with the whole subject into his voice.

Holdin's tone didn't elevate or drop, he answered as calmly as the question was asked. "Hell yeah, I'm pissed. Royally. But not at you or your mom. It's hard to tell what I'm more ticked about right now. I guess your grandfather, who I knew as John Taylor. Whatever he was running from stole your mother and you from me. How 'bout you? You angry?"

"Yeah, guess I am." Drifter acknowledged the question Jill couldn't believe Holdin had asked. "I've been angry at you for a while. I might have been wrong about that."

Holdin grunted, neither agreeing nor arguing, simply a male acknowledgment of fact.

Holdin's acceptance of Drifter's emotions without judgment made a tear slip down Jill's cheek. She was pretty sure they couldn't see it. Her eyes were closed and she'd almost stopped breathing as the quiet conversation beside her unfolded.

"So you married or anything?" Drifter asked.

"No," Holdin answered bluntly. "What else you pissed at?"

"Well, the accident and all. I'm pretty sure Mom thinks she might change if she has the surgery. The doc says if she doesn't, it could kill her. I'm glad she remembered everything and all, but I don't want her to change or lose her." Drifter heaved a sigh. "No offense, but I don't wanna be shipped off to you either."

"None taken. You don't know me." Holdin helped Drifter clarify his thoughts.

"The whole thing sorta screws with a guy's head." Drifter went on. "But you seem kinda cool. I was expecting an uptight bast....geek."

"Why's that?"

"Well," Drifter paused, "she's not exactly a player. I figured anyone she'd go for had to be like her. You act all cool in public, but I didn't expect much from meeting you."

Holdin chuckled. "Did you just call me a player and your mother a geek?"

"Ah, no. Well, maybe. She's sleeping, right?"

"Not likely."

"I'm resting," Jill informed them. "When did I become a geek?"

"It's not like you're a terminal geek, Mom. You're cooler than most guys' moms."

"Thank you, brat. Good to know I'm not a killer geek. What makes him so cool anyway?" Jill wanted to know.

"His truck. It's got a Hemi. Way cool," Drifter informed her solemnly.

Holdin chuckled again while Jill gave a mock moan. "I should have known. The two car freaks have been united."

"Sounds like we share an interest." Holdin sat up slowly to face Jill on the other bed. "Jill, since you're obviously not sleeping, can you tell me a little more about exactly what's wrong with you?"

"If I spoke big-word Latin I could," she murmured with a smile on her face. This was nice. The quiet conversation was relaxed, calm. Much as she'd imagined things could be.

"The English version is I tripped and fell. Hit my head in exactly the same spot that had been weakened before and a tiny bone chip fell into my brain. They say it could have been there before and the other hospital missed it. No one knows. In any case, I passed out. Drifter found me when he got home from basketball practice. We think I was out for a couple hours. I woke up in the hospital and had full recall."

"Okay." Holdin scrubbed a hand down his face. "So why the reaction to light in the soda fountain? Is the chip pressing on something? What happens if it moves?"

"Stress," Jill answered succinctly. "I'm pretty sure the headache would have happened without a chip in my brain. Come on, Holdin. I know this has been an overwhelming shock for you. Think of it from my point of view. Meeting you could have gone better if you hadn't shown up at the soda fountain this afternoon. But it still wouldn't have been easy. I've been stressing about it and the other issues since I woke up in the hospital. That's the main reason the doctors agreed to this trip. My stress level is too high."

Drifter sat up at the end of the bed, rubbing his face in an unconscious mirror of his father's move. "Yeah, another reason I was expecting a geek or worse. The doctor wants her calm and relaxed, confident is the word he used, before he does the surgery. She's been stressed off the chart over you."

"This whole deal is off the charts. I doubt it's all me." Holdin glanced at his lanky son. "Your mother is worried about a lot of things but the biggest is you, son. She's trying to make sure you're okay, no mater what happens to her."

"I know." Drifter shrugged. "She obsesses about junk."

Chapter Two

ಐ

"Yeah, junk." Holdin looked at the woman lying on the bed in front of him and dragged in a deep breath. Not that he expected it to help much. From the moment he'd glanced at "the booth" his world had shifted. It'd gone on shifting like a fucking Transformer figure. Each new configuration of facts came with a kick to the gut.

In the last fifteen years, every time he'd walked into the department store he very carefully avoided looking at the soda fountain. This time he'd gone in there to look at it. It was time to let it burn through him and be done with it. It'd still taken him twenty minutes to prepare.

If he looked at the booth, he was looking for her. Damn, he'd grown to hate it. Hate the desperate, helpless need to look for her. Fifteen years and then this sucker punch. He'd looked up over the selection of nails in the elaborate, old-fashioned display trays and there she was.

She'd sat in the booth, her back almost turned to the window behind her as if she huddled in the shadow she made. His teeth had snapped in a hiss of indrawn breath as he stared at her. Could it really be Jill? Her head was tilted down as she gazed at the floor but it didn't matter. He knew those honey brown locks, the curve of her skull, the way she sucked all the air out of a room. Jill.

Holdin blinked, trying to clear his head. Looking at that booth was supposed to erase its significance from his soul. It was supposed to be empty like every other time he'd looked at it. For the first few minutes he really believed his mind had conjured her. What convinced him differently was the furnace blast to his soul.

His feet had felt the flames first. He couldn't stop those feet from moving. When he was standing beside her at the booth, he'd felt the fire lick up his legs with her gaze. Still unable to believe it was her, he'd almost been shocked when she didn't shimmer and evaporate as she lifted her face. That's when the backdraft caught him and the world as he'd previously known it burned away. Whatever happened next would put an end to his questions, hopes, fantasies and the millions of explanations he'd made up for her. Answers. Answers would probably rip away the sweet angel in his memories but he had to have them.

Not even in his darkest fits of rage had he come up with what had happened next. Her answers had hit him like a mammoth defensive line, one after another. The center of that line had been his son. No, nothing could have prepared him for that.

There would be DNA tests for legal reasons but Holdin had no doubt who the boy was. Or rather "whose boy" he was.

Just when he figured he had about enough deep cleat marks up his back from being trampled, the killer answer rolled over him. That one came armed to the teeth and looking for blood. Jill. She could be taken away from him again and there was nothing he could do about it. Nothing. Again.

Discipline, control, none of it mattered. The person he'd made of himself in the last fifteen years, all of it useless. She lay there with her eyes closed in this dark room like a wraith from the past, and yet her power over him was now tenfold.

She'd never been that model thin he detested. Her lush little body had always fired him up. Now its curves shouldn't have moved the man with the same ripping intensity. Shouldn't have made him grit his teeth and struggle to control the physical signs so her son wouldn't notice the monster boner he was getting over the boy's mom.

Her heart-shaped face was pale. The skin around those closed eyes seemingly paper-thin as dark lashes partially hid the shadows there. Her pert nose rose above those sensual, full lips that formed a perfect bow he'd never been able to resist. When she was eighteen, her angel face had been an almost shocking contrast to the lush body below it. Those curves were made for sin and he'd been no saint.

She hadn't grown much taller, he realized. Her face had matured but not changed. Or was it stress written across it now? He couldn't be sure. She was still an angel face but now it seemed the angel had peeked into the devil's den. Innocence was missing.

Her body appeared richer, an opulent playground for a man who knew what to do with it. Full breasts had matured into an impressive bustline. Where she'd had a tiny waist and rounded hips, she now had undulating lines that tempted him to touch. Soft and lush, she looked like a Rubens' angel who could take a hardened male and make him beg for mercy. It wasn't a weak softness he saw in her. No, that would have been easy to deal with. This was a fully developed woman's strength. She was decadent temptation tucked into a neatly conservative T-shirt and loose jeans as if she had no idea how effective her charms were.

Her masses of golden brown hair were now cut to feather around her face in a charming frame for those huge eyes. It had been longer back then. He loved to run his fingers through it. When they made love, she had reacted strongly to his fist in her hair. He'd enjoyed that bit of caveman play and was glad she liked it. Sometimes he hadn't been able to control the fierceness of his response to her.

He'd always known why she had liked it and he knew why he'd needed it. Question was, did she? He'd never fully explained it to her, thinking he had time to show her how sweet her needs could be. He hadn't wanted her to be afraid of her spirit. Had she learned without him? Did she know herself as he knew her? That question moved through his mind, leaving an acid taste in his mouth.

As a young man, he'd been very aware of the sweet submissive living in her soul. He'd also known she hadn't had the benefit of a parent who understood her. Holdin's father had known his son's nature very early. His guidance had sometimes seemed harsh but as he reached adulthood, Holdin had understood exactly what his father had been so carefully teaching him. His nature made him strong in ways that could be dangerous if Holdin hadn't been completely aware of it.

Jill's father was not an insightful, nurturing sort who could help his daughter understand herself. No, he was a blunt man. One who expected Jill to be a good daughter but seemed to have little to offer beyond that. There was no mother present in the house and Holdin had never pressed for the reason.

Holdin had been sure he was doing the right thing by going slow and showing Jill how stunningly beautiful she was to him as the submissive she needed to be. He'd actually enjoyed the control it required of him to gently lead her down a path she often wanted to rush. He'd been so careful with her, believing they had a lifetime to make that journey.

When he turned sixteen, his father had been very direct about what was the wrong way to treat a woman. Honor and responsibility were the most important things about being a man. Rushing to gain his own satisfaction was being a selfish boy and Holdin had understood that lesson. His dad had made him read several books on his nature as a dominant, impressing him with both the dangers and the responsibilities of being who he was.

The fear that some clumsy fool had found the precious spirit in Jill and crushed her was crippling.

A seething wave of heat rushed up from his toes at the thought. Through the years, when he was in the middle of a bout of trying to forget her, he'd imagine her with another man. The outcome was always the same. Something in the room around him met its end and Holdin took out the remaining aggression by physically exhausting himself in a workout.

Holdin leaned forward to rest his elbows on his knees. Hands clasped, he took a few minutes to gaze down at the threadbare carpet. He needed to stop looking at her. No, he needed to think, and that involved not looking at her. It was damn difficult to look away. Irrational fear washed over him. He glanced up. She was still there. This was ridiculous.

"Drifter, let's give your mother a few minutes' peace and go take care of things at the motel office. There's a Dairy Queen across the road. Feel like something from there?" Holdin asked casually.

"Sure. You all right with that, Mom?" Drifter stood.

Jill's eyes opened to move between them, assessing. Holdin had the uncomfortable feeling she was reading his mind. He needed a few minutes but couldn't take the risk she'd be gone if he stepped out that door. Taking Drifter was like having her on a tether. She wasn't going anywhere. She said none of that.

"Thank you, Holdin. That's very thoughtful of you."

Holdin held very still to be sure he didn't jerk in offense. From an early age, control had been drilled into him. His father was very clear on that. Men do not lose control. The stronger his emotions, the more it became his responsibility to control them. Later that control had enabled him to build a career few were capable of. Right now it was all about Jill. Just as it had been from the moment she stepped into his life.

"Glad you think it's thoughtful that I'd like to spend a little time with my son," he growled as he stood. It didn't matter that his motives were not exactly clear. She'd put him on the defensive and he was aware this was a small part of it. This was a sharp, new pain she could inflict by treating him like a stranger.

Okay, he was a stranger to his son but whose fault was that? His brain was pounding as he had to answer himself that it certainly wasn't her fault. Best just do what he'd suggested.

"We'll be back in half an hour."

Holdin suspected there was no amount of time with his son that could make this more real, less surreal. The small measure of relief not looking at Jill gave him was nothing compared to the stark panic that came over him every time he glanced at Drifter.

How did a man become a father at this late date? What made him think he'd have been any good at it even if he'd been there from Drifter's birth? He would have been nineteen and green as spring grass. His life would have been totally different and he surely wouldn't have had as much to offer this man-child. Would it have been worth it? Could any part of this actually have happened for a reason?

Pointless questions shot through him in a maddening circle. The time passed too quickly and not fast enough then they were back at the room door.

The woman sitting at the small table in the motel room waiting for them was nothing like the one they'd left. Jill's small, round body was held erect, her head high. She'd gathered a regal calm about her that Holdin had never seen before. She was a shell of the girlfriend he'd known but so much more. And almost nothing remained of the shocked, pale woman who'd been lying on the bed when he left.

The curtains were open and the retro Fifties, draped in the Seventies, furnished motel room was brightly lit in all its faded orange and yellow glory.

"Ah, I hope both of you are feeling better," Jill greeted them. Deep in her gut, it felt as if the trembling never quit. Even though Holdin appeared interested in them, she couldn't trust it. This was too important. All the emotional issues were getting in the way and she would not let her son's future hang on that hook.

Lord, this was hard. She needed to be direct like a man would be. Managing that seemed monumental. Melting all over the man wouldn't get her the security she desperately needed. Desperate people had to do the hard things.

Drifter laughed. "Food always works, Mom. You know that. Looks like you're feeling better?"

"Yes. I should warn you, Holdin, he eats more in one sitting than I do in a week." Her eyes were laughing with her son when she turned to him. Then she sobered. "We need to discuss a few things. With your success, I assume you've encountered a lot of women who claim you fathered their child. We expect you to want a DNA test and will be happy to participate. We don't expect any support funds. The main issue is my health. If I'm not able to care for Drifter's future properly, I sincerely hope you would be willing to make arrangements."

She sat there with her hands folded in her lap and actually smiled at him after that little speech. Holdin's eyes bore into hers steadily. He'd thought they'd reached seriously fucked up before. He'd been so wrong.

"I think we have issues significantly deeper than my ability to make arrangements for Drifter's future." Holdin slowly sat down on the end of the nearest bed. "We need to discus them in private, Jill. As far as a DNA test, we'll do one to secure his inheritance legally. That's the only reason. I'd like to acknowledge him as my son now if that's all right with the two of you. Support is something you and I can work out and I intend to take a great deal of personal interest in your health."

Holdin paused as he studied her. "Do you think you're leaving after this conversation? Is that it?"

Jill's face tightened at his blunt question. "No. But I want us to understand each other. We don't expect…um…I know you're used to people wanting something from you. Not that we don't, it's just…ah, it's different…" One of her hands fluttered up to her neck searching for something at the V of her T-shirt. A nervous reaction to his stern tone and her battle to remain focused on her goal. She quickly dropped it back to her lap and resisted frowning at him. The reason for her nerves was his thunderous face.

"Really, Holdin. There is no reason for this to get ugly." She raised a brow at him. "I'm trying to make this as painless as possible for you."

"Are you? I don't see it that way. I see you trying to make this ugly and small."

Holdin glanced at Drifter who was standing awkwardly at the end of the other bed watching them. "You're belittling me, us. Making it sound like having a son is just another business deal. You're assuming you know me from what you've read." Holdin stood and paced to the door. Turning, he leaned his back on it. Blocking the exit was almost unconscious, but as he crossed his arms to glare down at her, he recognized it. She was not escaping that easy.

"You've told me your story. Now let me tell you how it was for me. Not the shit you read in the paper, this is what really happened.

"What do you think a guy assumes when his girlfriend disappears without a trace? No, don't answer that, I'll tell you." He forestalled her as her mouth opened to answer. "I had to assume your father had found out we were lovers. I didn't know if you told him or he just knew. I figured he'd taken you away from me.

"The day after you disappeared, my dad received new orders. We were moving to a base in California. I wasn't going to the college I'd thought I was. After some serious arguing, I accepted my parents couldn't afford to send me to an out-of-state college. My father wouldn't hear of my not going. So that meant a state college in California. I had no way of telling you where to find me. I needed you to be able to call me, which meant you had to know where I was. I couldn't stand for you not to know.

"I figured being in the public eye somehow would do it. I had to be famous so you could keep track of me. Football was the only thing I could come up with and still make it through school. I was a third-string backup that first year. I planned to be the starting quarterback by the time I was a junior. Do you have any idea how fucking ridiculous that plan was? No third-string quarterback gets to be a starter. I did it. I did it because I had to know you could find me. My junior year I was first string and we went to a bowl game. I waited for your call. You didn't.

"I made up reasons for you. You'd never been interested in football. You might not have realized mine was the name you read. It went on and on, I was damn good at thinking up reasons you couldn't call me. So the next year I had to get my face plastered in every paper across the country. I predicted we'd be national champions at the beginning of the year just to get the press coverage. It worked. But then there was the rest of the team and the huge weight I'd put on them by needing to get my face in the paper for you.

"The press called me Superman and a bunch of other smack for dragging that team to the top on my back. It was goddamned true. I needed us to be national champions and do it spectacularly so you'd see me. You had to know where I was so you could call me. You didn't.

"I figured perhaps college ball wasn't big enough. You wouldn't read the sports page and we were only front-page news a couple of times. You could have missed it. I had more reasons why you didn't call but you couldn't miss the Super Bowl. Everyone knows who wins the Super Bowl. At least they do the day after." Holdin sucked in a breath and grimaced.

"First-round draft pick meant nothing to me. It meant I was going to a shitty team and I needed to get to the Super Bowl. So I did it again. I hounded, I bribed, I bullied those men into practicing in the off-season, working harder, being better. I lived and breathed football. I drove them like a freaking obsessed fiend. My second year in the pros we made it to the Super Bowl but we lost. And you didn't call. The third year we won it all. And you didn't call."

Jill's eyes barely blinked as she listened. Drifter had plopped down on the end of the other double bed.

"I became the biggest thing in football, the best. Money, fame, a freaking household name and you didn't call. I took on the biggest charities I could find, did commercials. Became spokesperson for household products. If you didn't watch football, you had to have seen me in those commercials, I figured. I did every damn thing I could think of and you didn't call.

"Don't try to make us, this, finding each other trivial. You struggled with no memories, no history. I lived with them every damn day. I built my life around them, on top of them. I became the man you see now so you could find me. I've loved you, hated you and died because you didn't call over and over again. You drove me to the edge of endurance and then you pulled the impossible out of my soul. With each success and disappointment it drove me to imagine what I thought was every conceivable reason you didn't find me. Every reason except this one. It never occurred to me that you didn't know me."

Holdin pulled away from the door and took the two steps to her, sinking to his knees in front of her. He reached out and clasped her hands, which were folded in her lap. Holding them gently in both of his, he looked into her eyes. "Living with the memory of you was just as damn hard as living without the memory of anything," he said softly. "Give us time, Jill. Don't run away again."

"Oh my God, Holdin!" Jill breathed softly.

"I know, I know. I made you my obsession in ways that seem frightening right now. But I got over it too. I gave up. It wasn't 'til after the second Super Bowl ring. The third one I did for me. I stopped waiting for that call. By then the drive and discipline were mine and I was mad. Mad about the years waiting, hoping. It's not like the time was wasted but somehow it felt that way to me." Humor hitched up his lip briefly. "I'd become one of the richest, most admired men in the country and I felt like I'd wasted my time on a woman who'd never wanted me. Not like I wanted her."

"But..." Jill leaned forward, her face clouded with frown.

"I get it. I know you came back as soon as you knew, as soon as you remembered. For you it was a few days." His hands glided up her arms as she leaned into him. He shifted forward his eyes never leaving hers. "Give us some time, Jill. This time it's us. We have a son. We'll be in each other's lives."

Jill's head was cautiously shaking "no" as she shrank back from him. "I'm not her! Holdin, the Jill you knew, the one you waited for isn't me anymore. She died in that car wreck. The person I am now woke up and was alone, pregnant and unwanted. She had no one to turn to so she had to be an adult. Since then, this person has been making her own way while taking care of a child. The Jill you knew adored you and her father. But between the two of you, she didn't have a self-driven bone in her body. I hardly know that girl. Do *not* mistake me for the girlfriend you kissed goodnight at three a.m." Jill's body now pressed back in her chair, creating as much distance as possible between herself and Holdin.

Fear, panic, desperation, and now the unbearable weight of his loss, all of it pressed down on Jill. His story was almost unbelievable. She'd seen his celebrity as a block to reaching him, not an open door. It intimidated the hell out of her and she'd assumed it came with tons of insulation between him and the general public. He was *so* somebody now and she was a dental hygienist. When they'd met it'd been much simpler, more equal. Now she was the mouse staring at the roaring lion.

He didn't say anything for a long moment as he absorbed her argument. "Good. I can't be nineteen again so it's a good thing we've cleared that up." Holdin stood and smiled down at Jill. "So we both agree to start here? We've traveled a long way from the starry-eyed lovers who kissed goodnight fifteen years ago."

"What? The girlfriend you've obsessed over for fifteen years is gone and you just say good?"

"She was gone a long time ago, Jill. I knew it. I didn't know you'd lost your memory. For me, the person who never called was not the person I'd been in love with. Then when I found out the name I knew her by was an alias, I had reason to doubt I'd ever known that girl at all. I like the woman sitting in front of me a damn sight better than I do the other possibilities. You came to find me as soon as you were able. You faced your past and didn't slink away from it. This Jill is a hell of a woman who's willing to do whatever's necessary for our son. How could I not be impressed with her?"

Jill searched his face and slowly relaxed. This was good. He'd decided to listen to her. Nerves still rattled her insides but it could have been worse. "Okay. Then sit down so we can discuss this and get some things settled," Jill directed briskly.

"Is your surgery scheduled yet?" Holdin asked casually as he sat down on the end of the bed again.

"Yes, but that's not what I wanted…"

"When?"

"Um, next Tuesday. Now I thought…"

"Where?"

"Presbyterian, Dallas. Are you going to let me finish a sentence?"

"Not if it involves the garbage you started with when we came in here. Do you have to be there the day before for blood work?"

"Of course I do, and that stuff before was practical, not garbage. Let me remind you, I'm not at your beck and call anymore. The girlfriend who thought the sun rose with you is gone and…"

"You saying you worshiped me? Damn, you could have told me then. I'd have liked that." Holdin grinned.

"Ah, no, well, maybe. It doesn't matter! Stop trying to evade the issues."

"Quit trying to be a witch."

"What?" Jill scowled at his smiling face. He didn't want to deal with this now? The signals he was sending were so confusing.

"As I see it, we have four days before we go to Dallas. I'd really like it if you would consent to being my guest out at the ranch. Drifter deserves to meet his grandparents and see my home. Driving back and forth to town is a pain in the ass. Before you object, there is a three-bedroom guesthouse waiting for you. You'll be perfectly comfortable there.

"Things have changed, Jill. The ranch is now the home of a pretty well-off guy who has to bring in important folks occasionally. You don't expect me to make the guys offering me millions of dollars in contracts stay here, do you?" A wave of his hand indicated the neat but rather garishly threadbare motel room.

"Oh. Yes, I see." Holdin always sounded so reasonable. If she listened to him, she was being just plain stubborn by refusing to go out to the ranch. Not to mention denying her son his grandparents.

Jill looked over at Drifter. He'd forgotten to look bored but he wasn't looking excited either. "Would you like to go out to Holdin's ranch?" she asked quietly. "We've already paid for this room. We can stay if you'd rather not."

"Yeah, I'd like to go. But it's no big deal if you wanna stay here." Drifter shrugged. "He's only the most freakin' famous guy in Texas and junk."

Jill raised an eyebrow as Drifter continued. "It's not like I need to see what kind of cool stuff he has out there." Drifter grinned at his mother in a sheepish-boy fashion.

Jill glanced between the two males in the room. Two grins. They knew she'd go. It wasn't fair. Denying Drifter was nearly impossible when he got all smart and refused to ask.

Denying Holdin wouldn't have been as difficult but then she'd be the witch he called her. And she wanted to go, yet with the same intensity, she didn't want to go.

He confused her, thrilled her and scared her. This wasn't like it was before. They weren't the same people. But she wanted him and the man knew there was still a sexual fire burning between them. It singed the edges of every word they spoke. A white-hot flame they both tried to ignore with studied resolve.

What was it about him that still lit a blaze low in her belly after all these years? Was it his storied reputation? The wickedly sexy playboy who was charmingly generous with his time and money? Was it the modern gladiator who'd owned the gridiron and had done it repeatedly? Or was it a connection that had never died? That possibility snuck into her brain and wouldn't be forced out.

Breaking into the silence as she considered those questions, Holdin's cell phone rang. He pulled it out and looked at the caller ID.

"I have to get this. It's Mom." He didn't move away as he answered.

"Hey, Mom. What's up?"

"Is it true?" Carol Powell asked urgently.

Holdin didn't need to ask her what she was talking about. Enough people had seen him with them. He was sure one of those "helpful" folks had called his mother by now. "Yes."

"Where are they?"

"Right here with me."

"Well, hurry up. Apologize to Jill and bring me my grandbaby!"

"What? Why would you assume I have to apologize?"

"Because you do. Now quit wastin' time and git it over with! It appears I've waited fifteen years to see that child."

"Mom. It's not that simple."

"I don't care to hear the details, Holdin Thomas. I can do the math. She was eighteen and you need to apologize, son. Now beg for forgiveness and make it right. I expect to see both of them within the hour."

"Everyone's so concerned with the damn math! I used a condom. Mostly," Holdin growled.

"I told you I don't care to hear the details," Carol reiterated in amused exasperation. "But since you brought it up, big boy, apparently you didn't know how to use a condom properly. Sadly, your father and I had no idea you needed instruction on that. However I 'spect it's the times you didn't use one that got you in this lovely fix. Don't bother denyin' it. You were young. I know better, you're my boy and I know the kind of guy I raised. And don't think you're big enough to curse at your mama."

"Curse at you? Okay, okay, I'm sorry. I wasn't cursing at you, Mom. Believe me, I knew how to use prophylactics. You're probably right about the other time though. And I'm trying to bring them home but Jill isn't sure she'd be welcome. Perhaps you'd like to talk to her?"

"Certainly. Hand her the phone please."

Holdin held the phone out to Jill. "Mom wants to talk to you."

Jill glared at him as she took it. She didn't have to be a mind reader to know what the other side of the conversation had sounded like. He was blaming her for their reluctance to go out to the ranch. It didn't matter that it was the truth, telling his mother was playing dirty. Now she, the scarlet woman who'd had a baby out of wedlock, had to speak to his mother!

"Hello, Mrs. Powell," Jill greeted cautiously.

"Jill! I'm so glad to hear your voice. Please call me Carol. I hear you and my grandbaby are in town and I can hardly wait to see you both. Please feel welcome to come out to the ranch. In truth, there aren't two more welcome people on earth."

"Um…Mrs…ah, Carol, don't you want to know why?"

"The details? Of course I do, dear, but not as much as I want to see you both. I'm sure when we have a minute you'll tell Chuck and me exactly what happened, but right now that's of no importance. I'm simply too thrilled at being a grandmother to be concerned with the details. Getting you to come home is much more urgent. We have a guesthouse now, so if you'd like some privacy, we'll put you in there, but I'd rather the two of you stayed in the big house with us. You're family and I don't want to give up a minute of getting reacquainted and meeting my grandson. Please say you'll come out and at least see if you'd be comfortable. If the problem is Holdin, I'll put him in the guesthouse."

Jill burst out in a soft chuckle. "No, no. You don't have to put Holdin in the guesthouse. I'm sure everything will be fine. Thank you for the kind invitation. We'd be happy to visit you and Mr. Powell."

"You can call him Chuck, honey. I'll be looking for you. And welcome back, dear."

"Thank you, Carol. That's so kind of you. Goodbye." Jill held the phone out to Holdin. She felt overwhelmed in a whole new way now. She knew her goodbye had been stiff compared to the generous kindness Carol Powell was extending. Dealing with so many unexpected developments was stretching her resources. Even kind surprises were costly to her reserves.

Before, spending time at the Powells' family ranch had been a rare treat. It was twenty minutes from town. Usually Holdin spent time with her after they both got off work.

The ranch was the Powell family home. It'd been the Powell place since there were Indians to worry about. Charles Powell was an officer in the Navy, a helicopter pilot and instructor. At that time, the base outside Dallas was the first time he'd been assigned close enough to live on the family property and give his son a few years to finish high school in his hometown.

Jill fondly remembered the warm woman who was Carol Powell. The times she'd been out there, it had seemed to her

Mrs. Powell kept a house like June Cleaver in jeans with the attitude of Roseanne Barr. In her memories, she hadn't seen much of Charles Powell, he was always working. Her impression of him was a large man who seemed serious most of the time, but when he smiled she could see it in his eyes too.

The Powells hadn't seemed particularly wealthy nor poor. They were just so nice. Now, considering Holdin's recent profession and amazing success, she'd bet it was a showplace.

"Well, we have some visiting to do. That was a dirty trick, Holdin."

"No. A dirty trick would have been refusing to take you out there. She'd have been here in twenty minutes." Holdin smiled. "Believe me, this is better. We'll face her together, darlin'. You know I'd never make you do that alone."

Holdin captured her hand that went nervously to her neckline again, searching for the charm. Drawing her hand to his chest, he pressed her palm to him, covering it with both of his. "This is real, Jilly-girl, and this part is the same. Remember what I promised the first time I took you out to the ranch? If it got to be too much or too hard, I'd take you away, no questions asked. Same is true now."

* * * * *

Jill's eyes opened and she was staring at the bedside table. The soft blue numbers on the clock read 3:30 a.m. She'd been in the lavish guestroom bed since ten p.m. The ranch house had changed but it was still a ranch house, warm and inviting, though it was several sizes bigger now. Holdin's parents were just as amazing. Carol was bustling and full of effervescent emotions. Charles—Chuck to his wife—was large and quiet though no less intense.

The Powells had always planned on retiring to the ranch. Now that they had, they'd made it a working operation, it seemed. Charles had been reared a rancher so doing it now was pleasure. Not work.

Greetings, explanations, all of it was jumbled in her head as she gazed at the clock. It had gone well. Better than she'd hoped. But she should have known this family would be that way. There'd been no recriminations, no veiled doubts. Her biggest fear had been for Drifter. How would he handle all of this? So far he'd done it with a grace she hadn't realized the man-child possessed.

A tear slipped out of her eye as she thought about it. She had to think about it, go over each minute in her mind. Pain had awakened her. Sharp and pounding in her head, it brought fear on the jagged talons of torment. A thief who would steal her life and leave her in the dark that was nothing. She couldn't trust her own mind to be there for her. To let her retain all this. It could all go away so quickly and then she'd have nothing again. But worse, her son would have nothing. Jill dragged in a ragged breath as panic threatened to crush her.

A shadow stirred in the darkened room and she gasped. He shifted on the couch across from her and rolled off it to stride over to the bed.

"Holdin?" Jill questioned in surprise as he didn't stop. He pulled up the covers and slid into the bed, gathering her into his arms.

She was too taken aback to protest as he slid under her. She'd been lying on her stomach and now she was lying across his bare chest. He had shorts on, but that was all. Adjusting her easily across him, he settled with an arm around her. The other hand caressed her damp cheek where her face lay on his shoulder.

"I needed to know you were here, Jill. I didn't ask if I could sleep on the little couch over there because then you could have said no. You were crying and you can't expect me to ignore that. Relax and tell me why the tears."

Holdin's voice rumbled up from his wide chest to whisper around her. Deep and soothing, he surrounded her with comfort in a uniquely intimate way. There was nothing demanding about his hold on her but she couldn't call it impersonal.

It was so damn natural too. Their bodies had somehow picked up right where they left off. At least, how he treated her had. All afternoon and evening he'd been less than a touch away. Mostly, he was right beside her, holding her chair or opening the door. Handing her water or otherwise seeing to her needs as he always had while engaging in conversation and activities around them. He made his care appear a natural extension of his life.

The thin material of her nightshirt did nothing to disguise the feel of him. Hard and rippling, his chest supported her soft breasts. Flattened against him, her abdomen rested on his, angled to the side a bit so her legs straddled one of his thick thighs. The position was amazingly comfortable while reminding her how large he was. He'd not let her even brush the part of him she remembered as significantly large. As he settled beneath her, her leg between his shifted up naturally to rest against him. The shorts shielding his sac from her thigh might as well not have been there.

Straddling him brought steely thigh muscles up against her damp panties with firm pressure. She knew he felt her embarrassingly excited condition yet Holdin simply held her. He was too honorable to use her natural reaction to pressure her if she wasn't ready. However, there was no chance he wasn't aware of it.

Jill wanted to moan at the feel of him. This magnificent man who'd always burned her with a hunger she had no tools to resist. Then she wanted to rage at the reason she was awake to enjoy his attention.

Rage was pointless. She'd learned that a long time ago when facing the fact that no one would ever come looking for her. Now she was almost as alone as she had been then. This could only lead to more pain if the worst happened. Not her pain, his. He needed to understand how devastating things could get. This wasn't going to help him to protect himself.

"The reason I woke up was pain, Holdin." She needed him to face the ugly truths. "I was trying to remember everything about today, enjoy it because it could all be gone in an instant. The pain is a reminder. Nothing about present reality is secure for me. If I go back to sleep, I might not know who you are when I wake up. Do you understand that? We can't have a relationship. There is no foundation. No sure ground. What we're doing right now is just for this minute.

"I came here to be sure my son has a future. That's the only important thing. Oh God, I was so afraid I didn't have enough time to do that." Jill shuddered across his body. "What if you had refused to see me? You could have been anywhere in the world. I was so afraid."

"Hush, Jill," Holdin soothed as he cradled her precious body at last. Needing to hold her was undeniable and now the rest of his drives were clamoring at him. The one thing capable of controlling them was her need. It was always Jill at the center of the storm that was his hunger for her. Being held was what she needed. "You're panicking over the possibilities that don't exist anymore. Our son has a concrete future. He's safe. You did the right thing. You trusted the man from your past enough to come here. That's very important to me. I don't agree on our relationship issues though.

"Baby, we have unfinished business as a couple. What we're doing right now is part of that. I'm not asking more from you. This is Holdin holding Jill because she was crying. I need to do it. If you really think the time might be short, Jill, let us have these few days."

Her face was turned away from him on his shoulder and his lips nuzzled her hair. Dragging in the scent of it, he tried to flood all of his senses with her. She was still delicate as a night flower, the same and yet different, just like the lush body draped over him.

"What do you mean?" she murmured.

"You want our son to be safe, secure, right?"

"Yes."

"Then why can't we give him these few days with his family? A whole family. You and I have a connection that was never severed, Jill. I know you feel it. We're still a couple. We were so in love and so young. I naïvely thought it'd go on forever. I didn't have time to mention it, but I planned to marry you. I was going to ask, but thought it'd be a good idea to wait a year. That was the level of my commitment, Jill. There was nothing casual about it."

Jill raised her head and turned to look at him. Only a feeble bit of moonlight found its way in the double windows across the room but she could see him. His handsome face was drawn and serious as he continued.

"Things didn't work out the way I planned and then there was no ending for us, no closure and no future. What I'm saying is, right now we can give our son a family like he should have had. Our relationship is still open, Jill. Don't close it just because you think it might be done for us again.

"Let me be his dad who adores his mom. Not the guy who fathered him and who his mother was forced to turn to as a last resort."

Chapter Three

ஐ

Jill lay perfectly still. Her body was sprawled across him, her head lifted at a slightly awkward angle to see his face and it was all too seductive. He wasn't caressing her. No, it was the temptation to sink into his care that swamped her. She fought a sugar-sweet craving to let him be her boyfriend again. That was what he was asking.

If she agreed, where were they? She knew the answer. He would simply take over and deep in her soul that was such a temptation. To let someone else be in control would be so sweet. At eighteen she'd literally blossomed in his hands. Yet from the adult perspective she could see his gentle, unrelentingly sexy attention had been so complete that she'd not even realized the extent of his influence. She'd been his, body and soul.

"Holdin, how do we do that? I don't know how to answer. We aren't those people."

"I'm asking you to stop being defensive. Not give up your defenses, just stop fighting us. Let me hold you, Jill. I need to hold you. Let me help lift some of that burden you drag around. Lean on me, just a little. Is that so hard? Have I ever given you reason to distrust me?"

"We were hardly more than kids. Now we're adults. Huge difference, Holdin."

"I know. I don't want the eighteen-year-old Jill. I want the woman in my arms. We can't be those people anymore but we can let what we had give us a door to the future that might have been. Are you afraid of me?"

"Yes!"

"Why?"

"Everything! Don't you get it? *Everything*. What happens if we drop ourselves into a relationship again? What if we hate each other and just don't know it yet? What if we don't hate each other? That's worse. I can't lose everything again. I can't do it!"

"Jilly-girl," his tone was soft as his large hand pressed her head down to his shoulder, "you can't lose everything. It's not possible anymore. Even if you don't know us, both Drifter and I will be there. You'll never be abandoned again. Shhhhh," he soothed as she started crying into his neck. "That's what this is about. You were terrified and so alone. Not even a memory of being loved to comfort you. Oh damn, baby girl, I'm so sorry."

Jill sobbed on his chest in soul-wrenching, gasping explosions of emotions that gathered in force as she let them go. Her whole body jerked with each sob. He wrapped his arms around her to hold her grief-racked body to him and welcomed the outpouring of her heartache. It was the old loneness. The complete abandonment she'd suffered. It was all the emotions he should have been there to defend her from.

Pain marked his face as she poured out the depths of her loneliness, fear and desperation. Words couldn't have expressed the terrifying hell she'd awakened to in that hospital so long ago.

She'd been right. Between him and her father, she'd been surrounded. Not that either of them ordered her around. No, it was much more subtle than that. She was the woman of her father's house, in charge of it but completely safe in its shelter. When she was with Holdin, she'd been his in every way. He'd loved how they were. Loved how she let him be a man, expected it of him. Their relationship had been perfect and he didn't think it was the rose-colored glasses of time he was looking through.

It had been her nature to lean on him. It was his nature to accept it. They'd fed each other in ways few couples manage. And then she'd woken up alone. So very alone. Her soul had known that it was not her nature to fend for herself.

"Shhh, that's it. Let it go. It'll never happen to Drifter. I promise you, Jilly-girl. He'll never feel abandoned the way you did, darlin'. You've seen to it. He has a father, grandparents and a past. He's safe. You've taken care of our baby." Holdin assured her as the sobs continued but in a much healthier emotional cleansing. Not the complete meltdown she'd done to begin with.

The tears finally subsided and they lay there holding each other in a silence that was both sorrow and understanding.

"How did you know?" Jill asked into the peaceful dark that had settled around them. "I didn't even know why my soul was breaking until you put it in words."

"I know your nature, Jilly-girl. Then or now, it's the same soul and I know it," Holdin murmured. "Try to relax and go to sleep, baby. It's time."

"Time for what?"

"Time for you to let go of that fear. The two of you will never be alone like that again. No matter what happens between us, I will always be his father. His grandparents will always adore him. He's safe. It's time for you to be safe too. Be safe in me, Jilly-girl. I'm not going to lose you again. You can't drop off into nothingness a second time. Think about it. Even if you remember nothing after the surgery, you will not be abandoned. We'll be there. You'll have a history. You will have a future."

Jill let his words curl around her fears. He'd named the demon, the nothingness. That nothingness was the black hole of pain she'd give her soul to protect her son from. Holdin understanding that so quickly should have been shocking but it wasn't. He was right. He knew her nature.

Being in his arms felt like it always had. An overwhelming mix of edgy sexuality that could take her to the verge of endurance, tempered with the amazing certainty that she was safe in his care. The security he provided folded around her as exhaustion took its toll. Jill finally let go and relaxed into the luxuriant pleasure that was falling asleep in Holdin's arms.

Holdin lay there and felt her quiet down into sleep. For right now it was enough. Holding her, feeling her soft breathing on his neck was a need. The hard knot in his gut shifted a bit lower but he could live with that. The precious gift of her trust, her pain, giving herself into his keeping, even for this short time, fed the starved beast who'd hungered for her. He hadn't known that the last time he held her would be the *last* time. Hadn't realized it'd be fifteen years before he felt this again.

The part of his soul that was a vicious competitor had grown up on the pain of missing this, her. He'd been very careful to cover that wounded animal, hide him behind a mask of sportsmanship. Never once had he discussed where his relentless drive came from, not with anyone. It was private, that dark part of him that had held the memory of her in his clutches had grown into a ruthless opponent in every way.

Sometimes his drive to win had almost overwhelmed him, tempting him down a much more dangerous path. Each time the thing that'd held him back from the shortcuts of drugs or steroids, of bending the rules and taking risks had been the thought of her reaction if she ever found out.

Watching others get caught in sports scandals had convinced him that it couldn't be covered up. It'd be as public as his successes. He couldn't risk her seeing that.

She'd both driven him and guarded him. His demon and his angel.

* * * * *

Jill woke to the feel of her "mattress" trying to stealthily slide out from under her. She didn't open her eyes as she rolled over off him. "What time is it?" Jill asked as she hugged a pillow that suddenly slid up beside her.

Holdin was now sitting looking down at her.

"Six a.m. Go back to sleep, baby."

"Mmm, where're you goin'?"

"I work out in the mornings. Gets it out of the way." Holdin leaned down and brushed his lips over her cheek. "Is the headache gone?" he questioned into her ear as his thick arms braced him over her.

Jill opened one eye slowly to test her light sensitivity. The room apparently wasn't on the sunrise side of the house. It was still shadowed. "No pain," she mumbled, and shut the eye again. Her arms tightened around the pillow she hugged. Her knees came up slightly and her body relaxed into sleep. Just that quickly.

Holdin stood, hands on hips and stared down at her. He struggled with dragging himself out of the room. The raw view of her pain last night had gone a long way toward bridging the distance between them but it had cost him. The price of regaining a relationship would be steep for both of them. Each had been to a very dark place in the last fifteen years. Climbing out of that place was a journey that had built two adults who were strangers. He didn't even know if she was a morning person or not. Was this sleep one of deep peace or was it simply her habit in the morning?

"It's seriously creepy when you do that," Drifter commented from the door to the hall.

Holdin's head whipped around in surprise that didn't last long. "When I do what?" he asked as he strode to the door and out, closing it softly behind him.

"When you stand there staring at her while she sleeps."

Holdin smiled easily and put a hand on Drifter's shoulder, subtly drawing the boy with him as he strode to his own room. "Yeah? I guess I still can't believe she's here. I'll get over it. What are you doin' up?"

They stopped at the next door down the hall, Holdin's room. "I have a couple things I need to check on." Drifter glanced up and down Holdin's nearly nude body. "What were you doing in there?"

"I slept in there," Holdin answered honestly, a little curious where this would lead.

"You do realize the goal is less stress, right?" Drifter's tone said he doubted Holdin's ability to comprehend that. "If this is a problem, we have to leave. She can't afford it."

Holdin wanted to smile as he looked at his son. It was amazing, but the boy's unflinching attitude made him so damn proud. Little man was dealing with the facts, calculating possible outcomes and formulating a plan of action to deal with them.

"Relax. Your mother and I can handle our relationship. What are you checking on?" Holdin asked in a casual tone as he opened the door to his room and led the way in.

Drifter didn't follow, just stood in the doorway to reply. "If you're telling me it's none of my business, forget it. What happens to her is my business. Especially now. Will she be upset when she gets up?"

Holden grabbed a pair of sweats and tugged them on over the shorts. "No, she'll be fine." He barely glanced at the boy as he pulled a T-shirt over his head. "It's my business too and I take it seriously. But I'm glad to see you're concerned," he complimented gently while establishing a right to Jill.

Drifter nodded and turned to leave. "Hey, so what are you checking on?" Holdin asked as he picked up shoes and socks to follow.

"I need to check the car. I heard a sound outta the brakes," Drifter supplied as his long gate took him down the hall to the stairs.

Both of them descended as Holdin asked, "Think the pads are goin'?"

"Yeah, maybe. Not sure. The guy in your equipment garage said I could use the hydraulic this morning." Drifter glanced at his father. "Got a problem? I'm not taking your mechanic's time. I'll do the work myself."

"Course not. Mind if I look too? The Taurus 'bout seven years old?"

"Eight. Look at it if you want. I don't need any help." Drifter jammed his hands into his pockets as they headed for the back of the house where the kitchen door was the shortest route to the garages.

In the kitchen, Holdin dropped his shoes and socks by the table and detoured to open the fridge. "Want something?"

"Whatcha have?" A little of Drifter's defensiveness fell away as he peered into the fridge behind Holdin.

"I'm getting orange juice." Holdin grabbed it and stepped away from the open door. "Get whatever you want."

Drifter stood there a moment looking at the contents and then flipped the door shut. "I'll have a glass too." Holdin was already getting two glasses from the cabinet.

"Not hungry?"

"Naw. I'll have something when Mom gets up."

Holdin brought the glasses and juice to the table and sat to put on his shoes and socks. The move encouraged Drifter to participate by pouring the drinks. If they both were involved in some activity together, Holdin figured it wouldn't feel as if he were infringing on Drifter's space.

Drifter drained a tall glass and put the orange juice jug away after he'd shoved the other glass across the table to Holdin.

"You keeping track of her diet?" Holdin asked around his orange juice.

Drifter shrugged. "She likes coffee and caffeine is on the 'No' list."

"There's a list? The doctor gave her a diet plan?" Holdin asked as they left the kitchen through the mudroom and stepped out into the damp morning air.

"Yeah."

"She doesn't stick to it?"

"Doesn't like it."

"So? It's good for her." Holdin scowled. "How often does she go off it?"

"None." Drifter answered as he glanced around the large yard and outbuildings.

"Then why're you worried?"

"She forgets things. I just make sure. I gotta drive the car around to the garage. Since you're here, you could open the door for me." Drifter pulled the car keys out of his pocket, turned away to lope around to the front of the house where Jill had parked.

Holdin watched him, frowning. What had that been about? Was the boy afraid he wouldn't let him drive the car around to the garage? Not likely, Holdin had been driving equipment around the ranch when they visited from the time he could reach the pedals. Or was Drifter embarrassed about admitting he kept an eye on his mother? Another thing Holdin had no problem with.

Holdin shook his head and took off at a jog to make it across the nearly three acres of lawn to the garage before Drifter got there with the car. Entering the equipment garage, he activated the electric door. Drifter backed the car onto the lift skids as if he'd been doing it for years. Jumping out, the boy adjusted the fit and operated the hydraulic lift with an obvious knowledge of its workings. Holdin stood back as the car went up. He didn't offer assistance because he suspected Drifter needed to prove he could do this.

Being a father was a huge mystery but Holdin figured he knew how to be a friend. That had to be the place they started. He knew for a fact Drifter had no idea how to be a son, so both of them were SOL on that one.

Working in silence, they removed the front passenger side wheel to have a look at the brake pads. Holdin took the stance of assistant as if he'd seen Drifter do this a thousand times and had no doubt he could do it well. The dark clouds whirling around the teen's head seemed to dissipate when he realized Holdin really wasn't going to start trying to instruct him on how to do the job.

* * * * *

Jill was groggily aware of the door softly closing behind Holdin as she hugged the pillow and sank back into the lovely dream she'd been having. She'd heard Drifter's voice and that made her smile softly as she faded back to the past. She knew it was a dream and reached for it.

Eighteen again, she was at the movies with Holdin and several of his friends the first Friday night after her father and she had moved to Connersville. Her dad had been amazed she had a date already. He was exhausted from his first week of work at the factory. He was genuinely pleased she was making a new group of friends. It meant she was integrating into her surroundings, not sitting home alone feeling lonely and all "new girl".

The cool, late winter night enveloped Jill in loving arms as the present receded and she was sitting in the dark theater beside Holdin. Their shoulders were touching and tingles raced down her body at the contact that wasn't as casual as they hoped it appeared. First date and surrounded by others, it had been safe and exciting all at the same time. The shadowy dreamscape morphed him and her to a few months later to a warm loft over the foaling barn on Holdin's parents' ranch.

A private picnic evolved into hours of Holdin showing Jill how high he could make her fly. On this day, he'd stripped her clothes off in a long, languorous make-out session. His mouth ate her taste into him, loving her, drawing her soul into the shadowy loft as he growled his passion. When he was like this, she knew it'd be hours of progressively intense demands from her lover.

In the foggy dream reality, the memory poured over her, bathing her body in the fire Holdin had demanded of her that long-ago afternoon. Stretched out on the blanket, her body was his instrument and the more intense he became, the more finely tuned she became.

One large hand was molding her breast exactly how she loved to be touched. He could cup her, pressing down in slow circles as thumb and forefinger rolled a plump nipple in relentless rhythm. It was heavenly and maddening. His deep, slow kisses combined with that touch were driving her crazy.

He'd completely undressed her but only his shirt and shoes were off and her hands fumbled to reach his belt buckle. He caught them and drew them over her head, trapping them in one of his hands.

"No, baby," he growled, lifting his head from her swollen lips to look down at her. "Not yet." His breathing was ragged as he lifted his head farther to survey his prize.

"Damn!" Holdin murmured reverently as his gaze traveled over her body with arms restrained. Jill's delicious hips were gently rocking in invitation, the slick evidence of her pleasure glistening on her thighs as she rubbed them together, trying to give herself some relief since he hadn't touched her there yet.

Jill moaned, all she could manage was a plea. "More. I need it."

"It's comin', baby. Stay just like that, don't move." He released her hands and abruptly pulled his tube socks off. "Do you trust me?" he asked softly.

"Yes," Jill whispered back as she lay stretched out under his eyes. He stared at her a long moment without moving. Her body was burning with need. She arched her back slowly, setting the soft mounds of her breasts shuddering, and drew her legs apart for him. His body jerked in reaction to her visual tease as she knew it would. Her smile was a naughty moue.

Holdin leaned his face down to her ear. "I told you not to move, my wicked little wildcat. Now I'm going to see that you understand me." He sat up slowly and held up one of his long tube socks so she could see it then reached up and swiftly used it to bind her wrists together.

Jill gasped and he looked directly into her eyes as she heard a clink and click above her head and then she couldn't tug her restrained arms down. His fingers were trailing down the soft skin of her arms as she tried to twist her head up and see what he'd done.

"What?"

"Shhhh, Jilly-girl. Do you know how beautiful you are?" His fingers teased down the tender skin of her underarms, down to cup the full breasts. His thumbs both gently circling swollen nipples but not giving her the harder caress she wanted.

"But what..." Jill gasped.

"Do you trust me?" he interrupted again, not taking his eyes off her breasts this time as he teased them.

"Yes." Jill relaxed and stopped trying to look up at what he'd done to her wrists. His attention to her sensitive breasts was too distracting to worry about her hands.

He leaned down and lightly licked one plump nipple, carefully painting it with damp attention that wasn't the hard touch she was beginning to crave. He blew across his glistening prize and watched it distend farther for him before he glanced up into her eyes again.

"Are you uncomfortable? In pain? Is the position a problem for those reasons?" he questioned her in a firm voice that sort of startled her.

"No."

"Then this is the trust I need from you now," he continued as his knuckles grazed her soft belly in a circling pattern that was almost a feather touch to her sensitive skin. "If anything scares you, all you have to say is stop. You know that, Jilly-girl."

She nodded, her entire body beginning to tremble in excitement as she realized his intentions. Her legs were once again pressed together, rubbing in a vain attempt to create some friction for her needy pussy. Her hips continued to roll slightly as she squirmed. His large hand opened on her belly. He nearly spanned her from hipbone to hipbone, pressing her down and holding her still.

Jill started panting. His strength was always a turn-on, but this type of control was new. Something about it was amazingly hot. She wasn't afraid of him, she couldn't be. This was her Holdin and he always took care of her.

"Are you mine?" he asked her mysteriously as he began petting her belly.

"Yesss," she hissed, his fingers grazed the top of her damp curls and maddingly circled up again instead of sinking into where she needed them.

"You know I love you," he continued. He was kneeling beside her, his gaze on his own hand as he caressed her. "I'd never hurt you, never. Let me show you how much, baby. Give me your trust."

"Yes, please! Now!" Jill encouraged him as he just sat there watching his hand on her belly.

"Spread your legs, baby," he commanded softly. "Show me how much you want me."

Jill's legs V'd apart. "Wider," he insisted, and she extended them as far as they would go, digging her heels into the soft blanket beneath them to lift her hips up for his touch.

"No, baby. Put that sweet ass back on the blanket." His tone was firm again. "Turn your heels in and lay your legs open for me."

She did what he told her, laying herself open for him as she'd never been before. Soft lighting glistened on damp inner thighs, sparkling curls and the swollen folds of her most private flesh exposed to his view, at his command. Jill felt her body tighten in an unbelievable mix of embarrassment and excitement. It wasn't as if he'd never seen her before. His mouth had investigated every inch of her many, many times. But this was different and more intensely erotic than she'd ever experienced before.

"Yes, just like that," he approved. "That's my good girl. Do you want me, Jilly-girl? Tell me. I need to hear it. I won't touch you unless you ask me to. You have to understand you're not helpless like this, just so stunningly beautiful. God! You're so beautiful." His voice had gone reverent at the end.

"Holdin!" Jill moaned urgently. *"I need you. Don't make me think. You know I love you. Please, please, touch me."*

"Like this?" he asked as his fingers sank down to tunnel into the honey curls surrounding her sex.

"Yes! More," she demanded as he just stopped with his middle finger resting on the nub of her clit, the two fingers beside it curling down the length of her flushed outer lips.

"Tell me, baby. Tell me what you want," he insisted.

"No. I can't think. Just take me. I need so bad." Jill was desperate. The drive for release almost painful as her body burned for him.

"Are you asking me to take control? Are you giving me this body, Jilly-girl?"

"Yes! Please!" she begged helplessly.

"Say it, baby. Tell me what's mine. Only mine. Give me this sweet body," he insisted softly.

"Only yours," she panted, *"Always. You know that."*

"Mine!" breathed out of his mouth as his lips descended to the nearest nipple and his fingers spread her pussy lips and tormented her clit.

The explosion of sensation pushed a wail out of Jill as he took possession of her. His mouth sucked her nipple deep and hard. The hand on her pussy held her open in a fashion that was shocking even though no one could see her as his middle finger manipulated her clit. Jill wanted to scream but somehow she couldn't.

All she could manage were muffled moans as she endured pleasure that was torment. Then suddenly there was loud, pounding thunder.

No. Not thunder. Pounding. Where?

Jill jackknifed up in bed as her door opened and she stared at the face in it blankly. Still wrapped in the dream she was panting, her face flushed and her pulse skittering in alarm as the long-ago afternoon faded away.

Two faces in her doorway. Confusion and concern on them.

"Mom, you 'kay?" Drifter asked in concern. "You were moaning. Is there pain? Do I need to call Dr. Coates? You're flushed too and not breathing right."

"No, ah, no, I'm…" Her eyes flicked up to the worried man standing behind her son and heat flashed across her body. She knew the blush painted her guilty and trembling hands tried to hide her cheeks as she looked at Drifter again.

"No, really. Just a dream." She gulped back a moan when she realized the man behind Drifter smiled slowly at that confession. His eyes had always seen every detail, every nuance of her expressions, mannerisms. At one time he could simply glance at her and read her body. He wore that look now and he was right. She didn't like it.

"But you're trembling." Drifter's brow wrinkled in concern as he stepped farther into her room.

Behind him Holdin's eyes changed, the lids became heavy as his gaze dropped and Jill realized she was sitting up with the covers at her waist. Her thin nightshirt did nothing to disguise heavy breasts and the sharp outline of swollen nipples. Jill grabbed the sheet and clutched it up to her neck.

"I just woke up. I'm fine," she insisted. "Now shoo. I need to get up." Her voice wasn't as firm as she'd like it to be but she needed to get rid of these two.

"But…" Drifter started, still concerned.

"It's okay, son. Your mother was startled when we knocked," Holdin injected smoothly, a hand resting on Drifter's shoulder to pull him back out of the room. "Let's give her some privacy to wake up."

"I don't like this place," Drifter argued as he frowned back at Holdin. "It's too big. I can't hear her if she falls."

"I'm not going to fall. Stop worrying," Jill insisted. "There's no pain, hon. No headache. It was just a dream. I'll see you downstairs in a few minutes."

"My room is right next to hers. Remember?" Holdin added. "I'll hear her if she falls. Come on."

"But…? Are you sure?" Drifter asked again, worried as he searched her glowing face. He ignored Holdin's hand on him, looking to Jill for confirmation.

"Yes, yes. Go on." Jill avoided looking at Holdin. "I'll be down in forty-five minutes."

"Take an hour if you need it." Holdin grinned at her over Drifter's head as the boy backed out. "Breakfast can wait 'til you're ready." His eyes twinkled and he let them drift down again to where her legs were clamped tightly together. "As I recall, sometimes you needed a little extra time to," he paused and looked into her eyes again, "be ready," he finished the awkward sentence that had nothing to do with breakfast.

As Drifter turned, Jill mouthed "Beast" to Holdin.

Holdin held the door handle and leaned in so only his head was in the room and their son behind him. "Sexy beast," he corrected softly, and pulled the door shut.

Jill slowly sank back into her pillow and resisted the urge to groan loudly. Her body was damp with sweat and need. It trembled with the power of that distant afternoon and now she had to get up and face Holdin's family. Thank God, her son didn't know the signs like his father did.

She'd just resigned herself to a cold shower and was sitting on the edge of the bed when the phone rang beside her on the nightstand. Frowning at it, she wondered if it was a ranch phone. It didn't seem logical that Holdin would have his guestrooms wired with the public number.

"Hello?"

"What was the dream?" a familiar voice rumbled in her ear.

"None of your business. Does every room have its own phone number?"

"No, this is room to room, like an intercom but more private. It is my business. I think it's all mine, baby. You're flushed and damp, all the way to your toes," he drawled. "Nothing could be more my business. Now tell me. What were we doing to get you so worked up?"

"Who said it was about you?" she shot back.

There was a pause. "Don't play that game, Jilly-girl." Holdin's voice dropped even lower. "I know you're lying. You looked into my eyes and blushed from head to toe. Your body blasted out a wave of sexual demand and I could smell the want in the room. It was mine, woman. Don't hide behind another man. I'll not stand for it."

Jill's back stiffened. "Lying? I don't tell you what you want to hear and you call it lying? Then you think you can lay down some sort of command?" Jill asked in sarcastic amazement. "Aren't you just the king of everything? Get over yourself. I'm not one of your groupies and I don't work for you so take your judgments and orders somewhere else."

"Wait, Jill! Don't you—"

"Stop! Now. I'll be down when I'm ready and I don't intend to put up with this," she informed him with acid in her voice. "You don't get to order me or my son around." She put the phone down softly.

It rang again immediately. She picked it up and didn't bother putting it to her ear, simply held it in front of her and said, "Nor will I be bullied by this. If you insist on calling back, I'll take it out of the wall. My door opens in two seconds and you will see the last of us, Holdin. If I have to lock my door in your house, I don't need to stay here. We are not your possessions. If you can't manage to respect us, we're gone." Jill dropped the phone back in its cradle and eyed it. It didn't ring.

She sat on the bed five more minutes to make sure her door would not open at an awkward moment. Apparently he'd gotten the message. Acid turned in her stomach and ate at her as she shuddered in reaction. She hated confrontation. Now she began to suspect she might have overreacted.

She'd panicked when he called her a liar. Panicked because it felt like a slap from him. The emotional impact was too huge to deal with. She'd been teasing and he'd "hit" her. Well, not really, but just the fact that it'd hurt her so deeply had pitched her into a defensive shrew. One thing Jill did not do was lie. Never. Truth was too precious to her. Too difficult to see in the world around her. "*God*! I am a mess."

Holdin put his phone down very gently. He reached for control and securely fastened the lock on his inner demons. Possessive rage was pointless. She was correct on a certain level. They were not his yet. He coldly analyzed their exchange and acknowledged his words had been too strong. He'd reacted to her snappy reply and the vision of her dreaming about sex with another man had flipped him right into Neanderthal mode.

Time to go to the gym. He'd skipped the session this morning to spend time with Drifter. Right now that was the only place he could safely work through his reactions. His suite of rooms came with his own exit out the back of the house. Once outside he jogged to the farthest building across the wide expanse of lawn.

It was a steel structure thrown up on a concrete slab. Not fancy in appearance but inside were all the tools a pro quarterback needed to stay in form. This retired quarterback intended to make use of every one of those if he needed to. By the time he stepped back in the house, he had to be completely able to repair his relationship. To get to that place, he needed to run the "beast" into the ground. That bastard was not going to raise its stupid head again today.

Grimly he entered his private domain. He'd built it with his first signing bonus and it had been his sanctuary in his quest to be the best so Jill could find him. This space had seen him rage over Jill, weep over her and drive himself into the ground as he pushed himself to new limits. That first pro season he'd painted her name on the ceiling so he could look up to focus on the motivation. Several years later he'd painted over it but it didn't matter. The letters were still there, under the paint. He was always aware of them and often wondered if he should have scraped them off first but suspected that wouldn't have worked either.

His career, his physical abilities, they all were monuments to Jill. The quest to regain her had consumed his life for so many years. His journey had often been dark, even dangerous. He'd focused on winning and that meant destroying his opponents with all the ruthless zeal of a grudge match. Every single time. This space had seen him overcome pain, exhaustion, even several concussions. Here the relentless competitor had honed himself into a weapon.

Holdin started his workout. Pressing the timer, he whipped into motion. Pushing himself against the clock was extremely effective. Time didn't care who or what he was, it could beat an opponent without effort or emotion. Holdin needed the ruthless challenge of it right now.

And still she invaded his mind. The memory of her body poured over his last night rode him like a burr on a long-haired dog. He couldn't untangle his mind from the sharp prickles of need. Then there was the scent of her hair and that more personal perfume he'd recognized and realized he'd forgotten in the same moment. He'd been shocked that he'd forgotten it. Recognizing it last night had rattled his core so badly that he'd thought he might come just breathing her in.

He'd spent most of the night coldly forcing himself to breathe normally and sporting a tent pole under the sheets. A big old revival meeting tent too. He could almost hear the choir singing under there but it wasn't a hymn from the Baptist hymnal. This tune came straight from the temples of sin on Bourbon Street. The bluesy call to passion had throbbed with a thick backbeat that pounded up his veins.

Chapter Four

Holdin dragged his sweaty body back to the main house ninety minutes later. The exhaustion would pass, though he should have eaten something before working that hard. In the shower he tried to formulate an apology and decided confessing he was a witless idiot around her wouldn't be a newsflash to anyone. It probably wasn't the most reassuring thing he could say to her but it was honest. They had to start at honest.

Fifteen minutes later he strode into the kitchen. Even though the room was a large country kitchen, the two women sitting at the table took up all the space in the room. At least for him.

"Good morning, ladies," he acknowledged as he went to the microwave. It was a sure bet his mother had saved him a plate of food from breakfast and left it in there. There it was and he pulled it out without warming it. At the table, he took the chair beside Jill, who was holding a mug, as was his mother. Holdin made sure he took a stealthy look at its contents as he sat down and was pleased to see that it was green tea.

"Thanks for the plate, Mom. I'm starved." He picked up the fork that was still by Jill's elbow to start eating.

"Wasn't me." Carol smiled. "Jill set that aside before we all started eating."

"Oh?" Holdin glanced at Jill, who'd been studying her mug since he stepped in the room. "Thank you, Jilly-girl."

Jill didn't look up as she nodded. Then quietly, as he dug his fork into the eggs, "Holdin, I should apologize."

Holdin stopped and carefully put his fork back down, watching the woman beside him who hadn't lifted her eyes from her mug.

"I was rude. Um…sorry. I could have been tactful instead of reacting emotionally."

Across the table Carol pushed back her chair and stood. "I think there's something that needs my urgent attention. Somewhere. See you later, Jill. I'll be in the family room and we'll go over those things we discussed." She smiled and left.

Holdin reached over and gently pried one of Jill's hands off her lukewarm mug. After less than a second she let him have it. Her small hand rested on his and he drew it to his face, placing her palm against his cheek without saying a word. Pressing it there, Holdin closed his eyes as he dragged it down his cheek to his mouth. Softly kissing her palm, he opened his eyes to look into hers.

"You were afraid," he said into her flesh as their eyes met over her hand. "Still unsure if you can trust me so you reacted defensively to a hard push from me. It's not your fault. I'm the one who needs to apologize, baby."

Inside he felt deep relief. Her soul was reacting to his. Conflict with him was difficult, more than it would be for most women. It was that beautiful submissive in her. His need to protect the sweet spirit clawed at him. It really was his fault. Pushing her meant hurting her and he was so damn used to pushing for what he wanted.

Jill sucked in a gasp as his teeth nipped at her palm and then his tongue bathed the spot. Their eyes not leaving each other, he pulled her hand down his neck to the center of his chest. Holding the contact to him, Holdin asked quietly, "Forgive me? I have no right to question the years we were apart. I don't want to know about the men in your life. Everything else, but not that."

Her body was turned to face him as a little smile flickered across her lips. Even when they were sitting side by side, she had to tilt her head up to be face-to-face. Something about her leaning into him with her face tilted up moved the animal in Holdin. It was an instinctual response from eons ago, but the act of exposing her neck was so submissive a posture. It triggered the parallel aggressive response in him and he tensed to restrain the impulse to drag his tongue over the exposed creamy flesh.

His eyelids were heavy with the desire to consume and he couldn't hide it as she looked at him with those wide eyes and her tempting lips slightly parted. Her hand over his heart had to have picked up the increase in rate. Holdin dragged in a deep breath and regretted it. She invaded his every sense with her mysterious night flower scent. Lush and round, her curves had him salivating as her supple form swayed toward him a little.

"We have so much history, so much baggage." Jill sighed. "How do we get past it?"

Holdin leaned into her, his lips a whisper from the mouth he wanted more than life at this moment. "We can't. We have to deal with it."

Her body gave a slight shudder as her eyes focused on his lips. "I'm afraid. I'm not one of those perfect women you're used to. I'm...well, me."

"Damn it, baby girl. Don't you get it? They were never as perfect as Jill. Not the other way around."

"Really?" Her eyes flicked up to his as she reached for the sincerity in him.

Holdin's head shifted a fraction to the side, tilting his mouth to match hers though not touching. "Do you feel me wanting you? Desperate for the taste of you? You make me desperate, Jill. No one else. Ever."

"How do we do this to each other? Why do I want you so bad I burn every time I look at you? I tense up and pull back," Jill whispered into his lips.

"I know," he breathed. He let go of her hand to run his up the outside of her arm, around and under it to her side. Not touching her breast, he slowly stroked her rib cage. The effort not to pull her into him was a battle he was determined not to lose. "I'm not taking what I need, Jill. I'm trying not to scare you. Can you give me that? At least that?"

"What do you need?"

Holdin smiled that slow grin that had always made her catch a breath in sharply. "You know what I need, Jilly-girl. You've always known. But I'll settle for a taste. Tell me I can have a taste, baby."

"No." Jill pulled back and stood as Holden clenched his jaw and immediately took his hands off her. His eyes narrowed as he gazed up at her standing beside him.

"Testing me?" he asked tightly.

"Stand up, Holdin. I'm not having my first kiss over a plate of eggs and bacon. I want to feel you hold me. All of me."

Holdin's chair crashed backward on the floor. His big body was directly in front of hers as his hands rested lightly on her hips. His head bent and their lips were again a breath apart. "Meet me halfway, Jill. Don't make me take. Please, baby, don't push me that far," he growled fiercely, and stood still waiting for her.

Looking up into his amazing eyes as he literally vibrated with restrained tension, Jill let her hands rest lightly on his upper chest. Warm, breathing steel met her touch. His nostrils flared and she watched him endure the pleasure of her touch. As her hands glided up to his shoulders, his eyes changed, going dark and almost glassy. Jill noted each change as very slowly her fingers traveled his corded neck to tunnel under that golden crown of hair and cup the back of his skull.

"Could I step away now?" Jill questioned in a breathless whisper.

That's when she felt living steel tremble. His eyes squeezed shut and his lips brushing hers, he surrendered his strength to her. "No. My Jill would never be that cruel," he told her softly.

"No." Jill paused as he opened his eyes—no, she couldn't be that cruel to herself. "Please kiss me, Holdin."

His mouth came the millimeter to her lips. Slowly he brushed back and forth as both of them opened. His arms tightened around her to bring her body firmly against him as a hand slid to the small of her back. The other traveled up her spine to press her into him. Firmly, like a man savors the taste of fine food, he licked across her lower lip. His hand at her back moved up her neck to cradle the back of her head as he dragged his tongue over her top lip. He seemed in no hurry but the feel of his clenched body pressed into hers couldn't lie.

Jill moaned and closed her eyes. The hand low on her back moved down in a long, hard caress to span her bottom and press her hips firmly into his. He burned her through her jeans as that large hand pressed into her and went even lower to cup her curves. His middle finger had traveled the crease of her cheeks and now his fingers curled under to intimately press the ridge in the crotch of her jeans up into damp panties and suddenly engorged folds.

His mouth moved over hers, not pressing into her, sampling her in long licks and featherlight brushes. They were both open-mouthed and panting but he still didn't accept that damp invitation. His fist closed in her hair to hold her head firmly beneath him, but he didn't kiss her.

"Holdin!" sobbed out of her as he held her there. She felt surrounded, suspended in a hellish middle ground of razor-sharp touches that cut her with pleasure. Drowning in the emotional intensity of his tantalizing touch, her hands turned into claws as she tried to bring his mouth to hers. He had no trouble resisting and might not have noticed. "Holdin!"

"Right here, baby," he murmured into her mouth.

"No! More. Now!"

"I can't." His hand rocked between her legs from behind, shooting blistering sparks up her body as his fist in her hair turned her head fractionally so his open mouth could glaze over her cheek to her ear. "I need you too much, Jilly-girl," he confessed in rumbling growls, his mouth moving over her as if he needed to sample every inch of her for taste. "Don't let it scare you, baby. I promise, nothing happens you don't want. Nothing."

"I want, Holdin. I want already!"

His mouth moved around the base of her neck in nipping kisses and then he seemed to get stuck over her pulse, sucking tender skin into his mouth to bathe it with his tongue. Jill raked her fingers down to his shoulders as the beast in her arms ate at her flesh in maddeningly tender nibbles and shattering kisses. He was sucking her neck and he'd found the spot with a mysterious bundle of nerves just under her skin. Jill groaned loudly and her hips moved as if his lips had them on puppet strings.

"Oh God, don't! Holdin, please," Jill sobbed as he let go of the spot and licked it tenderly.

"Don't what?" he asked softly.

"Don't make me like this. You know where, how to touch me. Don't hurt me with it."

"Jesus, baby." His head lifted to look at the woman who inhabited his soul. "Why would you think that? This is me, Holdin. I'd rather lose a limb than hurt you."

Jill looked into his face. Her body trembled in his arms and her hands dug into his shoulders. "I'm afraid of wanting you this much. You haven't even really kissed me and I'm lost. What happens next? I've never been this lost since being with you and that was so long ago. I'm not young and firm. I'm not that uninhibited anymore. I can't handle this. I don't know what to do."

Holdin let go of her hair and wrapped both arms around her in a hug that was suddenly more comfort than seduction.

He folded her into his body as she buried her face in his chest, her arms now linked around his neck as she clung to him. "Shhhhh, Jilly-girl. Shhhh. You're so afraid, little one. Try to remember you're safe with me. Safe in me. I want you any way I can get you. God, I can't believe you're worried about this body. You're going to have to let me prove something to you."

Holdin shifted a step to put his back to the door. "But we'll have to prove it later. I believe company is on the way."

"What?" Jill's head lifted off his chest to glance up in alarm.

"Relax. No makeup dripping down your face. No clothes undone. Even the hair is good." He smoothed a hand down the back of her head. "Only problem might be the hickey." Holdin's head swooped down and he took her open mouth, swallowing the words of surprise and thrusting into her.

Jill's body responded to the dizzying invasion with a flash fire of reaction. This was what she'd been hungering for with the intensity of a starvation victim. Opening wider, she sucked him in and promptly forgot every word he'd just said. He invaded her with that kiss. Claiming her. Her arms tightened around his neck and her fingers sank into his hair again as she strained to get closer to him.

"How many rooms does a house have to have for y'all to find a private one?" Drifter drawled from the kitchen doorway.

Jill's body jerked at the sound of his voice but Holdin's didn't. He ended the kiss gently and smiled into her face. Blinking up at Holdin dazedly, Jill couldn't make sense of things for a moment. Holdin loosened his arms and stepped back from her while still holding her shoulders.

"Doesn't matter, buddy. You'll get used to it." Holden flashed a grin at his son as he pulled out Jill's chair for her. A bit unsteady, Jill sank into it. Holdin picked up his own chair and sat down to his plate again. "You get the brake pads?" he asked Drifter.

Drifter dropped a bag on the floor by the door and headed to the fridge.

"What pads?" Jill wanted to know as she watched her son, who'd eaten a huge breakfast earlier, pull out food and bread to start making a sandwich.

"That's how it is?" Drifter shot a glance at Holdin then turned back to building a sandwich while he casually asked, "You okay, Mom?"

"I'm fine. I assume you're asking about what you just saw?"

"Nope," Drifter interrupted her. "Do not make me hear any details. I understand the concept of kissing. No need to explain." Drifter brought his monster sandwich to the table and sat across from them. "I'm only askin' if you're upset or somethin' coz of the stress thing."

"Ah. Well, no. I'm not upset. What do you mean you understand the concept of kissing?" Jill added suspiciously, and leaned intently toward him across the table.

Drifter eyed her and a brow went up as he swallowed the huge bite he'd taken. "Mom, you have a hickey. Doubtful you can grill me at the moment."

Holdin choked on some bacon and Jill jerked back in surprise. Her hand flew to the right side of her neck, covering the sensitive spot that always drove her nuts.

"You didn't!" she gasped at Holdin, frowning fiercely.

"Now you've upset her," Holdin told his son as he gulped coffee to wash down the food.

"Holdin Thomas, did you give me a hickey?" Jill demanded.

Holdin put down his fork and laying his arm along the back of her chair leaned down to study her neck as if he were checking. "I can't tell. Let me get a closer look." His lips nibbled the other side of her neck and Jill squealed as she jumped. She would have fallen off her chair if his arm hadn't caught her.

"Hey!" Drifter jumped from his chair and half lunged across the table as Jill wobbled on her chair.

"Whoa, Jilly-girl. Easy now." Holdin steadied her, his arm securely wrapped around her shoulders.

"Geez! Huge rule. No falling!" Drifter was still standing, leaning over the table, both fists planted on it as his stiff arms flexed in tense energy.

"I got her. No one's falling," Holden responded calmly.

Drifter's face remained set in a grim scowl as he glared at Holdin, obviously placing the blame for the near fall squarely on the man's shoulders. "Do you? Do you not get that jerking, abrupt changes in body attitude or possibly rhythmic movements are mondo bad? Think of her head as light-bulb-thin glass filled with liquid and one lead marble."

"I will not hurt your mother." Holdin met the young man's gaze with calm confidence.

"Yeah? Your history says otherwise, man."

"Drifter!!" Jill gasped.

Drifter turned his head to the side and clenched his teeth, but his body didn't withdraw as he looked back into his mother's eyes grimly. "Mom, how is it I exist if he's so good at self-control? I know what happens when people exchange spit like the two of you were doing and it can't happen now."

"Drifter!" Jill repeated in sharp reprimand. "You will not speak to your father like that."

"No. It's all right," Holden interjected. "Those are legitimate concerns and in the circumstances he has a right to them." Holdin's hand squeezed Jill's shoulder in reassurance as he looked his son in the eye. "You're right. You have no reason to trust me. All I can do is tell you I have no intention of harming your mother or allowing her to come to harm. I understand your concerns and respect them."

Drifter stood up slowly, his face flushed and he glanced away from them. Once more he was a fourteen-year-old boy and highly uncomfortable with the subject. He sat down and picked up the sandwich but looked back at Holdin without taking a bite. His back still stiff, Drifter almost visibly steeled himself as he continued. "Do you get what I meant?"

"I'm well aware of your meaning," Holdin returned seriously. "However, my relationship with your mother is not up to you. We are together and I will guard her with my life as I would you. Do you understand my meaning?"

Jill glanced between to two males in outraged indignation. "You two will not discuss me like I'm some possession to be handed around. I can't believe this. Both of you!" She looked at Drifter in amazement. "How in the world did you become just like him without even knowing him? I am not your responsibility and I'm not his. I'm fully capable of looking after myself."

At her outrage, both males had the grace to look vaguely guilty. "Nobody is handing you around, Jill," Holdin defended them.

"You think I'm just like him?" Drifter asked casually around a bite of sandwich.

Holdin hid a grin, picking up the fork and resumed eating too.

Jill snorted, an inelegant statement in itself. "Apparently my genetic input has been completely ignored. You're a carbon copy," she informed him.

Drifter chewed and grinned at her, hazel eyes twinkling in satisfaction and remarkably similar to the ones concentrating on his last bite of eggs across the table from him.

Charles Powell walked in and came up behind Drifter, laying a hand on his shoulder. "Ready to get started?"

Drifter gulped the last of his sandwich as Holdin took his plate to the sink. "You two doin' the brakes?" Holdin asked.

"Yeah. We got pads earlier but I had a call to make when we got back. Thought we'd have a look-see," Charles added casually as Drifter busily cleaned up where he'd been sitting too. Getting the sponge from the sink, Drifter wiped the table as well as the counter where he'd made his sandwich.

Holdin watched his son clean up after himself as he washed and rinsed his own plate. Pleasantly surprised again, he wasn't stupid enough to comment on the boy's self-sufficient attitude. "Dad is the best mechanic around. A rancher can fix anything with an engine and most things without one."

"Mom, you hangin' around the house?" Drifter asked as he picked up the bag he'd dropped by the kitchen door.

"Yes. Carol wanted to show me some photos." Jill glanced at Holdin, who was leaning against the sink. "I'll be here."

Drifter nodded and left with Charles.

"I've got a few things to take care of in my office," Holdin said as they left. "I'd like to spend some time with you after, Jilly-girl. Think you can fit me into the schedule?" He came over to hold her chair as she stood and took her mug to the sink.

"I'll check my book." Jill smiled as his hand landed at the small of her back and they walked out of the room. "For heaven's sake, don't mind me. I'm sure you're a very busy man and have more than a few things to take care of."

Holdin's hand slid from her back around to her waist, tucking her under his arm instead of just walking with her. "Not anymore. I'm retired and I'm going to clear a few things up. We need some time."

From the arched opening to the family room they could see Carol across the space at a card table with several photo albums stacked on it. Holdin pulled Jill to a stop and into his arms, his mouth taking hers with firm pressure that made the kiss more than a peck. She opened to his lips naturally and then he was lifting his head.

"I'll be back as soon as I can," he promised as if he were going to some distant place. His arms tightened again and he took her mouth that had opened to reply to him in an even deeper kiss that moved as he explored the herb-tea taste of her.

Jill opened her eyes slowly as he drew away from her mouth. Her face was flushed and the pout of swollen lips glistened as she ran her tongue over her bottom lip.

"That was intense for just goin' across the hall," Jill purred.

"When weren't we intense?" he asked as with his hand at her back, they joined Carol at the table.

Five minutes later Holdin was in his office with the door firmly shut. First order of business was putting in a call to a Dr. Coates, neurosurgeon at Presby Dallas. Last night in all the talk, Jill had explained her condition to his parents. In that explanation, Holdin had carefully noted the name of her doctor and the medical facility she was headed to. There were questions to be asked and that was the man with the answers.

Ten minutes later the callback came. Holdin had known it would. There were advantages to throwing around his name when he needed to.

"Mr. Powell, what can I do for you? I hope it's nothing professional," a congenial low tenor greeted Holdin.

"Thank you for the prompt callback, Dr. Coates. I'm aware your schedule must be full and I'll only take a moment of your time." Holdin covered the mutual admiration required to get another powerful male to deal with him. Establishing respect for a man who didn't do heavy macho work was imperative. Otherwise they wasted too much of Holdin's time trying to prove they were just as manly as any pro quarterback. Or worse, they'd spend the same amount of time trying to prove they were smarter than he was. Both were an irritating waste of time.

"Getting right to the point," Holden continued. "Jill Smith is one of your patients, right?"

"Yes. Yes she is," Coates confirmed in a tone of surprise.

"I assume you're aware of where she was going before she would consent to surgery?"

"Oh, um, well, she did say in a vague way. You're not...ah...you are?" Coates floundered.

"I see she didn't mention the details, but yes. She was coming to see me," Holdin confirmed, and was very pleased to realize Jill hadn't gone into her story with the surgeon. Her silence respected him. "I'm calling because I need the whole story on her condition to ensure her safety. What are the biggest dangers to her health and how do you recommend ensuring her condition remains good?"

"Yes," Coates said slowly, and Holdin could almost hear the man's mind turning. "This must have been something of surprise for you. The two of you were hardly more than kids when you last saw each other?"

"We weren't kids. However, neither of us was aware she was pregnant when we lost contact," Holdin stated calmly to conceal his building irritation, and waited for his answers. He wasn't about to add any information that wasn't required on his history with Jill.

"Ah, the auto accident. Yes, of course. Most unfortunate. I can see why she was cagey about her story when she woke. If the press got a hold of this, it would be big news. I assume the paternity test is pending?"

"As I said, I don't want to take up too much of your time, Dr. Coates. I was calling about her condition," Holdin responded. "No need to bore you with irrelevant details."

The press and those complications hadn't occurred to Holdin. His focus had been so narrow on the amazing events of the last day that he'd completely overlooked the looming storm of media attention. Now that tangle of snakes and dragons bloomed in his mind. Damn!

"I see." Coates voice became slightly clipped. He recognized the smackdown in Holdin's response and wasn't pleased. "Jill should be in a hospital bed with restricted movement. That is the optimum insurance for her condition. Since we couldn't enforce that issue, all I can tell you is as little movement as possible. In fact, if the two of you have cleared up your issues as far as possible without the tests coming back, I'd like her to return immediately."

"Are you moving up her surgery from Tuesday?" Holdin asked as he frowned over the doctor's insisting on assuming he needed tests to ensure Drifter was his son. It was insulting but it was also how everyone else would react.

"No. Not unless her condition demands it. There simply is no reason for her to remain in your hair. Now that you have all the facts, I assumed you'd be ready to see her and her boy leave. Medically, I don't approve of this trip. Had I known where she was going, I would have opposed it for personal reasons as well. I'm sure it has been emotionally taxing on Jill and she needs to be calm and relaxed. So let's get it over."

"You've assumed quite wrong," Holdin stated using his low "furious leader" voice. The deep tone that had quietly and effectively berated young players into grasping that adult behavior was their only option. It was a combination growl and snarl and it came out naturally this time. "I'm calling to ensure she has the best possible care when I bring her in. Not to see how fast I can unload her. I will be involved with her care from here on out."

"I see. You do have a public image for being generous with charity. I can assure you that she will be very well taken care of here. We have one of the preeminent BrainSUITEs in the world and neurosurgical cases come to us from all over the globe. Jill is covered under her insurance and I don't see any problem with her receiving optimum benefit from every service we can provide. But it is nice to see chivalry is not dead."

Coates gave Holdin no chance to respond as he went on. "I was part of the national fencing team while at Harvard. A large part of that was appreciating the standards gentlemen used to be judged by. Your generosity is a credit to your profession, Mr. Powell."

Holdin sucked in a silent snarl at that obvious dumb jock insult that was meant to put him in his place. Apparently Coates wanted him to feel that *place* was considerably down the ladder from his own. Not likely. Also the reference to the fencing team was a male jab at proving he was as macho as any football jock but much more classy.

"Oh I agree," Holdin concurred in a silky smooth tone. "There's a lot to be said for a time when physical competition put an end to conflict between gentlemen. Pity we're not so civilized today. However, I can't imagine you, the surgeon, need to concern yourself with your patient's finances. But since you have, be assured Jill's expenses are covered. It's not charity when it's family. Thank you for your concern. I look forward to meeting you Monday, if not before."

"Indeed," Coates responded in as confident a tone as Holdin had used. There was not even a flicker of intimidation in it at the reference to physical competition. "Jill is an unusual woman. I take an interest in everything she needs. Right now she needs to be in the hospital. The sooner the better."

"Thank you. I'll see what I can do about that."

"I'll expect you then," Coates acknowledged.

Holdin dropped the phone in its cradle and eased back in his chair to scowl at the door across from him. The doctor was an irritating wrinkle. The man apparently wanted Jill and wasn't backing off. Holdin could smell competitive drive flowing through the phone when the bastard grasped the fact that Jill was neither charity nor an unwanted responsibility.

So his competition was a brain surgeon? Could have been worse, could have been a "rocket scientist". Holdin grinned harshly at his own joke. Didn't matter, Jill had been his long before the *king of the bastard nerds* had seen her. She'd be his long after too.

His smile turned into pure animal bared teeth after several more calls. He had a very clear picture of the fact that Dr. Coates was one of the finest neurosurgeons in the country. The bastard was extremely well respected and a bunch of other smack that made his reputation impeccable. This paragon had made it clear that his medical recommendation was to get Jill back in the hospital as soon as possible. Holdin couldn't ignore that. He hated it because it fucking scared him to death. The bastard might have made it plain that he had a personal interest but he still was her doctor and it was unlikely a man with his reputation would treat her medical condition lightly.

Holdin's problem was how to get her to consent to returning to Dallas right away. He wasn't in any position to order her back. He'd like to be in several positions with her, but not that one. Jesus! Anger rolled through him and he exploded out of his chair, sending it crashing to the floor. Pacing over to the fireplace and back across the large showplace study, he wanted to rip something apart.

There was also the publicity crap to consider. As soon as he showed up at the hospital in Dallas, someone would call the press. From there things would probably get wild if there was no information on why he was there. Even if the press were restricted from the hospital grounds, someone would pay an employee to get information.

His publicist would have to put out a statement explaining his involvement with Jill and Drifter. The thought of being forced to explain himself and invade his son's privacy like that, not to mention Jill's, caused bile to rise in his throat. If he said nothing, it would be worse. The press would make up explanations, printing them as if they were fact. After those were out, it was almost impossible to correct them. Pacing furiously back to the fireplace, he swore viciously.

Holdin's hand closed on some nonsensical item the decorator had carefully placed on the mantel when the study door opened and shut quietly. There was no need to turn around. She was in the room with him. The wild creature who'd been looking for her these last fifteen years felt her every breath. He would have known she entered the room even if it were full of people.

Chapter Five

"You're upset," Jill stated calmly as she stood in front of the closed door and looked at his big back. His head was bent and his arm resting on the mantel was tensed as he gripped the base of a heavy candlestick. He vibrated with energy and she wouldn't have been surprised if her hair suddenly stood on end in response to the static electricity snapping through the room.

Both she and his mother had heard a muffled crash then silence a few minutes ago. Carol had sighed and shook her head. Jill had chosen to investigate even though Carol had advised against it. Now in the huge, perfectly appointed office, she understood Carol's comment about letting the beast wind down first.

Here, in an overwhelming atmosphere of sophistication, hardwood panels and soft leather chairs, was the wild. It lived in the man as surely as it did in any remote wilderness den.

"Yes," Holdin answered in a quiet hiss. It was pointless to lie. He didn't want lies between them, not even small ones.

"Are you going to throw that?" Jill spoke softly as she would to calm any wild creature she couldn't avoid.

"I was thinking about it."

"It's a childish way to express emotions," Jill commented as if they were discussing the weather.

"Yes," he agreed with no excuses.

"I'd rather you didn't. It's a bit frightening to see you like this."

"I wouldn't throw it at you."

"No. I didn't think you would. It's still frightening. What has you this out of control?"

Holdin slowly released the candlestick. Turning to face her across the room, he shoved his hands in his pockets. Somehow he wasn't expecting the sight of her to still have gut-kicking strength. Maybe it was the situation that made looking at her so desperate. Pain knotted his stomach and he had to grit his teeth not to gasp as he looked at her calmly standing there. Her hands were clasped in front of her, her lush body tense as she watched him.

His eyes drank her in and he had to breathe deeply again to absorb the singular pain of looking at Jill. Fragile, precious and so possibly fleeting.

"I just spoke with Dr. Coates," Holdin told her with very deliberate calm.

Jill's head tilted as she regarded him. "So you need to smash something now? Is this a male thing that I'll never understand? Or can you explain it to me?"

"His medical recommendation is for you to get back in the hospital as soon as possible," Holdin told her flatly.

"Yes. He's an overly cautious sort," Jill agreed, and a little smile played around her mouth.

"It's not just caution, baby girl. He's your doctor." Holdin hated her smile when she mentioned the arrogant doctor. He had no right to ask her what it meant.

"Uh-huh. What does that have to do with your need to get violent?"

"I'm not violent. My reactions are magnified because of you. You make everything *more* — more important, more dangerous, more urgent." Holden walked slowly toward Jill.

The plush carpet completely muffled his steps as he moved across the room. Jill had the impression of a large golden cat stalking her as he moved. He flowed with silent power that rippled just beneath his skin. It was in the sensuous flex of perfectly honed muscles and nimble coordination that made him poetry in motion. Even just walking he was beautiful and now slightly dangerous. The edge of his emotional turmoil made him fascinating and frightening.

"What?" Jill nearly stuttered as he prowled into her personal space. Big, lean and intense, he was intimidating and exciting. Her lower body clenched as he rested a forearm on either side of her head against the door. His body felt hot as it pressed into hers, pinning her against the hard panels behind her. He had eased into her, slowly pressing himself up her. The controlled tension of his movements made them a caress.

Jill's hands fluttered to his hips, lightly resting on his belt as she sucked in air. He was looming over her, pressing into her and it became impossible to breathe as those unblinking eyes drilled into her. At last his head bent and he brushed his lips along hers.

Male lips nuzzled hers and the cat metaphor came back to mind. She opened to him with a soft moan. His arms left the door to move down her body as their mouths merged in a slow surrender to decadence. His tongue licked its way into her mouth while his large hands cupped her bottom, pulling her hips away from the door. She almost heard her nerves sizzle with each touch as they lit up like sparklers under his fingertips. His hands slid down the back of her thighs as the kiss deepened, his mouth molding hers in growing intensity. Very slowly he pulled her legs up around his hips.

Jill smoldered with his every move. His touch burned though their clothes as her V'd hips settled on the branding iron beneath his jeans. He was stealing her soul with the deep kiss. The gentle, insistent touch to her body was not exactly a request. It was more an acknowledgment of how much she wanted to give to him. He wasn't rushing, but he wasn't stopping. His command of her need and control of his own seduced her to the edge of surrender. She wanted to give up all thought and just feel. The hard evidence of his attention held in such tantalizing control was intoxicating.

Her back was pressed to the door as her legs locked around him and Holdin lifted his mouth from hers. His hands moved over her ass in firm caresses as he looked down into her face.

"Do you feel what you do to me? Every time I look at you, this is what I want," Holdin crooned into her ear as his mouth moved across her cheek and down to the soft spot just below her earlobe. "You go to my head and I can't keep you out." The deep timbre of his voice whispered around them between kisses down her neck.

"Perfect. So perfect. You fit my hands, Jill. You flow over my resistance with less than a glance." His hands moved up to the small of her back and slid around to her hips while tunneling under the loose polo shirt she was wearing. She wore it outside her pants to cover the curves she thought were too round.

His hard palms pressed into yielding flesh at her rib cage and kept moving up. The skin-on-skin touch made her gasp and his mouth was there to drink it in. He sucked her tongue into the hot depths of his mouth and explored it with his own. His palms moved over the stiff sides of her bone-reinforced bra and stopped. Not really cupping her, the heels of both hands pressed into the give of her breasts, pressing them together. His mouth lifted off her again.

"I need to touch you." His mouth moved down her neck again.

Jill leaned her head back on the door. She was sinking into the world he created and she had no intention of fighting it. He was magnificent, sexy and said he couldn't get enough of her. She wasn't stupid. He'd had the facts placed in his face as clearly as she could make them. Sexy beast was damn well able to make his own choices. If her choices were to get another taste of paradise in Holdin's arms…or do some idiot noble thing and "save" him from himself, well, noble was overrated.

"If you think this is fighting you, we need to talk about your life experiences," Jill panted.

Holdin smiled into her neck as his hands moved under her restrained breasts and lifted the weight of them. His mouth ate her lips again as he held those two heavy globes while his thumbs caressed cloth-covered nipples.

"How does that feel?" he asked softly.

"Mmmm. How do you know that feels so good?" Jill wanted to know. "Taking the weight off my body is almost as good as...well, it's better than chocolate." Jill's fingers dug into his shoulders as she arched into his hands. The arch pushed her pelvis into him as well. Damp heat rubbed up against hard flame and two zippers scraped together. Lifting and caressing her breasts at the same time was a sneaky move that she'd have to thank some brilliant woman for teaching him.

Holdin was smiling as they nibbled around each other's mouths, talking softly and touching. "I read about it once," he confessed. "Besides, the girls are so well strapped in, who could miss the bones required to support them?"

"Are you complaining about my bra?" Jill sank her fingers into his hair and pulled his head back so she could see his face. At the same time she flexed her hips and dug her heels into his ass to make sure the maypole in his pants would feel the damp heat her body was dying to drench him with.

"I'm admiring the enviable job it does," he insisted. His heavy-lidded eyes couldn't stay on her face and sank to the image of his hands moving under her shirt. "I'd like to admire it more closely."

Jill laughed. "I'm pinned to the door. No way this shirt is coming off."

One of Holdin's hands shot down to cup her sweet, generous ass again and support most of her weight. The other was suddenly around her shoulders, his palm cradling the back of her head in a firm grip as he swung them away from the door.

He carried her smoothly to the wide leather sofa that faced the enormous hearth. In slow motion he lowered her body so her upper back and head were supported by a pillow and the overstuffed sofa arm. Her legs were still wrapped around his waist as he lowered her. One of his knees deeply indented the leather seat while the other braced him on the floor.

When he was sure she was relaxed into the sofa, his hands went to the hem of the polo shirt and pulled it up to her armpits. Facing him was a blindingly white monument to modern engineering in all its boned and ribbed stiffness, thoroughly imprisoning the soft flesh he needed to touch. He gazed at it a minute.

"Whatcha gonna do now, bad boy?" Jill chuckled.

"Help myself to the goods," he answered, never taking his eyes off it.

"Holdin. Anyone could walk in the door. I can't get back into this thing fast enough to avoid serious embarrassment."

Holdin reached over her head to the end table on the other side of the sofa arm and picked up a cordless phone. He punched three numbers in with his thumb and put it to his ear, still studying the bra.

"Hey. How's the brake job coming?" he asked into the phone. "Really. Shit. Do me a favor, Dad. Insist on taking a look at the transmission while you have the car up. Yeah. None of your business. Make sure it takes at least another hour. Thanks." Holdin hung up and grinned.

His hands went to the shoulder strap clamps and flipped the little tabs up. A quick pull on the straps and both of them came free. He grabbed the tops of the cups and began peeling them down.

"Damn! Someone taught you that." Jill gasped as he slowly exposed her heaving breasts. "No one writes an article on the quickest way to get into an industrial bra."

"It's obvious," Holdin murmured distractedly as severe cotton gave way to pink, pouty nipples. He stopped peeling the cups down and let them hold her up for him from just under those enticing tips. "Jesus! Oh damn," Holdin breathed as reverently as a prayer while staring down at the amazing woman beneath him.

Her excited breathing made the generous mounds tremble. Their puckered tips danced brazenly before him. She was half propped up so the heavy globes seemed to strain over the peeled-down cups. Her legs, though still jean-clad, were spread wide to wrap loosely around his hips as he braced over her and she was once again his angel face with her sin-inducing body spread for his pleasure.

Jill looked into his glazed eyes and let the flames of his desire lick over every inch of her. He made her beautiful with his gaze. It was as if he invented the squirming wench who slowly lifted her arms and clasped hands over her head while arching her back to thrust nearly naked breasts up at him. The rumbling growl that moved up his chest as his body tensed above her was too gratifying. She drank it in and became what he saw when he looked at her.

He'd always done this to her. His hedonistic approval of her was like sinking into an enveloping chocolate-cream bath. Holdin's eyes on her was a richly wicked pleasure that painted a normally conservative woman in lavish excess. Heat gushed over her and need for his touch pierced her most private flesh with painful desperation. Watching this huge male tremble as he drank her with his eyes was almost more stimulation than she could take and it seemed she'd already passed the point where she'd refuse him nothing. It hadn't even been a speed bump.

"Holdin," Jill murmured softly. "I need you."

"Right here, baby girl. I'm here. There's got to be a few rules. We're not doing anything that endangers you. Understand?" He looked into her eyes and waited for compliance.

Jill regarded his stiff form braced with one arm clutching the back of the sofa and the other hand fisted beside her rib cage. He was very deliberately holding himself off her and not touching. "Tell me what you mean."

"It means you don't move your head." Holdin slowly lowered himself toward her trembling breasts. Need to taste became too irresistible.

"When have I ever been able to lie still? And how is this any good for you? You can't finish." Jill's voice turned into a mew of pleasure as she watched his fascination.

"This time you will and when has it ever been about me getting off?" His eyes flashed up to her face as he lightly licked over a distended nipple. The heat of his gentle tongue and the chill of his leaving her damp dragged a ragged moan out of Jill. "We were always so much more than that." He licked around the other nipple as he watched her face. "With you I was a man. Your trust fed me, Jill. Your innocence showed me how to control my own needs to see to yours first. You showed me what I needed, baby girl. Nothing was ever the same. You shaped my appetite for control. My pleasure is your pleasure."

His tongue circled and nudged at the peak of her breast. He toyed with its texture and taste without giving her a firm touch. Jill clenched her teeth for a moment as her hands clasped in white-knuckled tension above her head. "I may have gone overboard on that," Jill gritted out. "It wasn't intentional."

Holdin chuckled. His hands rested on her rib cage just below her breast. Hard fingers wrapped around her and his thumbs caressed the cotton-covered undersides of her over-stimulated breasts. She was fantastically sensitive there and he knew it. He knew every inch of her, every nerve, every reaction. Gently he pressed both thumbs up, causing her glistening nipples to strain toward his mouth.

"You were mine to protect and take care of, Jilly-girl. And the better I learned you, the deeper you burrowed into my soul. Every time I took a bit more control, the higher you flew in my arms. You were an addiction and a mystery…you fed my soul and drove me over the edge."

His mouth closed over a plump offering, sucking her deep and hard. He was rewarded with a gasping wail as fire shot through his woman. He could feel her light up in reaction as he pressed her nipple to the roof of his mouth and rolled it. Pulling his head back in a jerk shot a spike of pain into the pleasure and Jill shuddered as her hips slammed up in response.

Holdin released her breast immediately. His hands left her body to brace on either side of her armpits as he scowled down at her. "I told you not to move," he growled.

Jill opened her eyes. Tears glittered in them.

"Are you crying? Damn it, Jill!! You know better. It's your job to tell me what feels good and what's too much."

"No, this is being in the moment." Jill's hands unclasped and moved to frame his concerned face. "I'm emotional about this."

Holdin's scowl melted away. His head turned to lightly kiss one of her palms.

"Please, don't stop," Jill added softly. "It's just been so long, Holdin. So very long since we were here. Since you made me the woman you see. I wasn't expecting this, you. Not in my wildest dreams. I thought it'd be difficult to talk to you. Another battle. I was so busy getting ready to battle you for my son's future, it never occurred to me that you'd want us back. Never." Jill gulped in a hitching breath. "So the tears are not bad, they're just relief mixed with need leaking out of me."

Holdin stared intently into her face and gritted his teeth. She apparently had no idea how she moved him with these glimpses into her soul. How painful it was for him that she'd had to fight so many battles alone. "Baby girl, I'm all for you getting damp," he told her softly, hoping his response hid the flash of pain and fierce possessive rage her statement had triggered in him.

Jill managed to blush and look totally wanton at that. "Oh damp is not a problem." Her hips slowly flexed into his cock, rubbing up his fly. "But I was hoping you'd do something for me," she added in a husky whisper.

"What?"

"Take your shirt off." Her fingers curled into claws as she drew them down his shoulders and over his pectorals.

His grin turned wolfish. "Anything you want. But you have to lie still. Got it?"

He pulled the T-shirt up over his head and dropped it beside the couch. Jill could only moan her agreement with his demand as her hands landed on his hard chest.

He remained still as she explored him, but only for a minute. A pelt of golden hair lay over amazing ridges and valleys that were male muscle and tendons. He'd been perfect as a young man. Now he was ripped. She'd had no idea how primitive that term was until now. Saying something like he was built or muscled was too tame for this body. Power moved beneath his skin and there was nothing civilized about it.

Jill had almost forgotten her own exposed chest but Holdin hadn't as he leaned down to nuzzle the fragrant valley between her breasts.

His mouth moved over her in lazy licks that had Jill humming with sensations. Warm, sensual embers of constrained passion burst into flame with each touch. He kept the touches tender as he moved across her.

His hands molded her rib cage and slid down to the snap of her jeans. Pleasure burned her with his every touch. More than physical, it enveloped her mind with a heat that had been burning a long time. This was Holdin. Past and present melted together as he took what had always been his. Even when she hadn't known it, her body had been his. Waiting for him, needing him, needing this. Nothing had ever been more right than this.

She wouldn't have cared if she'd felt the snap of her pants give and the zipper slowly slide down. But she didn't. All her attention was consumed in the lick of his clever tongue over her sensitive nipples until suddenly a large, warm hand spanned her lower abdomen and hard fingers strummed back and forth over velvety skin.

Her legs slowly fell off his hips to extend down on either side of him. "Ohhhh," Jill moaned.

"Mmmm" was his agreeing noise as he sucked a nipple into the hot cavern of his mouth. Her hips tilted and his hand smoothly slid down to comb his fingers through the soft curls guarding her mound. At the top of her damp slit, he stopped to gently finger the sensitive crevice opening. Circling the spot she wanted him to touch.

Jill's hands fisted in Holdin's hair. She'd not even realized she was cradling his head to her breast. "More." Her moan was a demand.

Holdin's teeth clamped around her nipple in a small punishment and her fingers relaxed in his hair. A growl of approval rumbled around them and he was again sucking her abused flesh gently. Between her legs, slick fingers sank inside the folds she offered him. He still hadn't touched her clit and the tension singing up her belly was a trembling combination of excitement and frustration.

He sawed those fingers up and down, separating plump folds but not increasing the stimulation, carefully not touching the swollen bundle of nerves that would give her the push she needed to reach the next level.

"Head still," Holdin murmured as her mews increased.

"Yess…but I need more," Jill hissed back at him.

"I know what you need, Jilly-girl. Do you know what I need?"

"Tell me," she pleaded as her body moved on his hand.

"Your trust. That's all I ask. Give it to me." The deep bass of his voice drowned her as she sank into consuming sensations. It was difficult to make sense of that one.

"Holdin. I don't know what you're asking. What you want me to do?" Jill groaned in confusion. "Just tell me what you want."

Funny thing was, Holdin wasn't sure he knew what he wanted from her. Anything he told her to do would be worthless as proof she trusted him. She had to want to on her own. He needed her tied to him emotionally, physically, any way he could get her. Getting her back to the hospital was important. Not losing her to the prick with a stethoscope, imperative. Sealing his claim on her with her surrender was a primitive drive he had almost no control over.

His hand left the liquid heat between her legs and Jill opened her mouth to protest but let it out in a sigh of relief when he gripped her jeans and panties together and pulled them down her legs. He had to stand to slide her shoes and pull the clothing off. Already at her feet, he knelt on the sofa between them and, holding the leg on the edge of the couch, started kissing and nipping his way up it.

As he moved, he was spreading her wide, bending her knee and exposing her private flesh in the relatively bright office. He couldn't miss the changes of time on her lower belly, thighs and hips and she almost didn't even care anymore.

His maddening mouth moved over her inner thigh in stinging little bites that were injections of fire to already sensitized nerve endings. He was trying to drive her crazy. She knew it and loved it even more than she had in the past. Now, in this moment, as he finally licked the fold between thigh and cunt, she realized how unbearably erotic it was to know he would drive her nuts and control her in the same moment.

Just as he controlled his own strength, he mastered her need. A massive, powerful animal, he was careful not to mark her. With each touch she felt the tension in him and as it built, he became a lightning rod of concentrated energy. His control of that deadly need within himself drove her higher. It manifested in her as a euphoric rush. She was in the embrace of a feral beast and safer than she'd ever been before.

His tongue circled in the cream melting from her body. He licked it in as if it were his due, and it was. Then his wicked muscle invaded her and his lips sealed around her to suck hard. Jill bit her lip to stop the scream. Her hands fisted beside her on the sofa. He was eating her taste as carnally as it could be done. His hands held her thighs open with barely contained savagery and he was sating his taste for her. Her eyes closed and she panted, though from her shoulders up, nothing moved. Humming growls vibrated deep into her womb as Holdin took her intimate flavor and made it his possession.

Her thighs trembled under his hands and he knew she was close. But he wasn't about to cut this short. His head lifted as his hands moved to frame his prize. Pink and swollen, he marveled as his thumbs gently pulled her outer folds back to bare her to him. It was more than looking at the perfection of the female sex. This was Jill. She lay beneath him swollen and dripping and she was his. All his. Her distended clit told him how much she needed and he suspected she might be close to knowing how badly he needed this from her.

His hunger for her always had been more than sexual. The relationship between them had been more. It was more now. It made him and destroyed him. He'd taken it for granted once in the ignorance of youth. Not that he'd been lazy about it, but it had never occurred to him that this woman could be taken from him. This time he could see the thief at the door waiting to snatch her from him again. He'd thought it would have been better to know it was coming but he'd been wrong. Knowing was hell.

This could not be taken from them. Nothing could change this. His mouth lowered to drink her. He needed this moment more than he needed breath. To feel her fly for him. Only for him.

"Come for me, Jilly-girl," Holdin commanded.

His tongue flattened over her opening and slowly licked up to land on her clit. Then he took it into his mouth and gave her what she needed. Sucking gently at first, he absorbed her shocked jerk as her hips thrust up. His hands came up under her ass to hold her to him, he worked her most sensitive spot with concentrated intensity and she flew for him.

Jill's body suddenly combusted as flames shot up her body and exploded. It had been so long and she couldn't hold on. His wicked mouth took more as she gasped through the explosion. He sucked her clit in and rolled it gently then holding it between his lips, he lashed it with his tongue in hard, fast strokes that drove her into oblivion.

He didn't stop as she writhed beneath his mouth. Fully engorged, her contracting pussy only became more sensitive as every touch dragged her along the razor edge between pleasure and pain. She crashed into a second orgasm before the first had let her go and she couldn't hold back a low scream. Her hands clawed at his shoulders and he ignored them.

Gasping for air, Jill tried to shove him away. Her hands were ineffectual and his tongue a demanding beast that had made it clear he was not done with her. Her legs clenched around him, wrapping around his head and trying to arch her hips away from him. He held her in a vise grip and there was nothing she could do. She gave up and let her legs fall open as widely as possible while her body trembled once more in the fires he created for her. Release could only drag mewing moans out of her and then two fingers entered her in a hard thrust. He stretched her in a demanding invasion that shocked and drove her as nothing had before.

The finger-fuck was so dominant. He took her response, manipulating her while she knew he was not feeling a corresponding stimulation. His awareness of her reactions was unbelievably animal as his mouth worked her clit. He snarled and moved with her, never letting that screaming spot out from under his tongue. She rocketed into that place only

Holdin could take her. Each hard thrust into intimate folds forced her pleasure to staggering peaks. Her body gushed and clenched, taking him greedily. Hot shots of sensation speared through her with each deep penetration and yet she knew it would soon be more. He always took more than she thought she could give. His snarling excitement vibrated up her and Jill doubted she could stand it.

Holdin felt her surrender and growled into the heat of the cunt he owned. She may not have realized this surrender was to the primitive male who'd claimed her once before and never given up his position on her. That bastard had hunted her, driven him to become who he was for her. Now he had her back and no power would take her again. Well, that's why the bastard was primitive. He fucking didn't care what else occurred as long as he had Jill.

Reluctantly he let her spiral down. His fingers remained buried deep in her tight pussy as he licked around them, lapping up her taste greedily. He moved them lazily in and out and she clenched weakly every time he did. Watching for a moment, he smiled. Yes, this was his.

Finally his eyes traveled up her body. Over a trembling belly, tracking the mounds of her exposed breasts still half captured in the severe bra, to her face. He pulled himself up so he sat with one of her legs draped over his thighs, the other behind his shoulders on the back of the sofa and drank in the sight of her sprawled open to him. His fingers still moved in her and he enjoyed the slow fuck.

Her eyes half opened, sensing him looking at her.

"Roll your nipples for me, Jilly-girl," Holdin directed as he continued to slide his fingers in and out of her.

She tensed as her eyes focused on him, slowly surfacing from the fog of release and becoming aware of his view and his command. He was breathing heavily as his eyes moved over her, his jaw clenched and sweat glistened on his wide, bare chest. The damp evidence of her passion covered his face. His continued invasion of her body was gentle but insistent as was his hold on her leg across his thighs. She'd tensed and his grip tightened warningly. She was to remain as she was. No words were required, just the savage look on his face to tell her that.

Now the low-timbre command was pushing her. Taking her. He wanted her compliance and it had very little to do with sex. He was taking possession of her body. Her response to his command was overwhelming and immediately clear to him. His fingers deep inside her felt her body shudder and then liquid acceptance gushed around those digits.

He didn't smile. He bared his teeth and hissed as her fingers moved to the sensitive peaks of her breasts and slowly rolled them for him. Even though the act was surrender, sensation zipped straight down to her womb and shook her with little tremors. Jill's mouth opened in a silent gasp at the intensity of her response. Her body arched into his fingers and she reveled in the surrender he required. Everything else fell away and there was only this man in her world. He burned through her with his elemental control of her base responses.

A wicked cord of fear whipped up her body as he looked at her. It wasn't bitter. It was sweet seduction. He would have her as he wanted her. She knew he would. He'd make sure she loved his possession too. For this man it would be almost effortless. The fact that he understood the power he wielded was overwhelming. But not as frightening as the sure knowledge that he also knew how badly she needed it from him.

Suddenly there were three fingers in her and he was fucking her with them in hard thrusts.

Her hips lifted helplessly and her fingers pinched engorged nipples hard, pulling her breasts up to send drugging spikes of pain into the enveloping pleasure of submitting to Holdin. Looking into his eyes, Jill felt the whirlwind coming. His consuming need coupled with her desperate desire created such an overwhelming vortex of emotion and sensation. The power of it washed over her body with a roaring intensity that she couldn't control, couldn't resist.

"Help me," she gasped in panic. Fear and surrender crashed together and the storm of this moment was about to carry her away.

He heard it in her plea, saw it in her trembling body and immediately he was over her, the weight of his body holding her to the sofa as his other arm wrapped around her head and held her cheek pressed to his. The fingers in her cunt thrust into her with greater force and she gave herself into his keeping. The release erupted in what would have been uncontrollable abandon as she flew into the universe. He took her there and protected her from the power of it at the same time.

His low voice in her ear drove her higher and gave her an anchor to cling to. "That's my girl. Yes, let it go. So beautiful, baby girl." She convulsed repeatedly and he held her still. The world spun away and he guarded her soul with his body. His rigid control released her to abandonment and she was safe.

The full-body contractions finally began to quiet and his fingers in her slowed to gentle caresses as reality crept back into the room. Jill lay panting beneath him, afraid to open her eyes. The overwhelming pleasure she'd just experienced was as frightening as it was wonderful. It'd been about them, Jill and Holdin, in the most elemental way possible. Her pleasure had only been complete when she'd been willing to surrender even her life into his keeping.

Jill was still trembling as Holdin pulled his drenched fingers from her body. His cheek was damp with her tears as he turned to gently kiss them away. "Don't cry, baby," he crooned softly. "Don't be sorry this is who we are."

He was kissing her face with tender desperation as Jill opened her eyes to gaze at him in glazed amazement.

"Doesn't this scare you? Do you know what you did to me?" He'd shattered her and held her together in ways she couldn't even put words to. Her release had been as bound up in the symbolism of surrendering to him as it was about the sensations.

"I know what *we* just did and no, it doesn't scare me. What scares me is that you don't trust me now," he told her softly. "That is how we are. Tears on your face terrify me."

He knew she'd been completely his. Once again he'd held *his* Jill and given her everything he could. But now he needed to hear her say it, acknowledge that unique merging of souls that only she and he could achieve.

Jill closed her eyes again and tried to let their embrace calm her. He held her tenderly and again rested his cheek beside hers.

"Tell me why you're so afraid, Jilly-girl. You trusted me for a moment and then it was gone. What happened?"

"Reality happened." Jill dragged in a deep breath. "The past, the future, all of it. I'm afraid of going to a hospital again. Cutting into my brain is just piling on the terror factor. I'm so worried about Drifter and so afraid I can't help him deal with this. He's such a little man. He doesn't show me his fears anymore. He's too busy trying to protect me. Oh God, Holdin. Everything! I have to take care of everything and it's so much harder to remember that when you show me how it feels to…to not worry about anything." Jill turned her head into his neck as tears flowed again.

"Shhhhh. No, baby, no. Don't cry. Honey, how about you let me worry about a few more things for both of us? I'm trying to get you to see that you can do that. I'm the one you can lean on. I'll take care of you. I'll take care of our son. Your only job is to get through the surgery. That's it. Everything else is mine to worry about. Let me have it, Jill. Give me your trust."

Jill shuddered beneath him and the tears stopped flowing. He couldn't see her face but he didn't need to. Her body was tense. She was thinking about it but not really getting what he meant. She was withdrawing the gift of her soul. Somehow she couldn't take that step in the cold light of logic.

"It's not that simple," Jill stated softly.

"Why not? Have I ever intentionally let you down?" he prodded her again. Would she be brave enough to come to him? He steeled himself as he waited for her. She had physically returned to him voluntarily but could she make the rest of the trip mentally? Oh God! He wanted her so bad, so damn bad. Not just in his bed but at the center of his world. She was the heartbeat of his soul, a position that had always been hers.

"We're not so free anymore. Now there are huge issues to think about. There are estates and inheritance and guardianship. There are legal issues and moral ones. I can't just stop thinking as an adult. If it were just me, I could manage it. But as a mother, I have to think about all these things to protect my son. I can't let go. Not for an instant."

"Who asked you to stop thinking? Damn, woman! Of course you have to protect our son, but don't you see that you've done that?" Holdin's arms tightened around her as he ended the statement with soft kisses to the crown of her head.

Jill was silent and Holdin frowned. He could feel her resistance to what he'd just said in her body. Pain at what she couldn't say to him was surprisingly sharp. It was unrealistic to expect her surrender, that didn't mean he couldn't want it. Didn't mean he didn't need it. Anger was his initial response, fierce rage at the years that had been stolen from them, the life that should have been theirs. Those long wasted years of loneliness.

Damn, this would be so much easier if she were his wife already.

Holdin jerked in shock. That was it!! Baby girl needed security and he needed her. All of that could be tied up in a tidy bow with a marriage license. There would be no more questions of inheritance, guardianship, obligation or slick doctor bastards trying to steal her.

"Marry me." His deep voice made it a command instead of a request.

"What?" Jill's body stiffened.

"Marry me. Before we go to the hospital tomorrow. Let me call the preacher and have him do it. We'll file for a special license but I want to say the words and have it recorded in the church records now."

Jill's face left his neck and she stared at him with wide, shocked eyes. "You're serious?"

"Yes. Marry me," Holdin insisted again.

"No! We can't just get married! Are you insane?" Jill frowned at him as if he were suddenly some alien being.

"No. Think about it. Married is the one thing that takes away all the questions. I'm totally serious. We should have been married a long time ago," Holdin insisted logically.

Jill searched his eyes in consternation. He was serious and apparently convinced he was making sense. "Holden," she started slowly, intending to speak to him as plainly as possible. "People do not get married because they were a lovely couple once upon a time. Nor do they do it because they had a child. Getting married for any reason but the right one is insanity."

She grabbed his handsome face, framing it as he opened his mouth to argue with her. "No. Listen to me. You are a dominant. I'm well aware of that and what it means now. You need to take care of your family and that's wonderful. But I will not consent to marry you because you suddenly realized a marriage license would make controlling everything so much easier. Nor will I do it because you think I need it. Come up with the right reason and I'll consider it sometime in the future. But not now, not before the surgery."

"Jesus!" Holden snapped his teeth shut to stop the flow of frustration and carefully peeled himself off her to start gathering up her clothes. Shaking out her pants, he studiously concentrated on the job at hand while Jill pulled the bra cups back over her breasts and started fumbling with reinserting the shoulder straps in the little clamps attached to the cups.

He'd gone too far. Damn it to hell! Her "right reason" was kicking his ass, hard. She wouldn't believe a declaration of love now and he wasn't even certain the emotion he was feeling could be called that. Love was gentle, kind, long-fucking-suffering. None of that shit applied to the pacing beast dragging its claws in the dirt right now. That animal apparently had the mental capacity of a baboon. Holdin slammed the cage shut on the idiot and set about repairing damage.

Her pants were about as shaken out as they could get and Jill was still fumbling with the shoulder straps. "Let me, baby." Holdin gently took over the hooking up and deftly inserted the cloth straps through the clip slots. Pulling them tight required supporting each breast, which he did gently.

Jill glanced up at his face. His expression was calm as if a mask had dropped over it. He pulled down her polo shirt and picked up her panties from on top of the jeans he'd laid over the other arm of the chair. Jill was still half reclining on the sofa as he slipped them over her feet and glanced up at her with a raised eyebrow. She shifted so he could pull them up her legs.

"Dressing me?"

"Mmmm," Holdin grunted and grabbed her pants. Gently he helped her into them, going so far as to zip and snap them. "Don't get up. Remember you're not supposed to move around if you don't have to."

Jill let him do as he pleased. He seemed intent on the task. The explosive conversation that had ended so abruptly weighed on her. Would Holdin see her refusal to marry him out of convenience as a rejection? It was a rejection, but only of the reasons he was using. Or would he see it as a narrow escape? Even in her mind, she knew that wasn't fair. He'd been very clear that he intended to be involved in her life, not just Drifter's. Marriage was a huge step.

"I'll be right back," Holdin excused himself when she was dressed and strode across the room. Jill heard a door open and then water running. She couldn't see over the back of the couch but assumed he was washing his face in an attached bathroom. Jill smiled. He certainly needed to. She could use a shower too.

Holdin had returned and was just pulling on his shirt when a young voice echoed down the hall.

"Hey? Mom?"

"In here," Jill responded loudly.

Chapter Six

ಌ

"A family chat might be a good idea," Holdin said quietly. "We have to make some choices."

"What?" Jill whispered urgently as footsteps neared. "You are not talking marriage in front of everyone!"

"No. That's our debate," Holdin assured her as he went to open the study door. "In here," he called to Drifter who was peering into the family room looking for them.

"Hey, Mom," Drifter strolled into the room. "How ya feelin'?" His half smile turned to concern upon finding her reclining on the couch.

"Besides being stuck on the couch, fine. Holdin doesn't want me to move. So here I am." She laughed to lighten the mood.

Drifter glanced at Holdin. "Good. That's more like it."

Holdin returned to the sofa and sat down at the other end, carefully lifting Jill's feet into his lap. Approval from the boy was hard-won indeed. His hands caressed the soles of her feet naturally. He smiled at Drifter. "Have a seat, son. We should talk about a few things."

Drifter looked back and forth between them in concern. "What? Has something happened?"

"No, nothing like that. I called Dr. Coates though, and wanted to discuss what we do now in light of his medical opinion."

Drifter sprawled in the oversized wingback easy chair set at an angle to the couch. "Let me guess. He wants her back in the hospital now. Mom doesn't want to go."

Holdin grinned. "No one ever said you were slow. I figure between the two of us, she'll see reason."

Drifter smiled a slow way-too-knowing grin. "So what did you think of his non-medical opinions?"

"Drifter!" Jill frowned at him.

"Well, Robert isn't an idiot. When he realized who Powell is, he'd have said something," Drifter defended himself.

"So you know about that?" Holdin asked with studied calm. He could feel the boy working up to something and wasn't sure what his point was.

"Sure. He's the guy I called when I found Mom on the floor. Seemed logical. He's dating her and a brain surgeon."

"I see." Holdin's eyes swung around to Jill.

"Guess ya hadn't told him." Drifter raised a brow at Jill.

"We are not dating and there hasn't been a lot of time," she snapped. "Why are you in such a rush, young man?"

"He should know." Drifter shrugged and looked levelly at Holdin. "You've got a real nice place here and all, but that doesn't mean we're movin' in."

The studied boredom was back on Drifter's face along with a stiff undertone of stubbornness that was very familiar. Holdin regarded his son as his hands continued the gentle massage of Jill's feet. Drifter was feeling the need to push him. Almost a man and he wasn't ready to give up his position as Man of the House. Holdin supposed his physical possession of Jill every time the boy saw them today was a trigger. Smart little bastard had gone straight for the big guns too. No beating around with innuendoes.

"I'm aware Dr. Coates has a personal interest in your mother," Holdin agreed, tightly controlling his dark emotional response. "I'm a bit surprised you don't respect her privacy though." The gentle reprimand was all he could afford right now. The boy was deliberately looking for a rise out of him. Drifter's instincts were good though. He'd scored right on the fucking soft spot.

"What's the matter?" Jill asked. "Why are you being deliberately rude?"

"You mean it's none of my business, Mom?"

"I mean you're being combative. Why?" Jill wanted to know.

Drifter shrugged.

"Your mother and I do have issues. We both had a life for the last fifteen years and no one's acting like we didn't. Right now my concern is making sure she gets the best care possible. We'll work out the details of how our relationship develops as we go. And I agree with you, it is your business, son. We are your family."

Holdin used the term "son" deliberately. He was well aware of the distance Drifter was trying to create between Jill and him. This whole situation was moving too fast for the boy. In the last day and a half he'd gone from just worrying about his mom to the addition of a father in his world. Not just a man but another alpha. Even if Drifter didn't realize it, that was the problem.

Young lion was feeling challenged and it couldn't be helped. Holdin wished he could make it easier for the boy, but Drifter was the only one who could do that. It depended on what he decided to do about Holdin. Hopefully his mind was not made up yet.

Jill closed her eyes and bit her lip. She hated conflict. Yes, there were a lot of things she and Holdin should discuss. She'd not mentioned Robert because it was such a difficult subject. Seemed as if every damn thing were becoming difficult. God, she was so tired of it. Now Drifter was determined to stir up trouble. Well, not exactly stir it up, but he was on some male mission that made no sense to her.

The gentle pressure on the balls of her feet had never paused throughout the conversation. Holdin's touch was warm and tender. His massaging her feet felt amazingly good and it also somehow conveyed ownership instead of service as it would on another man. Perhaps that was what set Drifter off.

"Do you think we can all agree that it'd be a good idea to get back to the hospital tomorrow instead of a couple days later?" Holdin continued, including Drifter in his question. "That's a compromise, Jill," he added with a smile, hoping to get one out of Drifter with the reference to what he'd said in the soda fountain yesterday.

"Yes, I suppose that'd be a good idea," Jill conceded. "But I don't want to fly. Isn't there something about altitude that could be detrimental?"

"I'd only recommend it in an emergency," Holdin agreed. "We can go in the Navigator. It has a smooth ride."

"I don't want to leave the car," Drifter stated.

Holdin nodded. "Mom and Dad will want to come. Dad can drive it if you don't mind." Holdin directed the question to Drifter in acknowledgment of his need to have transportation. Even though Drifter wasn't old enough for a license, they both knew he could drive. Leaving the car would be emasculating, making him that much more helpless in a situation already difficult to handle. He needed some measure of control.

Charles Powell strolled in the room. "Did I hear we're going to Dallas tomorrow?" he asked casually while taking a seat across from Drifter in the matching wingback chair. Carol followed him and perched on the overstuffed arm of his chair.

"Yeah. You mind driving?" Holdin asked smoothly. "I spoke to Jill's doctor and he was very concerned that she get back as soon as she can. Coates is concerned and wants all movement of her head restricted. It's almost impossible to do that outside a hospital environment."

"Sure," Carol answered for both of them. "Y'all want to leave early?"

"We'll want to miss morning traffic," Drifter spoke up. "If we leave around nine, Central should be as clear as it'll get.

Only better time would be doin' the trip at four in the morning."

"Honey, I'd really rather not," Jill protested. "You're just determined to get me outta bed early."

Drifter grinned. "Like that's gonna happen. If I can't put a cup of coffee under your nose, nothin' will rise you that early."

Jill's chuckle with Drifter was full of their relationship. Close, just the two of them. "That's the only carrot that's makin' me want to do this," Jill confessed. "I get coffee again when it's over."

"I promise, soon as Robert says it's okay, I'll smuggle you a cup of the expensive French Vanilla stuff. Regardless of how bad it smells," Drifter added.

Holdin watched this byplay and saw the single mother who struggled to make ends meet on a dental hygienist salary. Saw a child doing what he could to make his mom's life easier. And he also saw Jill knowing her son well enough to let him look after her as much as he was able. Another window into a life he should have been there for. Painful bits of knowledge that stabbed him.

Drifter's continued use of Coates' first name told him the relationship between Coates and Drifter was tighter than he'd like. Another bit of barbed-wire knowledge.

He couldn't respond to any of it, but deep in his soul the beast was snarling. What he didn't know about Jill was understandable but unacceptable. What Coates did know about her was intolerable. The question that ate at him was one he didn't have a clear right to ask. He didn't think Jill would have allowed their relationship to get intimate if she was already in a physical relationship with another man but he needed to know for sure. Knowing for sure presented certain risks. What if she was involved with this bastard? Would it make a shit of difference? He doubted it. The only difference would be that it was over. He'd make sure all the parties involved were clear on that. Worse, what if she wanted to be? There was the question that would be a problem.

Just the thought of that possibility came armed with dangerous spikes of pain. It was unreasonable to expect she'd been untouched since he'd last held her, Lord knew, he wasn't, but logic had never had anything to do with his feelings about Jill.

Holdin reminded himself that Drifter was baiting him. He knew the boy recognized him for what he was. Be it subconscious or not, they were very similar.

"Good, we'll leave tomorrow around nine," Holdin said calmly. "Something else I want to talk about. We're going to run into the issue of my being a celebrity in Dallas. Someone will recognize me at the hospital and call the press. Soon as that happens there's going to be a million rumors about who you and your mother are." Holdin nodded at Drifter. "I'd like to let my publicist put out a statement before they start making things up. They will still call you my secret love child and probably some other garbage anyway. A statement will only make them look like they're reaching for a story.

"Next they'll stake out your home and be calling at all hours trying to get an interview. They might even break in if they think you're home. I'm still news in that town. It'll take a few years of retirement to wear that down. You'll become an instant celebrity and a target. Do you understand what I'm saying?"

Jill gasped. "Oh my God! I hadn't even thought of that." Her face was stricken with panic. "Do you think someone might try to kidnap Drifter because he's your son? Would they?"

Holdin's hands closed around her feet in a brief squeeze of reassurance. "It's possible. I'm not trying to scare you. I simply want both of you to understand. These are the facts of fame. It's not fair and it's almost never honest.

"Drifter, would you agree to stay at my place while we're in Dallas? It's a security issue. I'm not trying to take over your life." He spoke directly to his man-child. It was important to gain both respect and consent. Having to force Drifter to do anything would create a serious problem in their very new relationship.

"Oh honey!" Jill looked at her son pleadingly. "Please do that. I'll be so worried if you don't."

"Yeah, sure. Geez, Mom. It's not like it'd be easy to grab me." Drifter shifted in the big chair. "You really think it's gonna be that big a deal?" he asked Holdin.

"I think it's important to have a game plan. This shit gets out of hand fast. You look just like me. No way they're gonna miss that. It'll create a whirlwind to begin with," Holdin answered.

"Don't worry, no one is touching my only grandbaby," Carol declared confidently. "You just rest easy, Jill."

"I 'spect those paparazzi boys are gonna find themselves in danger shortly," Charles added as he patted his wife on the butt. "They should be warned. It's the humane thing to do." The tension dissipated at Charles' dry humor.

"As I said," Holdin continued. "It'd be best if there was a statement to give the press. Do either of you object?"

"No." Jill glanced at Drifter. "You?"

"Naw. Might be fun." Drifter shrugged again.

"Course we have to supply proof for the legal documents. Since we'll both be at the hospital I'd like to arrange the test. I want it out of the way fast. You good with that, son?"

"Whatever. It's just a cotton swab," Drifter agreed.

"Holdin, don't make that statement time specific. I'd feel more comfortable if it was vague. Can you do that?" Jill asked quietly.

"That's what the statement is for. To defuse while it says almost nothing. Don't worry, I'm not about to give the media facts they can research," Holdin assured her with a smile.

"Then it's all right with me if we have to," Jill agreed reluctantly.

"Good." Holdin got up to sit behind his desk and grab the phone.

Jill started to sit up. "Whoa there, missy!" Carol exclaimed. "Where you goin'? I thought you weren't supposed to move."

"Hey. Mom!" Drifter straightened in his chair. "Relax. What do ya need?"

Jill realized everyone was frowning at her as she glanced around. "It's lunchtime. I was just getting up to fix something," she defended herself.

"You just lay right back down. I'll bring a tray in." Carol stood up.

"I'm not hungry." Jill laughed as she slowly relaxed back. "It's the food pit over there who's going to start shrinking into himself soon." She waved a hand at Drifter.

Holdin released his breath and picked up the phone, trusting his family to handle the little mother.

"Ahhh. I know how to handle one of those," Carol assured Jill as she headed to the door. "You don't think the other boy in the room got that big all on his own. Come on, Chuck. I'm gonna need a few things from the freezer in the garage. Half an hour, Drifter. Your butt better be in a kitchen chair."

Drifter grinned at his grandmother's mild threat. "Yes, ma'am. You can depend on me."

Carol's head whipped around to laugh back at him as she left. Jill watched the open, uncomplicated connection between her son and his grandparents and smiled. That relationship had been amazingly immediate. Carol and Charles were the key. She'd known they were wonderful people. She hadn't known she could love the way they chose to show love.

Carol addressed Drifter as her "grandbaby" and hugged him like a long-starved grandma the moment she saw him. Charles Powell had gruffly told Carol to "let the boy breathe, for God's sake" and had promptly given Drifter a brief, manly hug that involved a lot of back pounding. They'd made it clear they were thrilled to have Drifter in the house. Then they proceeded to make her feel welcome. It had given her a few moments of nearly teary relief to begin with.

As the two older Powells disappeared, Jill looked at her son. Behind her at his desk, Holdin was on the phone and Jill assumed it was with his publicist. Drifter looked back at her and raised a brow in question without bothering to voice it. He was asking her how she really was and he meant about the man speaking at the desk.

Though his age was fourteen, Drifter had taken the job of being the man of the house seriously for some time now. It'd been disconcerting when she'd realized her baby didn't think like a baby. His maturity and adult outlook had given her many sleepless nights. Had she somehow stolen his childhood from him by being a single parent? Was she communicating her craving for safety in some unspoken way she had no idea about?

He wasn't disrespectful. He'd simply taken to treating her as his responsibility. A job he often took so seriously as to put aside his own wants to see to her needs first. How did a person scold a boy for being mature and unselfish? He could become bossy and demanding sometimes and they'd clashed over it, but honestly, his motives were usually her safety or health. In the end, she'd spent a lot of time trying to get him to stop worrying and let her be the parent. That had worked for a bit but not long. Now as she looked at him, she could see the wheels turning in his head.

Jill smiled. "Stop worrying," she told him softly.

"Not likely. You have a weird look. What's up?" he asked her.

"Is it a bad thing?" Jill pressed, still smiling.

"I dunno. You tell me."

Jill closed her eyes and took a deep breath, shifting slightly to press her head and shoulders back on the comfortable pillow. "No, hon, it's not a bad thing."

"It's too damn fast a thing," Drifter told her quietly.

Jill's eyes opened to regard the young man who should still be a boy. "Perhaps. Remember, we're not strangers. You're living proof of that."

Drifter grimaced and glanced away from her for a moment. "He is to me."

"I know. Give him a chance," Jill requested softly.

"He can't keep his hands off you. What do you expect me to think? You're my mom."

"Are you disappointed? Is that why you're attacking him?"

Drifter shrugged, again his eyes moving back to Holdin at his desk for a second. "I don't know. I knew he'd have some interest in me. I guess I didn't expect him to want you."

Jill's heart lurched as he said that. Her mother's heart heard the child's fear in it. "I didn't bring you here to give you away," Jill exclaimed in low tones.

"Really? Sorta felt like that." Drifter's sprawled body shifted uncomfortably.

"No! Never. Oh baby, how could you think that?"

"Relax, Mom," Drifter quickly reassured her. "It's not like I thought you wanted to get rid of me. It's just, if anything happened to you, that was the point."

"I see." Jill sighed as she suddenly got the rest of his statement. "What you weren't expecting was for me to want this trip for my own reasons as well?"

"Yeah, I guess. I didn't come here to give *you* away." Drifter scowled and glanced at Holdin. "There's no reason to rush into anything, Mom."

"Honey, it's complicated," Jill started, but behind her she heard Holdin end his call and put down the phone. She paused to see if he'd make another call. He did and Jill continued. "I never chose to leave him. He didn't break up with me. It's just not over for either of us, I guess. We have issues."

"You can't still be going steady. Isn't there some age deal on that? I mean, damn, if no one ever wants to card ya, it's too late."

Jill's laughter swept into the room as Holdin put down the phone a second time. The private conversation between Jill and Drifter hadn't struck him as funny up to this point. The two of them had been talking soft and seriously. A heavy cloud dissipated with the music of her humor. He hadn't heard her really laugh yet, he realized. Not this relaxed, natural way.

Moving around the desk, Holdin strolled over to the couch and casually leaned against the arm at her head. His hand stroked down her cheek as he smiled at her then looked at Drifter.

"What's the joke?"

Jill's eyes danced with amusement as she looked into his. "Since we technically never broke up are we still going steady? Drifter thinks there's got to be an age limitation on that and we can't be."

Holdin scowled and went back to the other end of the couch to sit with her feet in his lap again. Shaking his head in pretend dismay as he answered, "See, that's the problem. Going steady has no limitations without an official breakup. It's not like *just* dating a girl." Holdin grinned at Drifter who was again eyeing the way Holdin gathered her feet into his hands and started gently rubbing the soles. "She's still my girl," he ended on a more serious note as his son frowned for real.

"You're all over her like a rash. It's not cool, man. She's my mother. Have a little respect."

"Asking my intentions, son?" Holdin responded.

"I guess. Seems a bit early to even be doin' that. You don't know her or me. It looks as if you jump anything that moves."

Jill opened her mouth to speak and Holdin gently squeezed her feet while glancing at her. He wanted to handle this man to man without mom refereeing. If Jill had to mother every conversation he had with the boy, it'd never get anywhere.

"I respect your protective instincts, Drifter. You're a credit to the Powell men, but this time you're jumping to conclusions. It's you who doesn't know me. Your mother does. The relationship you see now is one that started a long time ago. It's not the same relationship, I'll grant you that, but it is the same two souls. My intentions have never changed where your mother is concerned. I planned on marrying her then and I still do."

"You do?" Drifter jerked in surprise.

"I thought that was a private conversation," Jill injected quickly.

"You two have already talked about it?" Drifter's eyes widened at his mother's comment as he glanced between them.

"Yeah. I asked her." To Jill, Holden added, "I wasn't planning on discussing it. He has a right to know though. It puts us in perspective."

"You asked already?" Drifter's voice squeaked in shock and he quickly cleared his throat. "Seriously?"

"Seriously," Holdin confirmed.

"Mom?" Drifter looked at her with both eyebrows raised.

Jill frowned at both of them. "This isn't something we need to rush into. Weren't you just saying that, brat? Right now the whole hospital thing is a big enough worry. I can't answer the question before getting through that. And just so you both know, I don't need the stress. Can you try to relax, Drifter? Try to get to know your father without making snap judgments. And you, football boy, stop adding pressure to the situation." Jill closed her eyes in frustration.

Holdin lifted a delicate little foot and softly kissed it just where the cute toes met the top of her foot. "Sorry, baby. I thought it'd make things easier if our son knew how I felt about his mother."

Jill's eyes snapped open and even though she tried, she couldn't glare at the man who'd just kissed her foot in apology. Kissing her foot should have been way over the top. Laughable even. When Holdin did it, it wasn't. Instead of being a humble submission, it was a declaration of possession. He had a right to kiss her anywhere he wanted. It was a promise of seduction. An erotic secret.

Watching them, Drifter laughed at the comical expression on her face. "He does know how to handle you, Mom. You can never keep a good mad going if I kiss ya."

Jill blinked and looked at Drifter in surprise a second. He'd just admitted to kissing his mother. In front of a male. "Yeah, that's because you never do. It's a shock tactic with you. And now I'm on to your game. That one will never work again."

"I think it's time I was in the kitchen. You guys coming?" Drifter stood and stretched.

"Not hungry." Jill smiled at the lanky boy. "You two go on. I'd like a catnap."

Holdin regarded her seriously for a moment. She was sending them off together and claiming she needed a rest. Probably true, but he didn't want to leave her alone. What if something happened like a seizure? Or she passed out. Who knew with brain injuries? On the other hand, he needed to spend some time with Drifter. Seriously needed too.

Lifting her other foot to his lips, Holdin dropped a soft kiss on her instep. "I'll be back in a few minutes. Don't do anything scary like have a seizure."

"No problem. I'll be the chick sleeping on the couch," Jill promised in as cheerful a tone as she could manage while she watched him stand. The beast needed to stop kissing her feet. She'd realized they were an erogenous zone during the long massage she'd just gotten. That instep lick had been wicked.

Holdin smiled his slow, bone-melting grin at her then turned to join Drifter at the door. Jill watched them disappear. He knew it. He knew the little flick of his tongue on the sensitive instep of her foot had affected her. Another thing some brilliant female had taught him no doubt.

Alone at last, Jill half sat up and glanced around. The study had been decorated in "manly" to within an inch of its life. She knew there was a bathroom attached. She spied a discreet door at the end of the bookshelves lining the far wall. Had to be it.

Sitting up slowly she tried not to hurry. There was no way she'd have admitted this need to a room full of people, but now it was urgent. As she got to her feet, a wave of dizziness accompanied stabbing pain in the right side of her head. It felt like someone had just jammed an ice pick in her ear.

Oh God. No! She was not going to pass out and make a puddle in this damn room! Very slowly she swayed across the room, clutching furniture as she passed for balance. She could feel the blood rushing through the veins in her head. It pounded at her. Nothing had felt like this before. She made it to the door and shoved it open. Just as she'd suspected, a spectacular bathroom opened before her. Or at least she thought it was. Things were getting a little fuzzy.

Jill gritted her teeth. *No passing out before taking care of business*!

Once done, she'd made it back out of the bathroom and was halfway to the couch when Holdin strolled into the office.

"Hey!" Jill was in the middle of taking another swaying, hesitant step before she knew he was there. "Jill! What's wrong?" Holdin was suddenly wrapping his arms around her, supporting her.

"I think tomorrow might be a bit late," Jill whispered, her face turned up to his but her eyes didn't focus on him.

"Jesus! Damn! You can't see me, can you?" One hand cradled the back of her head as it started to loll back even farther.

"Not so much," Jill admitted in the breathy gasp. She was breathing in short pants. A fine sheen of sweat covered her pale skin.

The staggering pain of this moment couldn't be dealt with. Holdin ignored it. Carefully he scoped her up into his arms. "Put your head on my shoulder and stay with me, Jilly-girl," he directed firmly. "Pass out and I'll spank your ass so hard you won't be able to sit for a week."

"Promise?" Jill teased weakly as he strode to the door. Holdin noted her surprising response and shoved it to the back of his mind for examination later. They'd both slipped into a very adult level of teasing they'd never discussed before.

"*Dad*!" Holdin bellowed down the hall at the kitchen as he strode toward it. A chair crashed to the floor and Charles Powell regarded them from the doorway.

One look at them coming toward him was all he needed. "I'll get the chopper." Charles turned to exit through the kitchen at a run.

Drifter stood frozen by the table, his face pale as Holdin entered with Jill.

Holdin knew exactly what he was feeling. Giving the boy something to do was the only way he'd make it through this.

Just as he needed to focus on getting what needed done to remain sane. "Drifter, run up and get your mother's purse. Any papers she'll need to be admitted. Don't bother about anything else. You know what she needs, right?"

"Mom?" Drifter breathed the words that were half a plea, half a prayer.

"Right here, hon," Jill managed. "Thank you for helping."

Drifter bolted from the room.

"I'll bring the Navigator to the back door," Carol stated briskly. "Stay there." She grabbed keys off the row of hooks by the door and hurried out. As the door closed behind her, they heard the high-pitched scream then muffled roar of a helicopter engine starting.

"Convenient to have a pilot on hand," Jill murmured. She could feel his big body tremble every couple seconds. It wasn't because of her weight or it'd be constant. The attempt to distract him was all she could do for her hero.

"Stay with me, baby girl. I mean it," he commanded in a low growl. "Nothing takes you from me this time. Nothing."

Drifter skidded back into the room with Jill's purse and a manila envelope. Carol honked the horn outside the back door. "Let's go. Hold the door, will ya, son?"

Jill wasn't clear on anything much until they were in the air. She was lying on a bed, she supposed, it was hard to tell. Holdin had an arm wrapped around her head preventing it from moving since she couldn't seem to do that herself. Drifter was clutching her hand on the other side. No one said anything except Holdin. He kept forcing her to talk. Asking her about stupid stuff like were the bills being forwarded from her apartment? Did her boss know she was not going to be in for a while?

"Who cares?" Jill whispered in frustration. "I think I'm going to take that nap now."

"*No*! You will stay with me, woman!" Holdin barked. "Do you understand me? You are not allowed to pass out, slip into a coma or any other damn stupid thing." His face was mere inches from her face as he snarled the words. "And if you can't manage it for me, your son needs you to remain awake, Jill. You will do it for him!"

Holdin glanced at Drifter. Tear tracks streaked his cheeks but he was breathing normally. Holdin knew he hadn't told Drifter she couldn't see. It seemed he didn't need to. Young lion allowed no indication of his emotional distress to show in anything she could hear.

"How did you come up with Drifter's name anyway? Why did you name him Drifter?"

"Yeah, Mom," Drifter agreed in a surprisingly strong voice. "You promised you'd explain it to me."

Up front the radio crackled as Charles spoke to airport towers about flight paths and then he was put in touch with the hospital ER. Emergency transport jargon flowed out of his mouth and it was clear he'd flown rescue many times. Carol sat close by, her face a resolute mask as she watched the struggle to keep Jill talking. There was pain and strength in her.

Jill's voice was barely a thread as a smile flitted across her lips. "I've apologized for that, brat."

"So, explain." Drifter leaned down as he demanded she speak to him. A tear dropped on her cheek and Drifter gently wiped it off.

"I was kinda a kid, you know," Jill started. She spoke in short, jerky sentences around the effort to breathe. "We were alone, you and I. No one was coming for us. That's what we were—drifters in time. No past, no future. So it stuck. Drifter, my beautiful traveling companion. You and I were the only people I knew. We'd been together from the beginning. So. That's it. I know, sorta silly."

Chapter Seven

The emergency team was waiting on the helipad when Charles set down the helicopter. They immediately took over in what seemed like controlled chaos of clipped questions on her condition and abbreviated instructions to each other filled with initials and medical talk that sounded like code. The white-clad group was a polite blur as they efficiently transferred Jill to a gurney and then she was gone in a flurry of activity. Holdin, Drifter and Carol hurried after them. Inside the hospital doors a young lady with a hospital ID identifying her as a student nurse met them and ushered them into a waiting room.

"Dr. Coates will be in as soon as he can. It might be some time though. He's evaluating Ms. Smith's condition. There are snack machines around the corner and of course the cafeteria if you need anything. You'll find a phone over there if you need to make calls." She turned to leave.

"Wait!" Drifter barked in a firm voice. "Where have they taken my mother?"

The nurse hesitated as she glanced between the large scowling man standing behind the young scowling face. "She will need to have several tests before surgery. I really don't know which one the doctor ordered first. Dr. Coates is an excellent doctor. He'll be doing the right thing."

The young woman's eyes kept darting to Holdin as she talked to Drifter. It could have been natural respect because though Drifter had asked the question, he was the adult male in the room. Holdin didn't think that was it though.

"I have to go. The doctor will be in shortly." The young nurse smiled and this time did hurry off.

Carol slipped an arm around Drifter's waist. "Come, sit down. I'm sure your Dr. Coates will be here soon." She pulled him to a sofa and Drifter went with her without protest. He was still clutching Jill's purse and the envelope. Carol gently took them out of his hands and set them on the floor beside her.

Holdin felt frozen. A deep February cold bloomed in his chest and radiated out. Suddenly everything around him faded as the reality that he didn't know where Jill was slammed into him. Old and icy, it was a familiar pain. This time it came with crushing guilt. Had he done this? He'd pushed her, demanded her body respond. His selfish need to connect with her had driven him with harsh determination. Damn it! He'd been pushing her from the moment his eyes landed on her bent head in the soda fountain.

How fucking self-involved was he?! Holdin shot a dark glance at Drifter and Carol and turned to stalk to the wide window. Standing with his back to the room, his legs spread in a stiff brace with his arms crossed over his chest, he glared blindly out the window.

Bitter self-disgust ate through his body with an acid kick of fear. Instead of listening to her and providing what she'd come to him for, he'd taken control and worked his own agenda. She had explained the situation upfront. How fucking plainer could she have made it? Drifter had kept trying to tell him how fragile she was and he'd not paid enough attention. He'd seen an opportunity to get the girl back instead of finding a way to ease her mind as gently as possible.

He deserved to have his ass kicked into next week — repeatedly. She shouldn't be the one in pain. It was his fault. He'd had her back in his life and been blinded by his own witless needs. He should have been taking care of her needs.

And he was damn well doing it again! Holdin turned to look at his son. Jill had literally risked her life to bring Drifter to him and he was standing here wallowing in his guilt. The only person in the room acting like a man barely shaved yet.

Drifter was squeezing Carol's hand and assuring her that Robert was the best doctor. Holdin took himself over to their seating arrangement and joined them. "You think a lot of the doctor. It'd help us trust him if you explained how you know him. What makes you trust him?"

Drifter still held Carol's hand and Holdin was aware his mother knew the boy needed to comfort her more than she needed comforting. Carol would have taken charge in an instant but she was no dummy. In some things, Drifter was a carbon copy of her other two men.

Drifter tried to smile but it was more of a grimace. "Robert is a friend of Dr. Tams, Mom's boss. Last year Dr. Tams let Mom have a few of his football season tickets so we could go when he wouldn't be in town. Robert's seats are right next to Dr. Tams' and he knew we had to be friends of Tams to be sitting there. He introduced himself. By the way, I saw you in three games last season." Drifter managed a real grin.

"Damn. Pointless to say I wish I'd known." Holdin smiled. "So you all met at the games. Kinda ironic."

"Yeah, we went twice on Dr. Tams' tickets and the last time Robert invited us. He's a great guy. I kinda told him about Mom's problem and he wanted to look at her files. She wouldn't let him. Said it'd be imposing and junk. She was mad at me for telling him when she was in the restroom. He took us to some basketball games too." Drifter shrugged. "Just a real stand-up guy. All polite and careful of Mom and fun to hang around with. I knew he was really smart and stuff but I didn't realize he was the best in his business until Mom had her accident. He knew what to do and everything."

"You're lucky to have a friend like that." Holdin looked Drifter in the eye, trying to reassure him that he wasn't going to lose it over the doctor. "They wouldn't let him wear the cool green outfit if he wasn't all right."

"Where is Mr. Charles?" Drifter asked Carol.

Holdin was amused at the way Drifter had chosen to address his grandparents. It was a compromise between stranger and grandparents. Understandable in the circumstances.

"He had to go park the helicopter," Carol responded. "Since they don't have a chopper parking lot here, he went over to Holdin's place with it. He'll drive back in one of the vehicles Holdin keeps at the house and be here in a little bit."

Dr. Robert Coates entered the room. He was perhaps six feet two inches, dressed in casual dress pants and a polo shirt under the white coat. He was a poster boy for relaxed confidence from his light brown eyes to the tips of the comfortable but stylish leather shoes.

His chin was so square the dimple in it just had to be there. Straight black hair was meticulously cut to stay right where he combed it, which was almost straight back from a high forehead. His gaze was direct and self-assured. His nose might have been too big except it was perfectly formed to complement his features. He was handsome in a well-groomed way that spoke of affluence, education and intelligence. The dark hair at his temples was slightly frosted, giving him an even more pronounced air of reliability.

Wide shoulders and narrow hips spoke of a personal trainer who knew all about body sculpting. He was Clark Kent in a doctor's coat. Holdin actually checked the V of his shirt for the telltale blue Superman suit.

Immediately everyone stood. Robert reached for Drifter who naturally moved toward him with desperate questions written across a young face. The tall doctor hugged the boy very briefly and then smiled into his face when Drifter stepped back. "Your mother is going to be all right. I'm seeing to it like I said I would." The doctor reassured Drifter while still grasping his shoulder and looking directly into the boy's eyes.

"Yes, sir, you did make that promise. I 'spect you'll be keeping it."

"Absolutely." Robert glanced up at the two other adults in the room and Drifter made the introductions smoothly.

"This is my grandmother Mrs. Powell and my father Holdin Powell."

"My pleasure, Mrs. Powell. Nice to meet you, Powell." Robert nodded at Holdin and included them all as he reported Jill's condition. "I don't have a lot of news right now. Jill is having tests done that will show us if the chip moved and if so, where. Depending on those results, we'll know if we have to go in today. It'll be over an hour, maybe several hours before I know for sure what we're going to do. I'd rather wait 'til tomorrow for surgery so we can monitor her condition overnight. Right now she's worried and a little freaked, which is natural, but not how I'd like her to be for the surgery."

Looking directly at Drifter, Robert continued. "I need a favor from you, buddy. When she gets out of the test they are doing right now, could you see her while they're takin' blood and things? I'd like her as calm as possible and looking at you is the only way that'll happen."

"Yes, sir. I'd like that," Drifter responded seriously.

"Good. I need you to be confident and cheerful for her. Your mom needs all the positive reinforcement we can give her. You have to let me know if you can do this. If you're feeling shaky emotional, I'll get you out of there. She can't be worried about anything, okay?"

"I get it," Drifter assured him.

"Is there someone you need to call? Or are you okay with the Powells?" Robert asked directly.

Drifter glanced at Holdin then reached over and took Carol's hand. "I'm fine," he stated firmly.

Holdin felt his heart expand painfully. His son made him proud and he'd had nothing to do with creating the amazing young man who could reach out to his grandmother so kindly.

"Dr. Coates, his folks are here for him. You don't have to worry." Carol smiled at the handsome doctor and squeezed

Drifter's hand. "Is there anything else you can tell us about Jill?"

"Glad to hear it, ma'am. I do think you should let Dr. Tams know, Drifter. He's been concerned. There is no more news until these tests are done." Coates looked at his watch. "It'll be another forty-five minutes at least for the one she's doing now." He paused then put his hand on Drifter's shoulder again and squeezed lightly. "Don't worry, I got this."

Drifter chuckled. "You're way too white and too old to say that."

"Yeah? Well, it's true. I'll see you later." Robert Coates nodded at Holdin and left. They all watched him disappear down the hall, a nurse hurrying to his side with a chart in hand.

* * * * *

Eleven p.m. and the hospital wasn't exactly quiet but it seemed calmer. Holdin slipped into her room. Jill was a lump beneath the hospital blanket and sheet. Her head and shoulders were restrained in a cushioned brace that seemed to swallow her. Holdin silently moved across the private room to the far wall, away from the door.

The light was indirect and shadows cloaked her in murky twilight. Around her machines blinked and glared into the night with red numbers and blinking points of garish electronic medical speak. Holdin leaned against the wall, ignoring the chair beside him. Somehow it was wrong to be even a little comfortable while she lay there beneath the IV and monitors. The needles puncturing her skin were obscene to him. They were the cruel teeth of the machines looming over her.

Tomorrow they would cut into her. It would be cold in the operating room. A sterile cold room full of strangers and steel equipment. She'd be alone again. Holdin had to breathe in deeply to suppress a groan of pain.

"You went home hours ago." Her soft voice floated up from the brace.

"I came back," he returned quietly. "Go to sleep, baby."

"You're worried." She was only whispering but he heard her clearly.

"I'm concerned." Holdin sighed and tried to smile. Her nature demanded she try to comfort him and he really wasn't up to her being brave for him. He needed her to relax and sleep. Let him watch over her. Just for a bit.

There was silence for a long moment. The noises from the hall were muffled but constant reminders of where they were.

"Would you mind holding my hand?"

"Will you try to sleep?" Holdin shoved the chair over beside her and sat, taking her hand in both of his. Being careful not to bend or move her arm because of the tubes, he cradled her small-looking hand in his. It felt slightly cold so he covered it with his other hand.

"I was thinking. Do you remember the first time?" Her gentle tones were both soothing and an insidious knife, paring away bits of his soul. Light as dust motes in the summer sun, her hushed voice lashed him with guilt.

"Which first time, baby girl?"

"That first weekend in June."

He knew exactly what she was talking about.

"Can't really call it the first time you made love to me," she murmured with a smile in her voice. "You made love to me so many times before that. Every time you touched me you taught me a new way to feel pleasure."

Holdin had to hide his face from her. He laid his cheek in her palm and closed his eyes, struggling to reply in a normal voice. "Yes, I remember. I'll always remember." His voice deepened with the effort to stay normal. He couldn't help it as the emptiness of those memories scraped over his soul.

Since Jill, he'd spent the first Saturday night in June alone because he couldn't forget. Every single year. He'd tried to ignore it several times but realized that was impossible. Those had been the darkest nights of his life. The first few years his drive to remain visible so she could find him had kept the demons at bay and he'd spent the entire night working his body past exhaustion in his private hell, the gym, either on the ranch or wherever he was. The last eight years had been worse. He'd lost a little more hope with each passing June. But he couldn't escape his memories. Especially that night.

"Do you remember what I asked you then?" she wanted to know.

"Yes." He couldn't keep pain out of his voice. The gloom surrounding them was nothing compared to where he'd been with the memory she focused on now.

"Aw, Holdin." Her fingers petted his cheek. He couldn't raise his head from them. "I asked you to love me enough to allow me the pain of loving you. I'd have been a virgin for the rest of my life if it were up to you." She was smiling again, her soft voice overflowing with amusement.

"Well, probably not the rest of your life." Holden kissed her palm then lifted his head to smile with her. "As I recall, I had a plan to take care of that."

"Mmm," Jill agreed with him, and they were quiet again for a long while.

Holdin thought she'd gone to sleep. Her little body was still beneath the sheet and her hand rested lightly in his. Out in the hall footsteps squeaked by and hospital employees spoke in what seemed like loud voices.

Then very softly her voice curled around him again. "I think that's my favorite memory. I've missed it. Have you thought of it over the years? It'd seem sad if you haven't. Like it was abandoned. As lost in nothingness as I was."

"God, Jill," Holdin groaned. "I've never forgotten one moment with you."

"But that night, that particular moment in our time together. Have you remembered? Have you ever held me again like you did then?" Jill whispered. Her voice trembled and a single tear slipped down her cheek.

How did he tell her? What words did one use to express a pain so deep it had almost robbed him of life? She wanted to know if he'd ever held her again like he did that long-ago night. Had he ever stopped?

He tried to keep the ragged torture out of his voice. "Jilly-girl, every single year, the first Saturday night in June since the one you gave me, I've spent with you. Only you." He was watching her face. The track of that one tear was a glittering silver ribbon as her lashes lifted slowly.

They looked into each other's souls for a long moment and then she smiled a tiny, sad little smile that understood what he couldn't find the words to say. "Thank you, Holdin. I would have been lonely without you keeping me alive."

"Every moment we had is mine, Jilly-girl. I never gave them up. Not to time, not to distance, not to silence. I never let you go and you were never alone."

Her eyes had drifted shut again but her hand tightened on his. "You were though."

"No. I had you. Not like..." Holdin stopped. He'd been about to say not like she'd been alone. Completely alone. Not even a memory of someone loving her. Not like she might be if tomorrow night she didn't remember her past again. "It's never going to be like that again. Even if you don't remember, I will, Jilly-girl. I'll be here this time. You will never be lost again."

"I know. You're a good man, Holdin." Her voice was a whisper.

"Now might be a good time to tell me your real name, Jilly-girl," Holdin suggested as softly as she'd spoken.

Jill sighed and her eyes opened. "I suppose it would. You know I told you my father was running from bad guys? He was, but he was protecting me. I witnessed a crime. He was involved with them, that was his business. He never meant for me to be involved. It was an accident that I saw what I did. They gave him a choice. Kill me or hand me over to them. Dad couldn't exactly go to the cops." Jill sighed again. "So I'd like my name to stay Jill. Do you understand?"

"Damn it! Are you still in danger? Is Drifter in danger if they figure out who you are? And if you left because they'd tracked you two down back then, remaining Jill Smith as opposed to Jill Taylor is not exactly a cover."

"I know. I haven't had time to check if the players are still alive. They could already be in prison. I should have told you back then but I was afraid. I couldn't give you up and I couldn't fix the problem. So I ignored it. I still don't know what to do about that. Coming to you was for Drifter. I never expected you to want me. Not like I wanted you. For me, our relationship was fresh, but I knew you'd lived in the here and now all these years. I couldn't worry about that past. The present was too important. Our son's future was all I could worry about.

"I was Carmella Capizzano, daughter of Stephan and Margo Capizzano."

"So you're my belladonna," he drawled in a goofy Italian accent. They both chuckled for a moment. Then Holdin let the humor slip away. "All right, now you've told me. I'll deal with that, baby. Don't worry about it. There is something else I've wondered about over the years. You wouldn't talk about your mother back then. Is there anything you'd like to tell me tonight?"

"She died right after I was born. I have no memory of her." Jill smiled at him. "Now you know everything."

Holdin kissed her hand as he looked into her face. "No. Not everything."

Jill's eyes closed and she breathed in deeply again. "I think I'll go to sleep while you hold me on a warm June evening again. Take me there, Holdin…talk to me like we did then. Pretend for me a little."

His voice was low and a little uneven with emotion, just as it had been that night. "Jilly-girl, come out to the foaling barn, I have something to show you."

* * * * *

Fifteen years ago…

In the barn were two new foals. Sweet, fuzzy little creatures on spindly legs. They were all big eyes and adorable wobbles. Jill was enthralled as Holdin let her in a stall with the large mare and her new babies. Delicate little noses were soft as velvet and after a moment investigating the strangers, the babies became comfortable with them and let her pet them as they did what little horses do.

After twenty minutes, Holdin pulled her out of the stall. "I have something to show you," he said again with his slow smile.

Jill was confused as she glanced back at the foals. Holdin steered her up to the loft and to the back. There was a blanket spread out and beside it, a clean bucket with a couple bottles of soda along with some bottled water.

They were kissing as they sank to the blanket. Hot and hard, they took from each other with open-mouthed greed. Jill moaned as they rolled and Holdin landed on top of her, giving her the heavy weight of him for a few minutes. She loved the feeling of him over her, surrounding her. The weight of him always turned up the excitement for her. It wasn't that he crushed her, no, but he did firmly control her in this aggressive position.

His mouth sealed to hers, his tongue was deep inside her as his hips bore down on hers. Naturally her legs spread for him, wrapping around him to notch his erection directly over her already burning pussy.

Necking with Holdin was possibly the most exciting pastime this side of nirvana. He was so big and strong. His muscles flexed and strained above her as she petted him. Her hands were very busy pulling his shirt out of his jeans and skimming up his bare back. Holdin groaned into her mouth. The smooth rocking of his hips into the cradle of hers increased.

Nimble fingers went directly to the buttons of her blouse. He lifted his head long enough to shove it off her shoulders. The blouse fell open and soft, shuddering globes spilled over the top of the cheap bra. Holdin arched up, using the powerful muscles in his back to lift his torso so he could rip his shirt off over his head as his eyes feasted on her breasts.

"Finish it for me, Jilly-girl." His hands landed on either side of her as he supported himself above her. "Take off the blouse and bra for me."

Jill's body clenched in excitement. She loved it when he did this. He'd stop and take control of the sexual frenzy. It wasn't as if he stopped wanting her. It seemed he wanted her more. She could see it in his face. The way he became almost harsh as he held back the desperation was such a turn-on. He'd never broken under the pressure, never lost it again to return to the abandon that started their touching. He became more demanding and oh-so sexy as he showed her how much he loved her body.

It was his control that had allowed them to explore each other in slow detail. Their times together had become more intense as Holdin guided her, commanded and demanded she come for him over and over again. She loved touching him, making him groan in pleasure as her hands and mouth explored the hard planes and ridges of his body. Sometimes he let her do it for a long time.

Then he'd take command again. And, oh mercy, he knew her, knew her body and its responses. Mostly he'd taught her how she could respond. He always seemed to know what would drive her that little bit more crazy than she'd ever been before. Always guiding, controlling and demanding she feel more, experience more. But there was one thing Holdin was very firm on. They'd never included intercourse in lovemaking. His reason was simple. He'd have to hurt her to do it, especially the first time.

Jill smiled up at her lover and shrugged out of her blouse. That left the bra. Her hands cupped her breasts, caressing them as he watched. His jaw clenched and his eyes narrowed. Jill slowly unclasped the front closure of the bra and peeled the cups back.

"That's my girl," Holdin growled roughly as he dropped to his elbows so his hands could cup her. "Such a prefect handful you are." His head swooped down and he roughly sucked a sensitive nipple deep into his mouth. Jill moaned and arched as he pinched and rolled the other nipple.

Holdin was always careful with her, but that didn't mean he was gentle. Jill found the more demanding he became, the more intense the connection between them. His firm tugging on her sensitive breasts sent stars spinning down to her crotch. There his stiff erection ground into her through two sets of jeans. Her hips arched up a fraction more, inviting the stimulation. Jill moaned as he let her breast pop out of his mouth.

"Such a pretty baby. Look at you all red and swollen. Damn, I love your breasts." He leaned in and licked around the nipple he'd been tormenting in his mouth. "We have got to get some of that edible oil. I wanna see these glistening," he murmured as he watched himself stroke her other nipple from root to tip in a pull that stretched her.

"Holdin," Jill moaned to get his attention back in the present.

"Patience, Jilly-girl." He smiled as he shifted to his knees beside her. He knelt there, hands casually resting on his thighs, elbows pointed away from his body. The position emphasized the width of a very developed male chest and shoulders, outlining his torso as the lines undulated down to tight hips and then the hard mass of powerful thighs jutting out widely as he rested on his heels. "Shuck off the pants for me," he commanded softly.

Jill stood and toed off her shoes then slowly unzipped her jeans. His command to strip for him wasn't new, but it was one that swamped her with conflicting emotions. She felt shrinking shyness battling with screaming excitement. The shyness always lost the major battle and Jill did as he'd directed, but she couldn't look at him as she did it.

Panting in short breaths to deal with this, she slid her hands down her hips, dragging panties and jeans off. Stepping out of them, she stood before him. Hands fidgeting in front of her, her legs slightly spread, she thrilled to the burn of his eyes moving over her as he knelt looking up. He should have looked like a supplicant at her feet but he didn't. He was too hard and big, too perfect.

"Come here." His voice was guttural, a low rumble of command that shot reaction through her lower abdomen.

Jill knew what he wanted. She stepped in front of him, placing her feet on either side of his thighs, spreading her legs for his inspection. Exposing herself to him sent a gushing spike of excitement and embarrassment through her. The intoxicating mix took her to an edge that balanced her between the conflicting emotions, yet it would be impossible to do anything else. Submitting to his intimate attention was emotionally binding for Jill. For Holdin she'd do anything, it seemed.

Big, rough hands glided up the backs of her legs to cup her bottom, squeezing gently as he pulled her hips forward. His mouth moved over her belly, licking, tasting, and gliding over the tremors his attention induced. He turned his cheek to rub the short, soft curls of her mound over it as his growls of pleasure surrounded them. He'd trimmed her there himself, showing her how he liked it. His intimate attention to the details of her body had been shocking at first but he'd explained it to her so well.

First he'd asked her, "Are you my girl?"

"Yes." She'd frowned at the question.

"Then this pretty mound is mine. I'd like to see it shaved but for now this is fine. There is no shame in this, Jilly-girl. I take care of what's mine."

Indeed he did. There seemed no detail of her life he wasn't interested in. His attention enveloped her, cushioned her life in ways both dreamy and exciting. Like now as he nuzzled her intimately and his tongue pushed between outer lips to nudge her clit with light licks. The act of forcing her folds apart heightened the sensation of him invading her. He was entering the damp portals of her body. Jill moaned, her hands sinking in his hair as his approval rumbled around the prize he'd found.

Heat swarmed over her as his tongue teased. Her legs trembled and his hands on her butt tightened in warning. He wanted her right where she was, not collapsing. The force of his will shot another thrill through her. She didn't know why, but the feel of him like this was such a high. Her knees started to buckle and he supported her weight 'til she gathered enough control to do it herself. His ability to gently but forcefully command her compliance was as much a turn-on.

His mouth was open as his tongue ran up and down the valley between plump outer lips. Reaching under her from behind, two fingers swirled through the cream gushing out of her opening. Jill trembled in mounting anticipation as he coated those digits while licking over the bundle of nerves above them. He wasn't giving her the touch to push her over, just building the sensations. Knowing what was coming increased her need and she pressed into his face, bending her knees slightly to widen herself for him.

Holdin's tongue flicked over her as those fingers circled and stroked in repeated demand. Jill moaned. He was taking so long. Playing with her while she was already on the edge. Finally he gave her the touch she'd been waiting for.

His fingers dragged liquid back over sensitive skin to tenderly circle her anus. Jill was gasping at the dual sensations as he told her with his fingers that he intended to have her there as well. It was both the wicked, forbidden embarrassment of his intentions and knowledge that she wanted him demanding this from her that wound her to a new level of anticipation and desperation.

"That's my girl," he approved softly between licks. Her knees bent farther as she helplessly thrust her hips into his face. "Yes, pretty baby. So ready." His deep voice crooned as he resumed flicking her clit in maddening licks. The fingers circling behind her dipped in a bit, gently pressing her anus but not entering.

Recently he'd introduced her to this sensation, painting her with her body's lubricant while pleasuring her to madness with his tongue. He'd forbidden her to come unless he'd entered her ass with those slick fingers. The first time it was only one finger and he'd taken so long teasing and eating her, as soon as the thick digit slipped into her body, she'd crashed into orgasm. Those new sensations of invasion and the tiny burn had mixed with the shattering pleasure and become addictive. She'd come so hard, her muscles ached with strain.

She'd been shocked after but he'd smiled his lazy smile as he held her still trembling body, "Aw, Jilly-girl," he'd soothed her. "You're mine. All of you. It's not wrong or dirty to give me all of you. Did it feel bad?"

She remembered she'd blushed wildly that late spring evening, which was silly considering on that occasion she had been lying in the back of his pickup with him, on a blanket and naked as the day she was born. "No," Jill had whispered.

He'd chuckled softly. "Just no? Aren't you the brazen wench who just screamed for me? I was sorta concerned we'd draw attention even though we're twenty miles out," he teased gently.

That night she'd learned how to make him bellow in pleasure. Actually he'd taught her after she'd insisted, determined to be woman enough for him. It seemed her mouth could make him as crazy as he made her.

Since then she'd found she craved the new sensations. How did he know what sweet, aching pleasure it was? His command of her response in that way made her feel even more his. Then he'd instructed her how to accept him. Now she complied with his touch as if it were a command.

By now the sensation of his fingers circling her bottom entrance triggered another level of excitement. She gasped and willfully relaxed for him. His hands left her for a few seconds and she knew he was slipping a condom over his two fingers. It made cleanup easier and ensured he never injured her with fingernails when inside her body.

Jill's body tightened in anticipation as his mouth never left her sensitized folds. He was relentless, sucking her with hard pulls then releasing and petting her with his tongue. The muscles in her legs trembled as she held her knees slightly bent, feet pointed away from her body and tilted her pelvis to his mouth.

Holdin lifted his head from the center of her need and kissed down a straining thigh, he glanced behind her. "Move back. Hook your arms over the beam." He instructed softly.

Behind her was a divider, a few boards nailed to the support posts and stretching back to the exterior wall. The center board was just the right height for her to hook her arms over behind her and lean her upper back against it. Jill stepped back and adjusted her position. The support helped but now she felt somehow restrained with her arms behind her to hold on to the beam.

"Spread for me, baby," Holdin growled as he watched her. "That's my good girl. Look at you. So beautiful."

He'd followed her body and was still kneeling between her legs. His hands pushed her knees farther apart as his wide shoulders inserted between them. Again his mouth sucked her in but this time he was fierce, almost snarling into her as he nipped and licked over exposed flesh. His coated fingers dragged through the liquid surrender between her legs. He teased her by playing around her pussy opening for long minutes before moving back to the other entrance.

Jill's head fell back on the beam as Holdin sucked her clit into his mouth and pushed two fingers into her ass. Powerful, burning pleasure shot through her. It was a potent mix of emotion and sensation. The complete surrender of the new position had already excited her with its subtle bondage and the way Holdin's entire body had reacted to his view of her. His cheeks had sucked in as his nostrils flared. He'd bared his teeth in a grimacing growl and fell on her like a slightly wild beast. She wasn't afraid of him, but she was very aware of his fierce desire and the control he exerted at all times. His muscles bunched and clenched but he never crushed her, his touch was often firm but never painful.

"Not yet!" he snapped at her as her body tightened in response to the new edge they'd put on their lovemaking. He could feel her hovering on the edge of orgasm and knew his control was what she needed to sink into the pleasure of being who she was. Commanding her to wait gave her the freedom to explore sensations, stretch her sensual limits. It released her from responsibility on so many levels and let her simply be his.

With his fingers buried deep in her ass, he looked up from her crotch at the lush shudder of her large breasts. Pulling the fingers out slowly, he watched breasts jiggle with her gasping whimper. Pink nipples were distended in pouty excitement as her chest was forced up and out by the position of her arms. He pushed back into her ass and her bent legs tensed. She was stretched and spread in a position that showed off her body in stunning detail. She'd never been more beautiful, more wanton, more druggingly sexy.

"That's it, baby. Feel how good it is." His fingers began to move firmly in and out of her and he wondered if she was to the place where she could come with just that stimulation yet.

He'd been very careful introducing her to the pleasure of her ass being invaded. The completeness of submitting to his control in this way was a classic mix of embarrassment and gratification. He wanted her to have both those pleasures, but he also wanted to be very sure he never damaged her physically. This entrance to her body could be trained to take a cock, stretched to ensure her pleasure the first time he took her that way.

"Yes, yes. Please, Holdin," Jill moaned softly. "I need more."

"I know. I'm looking at you, Jilly-girl," he stated in a deep growl. He never used crude words when making love to her, but had found telling her how much he enjoyed her submission heightened the intimacy for both of them. It was part of the amazing relationship he'd been carefully introducing her too. Showing her that this was what he needed with her. She needed the safety of surrender in the same way he lived for the sweet pleasure of seeing her fly to a new height.

It wasn't new for Holdin, it'd just never been perfect like this. His other experiences had been a game to his partners and that was all right with him. He'd not intended to keep any of them. Jill was completely different. There was no game in it for either of them and he intended to keep her forever.

Loving Jill made Holdin a complete person. He knew it. Her submission in response to his dominance stretched his limits every time. He knew she wasn't aware of how she taught him. Actually drove him to learn more about himself as well as her spirit. Guiding her, protecting her, teaching her…these were his pleasures, his obsessions and his greatest fears. Doing anything that might damage the growth of her beautiful submissive was the fear part.

His constant concern had hammered home control and patience. Learning the concept was one thing, being aware he had the power to hurt her made those principles an imperative. Those were his responsibilities and he'd learned them well now.

"I'm looking at those gorgeous breasts bounce with each thrust into your body. Do you see how they dance for me?" He straightened a bit to capture a nipple in his teeth, passing his tongue back and forth over the tip as his fingers jammed into her ass with more force, making her body bounce and her breast strain on the nipple he held.

Fire exploded in her breast as the captured nipple felt the bite of teeth coupled with a tongue-lashing. Pain and pleasure. He mixed them so skillfully that one was not as intense without the other.

"Please, they're yours," Jill gasped as he captured the other nipple for the same torment.

His fingers fucked her ass in a steady rhythm as he let the other breast go. "Yes. Mine. All of you, Jilly-girl." He sank back to his heels and smiled at the view. "So pretty, baby. Straining open for me." He leaned forward and flicked his tongue over her clit in light licks.

"Holdin!" Jill gasped. "Please."

"Now!" he commanded, and opened his mouth over her clit, clamping down on it with firm lips and tugging gently.

Jill screamed as her body clenched in release. Her feet came off the ground to pull knees up in an effort to get more of him in her. And then she was flying. Jerking through shattering contractions as popping explosions raced up from pussy and ass, her feet landed lightly on the ground as he continued to pump into her. His mouth worked her hard and Jill suspected she might pass out soon.

Then she was sagging by her shoulders, gasping for air. Holdin pulled out of her, stripped the condom off, turning it inside out as he did. He leapt up and grabbed her, supporting her body so she wouldn't strain her shoulders. He picked her up and carried her to the blanket, laying them both down as he held her shuddering body.

Tears were streaming down her face as she clutched him. "Shhhhh, baby. Shhhhh. Did I hurt you?" he asked softly, his lips moving over her face, kissing away all evidence of her tears.

"No. It was just...more." Jill's voice was small and shaky.

"You are so beautiful. Every damn thing about you is amazing. You know I love you. Right? I'd never hurt you, baby, never. At least not so you didn't love it."

He smiled into her eyes as she bit her lip. There was something so naughty about him knowing that the mix of a tiny bit of pain with her pleasure was the thing that sent her off. "You know, don't you?" Jill asked shyly.

"What do I know?" Holdin purred as his hands smoothed down her back.

"That I need both sometimes."

"If you're talkin' about a little rough lovin', yeah, I know. You drive me nuts with that. It's the sexiest thing I've ever seen."

Jill was staring into his collarbone, unable to meet his eyes. "Do you think it's bad of me?"

"I think," Holdin put a knuckle under her chin and raised her face to his, "you are the most amazing woman I've ever known. I love you, Jill. I love everything about you. But the part that turns me inside out is how you respond to me. Get it?"

Jill searched his eyes. "I make you crazy? You never lose control or, I don't know, act nuts. You've never even asked me to make love properly. Don't you want to?"

Holdin frowned darkly. "How can you doubt that?" He abruptly rolled over on his back and unzipped his jeans. Out sprang his cock. It stood up from his body—long, thick and hard. The shaft was thick all the way to the tip where it narrowed a tiny bit just below the flared head. The ridge on its underside was thicker than her index finger and stood out firmly. "Wrap your hand around the base of it, Jill," he directed in a very firm voice.

Jill half sat up on her hip, one hand supporting her and reached for him. She grasped him and his hand covered hers from the other side, she couldn't close her fist around him.

"What do you think that would feel like in your little pussy? You can't even close your fist around it," he demanded harshly. "I can prepare your ass, make sure you feel nothing but pleasure there. I can't do that with your cunt." Holdin sucked in a ripping gasp as her hand on him and the subject he was arguing almost became too much. "Your body was made to take a man there, but the first time will not be easy, baby."

His hand tightened on hers, stroking up and down lightly. It wasn't the first time she'd seen him or even touched him.

"That's what I want to know," Jill responded softly as she watched both of them caress him. "I want to feel you in me, Holdin." Before he could answer, she leaned down and took him in her mouth. He stretched her jaw and she couldn't even fit half his length in her before he hit the back of her throat.

Holdin barked out a startled groan as her head sank down over him. "Damn!"

Jill closed her lips and began sucking, letting her head bob on him as she pumped the base. He was so hot. The velvet flesh was pulled tight over pulsing steel as his hips jerked for her. Oh yes, he felt her. He couldn't quite control his reactions.

"Jill!" Both his hands fisted in her hair to pull her off him and turn her face up to his. Her lips were swollen and her nose was a little red. She looked as if she'd just been sucking on a cock and he had to pause. She was so damn sexy. "Jill. I will be your first lover and I will be your last lover. I just don't want to hurt you. Don't you get it? Guys sometimes lose control. It feels so good they just… I might lose control. I might hurt you real bad. What if I can't stop and you want me to? Damn it, Jill. I want you too much to risk it. I'm twice as big as you and I could hold you down with one hand and take what you're not willing to give."

"But you wouldn't." Her eyes were steady as she stared into his.

"You're so sure?" he questioned softly.

"Yes."

Holdin groaned and pulled her into his chest, wrapping his arms around her in a fierce hug. "Don't ask this of me. Not now."

"If you plan to be my lover at some point, how were you thinking to get there?" Jill wanted to know as he held her.

"I thought I'd wait 'til you were a little drunk some time. Alcohol deadens nerves," he confessed in a low, fierce tone. "I couldn't think of another way without hurting you the first time."

Jill lifted her head off his chest to look into his beautiful, stressed-out face. "I don't want to be drunk and I don't want to wait. Make love to me, Holdin. Make love to me now."

Holdin framed her face with his hands. "I did, I have and I do, damn it. Don't, Jill. Please."

She looked at him a long moment. "Love me enough to let me feel the pain of loving you."

"Baby, have mercy," he breathed softly.

"Mercy refused," she whispered back.

Holdin's eyes closed as he sucked in a deep breath. She was demanding the one thing he wanted. He wanted her spread under him so badly it scared him. There was nothing but ferocious need when he indulged in that fantasy.

With other girls, the desire had been strong but nothing like he experienced over Jill. His needs with Jill were animalistic and base. He knew it. Entering her body in that most intimate way would be releasing an unknown element within himself. Taking her virginity might be more than either of them was ready for. How could he protect her from himself when he didn't know what the threat would be? If there even was one?

His hands tightened around her face for an instant. When he opened his eyes, his face was set in a fierce mask. "You will do exactly what I tell you too. If we're going to do this, I will be in control. Do you understand? You can't fight me, baby. I don't know if I could stop."

Chapter Eight

Jill nodded in agreement.

"No. Say it, Jill. I want you to say the words so I know you get it. This isn't something we can undo. You will give yourself to me in every way if we do this, baby." He lay there waiting for her response as her big eyes blinked a moment.

Jill's already tingling body heated at his demand. The firm, decisive tone he took was such a turn-on. "I'm yours, Holdin. I'll do exactly what you tell me too," she stated as firmly as she could manage.

Holdin suddenly rolled them over and loomed above her. Jill gasped as he roughly shoved her knees apart with powerful legs. His huge body covered her as his hands jerked her arms over her head and grasped her wrists in one of his. He was big and heavy. He smothered her with no effort and she couldn't move. Jill's eyes were huge as she looked up at his face above her. She was breathing roughly in reaction to the sudden shift. His cock felt as if it burned as is now rubbed up her mound and belly.

Holdin was breathing hard through flared nostrils, a tight grimace almost clenched his teeth together as he asked her, "How does that feel, Jill? You're completely helpless beneath a guy who can take what he wants. Is it too scary? Tell me now, because I'm not going to hear you later."

Jill's eyes softened as her lids lowered. Her lips parted in short pants as she gazed up at him. "Don't you feel how you turn me on when you do this?"

Holdin's forehead dropped to hers and his eyes closed for a long moment as he sucked in a several deep breaths. Then his hand released her wrists and he peeled himself off her.

Briefly sitting beside her, he pulled his boots and socks off then stood looking down at her steadily as he shoved his jeans down and off. Straightening, his fisted hands rested on his hips while jutting between his legs his cock appeared huge.

"On your knees, Jill. Give me your mouth and we'll see if you can take it." His command was hard, as were the male eyes that stared down at her.

Jill came to her knees. Her eyes were on his cock as her hands rested on his thighs and she leaned into him, opening her mouth.

"Hands behind your back. Spread your knees and get your eyes up here. I'll tell you when you're allowed to suck that," Holdin snapped harshly.

A powerful shudder of excitement rushed through Jill as she looked up into his intense face. He'd never been so demanding and she'd never wanted to taste him so badly. She quickly placed her hands behind her and shifted her knees apart as he looked down at her.

His foot tapped a knee. "More, woman. I said spread. Rest ass on heels and straighten your back."

Jill swallowed as saliva flooded her mouth and creamy excitement gushed in her contracting pussy. She spread her knees as far apart as possible, straightening her back so her breasts thrust forward as her shoulders were pulled back. Her hands clasped behind her in clammy anticipation. With her face turned up, she was shockingly exposed to him. The feelings rushing through her were almost too many to distinguish but what burned brightest was a dark pleasure as his eyes moved over her.

She'd had a taste of this kind of domination several times before, but never like this. Kneeling before him as he examined her exposed body was something new. Embarrassment that was not shame shot through her and heated her breasts. The tips actually ached as they swelled under his gaze. Deep in her belly it felt as if her soul trembled as she waited for him to speak, and she realized the thing she wanted more than anything was permission to put her lips to his cock.

Her reaction to his orders had been to make her hungrier for him. Did he know he did that to her? He must, she concluded as she felt her womb contract in empty protest as he looked down at her and didn't give her permission to take his taste into her mouth.

"Do not move unless you're told to, Jill," Holdin growled as he watched her closely. At his words, she trembled again and he saw her body flush in a rush of excitement. Her reaction was further confirmed as he stepped back to get a better look. Her belly shook in uncontrollable shudders and as he inspected her, the folds of her pussy flowered in excitement. Swelling lips were pulled apart by her stretched stance. As he watched, fluid dripped to the blanket below her.

Holdin gritted his teeth. He'd meant to scare her. Give her another chance to change her mind. The flushed, trembling Jill kneeling before him was so excited she was making a puddle. He'd never seen anything as sexy as the vision she made right then.

His eyes shot up to her face again and he watched her swallow. Amazement washed through him. He grabbed her chin. "Open. Do not swallow without permission."

Her breathing increased as she opened her mouth for him. He was watching her with a very stern look on his face as he held her jaw open. Suddenly Jill realized she couldn't control the flow of saliva. He would see how badly she wanted his taste. The command not to swallow meant she couldn't hide it. Saliva quickly pooled in her mouth and spilled down her chin. Holdin's thumb moved slowly back and forth through it as it dripped onto her shuddering breasts.

"Look at you," he breathed. "My girl is dripping for it. All over. Do you see how that needy pussy is wetting the blanket, baby? And look at your mouth. You can't help it, can you?"

Jill moaned in a strangled admission. Embarrassment swamped her. He gazed down at her drooling face and saw her needs. It was almost too much as he smiled tightly and released her chin.

"Swallow," he commanded softly. "So perfect, my sweet baby. Do you know how beautiful you are to me?" Even though he'd meant to be harsh, encouraging her with his approval was an imperative. She'd shocked him again. Teaching him with her response in ways words could not.

His damp fingers went to his cock and he stroked it slowly in front of her face, coating it with her saliva. "Is this what you want, Jilly-girl?" he asked.

"Yes," Jill admitted softly.

"Yes, what?" Holdin pressed her just as quietly but there was steel in the low tones. "Ask for what you want, baby. Say the words. This is not wrong or dirty. This is what we both need from each other. Now be who you are, Jill. Be needy. Don't try to hide it from me."

"Yes, please, Holdin. May I...ah..." Her face was already flushed. She couldn't blush any more but she had to swallow again to continue. The electric current of sexual excitement snapped around them as he required she ask for him in her mouth. She didn't have time to marvel at the way he turned the level of her need up with each demanding, unbelievably embarrassing and at the same time almost painfully exciting command. He had barely touched her and she could feel herself almost dizzy with want.

Jill glanced down to give herself a little emotional space as she begged him for what she needed. She had no idea how she'd gotten here but was pretty sure he'd brought her to this place where feeling his cock in her mouth was something she was willing to beg for. "Please let me suck you."

"Can't say the words, Jilly-girl? Look up at me and say it again. Show me you're mine. That mouth is mine and so is every other needy opening in your body." His chuckle was low, almost a snarl. "I'm going to fuck your face, little one, and you're so wet you drip. What a beautiful little bitch my girl has become."

It was the first time he'd used such a word with her. Jill heard it, but it didn't mean the same thing she'd always thought it did. He'd called her his, called her beautiful bitch and she loved it. She was one. He was right about the level of her excitement. For him, that was exactly what she was.

Both his hands cupped her head and his fingers curled into her hair, holding her face up to his. "Look at me," Holdin paused as her eyes rose to his, "and ask."

Jill couldn't breathe through the excitement for a second as he looked down into her soul and dragged up her needs for his examination. Yes, she needed to feel him in her mouth. "Please, fuck your girl," she whispered, and immediately he firmly pulled her to his cock.

"Remember, hands behind back, baby. This is how you get it this time." The fat head teased her lips, Jill opened but he didn't enter her. He followed her lips with the damp tip, painting them with his pre-cum. Her tongue flicked out to lick at the taste and he smiled.

"Hold that tongue out for me, Jilly-girl. Open wide and put it out there," he commanded.

Jill did as told, her eyes on his face as he watched her. Holdin placed the tip of his cock on her little pink tongue and watched as a drop of pre-cum pearled for her. Jill's body shook in reaction. "Swallow," he commanded again, and withdrew his cock.

His fingers caressed her scalp as she gulped his taste into her body. "Good girl," Holdin approved and her hips jerked in response. Looking down and making sure she saw him do it, he smiled at the dark, damp mark on the blanket below her. It was spreading.

"Eyes on me. Now open." His thick member rested on her lips again. Staring fiercely down at her, he was pressing into her, holding her head and controlling its movements. He'd never done that.

His complete control of her had an amazing effect on Jill. Instead of feeling constrained, she felt relieved. He wouldn't let her disappoint him. All she had to do was exactly what he directed and he'd even taken over her need to think about body movement. He'd left her one job, enjoy being what she was. She was free to sink into this amazing pleasure and let it consume her.

His fingers firmly cupped her head as he nudged to the back of her throat. Jill closed over him, taking all she could and sucking. One of his hands went to the base of his cock to stroke himself as his hips began to move.

His strokes into her were short jabs as his fist worked the thick base. Jill tried to lick him but she had no control and soon realized her job was to suck what he gave her as he gave it. He was truly fucking her face and it was driving her nuts.

His fist in her hair holding her for each thrust into her mouth, his intent gaze as he looked down at his cock sliding in and out of her. All of it was so amazingly new and yet completely as it should be. He made her feel hungry for him this way, and now it was a new pleasure to feel him move in and out of her.

Soon he grimaced and she felt him swell even larger, and then he pressed to the back of her mouth and held himself there as his fist worked his shaft.

"Swallow," he commanded harshly, and jets of semen flooded her mouth. Jill swallowed as fast as she could, blinking back tears as the sensations overwhelmed her. He held her to him as he shuddered and jerked. It was difficult to breathe and yet amazingly erotic. She shook in reaction as her eyes turned up to his face, she watched her astonishing Holdin lose control to her. That was a new thought. One that sent little flicks of heat down her body. She was the one who'd given him this orgasm.

He stilled and then slowly withdrew from her. "Relax, baby," he breathed. Holdin backed up to lean against the support post as Jill slumped down off her heels.

Jill couldn't look up at the magnificent male panting as he leaned against the post. She felt like a mess. Shy glances told her that the way he was looking at her should have made her feel like a beauty queen, a very naughty one though. Desperately she tried to gather her scattered emotions. Her scalp was a little sore from where he'd held her, her jaw ached and she had both saliva and cum dripped onto her breasts. All of those things made her both embarrassed and proud, and she didn't understand how that could be. The reasons were the same and they were producing such conflicting emotions.

Embarrassment won and Jill nervously glanced around but couldn't find anything to wipe up with. She very carefully didn't glance up at Holdin. It was difficult to understand what had just happened. What must he think of her? She'd begged to perform oral sex. She had drool and cum on her and she was embarrassingly turned on. Her hand went to the telltale drops on her breasts but he stopped her before she could touch them.

"No. Leave them," he commanded. His voice was soft but the tone was not. Jill froze in confusion as he strode to her side and paused as he looked at her. A little smile touched his lips.

"You are so beautiful like that. Naughty looks amazing on you." Once again Jill was swamped with the conflicting emotions. Proud of herself because Holdin enjoyed looking at her like this. And equally embarrassed to her bones because she was proud of herself for looking like this. It made no sense. What didn't confuse her was the warm flush that zipped around her body.

"Come with me, baby," Holdin said quietly as he bent to put a hand under her elbow, the other grasping her hand to help her up.

"Where?" Jill let him pull her up.

"Put on my shirt. It'll cover in case anyone wanders into the barn." Holdin picked it up and pulled it over her head then scooped up his jeans.

The shirt reached the tops of her thighs, barely long enough to cover her bottom. She was pulling it down in a useless attempt to make it longer as Holdin chuckled. Jill frowned up at him as he zipped his jeans.

"This isn't much covering."

Holdin pulled her against his body, cupping her ass cheeks under the shirt with gentle hands. His handsome face was filled with humor and approval as he looked down at the curvy bundle in his arms. "It'll do. Remember, you're doing as told, Jilly-girl. And I like how you look in my shirt. We're only going down to the supply room. There's a shower. My baby needs some cleaning up and I'll be taking care of that." His hands squeezed a little at he dropped a kiss on her nose.

His arm remained around her as they descended to the ground floor. Jill felt strung up on adrenaline and potential embarrassment. His big body almost held her up as she moved with him.

The T-shirt did cover her but not decently. It stretched over her breasts, which swayed beneath it. Her erect nipples were clearly visible. In front, it did touch the tops of her thighs, but behind she suspected it gave an explicit view with every move she made. Holdin was very firmly leading her down the main aisle of the barn now and she didn't have a chance to be sure no one was at the other end.

They both were barefoot but the foaling barn had very little debris on its floors. They reached the supply room without incident and Jill gratefully slumped against the wall.

It was a combination room holding what was needed to assist a horse's birth and clean up after. The shower stall stood in one corner, beside it a toilet. Neither was cut off from the rest of the room. The wall facing them had floor-to-ceiling shelves beside an old stove. Next there was a large utility sink and several big pots were turned over on the drainboard. Though the ranch was not a working one at present and the horse herd small, this room had been kept stocked these last few years.

Everything was very neat and clean, even the shower and toilet, but there certainly were no frills here. Holdin set a pot of water on the stove to heat and then smiled at her. "Come here, baby. Let's get you cleaned up."

"Someone could come in," Jill worried as Holdin turned on the shower. Jill stood in front of him as he shoved off his jeans.

"No one is coming. The two ranch hands have the afternoon off and my folks are in the house. They wouldn't show up, baby." He pulled the shirt over her head, hanging both the jeans and shirt over a towel rack on the wall. "In you go." His hand landed on her bare bottom with a smack. Jill squealed and had to step into the shower to move away from it.

"Hey. What was that for?" she demanded as he followed her in.

"Coz your pretty bottom is such a sassy, round one and I wanted to." He chuckled as he turned her to stand directly below the warm spray of water. Jill gasped and gulped water as his hands started to move over her. He rubbed over her breasts gently, making sure they were rinsed as he smiled down at her. Then soaping a washcloth, he turned them so his back was to the flow of water and carefully washed every inch of her.

They'd never done anything like this before so Jill had no experience to go on, but she was pretty sure the way he was taking care of her was not how a guy usually treated a girlfriend. His careful hands caressed, rubbed and fingered every inch of her as he told her to move or turn or lean her back against his chest. The soapy petting was slow and sensual as they both watched his big hands move over her, around her and in her.

Jill was hardly aware of the soft mews as he touched her, her back on his chest as his big arms reached around her to glide over breasts, under them, down her torso and slowly between her legs. Again it was his firm control edged with her shy embarrassment that set her on fire. He kissed her neck in loving nibbles as his soap-slick fingers investigated each fold between her legs and had her thighs trembling again when he whispered in her ear, "Still determined to have cock in this pussy?"

Jill's head was lolling on his thick shoulder as she smiled hazily. "Oh yes."

"What happened in the loft didn't scare you?" he wanted to know as he twirled a fingertip into her belly button.

"You mean when you get fierce and demanding?" Jill licked up an interesting tendon in his neck as he bent over her shoulder, watching his hands make soapy mounds of her breasts that were beginning to burn as he fondled them.

"Yeah. Were you afraid?"

"No. Here's the big secret," she whispered to him. "I feel safe when you do that. Not safe in every way, um…it's hard to explain. I'm safe with you and terribly excited."

"Explain it to me," he urged as he directed. "Bend over, hands on the shower wall and spread for me, baby."

Jill gulped as his hands firmly encouraged her into the position he wanted with an arm around her waist and one hand at the back of her neck. There was no chance of her falling as he held her, but he was also ensuring she did as instructed.

"Explain what?" Jill gasped as he gently pulled one of her cheeks open and proceeded to slowly drag the washcloth down her crack, circling her anus as he gave himself a good view of his actions.

"The not safe part, baby," Holdin questioned then added as he continued the meticulous cleaning, "I take care of what's mine and every inch of you is mine, Jill." The washcloth disappeared and it was just his soapy fingers now. Still carefully holding one bottom cheek open so he could see what he was doing, he rubbed her puckered opening then firmly pushed the tip of his finger into her to gently circle just inside her.

Jill laid her cheek on the damp shower wall and gasped through the swirling mix of sensations and emotions. His finger wasn't painful. It was a guilty pleasure. As was the knowledge that he watched as he did this.

The fact that she voluntarily arched her back and presented herself just as a bitch in heat does to a male animal was shockingly nasty. That mix of embarrassment and pride assaulted her again. Pride because she'd heard Holdin's growl of approval as she shifted. Embarrassing because she was proud of being this eager to please him. She wanted his attention like this and her body knew it, as did he. He couldn't help noticing her involuntary push back on him, or the way her feet shifted so her toes turned in and the space between her thighs widened. Somehow she'd become the bitch in heat presenting to him.

"It's this," Jill whispered in a shaky moan. "What you're doing right now. I'm embarrassed and excited. You take me to the edge. Don't you get it? You're looking at my ass, playing with it and I feel helpless, so exposed. At the same time I'm safe. It doesn't make sense."

Holdin stopped moving, his finger inside her. Her body was trembling in minute tremors as he looked down at her. "Jill, you love this. I can see you shaking in excitement." His finger twisted in her again and then he pressed a second slippery tip into her.

Jill gasped as her head sank down between her shoulders.

"Push back on me, baby," Holdin instructed. "Open your ass for me by pushing back. I want to see my fingers fuck this tight little hole while you explain how that makes you feel."

Her body bore down on his fingers and her tense opening flowered for him. A third finger entered with slick ease and he twisted them. She shuddered hard.

"I can't. I can't explain it," Jill sobbed desperately as fire rushed up her belly. The three fingers in her anus stretched her but there was very little pain. The burn was a quick spice to the pleasure and helpless embarrassment.

"Try," he demanded as his fingers pressed in a little farther, widening her opening and forcing her to relax.

"I'm ashamed that I love it," Jill confessed in gasping desperation, and he slowly rotated in her. "I know you're looking at me and it's so…embarrassing. But I want it. I want it like a drug or something. When you get like this, I can do anything you ask and be embarrassed about it and still be turned on. I am free of my inhibitions because you don't let me have them."

Holdin chuckled darkly. "So my little Jilly-girl can be a bitch in heat for me and still a lady in public. Is that it? You get to enjoy both and not be responsible for the bitch part."

"Oh God. I guess," Jill agreed.

His hand released her cheek and snaked around her waist again, supporting her weight. "Back up." Holdin was already pulling her off the wall. "Grab your knees and spread your legs wider." He positioned her directly over the shower drain and made sure she was steady, three fingers remaining in her. Then he reached up and grabbed the showerhead that was on a long hose so it could be moved around.

"Now hold still, my sweet little bitch," he crooned. "I'm going to give you an interior bath." He smiled as she quickly adjusted as his hands directed her. "That's my pretty bitch doing as she's told. Good girl."

The three fingers in her spread slightly, holding her open as he directed the firm spray of warm water up into her body.

"Holdin! What are you doing?" she demanded as water shot up into her body and she had no control of it gushing out again because he held her open.

"I'm taking care of my little bitch and making sure she's ready for me," Holdin replied calmly as he quickly put the showerhead back after making sure everything was rinsed. He then grabbed the soap and one-handed rubbed it over her bottom cheeks. Placing the bar on the top of her bent form, he lathered the soap he'd rubbed on her then drew the lather down her crack again, washing her quickly while still holding her ass open. His hand sluiced down both legs and back up. Then the soapy hand went to his cock, stroking over it in quick strokes she couldn't see.

"You need to be ready because I can't wear a condom the first time," Holdin continued. "I need to feel you, know if I'm hurting you. I can't come in that sweet pussy, but I don't think I can keep from coming in you, Jilly-girl. So I've made sure you're ready for this." His fingers pulled out and before her stretched hole could adjust and close, the fat head of his soap-slick cock slid into her easily. He gripped her hips as he pushed into her.

Jill's head snapped up in a shocked reaction as her body clenched. Thick, hot and slippery even though she tightened, Jill couldn't have refused the hard intruder. New sensations rushed through her like a firestorm. Foremost was harsh excitement. It clawed at her with fiery fingers as he took her ass.

"That's it, feel it, baby," Holdin hissed, and pressed into her tightening entrance. The careful stretching of her anus had paid off and she took him with relative ease. His soapy cock slid slowly into her. "Jezus, you're so sexy. Such a beautiful slut. Relax, honey."

Holdin gritted his teeth as she closed over him. Watching her take him like this, feeling her contract on his cock as he took her ass was so damn good. Her hot body was made for fucking and this was even more intense than he'd expected.

Encouraging her with the words was difficult when he thought his head might explode as he watched her submit to his body. But still, he needed to know for sure how Jill was feeling. One of his hands snaked around her hip and calloused fingers strummed plump folds. With a shallow thrust one finger entered her constricting pussy and Holdin groaned out a chuckle.

"Good girl. Feel how you love it. Damn, Jilly-girl, you're gushing."

His voice stroked her with praise that made her see what he saw. She loved it, she wanted it, but more than anything, she loved that he loved it.

His cock was a hard, thick monster that subjugated her with its intrusion and still took her without pain. Finally, seated all the way in, both of them moaned. Jill felt as if the world were spinning beneath her feet as she gasped in guttural moans. Hot excitement burned through her and emotions whirled out of control.

Bent in front of him as he took her like this was so sharply humiliating. Loving it and pushing back on him in eager excitement meant she was a nasty slut. Oh God. Was she that slut? The answer was yes. For Holdin she was anything he wanted. Not because he wanted it any more than she wanted it though. What Holdin wanted showed her how much she loved being his. He knew she'd want this and he'd taken her.

How could she not have known this about herself? How had he known it? That's when she realized it didn't matter. He knew her. He knew her to the depth of the woman she couldn't face. That creature was this person.

Jill sobbed in surrender and felt herself shudder in unimaginable excitement as he played with her pussy and drove his cock into her ass. The new stimulation of his cock fucking her ass was amazing. The thrill of loving his possession, his control, his complete understanding of how nasty she really was almost drove Jill over the edge into orgasm. He even knew that.

Holdin gave her a few short thrusts and pulled out as he reached for the showerhead again and immediately pointed the spray into her still-open ass, effectively rinsing the soap out of her then washed himself again.

"Stand up, baby. That's it. Good." Holdin reattached the showerhead and pulled Jill back into his arms. His forearms crossed as his big palms each cuddled a breast while holding her to his chest. They stood under the spray a few minutes shuddering. Jill was shaking in reaction to the experience and Holdin shaking in reaction to pulling out of her.

"Okay, baby?" he softly asked eventually.

"Yes." Jill turned around to bury her face in his chest as her arms wrapped around him and clutched him to her. His hands moved up and down her back, gently caressing her as she pressed into him. Her breath started coming in hiccups.

Holdin cradled the back of her head as he kissed her neck. "Tell me what the tears are about."

"Nothing. I just... This is so intense." Jill's muffled explanation into his breastbone was halted and jerky.

Holdin smiled into her damp hair. "Okay, you just let it out. I'll take care of everything." He picked her up to step out of the shower. Putting her down, he kept an arm around her as she still huddled into his chest while he flipped the shower off and grabbed a towel. Her sobs were short little hiccups of emotion, much like a tired child who is trying not to cry.

He dried all of her he could reach while she hid in his chest. Comforting her with the safety of his touch. "We need to talk about this, baby," he started as he rubbed her hair. "I understand those were not tears of pain or fear. Crying is a very strong statement to me."

Jill dragged in a deep breath as he gently set her away from him and ran the towel over her. "It's hard to explain. I feel so dependent on you somehow. What we did just now felt so good and yet I can't believe I do whatever you say when we're together. It doesn't seem right but I want to so badly. I'm not making sense, am I?"

Holdin wrapped the towel around her, tucking it in under her arm. He grabbed one for himself and quickly wiped the water from his body.

"Well, it does make sense actually. You're feeling conflicted about our relationship and don't understand your responses to me," he told her calmly. "Part of you is fighting it. The internal struggle is deeply emotional. Your basic desires that you surrender to me are battling with what you've been taught is the right way to be."

"I feel guilty and excited, sorta embarrassed and so free. I feel all mixed up." Jill shivered slightly.

"Nothing is wrong with you. We're just different than you expected a relationship to be." Holdin pulled on his jeans and went to the stove, shutting off the burner. He took a mid-sized rectangular metal box off the shelf. It had a metal top and was the type of item often seen in doctors' offices. In it he dropped a short stack of clean washcloths from the shelves where they were stored then poured enough hot water over them to soak them. He sealed in the heat with the lid. "Jill, what's between you and me is different. A relationship like this isn't bad or wrong. It's something that's been going on a long time between really honest people. People brave enough to be who they are and lucky enough to have found each other."

Holdin set the box down and leaned against the counter. Jill was standing in front of the shower where he'd left her. He didn't want to crowd her for this conversation. It was too important. "Here's how I see it. We fulfill needs on a very basic level. I need to be in control and it turns you on when I am. I think that takes us to a much deeper level of intimacy than most people reach. The more turned on you get, the better it is for me.

"So we sorta drive each other. My control becomes stronger and your submission to it becomes deeper. You relax and let yourself enjoy what we're doing without having to think about it. That surrender drives me nuts and also controls me. Your trust is the most amazing thing I've ever experienced. I'm so damn proud every time you give it to me. Saying I love you seems small compared to the way you make me feel."

Holdin gripped the sink behind his butt to keep from reaching for her. She had to understand how deeply he felt about her. How much he valued her gift. It was more than just loving her. He treasured her. Pulling her into his arms would be influencing her with the sexual heat that flashed between them so easily. That would be unfair and playing dirty. He wasn't about to do that, but it was damn difficult to stand here and not touch her.

Jill's head tilted and her hands clasped together in front of her nervously. "When I think about how I am with you, I feel like a spineless idiot. That's usually long after I'm at home in bed. When I'm alone, I can't imagine what you see in me besides a stupid robot who follows orders like she doesn't have two brain cells to rub together." Jill shrugged and looked at the floor as she confessed the rest. "I promise myself I'm not going to be like that anymore and the next day it happens again."

Her head down, Jill looked up. "You're waiting for me at work and before I can say anything you put an arm around me and give me that quick kiss. I'm an idiot again. I want more. You know it and, and…"

"And I tell you where I really want to taste you," Holdin finished for her with the same wolf's smile he usually had on his face in the mornings when he whispered what he wanted in her ear.

Holdin always found those first few moments in the morning difficult. They both worked the early morning shift, starting at six. Every morning he battled the urge to rush to her. Mostly he wanted grab her and take her on the spot. There was some strong, basic wiring in his brain that demanded he establish possession both physically and mentally after being away from her overnight. He did it with words, but not "I love you" or some other lame crap like that. No, he needed her to feel his possession and her surrender to it on the same primitive level he wanted her on.

He worked stocking so there was usually a truck to unload. Strangers or staff were around and being hot to get his hands on her definitely wasn't cool. So he'd solved his problem by murmuring explicit instructions or questions in her ear. Jill would blush and step under his arm, obviously eager to be close to him. Worked real well. It'd never occurred to him that she'd be embarrassed about it.

"Yes." Jill smiled helplessly. "I just lose my mind and then I'm right back where I started."

"Jill, you don't lose your mind. It's just when I see you in the morning, I've missed you." Holdin gritted his teeth. He didn't really want to confess making sure she lost her mind around him. "You're my girlfriend. Wanting to be with me isn't wrong or bad."

Jill walked into his body, her hands petting down his bare chest and around his waist to stroke his back in open-handed caresses. "No, but needing you is. I don't mean just wanting to be with you, Holdin. I *need* you. I can barely walk up those steps in the morning. I want to run. That's just pathetic!"

Holdin wrapped his arms around her, one hand tunneling under her damp hair to cradle her skull, the other sliding down her bottom to pull her against him. He chuckled softly, "Oh damn, baby. There isn't a morning that I don't want to leap down those steps and grab you. Waiting for you to walk to me is torture. So we both are losing our minds. Don't tell anyone, okay? We're way too cool a couple to be the desperate idiots who slobber all over each other in public."

Jill's face lit up. "You want to rush to me? You feel just like I do?"

"Oh yeah. I want to do a damn sight more than get that little puritan kiss. Someday I'm going to wake up beside you and show you how I feel in the mornings." His hips nudged into her pelvis for emphasis. "I'm a morning person," he teased as his head dipped down to taste her neck.

"I could have sworn you're an afternoon person." Jill tilted her head to enjoy the neck nibbles. He knew he could make her tingle from that touch alone.

Holdin growled in a low rumbling complaint that was all male. "Texas men take what we need and don't whine about the rest. It's what I can get with you, woman."

Jill laughed softly. "I feel much better, you know. I needed to know it wasn't just me."

"Baby," Holdin's head came off her neck so he could look her in the eye, "I am more into you than I know how to say. I act all casual most of the time. But you'd be embarrassed if I didn't." He grinned his lopsided smile. "And sometimes I need you to blush for me but not because I'm acting like an idiot." His hands both dipped beneath the short towel and came up her thighs to cup both bottom cheeks. Very slowly he separated them and Jill blushed hard at his suggestive handling.

"Yeah. Just like that, so I know you understand whose girl you are. No one else, Jill. *Mine*. It's not wrong and it's not shameful when it's between us." His voice was barely a whisper into her mouth as she strained up on her toes. Hard male lips crushed down on her mouth as his hands slid down her thighs again and lifted her, wrapping her legs around his waist as they moaned into each other's mouth.

Holdin lifted his head. "Time to go back upstairs, Jilly-girl." Her body tensed to get off him. "No." His hand spanning her bare bottom gripped firmly. "Stay right there."

He picked up the square tin in the other hand and stepped over by the towel rack. "Grab my shirt," he directed. Jill picked it up and they were out the door.

Holdin strode down the brightly lit barn ally. It was late afternoon and the center of the barn had been roofed in a material that let sunlight filter through. Jill relaxed in his arms completely and realized she was smiling. This was exactly where she wanted to be and he'd just freed her from any lingering guilt over it.

Back at the blanket in the loft, Holdin knelt carefully and laid her down. Jill's smile was sensual as she arched her back and stretched her hands over her head. Holdin carefully put the tin container down, shucked off his jeans and moved to kneel at her feet. Picking up one of her feet, his thumbs started massaging right below her toes with firm pressure.

"What are you doing?" Jill wanted to know as she purred at the new sensation. It wasn't even sexual and it made her feel amazing. He was just kneeling there rubbing her foot as he smiled lazily. His eyes were moving over her towel-wrapped body with every indication of pleasure.

"I'm looking at you, touching you," Holdin answered almost absently.

"I'm not even naked."

"No, but you will be."

"You can't reach the towel from down there."

"When you're ready, you'll take it off, baby. It's your choice."

"I will?"

"Yes, you'll do it for me because you want to. Or you won't because you don't want to. Either way I get to do this and enjoy looking at you."

Jill came up on her elbows. The foot massage was making her leg tingle with contentment. He picked up the other foot and started on it. "You mean you like rubbing my feet? You do it for me because you want to."

"Yes." Holdin nodded. "I want to because I know it feels good. You are mine. From these toes to the top of your pretty head and I take care of what's mine."

Jill bit her lip as she looked at the big, magnificent male kneeling at her feet, rubbing them. He wasn't touching her sexually or encouraging her in any direction at all. They were here because she wanted him to take her virginity. He hadn't said no but he'd argued against it. Now he was giving her time—again. Not ignoring her and not arguing with her, just taking care of her while he waited for a sign that she was ready.

Warm hands took her to heaven on cottony clouds of sensation, gently, firmly and oh-so tenderly. His heart was as committed to making her moan with drowsy relaxation as it was to making her scream in sexual frustration.

Lying there in the shadowed hayloft, Jill felt a painful certainty slowly flow over her heart like molten metal. It engulfed her and secured itself in place. Encasing that beating organ in unbreakable walls with no seams, no locks. A smooth prison with only one escape route. The key rested in the rough hands moving over her instep. It lived in those hazel eyes that burned for her below lazy lids. It didn't matter how old they were or what lives they'd lived to this point. Here was the man who'd own her forever. The one man, the only man.

The man she would have to love enough to leave. At some point and probably soon, his life would depend on her leaving without a trace.

Jill sank back off her elbows and her hands rose to cover her face. Gasping through the rapier cuts her thoughts inflicted, she didn't want him to see. The only thing she had to give him was whatever time they had left. If he knew, he'd die with her every day. It was too late to break up and spare them both. She wasn't strong enough to do it. Somehow she'd passed that moment and not even known it was there.

He was only marking time working at the store. His plans were college in the fall and she knew she'd probably not even been here by then. At first dating had been just for fun. How quickly everything had changed.

"What?" Holdin asked in concern, his hands still holding her feet in his lap, his body leaning toward her.

Jill composed her face. She would have this moment. Everything else dropped away as her hands left her face. There was only him and she let the decadent pleasure of being his woman flow over her face, concealing the desperate anguish that lived in her soul. Love was a small word for where they were and there were no words for what came next. There was only now.

Holdin sucked in a sharp breath as she looked at him and slowly pulled the towel away from her body, holding up her arms to him.

"Yes," Jill breathed.

Holdin prowled up her body on hands and knees, his eyes never leaving hers as he settled over her.

Her soft voice continued. "You will hear my yes when time ends and there are no more days. There will still be my yes, Holdin." His mouth crushed down on hers as the urgency of her mood surged over him. His arms tunneled under her body and he pressed down into her as he pulled her up. Arms and legs wrapped around him, she clung to him with all the desperation that was swamping her.

His kiss was long and deep as he tried to draw the mysterious pain he felt in her out of her into his own body. He could feel it moving through her soul but couldn't find the cause. Her small body clung to him with it and somehow it felt as if the end of time she'd spoken of was called down on them.

The fragrant air became laden with soft moans and rumbling growls as his mouth finally left hers and dragged down to her sensitive neck. He was fierce and tender. Living rock that held her on the edge of forever with hard hands and burning eyes. Urgency was held in ruthless control as he molded her trembling breasts, plucking the tender peaks, twisting them and moving down her body to lick the sting away.

Her head spun with the sharp pleasure he gave her so easily. Each touch severed another artery as he deftly removed the heart he owned and took it into his keeping. By the time his hands shoved her knees up to her chest to open the center of her body to his ravishing mouth she was nothing but a moaning body of sensation. His possession to please or tease as he wished.

He knew it. He was hunger and will, wrapping around her in driving demand. He took her moans and required more. His mouth opened over her swollen pussy and he snarled in satisfaction as her body gushed for him. Tangy sweet, her body gave him his due and he took it from her with slowly unraveling control. His tongue moved over her in demanding strokes that became animalistic as he gorged himself on her essence. Lapping at her, he petted each fold, driving her sensitive center wild with need. Controlling her with touches that wouldn't let her reach the release her body was craving.

The sound of him greedily slurping between her legs with animalist enjoyment stabbed Jill with spikes of guilty pleasure. Embarrassment became another face of pleasure as he ate her. His pleasure added a dimension to her sensations that she couldn't name. He was driving her wild with it and she loved how he took her. Wanting to please him became the center of her world but he wouldn't let her focus on it. His clever tongue kept lashing her with the realization that she loved being spread before him. The nasty slut in her eagerly offered her most intimate secrets for his examination.

Soon that was not enough and his fingers trailed around her vaginal opening then slowly thrusting into her shallowly as he played with sensitive folds.

Jill couldn't remain still as he teased her. Shifting beneath his mouth, she tried to center him where she needed him. Holdin snarled as he turned to nip her thigh and Jill yelped. The sharp reminder of his absolute control shot through her. It was harsh and insistent. She was his to do with as he pleased and that fact made her gush with guilty intensity. Stretched before him was not enough. He required she surrender to his demands and she loved it. Needed it. The red mark on milky white flesh glowed as he licked it and then returned to her contracting cunt with renewed interest.

Moaning, Jill clutched the blanket below her as he sucked a damp fold into his mouth, lifting it from her with a shake of his head. Then took the other and growled as he shook it gently. Her body obediently shifted back to where he wanted it and he grunted in satisfaction, stabbing his tongue into her opening in reward.

Contracting around him, Jill howled in reaction. The intensity of his demands, his dominant control and the stab into her over-sensitized channel drove her harshly up the last bit to painful need. Her entire body was convulsing on his tongue and she couldn't hold back another second. Of course he knew it. Pulling his tongue away from her, his finger grasped her clit and jerked it up in a harsh twist. The new pain forced her release back but not by much.

He refused her release in the most dominant way possible. Using her body like the plaything it was for him. He let her clit go as Jill panted off the desperate high. Her body shuddering as muscles contracted in protest. The rushing whirlwind didn't let up as licking gently then roughly he drove her right back up that desperate hill until Jill started begging.

"I need it, oh please. I need to come. Anything, Holdin. Anything you want but let me come."

His response was a rumbling growl as lifting off her, his thumbs peeled back her labia and he blew down pink center folds.

"Please, please." Jill's ass had jumped off the blanket as his warm breath washed over her in contrast to the animalist fervor of the last few moments.

"Please what?" His clever tongue licked around her clit, circling it roughly. "Say the words, Jill."

"Please, Holdin. I need you. I need you in my body," Jill moaned.

Two fingers swirled through the cream flowing down the crack of her ass then pushed deep into that small hole, hard and fast.

"Like this, Jill?" His lips were peeled back from his teeth in a predatory snarl as the guttural rumble of his voice made the words almost indistinct.

Jill arched into the invasion, her head thrashing as he pulled out and rammed his fingers back into her ass again. The thrill of him entering her there rocked her. Those new, shameful sensations shot unbelievable pleasure through her womb as if there were some direct line connecting them for her.

"Oh God," Jill gasped as he continued to thrust into her contracting opening. The abrupt entrance and demanding strokes shot burning arrows of intense need deep into her belly. It didn't matter, she wanted him to take her. "I don't know. However you want."

"Yes, baby. I'll get to that hungry ass soon. Now say the words that you need to say."

He rose up over her body, one arm bulging as he supported himself above her face again. The hand between her legs added a third finger twisting as he continued to thrust into her ass. "You know, Jill. You know what you need. I will spank your ass like a five-year-old if you refuse to say the words again. You will not hide from me this way. You are mine—every emotion, need and desire. Mine! Give them to me!"

Never. He'd never been like this and it shot her into some amazing place where she was only his. Nothing else mattered. She was free to be the woman he'd made her in his arms. The woman who needed him just like this because he knew she wanted to feel his possession of her ass, her cunt, her body.

There was only Holdin and she would do anything to have him.

"Please, fuck me, Holdin. I don't care how you do it. I am yours. Take me, I beg you. Just fuck me, please. I need it so bad." Her voice was splintered with desperation.

"Then be mine." Both his hands came up to hold her head as his body adjusted over hers. The fat head of his cock dragged down her burning folds to rest at the contracting opening to her very soul. He nudged gently, pressing in so her tight channel held only the wide head. "Look at me, baby."

Holdin teetered on the brink of forever. In her eyes was his future and he needed her in it with him. Loving Jill was more than taking her this final step. But this step was one that closed the door to the past for both of them.

Her eyes gazed up at him in watery devotion and he knew the woman she was about to become was the center of his soul. His commitment to her now was reverent and total. She was giving herself into his keeping and he wanted that responsibility more than anything he'd ever known. "Mine, Jill. You are mine."

His hips abruptly thrust into her. It was sharp and hard and took her so quickly she didn't have time to feel the ripping pain. It was mixed into the shocking intrusion as he forced her to take him to the hilt. Merciless and thick, he burned into her body and held himself there.

His hands still held her head so she couldn't turn away from him as pain washed over her. A single shocked exclamation was forced out of her as tears suddenly streamed down the sides of her face into her hair.

"Yes, Jilly-girl. Pain," Holdin hissed in fierce response. "This is the price of your gift. You've given it, now it's over. There will never be another time like this, baby. Not like this where pain has no part of the pleasure." Holdin kissed her tears, licking the salty taste of her virginity and its price. "You're mine now, mine in ways that can't be undone."

His thumbs stroked down her cheeks as he held his body in her. There was fear written across her face with the pain. It started to fade as he held not only her body but demanded her mind as well.

"That's my girl," he approved in gentler tones, still kissing away the tracks of her surrender. "My beautiful girl who's become a woman. Fear is not part of this, baby. It's a healthy emotion but it's not between us. I'll take care of you. Don't be afraid. You've given yourself into my keeping and nothing can undo that. Nothing. My sweet slut. My precious lady. You are both and you are mine."

Jill gasped in gulps of air and her body suddenly contracted on him. Holdin smiled in understanding. His woman. His slut. She was that slut at heart and only just coming to grips with it. Even in this moment, she'd responded to him on that reminder. He'd known what he was for a long time. The dominant urges were the only way he'd ever expressed himself sexually, but Jilly-girl hadn't had the freedom to recognize who she was. She'd never understood that side of herself.

His experience was not vast but it was informed. Tying up girls on the school playground at ten had pretty much been a clear sign to his father of what type of son he was rearing. Charles Powell made sure his son came to understand his own nature and did not express it inappropriately again.

At first he'd not explained the sexual side of it, but by fourteen Holdin had read enough to know what he was. Charles was a firm father but always fair. Bringing questions to him might have been a little uncomfortable, but Holdin knew he had a responsibility to protect the very ones he might hurt if he didn't understand.

There was a sharp cost to protecting his little slut. Her body was begging him for the hard use they both wanted. That tight, tender pussy pulsing on his cock shrieked at him in female demand. Not giving in to it was the hardest thing he'd ever done.

His head snapped back and a strangled roar erupted from him as his eyes squeezed shut. But he didn't move. Her body released slowly and then contracted again and he concentrated on the control her submission required as he bent his head to her in gasping agony. Pleasure flayed him. That sweet, tight tunnel sucking around him was nearly his undoing. Shuddering, he looked into her face again.

"You're not moving," Jill whispered desperately.

"I want to. More than anything in this life, I want to," he told her tightly, "but not more than I love you, Jill. Never more than that." The urge to pound into her became pain as he looked down into her precious face. But it was a pain he'd take for her. This time he could not surrender his own control, not under any circumstances. If he couldn't take care of her now, he didn't deserve her.

"Help me, Holdin. What do I do?" Jill whispered as her body now adjusted to his possession of it was once again demanding sensations she was afraid of. It had hurt the first time he entered her. How could she want him to do it again so desperately?

"I'm here, baby." One of his hands released her hair and snaked down between their bodies. His fingers found her clit and played over it lightly. Jill's mouth opened in silent reaction as he fingered her. He was pulling sensations out of her when she thought there was nothing but hard, burning pain. Heat surged up her in waves of pleasure that sparkled with the pain of needing him. Wanting more, shocked and enthralled. Jill's fingers dug into his shoulders as she held on to him in shuddering confusion.

"That's my girl. Feel how tight you are, how perfect," he growled into her ear as his head dropped. His lips moved over her neck in licking nips as he whispered to her, "So perfect, Jilly-girl."

He filled her up. Her body adjusted, expanded around him and then there was sensation. Amazing new sensations. He held himself still inside her and every nerve ending in that sensitive channel was wedged against him. The discomfort was changing, not lessening, just changing. Stabbing shots of excitement from knowing fingers took over, mingled and twined around the heat of accommodating him lodged within her.

Her body was already trembling, the interior muscles clutched in growing excitement as he forced them apart. "Yes, baby. Give it to me. So good." Holdin held her eyes as he took her to a new place. "That's it, look at me. Don't look away, baby. The beautiful slut in my arms is all mine. Everything you are, everything you feel. Look me in the eye and give it to me," he continued firmly, giving her commands to hold on to as she found a new way to be. He'd have her soul and body. He intended she know it.

Jill panted harshly, reacting to both his words and his touch. The incredible sensations of his possession, thick, hard, and deep were now sending waves of heat spiraling through her. He was burning her mind and body, branding them with his imprint.

"That's it, feel how good it is. My pussy, Jill. My sweet, tight pussy. I will always take care of what's mine, baby, and you've given all of you." Holdin felt her body slowly tightening around him again. She was responding to him but he couldn't be sure of her pain level. He was damn sure of his pain level.

Buried to the hilt in her hot little pussy and not being able to move for fear of hurting her was introducing him to the fierce basic man within himself he'd hardly known existed. A roaring aggressor who was driven with the need to possess Jill. There was little logic, nothing but the primal drive to ensure possession through any means available. The screaming demand to fuck grew with each second. He'd never needed anything as badly as he needed this.

Desperately, Holdin held on to control as the small body beneath him trembled in his arms. This was her first time. He couldn't let her first time be a painful, ripping experience with a raving beast taking her like a mad man. The conflict cost him almost every bit of sanity he had left. Abruptly he realized he was about to lose the battle.

He knew she wasn't going to be able to reach orgasm this time but he would. It wasn't fair but it was who they'd become. She was his woman and he'd done everything he could to prepare her for this. Now he needed her to understand that.

Holdin gasped as his need to possess her ate through his resistance. "Your body is mine. When we can, I'll show what that can mean." He gritted his teeth and sucked in air as he fought for just a little more control. "But this time is mine."

"Yes," Jill answered. Her eyes burned into him as if she could see his struggle. "Now, please, Holdin. Take what is yours. Always yours."

Her acceptance was more than he could take. It was surrender and understanding. She knew her surrender was the one thing that he could not resist. His response to her was savage as the aggressive conqueror within ripped out of his cage.

Pulling out of her, he dragged the head of his cock down that delicate bridge of flesh to her lower opening. Groaning, there was almost no time to reassure her, but he had to. "I love you." The words were almost unintelligible as the primal demands of his nature roared with impatience.

"Love me more." Her whispered demand slipped the last gate open and Holdin was lost.

His hips powered forward and he plunged into her hot little body. This time there was no restraint. He'd prepared her for this possession and now he took it. Hard and fast he jacked in and out of her. The tight opening and velvet channel beyond it robbed him of any higher thought process as he fucked her ass relentlessly. All he could feel was how damn good it was as she accepted his cock. The hungry, primal man within screamed in satisfaction and drove him even harder.

The demanding dominant she made him needed more. His body rose up and both hands grabbed the back of her knees, jerking her legs up to press them against her. Holding her open to him and taking her complete surrender was what he sought. He needed her surrender, craved the proof that she accepted him completely and welcomed his control. She gave it to him by grabbing her own knees to hold her legs up under her breasts.

"*Mine!*" he roared as his balls tightened and he felt the fire of release barreling down on him. Then there was nothing but shattering oblivion as powerful, jerking thrusts of his hips slapped her ass and his mark jetted deep into her body. He couldn't stop. Nothing had ever felt like this mind-bending pleasure.

Slowly the fog of release let him go and he collapsed down on her, still jerking as her body tightened on him and then relaxed. Holdin was breathing hard. His balls ached and his head felt light. He didn't like the slightly dizzy feeling and raised his head to shake away the haze. Looking down, he became aware he was still lying on Jill.

Then the magnitude of what they'd just done rolled over him in hot waves of intense pride. No other would ever have his Jill. Not that it was even a possibility. He needed to say that to himself as he looked down on her. His woman in every way. Holdin pulled out and she moaned. Her eyes remained closed as his body slid to the side so he could look at her.

She wasn't moving, just lying there panting with her eyes closed. Oh damn! The reason for her lethargy punched through the preening beast in his brain. He looked down her body and felt his gut clench. He'd known there would be blood. Actually seeing it paint her thighs a filmy rouge as it mixed with other liquids was shocking. Had he hurt her more than he had to? He'd been a senseless animal at the end.

The unbelievable euphoria faded and he reached for the tin of warm washcloths. Sitting up, he very gently lifted her leg and ran the warm, damp cloth down her thigh to press it over her. The heel of his palm carefully pressed it against her tender opening and he tried to see if there was new blood farther down. He needed to be sure he hadn't damaged her there. He'd had little control at that point.

Jill said nothing as he carefully removed the bright red evidence of her innocence. The second cloth finished the job and the third one he pressed to her bottom, holding it there as he reverently kissed her knee. She'd jerked a little but didn't shrink from his touch. That was good. She had to accept his touch in aftercare, know she could depend on it no matter what they did.

"Jill?" He needed to hear her voice. The possessive dominant needed that connection from her as much as she had to know he would always take care of her.

"Mmmmm?"

"Jill. Tell me how you feel, please." Holdin turned to his commanding voice. He wanted to say so many other things, but it was more important to know if she was physically all right.

"Tired, a bit sore." Her voice was softly subdued.

Finally done cleaning her, Holdin lay down beside her and wrapped his body around his precious woman. He was half lying on his side as she still lay on her back. Both her legs were propped up over his hip as she often did when they cuddled. She said it let her back straighten and felt good after the weight of her breasts on it. She'd told him that bit of information in early May when he'd taken her on a picnic. Since then, he always arranged her like this when they had a chance to lie down. "Baby? Talk to me."

"Sure." Jill gave a little mewing purr as she adjusted into his hold.

"I didn't mean to hurt you any more than I had to." Holdin's arms tightened around her. His lips said the words into the top of head.

"I know. It was amazing." Jill's eyes didn't open as he looked down at her face trying to read her.

"When you're not sore, we'll do it again. You'll understand," he continued.

"Holdin?" Jill interrupted him.

"Yes?" He held his breath. This was where she could try to reject any next time. That would be a problem between them. He didn't want to force her on her second experience but he would if it was the only way she'd get past the pain of the first one. He'd not let her live with an expectation of pain with intimacy any longer than he had to.

"Shut up and hold me," Jill directed calmly.

Holdin jerked in surprise when the words sank in. "What?"

"You heard me. Shut up. I love you, you love me. We made love and you want to do it again. That makes me one freaking sexy woman and I like it. I am possibly the most contented female since Eve. Don't make me gag you to get some peace and quiet so I can enjoy this."

Relief nearly choked him. A deep, burning smile unfolded in his soul and the primal male he'd just become aware of growled in satisfaction. Holdin bent his head so his cheek brushed the top of her head and relaxed. "No problem. Let me know when you're done enjoying, baby. I have to take you back to town sometime."

Chapter Nine

The air was not sweet with the smell of hay anymore but heavy with antiseptic reality. Those images would never fade into the soft focus time gave most events. For him they'd been razor sharp, carving into his heart each June with relentless clarity. The two of them had entered a door that day, one he'd never been able to close.

The gift of her submission in every way had taken up his world and made her the center of everything. Everything he became from that moment forward was about Jill. Even the things he was not were because Jill was in the world. He'd become her man. She'd become his universe.

He'd given her the necklace with her name spelled out in gold the next evening. The moment he clasped the chain at the back of her neck, he'd felt a calm satisfaction. Their relationship had changed and the necklace was an appropriate symbol, if only between them. He'd gently grasped her shoulders and turned her to survey the gift against her skin.

"Beautiful" was all Holdin could say as she looked up at him.

Jill's fingers had naturally gone to the new ornament she wore. "Thank you, Holdin." Her voice was slightly shaky as she smiled into his eyes. They were both moved by emotions deeper than either had expected.

"You're mine, Jilly-girl. Don't take it off," Holdin instructed in a quiet growl.

"Never?" Jill asked, trying to inject a lighter mood.

Holdin's tone remained calmly serious though his lips bowed in a pensive smile at her. "Never."

They hadn't discussed it again, but to his knowledge she'd never taken the thing off. That pleased him now. Tomorrow they would remove it before surgery.

In the distance a buzzer went off and then running feet rushed past the door. Close by someone was losing a battle with the mortal enemy. He heard codes being called and clipped voices barking instructions as the fight for life raged. So close. She shouldn't be so close to the Reaper's haunts. In this place, death knew every soul and it felt as if both darkness and light were here, eager to claim another convert. He wanted to gather her in his arms and run from this place.

A cold shiver ran down Holdin's back, the passing of eternity perhaps? Whatever it was, it could keep on going. No one in this room was walking into the light or drifting down to the dark. The urge to bare his teeth and snarl at the shadows was primal. The predator within paced the perimeter of her bed, securing it. Guarding against unseen adversaries didn't seem anything but logical to that elemental warrior who lived on this woman's emotions. Her heart beat for both of them and nothing was taking her tonight.

If only such promises could be true. For Holdin there was no comfort in wishes. Fate was a cruel mistress who'd already amused herself in their lives. However, just because he'd suffered in the past, as had Jill and Drifter, there could be no expectation of mercy as fate rolled the dice on them once more.

Lifting his head from their clasped hands, he focused on her face. She was sleeping at last. Even though he knew there was nothing he could do here, the thought of leaving was not easy. He could no more guard her than he could take her illness into himself, no matter what the focused creature in his soul said.

Glancing at the clock, Holdin sighed. It didn't matter what time it was. He had things to do that were about protecting her in the real world. He couldn't fight the medical battle for her but there was one he would take care of. The world of stalking hit men and shadowy mobsters was getting a brand-new player.

At its core, every battle was a game of strategy. Strength was only a tool, a component used by the game planner. In this game there were no rules, no monitors and no holds bared. The men who ran the game were professionals and Holdin respected that. Respected it, but wasn't half as intimidated as he probably should be. It was just a new arena, not really a new game to a born contender.

Kissing her hand as he reluctantly released it, Holdin slipped from the room. He needed to make a phone call and he didn't want to do it in this building. Making his way out the maze of hallways, he headed for a side entrance. He didn't think the press would be waiting for him at the front door yet but just to be sure he went out a service entrance and jogged around to his SUV.

The night air smelled fresh, even in the city, as it washed the hospital scent from his lungs in the short jog. It felt right to jog onto this new field of conflict. No moon lit the night sky and though the parking area was brightly illuminated, Holdin kept his head down to create a shadow over his features. He was aware of several suspicious cars parked near the hospital's front door in the fire lane with engines idling. Looked as if the press were here.

Quickly entering the SUV, he pulled out and exited the hospital property. Two of the suspect cars followed soon after he'd fired up the SUV. Holdin made sure it wasn't obvious he was hurrying, but headed out as if he were driving back to the ranch, not going to his place north of town.

Cold gold-green eyes watched in the rearview mirror as both cars gave up shortly after they recognized his route. No beat reporter wanted to drive out that far at this time of night. They could get a few hours of sleep and file a story in the morning. The news was in town, not at the ranch.

As soon as they were gone, Holdin snapped his cell into the dashboard holder, activated the hands-free on it and dialed a number. He continued driving in case there was a car he'd missed. That would be the car he most wanted to leave behind. The one not interested in reporting news. Even at this hour, the road was fairly busy and it would be easy for a vehicle to hide in the headlights behind him. But perhaps the traffic would make it more difficult to pick up a signal from his cell if they were trying to listen on some spy device.

A groggy voice answered on the fifth ring. "This better be important." The low growl wasn't exactly friendly but even half asleep Matt Moholand was too well trained to use a name in greeting.

Holdin's first year of college, Matt had been a junior and a defensive end. He'd been injured late in the season and it was clear pro sports were not in his future. So he'd finished a degree in criminal science and went into a career in law enforcement. For ten years Matt had been one of New York's finest, making it to detective relatively young. Now he ran his own agency.

They hadn't been buddies but Holdin had seen strength of character in the man. It was later as a public figure and professional athlete that Holdin found having a friend in Matt could be extremely helpful.

Their connection was not known to the public and almost untraceable since they'd never actually taken the field together. Matt had left the football program long before Holdin became a starter. But between them, the comfort of knowing where each other came from had allowed them an immediate level of trust later in life. Matt was the investigator Holdin had used when he discovered Jill Taylor wasn't his girlfriend's real name.

"Charge me extra for aggravation," Holdin responded in tense tones, hoping Matt would read him and stop talking already. "It's important."

"You can fuckin' afford it," Matt grunted.

"Yeah. Here's the deal. I need information on a guy. No one can know I'm asking. That's crucial. The guy died fifteen years ago but I need to know who he was and who he associated with. Also how connected his associates were. Someone was chasing the guy when he died. Whoever that was, I'll want to know."

"The world is full of dead *guys*. Gonna give me a name? Location to start from?" Matt was obviously getting out of bed as he spoke. Holdin could hear the rustle of sheets and creak of furniture as the big man moved.

"Don't write it down," Holdin instructed. "If this crew gets a whiff of you snooping, you don't want them to find a trail."

"Now you have my attention," Matt responded seriously.

"The dead guy was Stephan Capizzano, his wife, who is also deceased, was Margo. I don't have a location, but start looking in New York City. Then try Chicago and Miami. I doubt he comes from L.A. or Las Vegas because he was headed west when he died. He wouldn't be running to the guys chasing him. You won't find an obituary on Stephan. He was using an alias when he died but you will on Margo. She died about thirty-three years ago."

"Shit. Tell me this isn't related to who I think it is," Matt asked, referring to the last time he'd attempted to find someone for Holdin. The girl who'd turned out to be a ghost.

"It is," Holdin confirmed.

"Well, you got trouble," Matt snarled.

"Yeah, the last name is distinctive."

"You found her? She gave you the info?" Matt wanted to know.

"She found me," Holdin confirmed. "I can't get more information right now but I need to know the facts and I need them right now. I want to know if the people who were involved with Capizzano are a threat."

"Your little friend should know. Ask her."

"I'm not in the mood, Matt," Holdin snapped in frustration. His patience level was dangerously low and the sharp tongue of a New York native was difficult to appreciate at the moment. "I said I can't get more info from her. I need to know if she's in danger. If she is, so is my son. Get the picture?"

"Shit! Seriously?"

"Dead serious."

"Hell, if she were in danger, she'd have been taken care of by now. I'm not being a smart-ass about that. The people you're talking about don't wait that long to take care of business."

"Okay, I'll explain. Fifteen years ago she and her father left town as I told you before. What I didn't know was they had a car accident the next day. Stephan Capizzano was burned to death, no way to identify the body. She was pulled from the car but she had a head injury and was unconscious. So they were John and Jane Doe to the authorities. When she woke up, she had no memories. Not 'til she sustained another head injury about a week ago.

"She came to find me with my son. Tomorrow she's having brain surgery. There hasn't been a lot of time to talk. Tonight she told me her real name and the fact she and her father were on the run from people she called 'bad guys'. That's why the alias and disappearing act. The other thing she said was that it wasn't her father who was in trouble. She'd witnessed a crime by her father's associates. I need to know if the bastards will still want her when it hits the papers that my former girlfriend is in Presby Dallas."

"Damn. A son? You didn't know?"

"Yes, and no, I didn't. Damn it! Are you going to do it or not?"

"Stop being an ass. Course I am. Give a guy a minute to get over the shock. That story is pretty fucked up. You sure that's your son and she really didn't know who you were all this time?"

Holdin gritted his teeth as he grimaced. That question would probably tick him off every time he heard it. And it would be a while before he stopped hearing it. Still, it put more snarl in his voice. "I'm sure. Minute's up. Get to work on the other."

"I'll talk at you later when I have something. Shouldn't be more than a few hours now that I have a lead to work with." Matt hung up.

Holdin pulled off at the next exit and turned around. There were no visible tails on him and he figured it was time to try to get a few hours' sleep. He briefly considered going back to the hospital but knew he'd add tension to the room if he stayed in it with her. She'd feel it even as she slept and wouldn't be able to sleep deeply. He didn't have much hope of rest for himself but the least he could do was not infect Jill with his worrying.

When he was finally stretched out on the California king in his master bedroom, Holdin resignedly stacked his hands behind his head and stared at the ceiling. His body was exhausted but not because of the physical demands of the day. Emotionally he'd left almost every bit of his soul on the ground. He wished he could feel empty. That would be a relief compared to what he knew would be a long night packed into the few hours of darkness left.

The fire in his soul burst though the control he'd been maintaining so carefully. He'd had her in his arms last night and tonight he didn't know if he'd ever hold her again. White-hot shards of pain made him suck in a breath through clenched teeth as that thought cut through him. The suspicion that it was his fault sliced up what was left of his flesh. Had he been blindly selfish? Pushed her too hard for a physical commitment? The sweet release she'd given him could have been the price of her future.

Bitter guilt added an acrid taste to the torture. It wasn't that he'd had no right to her. His possession of her was not the issue that was eating through his intestines like a parasite. Jill was his woman. What he couldn't defend himself from was the knowledge that he could have confirmed the connection between them another way. He'd needed her surrender so badly, had it blinded him to her needs? What kind of bastard was he if he couldn't put her needs before his own? He despised that sort of male. They were weak idiots who couldn't control their own urges.

If he was one of those, even if it was only this *one* time, he'd senselessly used up his family's future for a few short moments of possessive gratification. It made him no better than the male garbage who destroyed their families for drugs, gambling, whatever the addiction was they couldn't resist. Jill was his addiction, he knew that. It had been his responsibility to protect her, even from himself. Perhaps mostly from himself.

He'd thought he'd endured pain in the past, it was nothing. Beyond the personal guilt was the knowledge that he was helpless to protect her, help her through tomorrow. That was agony on a new level. It cut him to the bone, denying his nature on every level. There wasn't even the meager comfort that he was doing something. When she'd been lost, he'd at least been able to "do something" to help her find him.

He'd always been certain Jill was in the world. That she was part of the human fabric flowing around the globe, he'd felt it instinctively. Believed she was here, somewhere, because he had no other choice. And he'd been right. Tomorrow could possibly bring a new reality, one he didn't know if he could deal with.

Holdin squeezed his eyes shut and willed the fates to smile on him one time. He'd make any deal they required, sacrifice at any altar they directed. Nothing was sacred except the life of this one woman and her son. He believed in the

Christian God, but he knew there were forces in this world he didn't understand.

Superstition was a part of every professional athlete. They saw to clearly that talent and desire were not enough to make a champion. Luck, fate, kismet, whatever one called it, was the fickle bitch who played with them. Perhaps the ancients had been right in the practice of worshipping many gods. Who knew?

* * * * *

Holdin and Drifter were in Jill's room by six a.m. Surgery was scheduled for eight-thirty and preparations were underway. A patch of her hair had been shaved and the rest pinned out of the way. A skullcap was fitted over her to secure it. The opening for surgery was neatly cut out of it. She was silent as the technicians worked around her. Jill's only demand had been that they let her hold Drifter's hand as long as possible. Holdin stood against the wall watching as the nurse reached around her neck to remove Jill's necklace.

"I'll take care of that." Holdin stopped her as he went to Jill's side. The nurse stopped in surprise and nodded, moving aside as Holdin bent over Jill.

Looking up at him as he reached around her neck for the clasp, Jill bit her lip. Her free hand rose as if to hold the charm on.

"Shhhhh, baby girl," Holdin soothed while smiling into her eyes. "I'll keep this for now." The gold was warm with her life energy as his hand closed over it. Jill gulped in a hitching breath. "It'll be waiting when you come back," Holdin assured her.

At those words, Jill glanced away for a second, the uncertainty of her returning clouded pretty brown eyes as she met his again. "Thank you."

Holdin slipped the necklace in his pocket. With the crowd of strangers in the room, Holdin couldn't say what he needed to. The words to take that cloud from her eyes escaped him as he desperately searched for them. And then someone was asking him to step aside so they could continue.

Her smile trembled as he backed up. Their gazes clung to each other for that moment and then it was gone.

Jill's attention focused on her son. As she should be. Yet Holdin felt a ragged stab of loss and the need for some commitment from her that she'd be back. That she believed it. She had to believe it for it to happen. He stood there and watched her be brave and couldn't find a way to help her.

Control was once again Holdin's battle as he contained the need to tell her that she was his. Nothing would ever change that. No power in heaven or earth could touch it. Nor could it change the fact that she was her baby's mama. But he remained silent. He had no promises to offer, no assurance, nothing that could alter the battle she had to fight alone.

Watching them prepare her for surgery was a drawn-out lesson in what it was possible to endure. This time he knew what was taking her and still had to stand back and let it happen. Help them if he could. Helpless rage boiled in the pit of his stomach. Raw and senseless, it urged him to snatch up the woman who was his and leave this place.

What was the use of being rich and influential if he couldn't use it to fix things for the people he loved? Wasn't that what rich men did? They bought, they bribed, they blackmailed the world to bend it to their will. He'd failed, even on that callous level he'd failed.

In a hospital room, no one had status. It was the great equalizer. Rich or poor, brilliant or barely finished grade school didn't matter. In this building, every family had to stand by helplessly and pray when the gurney was wheeled away. There was no mercy to be purchased when that small group of orderlies and nurses disappeared.

Watching her vanish out the door took every ounce of willpower he possessed to hold back a bellow of denial. He wanted to charge them and beat the malevolent men to a pulp for trying to take her. Gritting his teeth, he actually visualized squeezing the life out of each one with his bare hands around the white-collared necks.

Holdin glanced at Drifter and noticed a slight tremble in the boy's stiff-legged stance as the door shut behind the rolling bed. The space between them where her bed had been was now empty. The absence of a bed in the hospital room suddenly became unbearable and both of them avoided looking at the space. In fact, Drifter remained facing the door. His breathing had picked up as he glared at it.

The tall young man's hands were fisted at his sides and Holdin recognized the struggle for control in his son. Again Holdin was helpless. There were no words that fixed watching one's mother being wheeled off by white-clad orderlies. It was a stark reality that could not be soothed and he wasn't about to insult the boy by pretending it could. Holdin reached a hand toward his son's back, unsure what he'd been about to say when the door opened again and a smiling student nurse invited them to follow her.

Holdin and Drifter were ushered into the surgery waiting room where Carol and Charles were already present. Drifter sat beside Carol and smiled weakly at her as she took his hand. Charles was standing with his back to the window and Holdin joined him.

"So she went?" Charles asked. It was a pointless question whose real purpose was to fill the silence.

"Yeah." Holdin nodded. "Shouldn't be too long. Just in and out then an hour in recovery." Everyone knew the schedule. Holdin needed to repeat it for himself mostly. Two hours, that's all it should take. Three hours on the outside because he hadn't taken into account prep time right before surgery, so four was probably realistic. He knew he was stretching it, trying to force every eventuality into the "okay" slot.

She had to be okay. He'd refused to think of what happened if she wasn't. For Drifter he'd acted as if he'd considered it and had a plan, but within himself he hadn't. Having Jill back was too big, to consuming, to allow her to leave again. If it happened, he'd deal with it. Hopefully gracefully, but he didn't hold out much hope for that.

It was a good thing his mom and dad were here and that was just sad. It felt like a failing that he needed them to ensure he behaved if the news was bad. He needed them for Drifter, not himself.

They were insurance that someone present would be sane enough to help his son. He had little faith for himself in that situation. At least he was honest enough to face his failing. He'd been in love with Jill too long, too hard. He'd seen himself when he lost her the last time. This time would be worse.

They were all silent as the minutes ticked by. There was nothing to say. Everything seemed trivial. Holdin couldn't sit, he couldn't pace. He simply stood and stared at the door. In the background, he heard Carol try to distract Drifter with a drink of soda or something to eat. Charles went to sit with them. Holdin's eyes moved to the family unit and he knew it was his job to join them.

So long he'd been alone with Jill. That was a strange way to put it but there it was. He'd mourned her alone, missed her alone. He'd never been strong enough to share her memory. Not with his parents and certainly not with anyone else. She'd driven him to be the man he was and yet it'd just been the two of them in his mind.

She'd spent the last fifteen years without him, completely. He'd spent them with her. Only her.

Including Drifter in their relationship was something he'd not realized would be so difficult. Even when he'd grasped the fact that he had a son, it'd not occurred that he'd have to share this most intimate part of himself with his son. His pain had been his alone. Now it was selfish to hold it in. Suddenly he recognized that Drifter felt the same way.

Drifter had never had to share his mother. Their relationship had been uncommonly closed in a way that could not be opened by anyone other than his biological father. Even if Jill dated, Drifter didn't have to share her as he would have to with Holdin. Of course the boy was not enthusiastic. How could he be? Holdin represented a threat, someone who could take his mother's attention from him. In a child's mind, attention equaled the level of love they received.

Holdin slowly walked over and sat down across from Drifter and Carol. Leaning forward he scrubbed his hands down his face, consciously relaxing, letting his face show at least some of his emotions. The boy needed to see it in him. To know they shared this pain, regardless of what it cost Holdin to do it. Bent with elbows on knees, Holdin faced his son. Even his sitting position was an effort to convey their equality in this moment.

"Neither one of us is very good at sharing her," he started quietly.

Drifter regarded Holdin blankly for a moment. "What?"

"I shared a little with you in the hotel room. Telling you what your mother meant to me all these years. I'd never told anyone that." Holdin straightened in the chair but scooted down so his butt was on the edge of the chair, stretching long legs out in front of him, remaining at eye level with Drifter. "But I didn't get what it would mean for you to share her with me. I doubt either of us really got it. She's been mine all this time, if only in my mind, but still, just mine. Our connection was so strong, so deep, it didn't fade with time. Her loving you is an elemental connection of a mother with her baby. I know you're not a baby anymore. But you will be her baby forever." Holdin's eyes flicked to his mother beside Drifter. "Come to terms with it, son, we both have strong women for mothers."

Drifter grinned and glanced at his grandmother too.

"He's right," Carol agreed. "I don't care how big he gets," she nodded toward Holdin, "he's still my baby and he'd do well to remember it."

"Yes, ma'am," Holdin confirmed, chuckling. "See what I mean?"

"Yeah. So?" Drifter regarded Holdin with the bored expression again. Holdin knew it was a defense. Passive aggressive, it was one of the few tools Drifter had to deal with this situation.

"So I'm saying, the way I love your mother might be something both of us have to adjust to. You're not used to having a father and it never occurred to me that I have a son. We have to share her in ways neither one of us expected. Even if she'd married someone else, that man would not have the connection she and I have. Not with regard to you. I get it that you're enough like me to resist sharing her with me. I'm sorry it's difficult. It shouldn't be. But what we should have had isn't important. Right now is the only thing we have to work with. We've got some time to kill. Getting to know each other would be a good way to spend it. Can you meet me halfway and do that? I'd really like to hear how you know so much about fixing a car."

"You just figure out that there's no getting rid of me so now you want to know me?" Drifter asked in disdain.

"No. I wanted to be sure you understood that you aren't getting rid of me. I want to know you because you're my son. I'm trying to make it easier for you by explaining how similar we are. Your reactions to me are ones I'd have if I were in your position."

"You sure talk a lot when you're trying to make a point," Drifter observed. Silence stretched out after his statement.

"Well?"

Drifter's face twisted in a bitter grimace. "You do know it was Mom who insisted we go find you? I did it because she needed to." Drifter glanced at his grandmother and Charles, who'd sat down on the other side of Carol as he tried to soften his resentment for his grandparents. "Not saying it was a bad idea." Then his gaze returned to Holdin and all softness disappeared. "But I figured the chances of you being that interested in me were low. It was never about you and her." Drifter slid a little farther down in his chair and glared at Holdin belligerently.

"I know. You didn't plan on me impacting your life. But consider this. Your mother did. She knew me well enough to know I'd be very interested in you. Can you respect her wishes and make an effort?"

Holdin knew Drifter was scared. Right now that fear was translating to anger and he'd become the target. If he let it go, being the bad guy would continue to grow. If he couldn't reach Drifter and find a common ground to make this an event they got through together, their relationship might never grow beyond that anger and resentment.

"Your mother's first concern is always going to be you. I don't want to change that. It's why she risked her life to bring us together. Our relationship is so important to her that she was willing to die for it. I can't take that lightly. I hope you don't. She didn't expect anything out of our meeting for herself. You got that, right? When she wakes up, she'll need our support as much as she needed it before. Seeing us struggling with each other will create stress she doesn't need. Her main concern should be recovering, not refereeing between you and me."

Holdin paused, hoping what he was saying was making an impression on the angry young man. "I'm not saying you have to pretend to like me for her. All I'm asking is that we get to know each other. We both want what's best for her. That's a place to start, to try for her."

Drifter regarded Holdin in silence a few seconds and then the need to move forced him out of his chair. Holdin watched the rangy young man pace over to the window. He stopped to stare out it, arms crossed over his chest, legs stiff. Tension flowed around Drifter in angry waves as he stood with his back to them. Carol moved to get up but Charles gently laid a hand on her arm to hold her back.

Holdin went to the other side of the window, standing in a mirror image of his son, gazing out blindly at the bright summer morning outside. After a few minutes, Holdin began talking. He wasn't looking at the boy as he started telling him about how it was to be fourteen and reared all over the world. The Powells had been a Navy family. There was no money for extras. His interest in cars could only be fed through magazines.

The information flowed out of Holdin in a steady stream that wasn't complaining, it was more a humorous, self-depreciating story of a boy whose interests were very similar to those Drifter harbored. Shortly Drifter was interested enough to ask questions. They weren't exactly having a conversation but it was getting there. In the telling, Holdin included the recounting of some of his young antics that had gotten him into trouble. Carol and Charles naturally joined the conversation, adding details Holdin left out.

Eventually Drifter began telling them how he'd learned about cars. Their apartment building was next to a family-owned service station. The owner was a mechanic as were his sons. Hector Chavez knew a boy who needed to be involved when he saw one.

The Chavez family was a hard-working bunch who'd built a reputation for good work at reasonable prices. They didn't have much to share but what they did have was male companionship and an appreciation for the willingness to learn. They'd apparently folded Drifter into their lives and by extension, his mother.

Holdin mentally made a commitment to find a way to repay the debt he owned them. Perhaps repay was reaching too far but he certainly owed them his thanks. There really was no way to repay the generosity they'd showed his son.

Charles Powell looked his son in the eye and raised a brow. Holdin nodded. The Powells owed a lot to the Chavez family.

Time passed. The conversation didn't make it go faster. Everyone watched the clock. What it did give them was some ground to meet each other on. Drifter wasn't a stiff, defensive mass anymore and Holdin found investing in Drifter's comfort was more rewarding than he'd thought it could be. It wasn't painful to acknowledge the life Jill and Drifter had led. It was simply the facts. Reality.

Letting those years they'd struggled alone bother him was a selfish point of view, one that revolved around him and what he'd lost by not being there. Parts of the story gave Holdin a heavy heart but for the most part, he had to admire how Jill had reared their son. Accepting that nothing could change the past gave him a small measure of peace. The future was the only thing he could be involved with and nothing would keep him from that task.

But he couldn't afford to even glance into the future right now. The unknowns were too great. Knowing he was a selfish bastard about Jill didn't make it go away. The possibility of her not knowing him after surgery was too painful to deal with. Focusing on Drifter gave him some satisfaction. This would never be taken from him. His son.

While they were talking, a technician came in to do the DNA swabs. A long-handled Q-tip was used to gather cells from the inside of their mouths. It was quickly done and the tech left.

Drifter regarded Holdin seriously as she disappeared. "What if it's not you?"

Holdin smiled. "Give up that hope, buddy. Didn't my mom show you the pictures of me at your age?"

Drifter shrugged. "Yeah. I know. It just seems too strange."

"What's so strange about it? You knew there had to be a guy."

"But you're you. This famous, rich guy from TV. It's strange."

"It'll get stranger. Wait 'til everyone knows you're the son of the famous, rich guy from TV."

Drifter laughed. "I guess it could be worse. You could be a teacher or something. You know, geeky nerd."

"You've thought about that, haven't you? Wondered who your father was. Were you worried someone would just show up someday?"

Drifter jammed his hands into his pockets. "I figured it was a possibility. Could have gotten ugly if Mom didn't remember him and junk."

Holdin nodded and glanced away to give Drifter some emotional space as he asked the next question. "So what was your plan?"

"I don't know. I sorta thought we might have to run away from him at first."

"You ever talk to your mom about this?"

"Naw. She'd have told me not to worry about it. She thinks I'm still a baby sometimes. I talked to Mr. Chavez about it."

"What did he say?"

"He said the guy couldn't take me from Mom and if he became a problem to let him know. Mr. Chavez wasn't always a mechanic, you know." Drifter continued ominously. "There was a revolution where he comes from in South America. He used to be some sort of military. Anyway, I had him watchin' our back."

"Sounds like you took care of the problem," Holdin responded, being careful not to imply judgment one way or the other on this surprising development.

Drifter and Holdin had sat down after the DNA test. Carol and Charles had left the waiting room to bring back some soft drinks for everyone and it was just the two of them.

"Mom doesn't want me to learn how to use a gun. Mr. Chavez thinks I'm ready but it scares Mom to death. He promised to teach me when I turn sixteen if she says it's okay and I still want to."

"Protecting your family is very important, I agree with you." Holdin weighed his next response. He understood the man-child's frustration when he'd realized he wasn't strong enough to protect his mother. That must have been a frightening insight when it occurred to him. Normally there should have been a father to fulfill that role for a boy. If everything had been as it should have been, he'd have naturally taught his son how to be his partner protecting the family.

The personality Drifter was displaying was all too familiar. He came from people who'd come out here into the unknown west with barely more than their wits to protect them. They'd brought their families and carved a life out of the ground. Protecting home and family was imprinted on males from birth apparently. The instinct had bloomed in the boy when he was too young to have resources to handle it. But Drifter had. He'd looked around his world and made arrangements.

Drifter nodded and glanced away as Carol and Charles returned. A few minutes later Robert Coates entered the room. The tall doctor was still in surgery scrubs, eliciting an air of confident control as he regarded them and smiled. Holdin's first reaction was fear then relief as he rose to meet the man at eye level. He needed that small measure of control.

"The surgery was textbook," Coates informed them. "Jill appears fine. She's said a few things to us in recovery when asked questions, so she's lucid. As for her memory, there is nothing we can do now but wait and see. She'll be out of recovery in under an hour. Then she'll need to sleep as the drugs wear off."

Holdin realized he'd been unconsciously holding his breath and let it out. She was alive. That was the most important concern. Deep in his soul fear still churned in burning intensity, this news only relieved a small portion of it. Life didn't mean she was fine. All it meant was there was hope.

Everyone had stood up expectantly when Coates appeared in the door. Drifter walked to him. "When can I see Mom? I don't care if she's sleeping. I want to be with her as soon as she wakes up."

Robert put a hand on Drifter's shoulder and squeezed affectionately. "I know you do. As soon as we can, I'll get you in the room with her," he promised.

"What did she say?" Drifter wanted to know.

"Nothing that tells us much more than she's conscious and functioning. This is not the time to stress her. She can move toes and fingers, which means she'll have full function. She can respond logically. That's all very good news. It's what we want to see right after surgery. She needs rest."

"So you're not worried?" Drifter pressed for reassurance.

"Son, she is alive and functioning. That was the motive for this surgery. Without it, she'd have sustained brain damage and possibly died. As her surgeon, I consider the procedure a success." Robert sighed and glanced at the adults behind Drifter then focused his attention on the boy again. "Personally, I have no doubt that she'll know who you are. The area of the brain the bone chip affected was not a primary memory center. Try to relax. She'll need to know you're okay when she wakes up."

There was little more Robert could tell them but Holdin had difficulty focusing on it. The bit of information Robert had been reluctant to say was huge. The doctor had used the information to soothe Drifter and obviously been unsure if the adults in the room would understand what he was saying in light of the whole case. Jill's memory centers had not been affected by the recent trauma. Coates agreed with the original diagnosis that her loss of memory was not a medical problem. It had been due to some other cause. She'd told him when they met in the soda fountain that the doctors had "expected" her memory to return.

The reasons someone's subconscious "chooses" to wipe the slate clean and start over were all dramatically bad. If Jill's mind had played that trick on her, the situation she'd told him about last night was much worse than he'd understood it to be. Damn! Holdin felt it like a hit to the torso. The new understanding of her desperate situation was shocking.

"Now if you don't have any more questions, I'll get back to the patient." Robert looked at each of them. Drifter shook his head no and Coates focused on Holdin, raising an eyebrow in unspoken question.

"Not about the surgery," Holdin agreed, "but I'd like some of your time later when you have a moment."

Robert nodded. "We'll chat."

Holdin reached out to shake Robert's hand. "Thank you." Her life was the most important issue and this man had saved it. He'd given her back a future and Holdin would be grateful for that no matter what else occurred.

* * * * *

As soon as Jill was released from post-op and returned to her room, she asked for Drifter. He was the only one allowed in to see her, but when he came out he was all smiles. For him the waiting was over. His mother was still with him.

Holdin was relieved for his son. She was tired and wouldn't be in any shape to speak with anyone else 'til tomorrow but it was an incredibly good sign. However for him, the darkness of uncertainty was a roiling mass that would not settle. He needed her and there was no way to tell if she still needed him. When he had her in his arms, there was no question where she belonged. But like the last time, she'd had to go places he couldn't go with her. That's when she slipped away from him and he hated it. He hated not being able to take this from her, spare her in some way. It was illogical and physically impossible but that didn't matter. He should have protected her.

Deep grooves marked Holdin's face as he struggled to be happy for his son. Drifter's world was secure and that was something to hold on to.

Shortly after Drifter came out, Holdin's phone vibrated. He stepped away from the group to answer it. The only call he was expecting was from Moholand.

"Yeah, what have you got?" Holdin was standing in the hall, away from the rooms on the second floor. It was a glass-enclosed walkway that was relatively quiet since it was separate from the patient activity.

"Good news, I hope," Moholand responded. "The information comes from location and public records only. I assumed Capizzano was involved with the crew nearest his home location. I didn't ask questions yet because you wanted it quiet. Soon as someone starts asking about something this old, word will get out. So far, your man appeared to be involved with some heavy hitters but the leader at the time was gunned down a few years ago in some sort of dispute. His second is now the main man. Your guy is barely a speck in the past."

Holdin grunted in male acknowledgment and waited for the rest. There always was something else, especially when the news was good.

"Don't know if this means anything, but the second was arrested twenty years ago for a murder. The charges were dismissed for lack of evidence. Right now he's a guest of the federal government in another case that's in trial. Murder again, very high profile. The jury is out right now. If it's guilty, he'll be going away, possibly with a due date on his soul. It'll probably hold up in appeal if they get him convicted."

"Damn, how long has the jury been out? What's the feeling? Do they think it's gonna stick?" Holdin wanted to know.

"They've been out two days and I can't tell you how it'll go. No one seems sure."

"Let me know as soon as it breaks."

"You'll know when I do. It'll be all over the news," Moholand returned.

"No, I'll probably have no idea. Surgery was today. It looks good but I'm not going to be free here for a while. Call me."

"Fine, I'll hold your hand. But I'm gonna bill ya for the effort."

Holdin grinned. "Those aren't bills you send me, they're love notes."

"Yeah, well, this time you get the full rate. Cuttin' you a break seems to give you a foul mouth."

"Just saying, I'd rather you felt it was worth your time. Doin' me this favor might be dangerous."

"Notice I figured out fast that I'd rather stick to public records? If I were you, I'd keep her face out of the media and the details on how you met sketchy. Make something up. You're a popular guy, everyone will believe you were doin' someone your first semester at college. Change the boy's birthday so it matches that story. Mentioning the old girlfriend at all is a bad idea. A person being in the federal hotel doesn't mean he can't reach out. Don't give him a reason to."

"That your professional opinion?" Holdin asked. Moholand's words of caution said much more than the facts had. He was worried.

"Yeah. No amount of security gizmos or bodyguards will make a shit of difference if you draw this person's attention. These are the bastards who put the fear in professional."

"Then why is he hung up with the government now?"

"Government got lucky, though I think they had some help from this guy's real competition, the other pros."

"Damn." Holdin rubbed his forehead. "Okay, buddy. Thanks. Don't do anything else for right now. Until I know for sure that's who we're lookin' at, I don't want you stickin' your nose in."

"Don't worry. I've already deleted the search from my hard drive. Thinking of swapping it out and destroying the one I was using. I'm real happy to go eat donuts and look ignorant on this one."

"Call me," Holdin directed before he hung up.

Standing in the deserted hall, Holdin gazed out the glass front at the surrounding parking lot. Shit and damn! According to Moholand, no one could protect her if the past came back looking for her. Assuming her father had been just as bad as the boys he ran with, he was probably the only person who was capable and that bastard had died on her.

Realization hit Holdin hard. With her father dead, her only chance of life had been to disappear. So she had. It'd been bothering him that she'd never even hinted anything to him back when they were together. As close as they'd been, that hadn't made sense.

He'd wondered about the nineteen hours before the crash too. She could have called him from a restroom. They'd have stopped once in a while. But she hadn't called. Which meant she'd agreed with her father about leaving him cold. Made sense now. Ignorance was her only way of protecting him.

So if her memory loss was not medical, the only reason she'd allowed herself to remember was because Drifter needed a future. She'd been just as scared for her son and had little time to make arrangements. Which meant that now that the danger to her health was past, could she slip back into the safety of anonymity? Even if she didn't want to?

No, she had to know that memory loss now would endanger Drifter by taking away her ability to protect him with knowledge. So now she would be even more afraid for her baby. Holdin had to reassure Jill that he had a plan to keep her detached from the young woman on the run she'd been before she came up with some plan on her own to distance herself from him and their past again. She'd already created a pattern of trying to bury his connection to the person she'd been. It was how she would try to protect both Drifter and him again. And most likely why she'd tried to keep him at arm's length before the surgery.

The thing that gave him hope was her inability to stay away from him emotionally, even when she was fighting it. They'd made love at the ranch. Nothing about what they'd shared had been as simple as sex. She was his and both of them had known it.

Maybe he shouldn't have pushed her, but in a sense he'd had no choice. Just as she'd not been able to deny what they were together. The relationship between them was not entirely physical but it was expressed that way between them. If he were better with the words, perhaps things would be different but he doubted it.

Holdin turned and strode back to her room. He had to get to her fast. Tell her about the new story they were going to use and reassure her that he'd be protecting both her and Drifter. There would be no running from him. This time they'd have a future together, he'd make sure of it. If this plan didn't work, he had another one in mind. One he grimly hoped he wouldn't have to use.

It was suppertime and Holdin asked his parents if they'd take Drifter out for a meal. He didn't want them to know he needed a few minutes alone with Jill, even if she was groggy.

Drifter had been reluctant to go but Holdin promised to call if anything changed. He waited until they were out of sight before slipping in her room.

She was lying so still and apparently sleeping as he gazed down at her. Tubes went in her nose. There was a catheter, an IV ran into her arm and she was hooked up to what seemed like a ridiculous number of monitors. Once again the light was dim and shadows crept around the walls of the room. The summer sun was up in the early evening outside but here the drapes were drawn and night seemed a stalker slowly drawing nearer with eager intent.

His primitive core was crawling the walls in aggressive fervor at the knowledge that she was in danger. Even though he felt the threat was distant, it was difficult to tolerate the possibility. But that was nothing compared to the deep, piercing pain of knowing she'd sacrificed so much to protect him.

Turning her back on her past had been for her own protection as well but he'd bet the memory loss had been because she didn't trust herself to remain anonymous. She knew the effort to keep away from him would become too great in a weak moment and she'd been unwilling to allow herself even the possibility of endangering him. He wasn't flattering himself that she would miss the sex that much. It was her natural, submissive need for security that would do it. It would not have been possible for him to keep away from her if the positions had been reversed. He knew that for a fact.

Holdin pulled a chair up and took her free hand. "Jill?"

Her eyes opened but her face didn't change as she regarded him silently. Holdin refused to let her lack of welcome bother him. She was trying to protect him again and he simply was not having it.

"Hi, Jilly-girl." He smiled and lifted her hand to his lips for a second, needing the intimate contact. Even if it was only a kiss to her palm. "How's my girl?"

"I have a hole in my head," Jill informed him in a husky whisper. "Things could be better."

"I know, baby. There is something that is better. Just listen to me for a minute. Can you manage that?"

"Sure. If I fall asleep, don't take it personally. It's the hole in the head. Things fall out." Jill smiled faintly at her own joke.

"Hush and listen. You're not supposed to be a smart-ass already." Holdin kissed her hand again because he had to then got to the problem and his solution.

"I know why you had to stay away. Why it was so important that you protect both of us by not remembering us. Don't get upset, I haven't been digging around your past in a way anyone would notice. There's good news though. The man who was the head of your father's gang is dead. His second-in-command is currently in jail for a murder two years ago. They aren't a threat." Holdin studied her as he went on. "Even so, we'll change the facts about when we met. All we have to do is move Drifter's birth date a couple months. I can make sure anyone who knows different is silent. It's not a problem this time."

Holdin had absolutely no difficulty withholding some of the information from her. Jill needed to relax and concentrate on recovering. It was his job to worry about everything else. When they were younger, he might not have had the tools to protect her, that didn't apply anymore. He was not going to lose her again, not to her efforts to protect him and certainly not to some fucking thug. Nor was he going to let said thug have one more minute of his life. That bastard had stolen the future from them once.

If the Feds couldn't take care of business, he'd see that someone did. He knew that sounded as if he were willing to take out a hit on the man and he supposed basically that was exactly what he'd be doing.

He was perfectly willing to use the services of a little-known company out of Miami that was in the business of security. Holdin had met the owner some years ago. That man was the definition of scary bastard. Holdin had immediately recognized a cunning predator walking in the skin of a man, a familiar spirit.

The meeting had been a chance one, both at the same place for different reasons, but they had been comfortable with each other immediately. This was one dominant male who had no need to prove anything to the pro quarterback. Holdin had enjoyed the interaction as they were in the company of a mutual friend.

When they had parted ways, the tall Native American with ice gray eyes had shook his hand and nodded as he said quietly. "I'm in the business of making problems go away. Call me when it's time."

Holdin had been troubled as he watched the large man's form disappear into an elevator. Now he had a feeling that those unsettling white-gray eyes saw things in ways it was best not to question.

Jill's eyes drifted shut as if she couldn't hold them open but her hand squeezed weakly in his. "That's a flimsy cover story," she stated in a near whisper.

"Sticking to the truth as closely as possible is the aim, darlin'. Total fabrication is impossible to support in the long term. We can say we met my first semester of college. You were waitressing in a local bar. It'd be very hard to track you. You didn't have a close girlfriend in Connersville who'd be certain you're the same girl. I don't think there's even one photo of you. You always managed to avoid them. I know because I've tried to find one.

"Fifteen years is long enough for people to think you sorta look like the Jill I dated, but they will not make the connection if there's a whole set of logical facts leading them in a different direction."

"People saw me and knew enough to call your mother. I've been recognized, Holdin."

Her eyes were still closed and she hadn't moved, but she was arguing with him about the truth and logically handling the facts. She knew exactly who he was.

Holdin struggled to keep the relief and subsequent euphoria out of his voice. She knew him. She remembered everything about them. There was no gap between past and present relationship. She had them in the right order.

The dark fear in his soul screamed as it dissipated. He'd been guarding it so closely, holding it away from everyone in ruthless determination that now the freedom of releasing it was painfully wrenching. Fierce, possessive impulses pounded up his body as the fear exited. He had to fist his free hand around a bar of the hospital bed's protective side railing to keep from lunging over it and gathering her into his arms.

He didn't want her to know how relieved he was. Acting as if he'd never expected anything different had made it so and he was superstitious enough to believe there was power in that. Preparation allowed one to capitalize on the opportunities luck offered. Holdin had willed his success over and over again. Willed it because he needed Jill. Willing it now was natural and also the most important gamble of his life. If fate had denied him, things could have gotten ugly.

"The woman who called my mother had no idea who you were. She is a friend of my mom's and knew me when I was Drifter's age. She recognized me in Drifter. That's what everyone's been talking about. Apparently they think you're someone I met after I went to college. Half the work on the cover story is already done."

Again Holdin didn't spend time filling in all the blanks for Jill. His mother had known with a mother's knowledge of such things that the only person who could possibly have had her grandchild was Jill. Carol's confidence in that fact was the reason she'd known who was in town before she called Holdin.

Jill's eyes opened to gaze at him for a long, silent moment. "I hope you're right. I have no idea what else to do."

"It's about time you let me handle this, baby. Your job is to recover. Trust me to take care of my family."

Jill closed her eyes again but a faint smile touched her lips. "Not much else I can do."

"Damn right," he assured her, putting as much flat confidence into the statement as he could. She had to see him as capable of protecting her and Drifter's future. It was imperative she accept it now.

The door opened behind him and Dr. Robert Coates strolled into the room.

"Good evening," he greeted them both as he raised a brow at Holdin.

Holdin's hand tightened on Jill's and he smiled at the doctor. The smile didn't touch his eyes as he regarded Coates.

There was one thing Holdin had worked out very clearly. No matter what was between these two, Holdin was here to fight for Jill. Any altruistic thoughts of letting her go if that made her happy had died a silent death at the hands of his possessive soul. Her surrender to him at the ranch had sealed her fate and killed any questions he'd had about her still feeling the same way about him. Jill was his now. Nothing else was acceptable.

Chapter Ten

"Jill needs to rest and I believe you wanted to talk to me. Why don't you wait outside a minute and then we'll have that chat," Coates directed smoothly while picking up Jill's chart and glancing at the top page.

Holdin clamped down on the immediate rush of fierce possessiveness. This man was her doctor and had saved her life. His smooth command was meant to convey dominance and control of Jill. Coates knew exactly what he was doing by directing Holdin to leave. If Holdin stood up and meekly left, he'd be submitting to Robert's superior position. It was petty to want to smash Robert's face, but that was Holdin's first reaction.

Holdin gently squeezed Jill's hand and leaned over her as he rose. "I'll be back, baby girl." He dropped a kiss on her lips and waited for her smile before he stood. Turning to Coates, Holdin nodded curtly and exited the room before he did something stupid like challenge the man. This was Coates' turf. Holdin needed Coates giving Jill his complete attention as her doctor, not nursing a broken nose.

Robert joined Holdin in the hall five minutes later. "Come on, we can talk in my office," Robert offered, and led the way.

Neither spoke until the office door closed silently behind them. It hadn't been a long walk, the hospital provided offices on the same floor for the surgeons. Robert waved Holdin into a comfortable leather chair in front of his desk as he moved behind it to his own seat.

Choosing to speak in his office put Coates in a position of authority but Holdin supposed that was his due. He was one of the finest brain surgeons in the country. He'd earned the honors surrounding him on the walls in neat black frames. The office was understated perfection, decorated with class while not being showy, very like the tall doctor sitting behind his desk.

"I believe you have some questions." Coates regarded Holdin levelly.

"Correct. First I want to thank you," Holdin stated calmly. "You've done more than be Jill's doctor and I appreciate the kindness you've shown my son. It made this easier for him."

"I became acquainted with Jill and Drifter some time before she had the fall," Coates acknowledged while carefully including Jill in his life outside the hospital. His answer didn't accept Holdin's thanks nor rebuffed it. Holdin grinned internally as he chose words for this battle of wits.

"Yes, Drifter has a lot to say about you. As I said, his confidence in you was a comfort to him. It's been a difficult couple of days for all of us." Holdin paused as Robert nodded. "I have several medical questions you should be able to answer."

"Of course." Robert's confidence sounded in his voice as he waited for Holdin to continue. He didn't acknowledge Holdin's turn of phrase that subtly questioned his ability to respond knowledgably.

The question that had been eating at Holdin was a handy place to start. Now that Jill was out of danger, it would serve several functions. One was to let the doctor know who was in possession of the woman. "Jill went into trauma shortly after we made love. Her head didn't move during our interaction but her releases were intense. She was fine directly after, but a few minutes later the pain started. Did her orgasms cause the bone chip to move?"

For a second Robert's expression didn't change as he regarded Holdin. Then he shifted back in his chair, visibly relaxing as a smile touched his lips. "I could be an ass and tell you that's exactly what caused the episode. But honestly, it was going to move anyway. The only way she could have possibly avoided the movement would be for her to have remained absolutely still and it might have moved anyway. The entire trip was the cause."

Holdin nodded and let his relief show. Robert Coates had earned a bit more respect and Holdin relaxed. They both knew possession was established and Robert had bowed out. That also told Holdin Jill had never been intimate with the doctor. A point that was exceedingly pleasing to his dominant side.

"Is there any danger of recurring problems?" Holdin asked seriously.

"There are no guarantees, especially in medicine, but she's a healthy young woman. We've seen no evidence of another weak point on her skull and it looks like she'll make a full recovery physically. So far, I've seen indications that her memory is intact. At least where Drifter is concerned she appears to have total recall."

"She has full recall," Holdin informed Coates. "Is it correct to say you don't feel her memory loss was due to medical reasons originally?"

"Really? You're sure of her recall?" Coates leaned forward across the desk.

"Yes." Holdin nodded without explaining how he knew.

"Not going to tell me why you're so sure?"

"It's better if you don't know. Actually, safer for you," Holdin answered seriously. "Jill would be upset if I put you in danger by telling you."

Robert frowned. Surprise and concern entered his voice. "She and Drifter are in danger?"

"Could be, I don't have all the information I need but I will soon. Which is part of why I wanted a word with you. Can we keep the number of people who need to enter the room to a minimum? I'm not suggesting putting a quarantine sign up over her door but I'd like to. Also so you understand why I'm not leaving until she does."

"There's no way to do what you're asking unless you go loud with guarding her. Am I reading you wrong in assuming your keeping it quiet for some reason? I'd be more help if I knew what you're worried about. I'm not just a doctor, I'm a military doctor. Not exactly helpless."

"I know. You're a credit to your profession, Coates." Holdin grinned as he used Robert's words.

Robert returned the tight smile. "You've done your homework."

"Absolutely. Thanks for your service to the country. You volunteered after residency and were assigned overseas during difficult times. As I said, a credit to your profession."

Robert nodded and waited a few more seconds to see if Holdin would add more information. "Since you're being a dick about explaining why you want her guarded, back to your question on her memory. No, her memory loss had no apparent medical cause. The recall could have been triggered by the trauma of her fall but again I'm doubtful of that." Looking Holdin in the eyes Robert raised a brow. "You're not surprised, are you?"

"No. She had reasons. I believe her subconscious was trying to protect her."

"Protect her from you?"

"If that were the case, she wouldn't have come to me when she regained her memory." Holdin grimaced. "Circumstances have changed and she knows I'm fully capable of taking care of the problem. The threat is the same one she faced before the first accident, though less urgent. I'll be eliminating it shortly."

"You're certain of your intentions then?" Robert asked with undisguised concern. "Jill and Drifter can depend on you? In light of what you refuse to tell me, I have a right to know."

"Yes, Jill's my wife. We just don't have the papers yet."

Robert smiled easily this time. "I had to ask. You're a lucky man."

"Yeah, I am," Holdin agreed. He couldn't relax and return Robert's smile but he appreciated the unspoken confidence it implied. Coates didn't waste time questioning him on how he planned to eliminate the problem. "So when can I take her home? It'd be better for her if she weren't in a building open to the general public. I'll hire nursing assistance for as long as she needs it, but I want to get her in a controlled environment as soon as possible."

"If you stay in Dallas so I can see her regularly for the next two weeks, you can take her to your place tomorrow evening at the latest. We'll know if she's got an infection by then. That's the only medical danger I foresee. Her procedure was relatively simple. If she needed nursing care, it would be because she suffered a complication. We wouldn't let her go in that case, so don't worry about hiring someone."

"Not a problem. We'll be here in town." Holdin stood. "I appreciate your time, Robert." He held out a hand. They shook briefly and Holdin turned to leave.

"You know, if you screw up with her again, she's not going to be available a third time," Robert stated quietly as Holdin opened the office door.

Holdin looked back and smiled darkly. "Reason she's mine is I never screwed up the first time. Don't hold your breath."

Holdin walked casually down the corridor toward Jill's room. He'd enjoyed Robert Coates after they'd established boundaries. He'd been completely sincere in his admiration for Coates' service record and the character the man displayed. Coates was trustworthy and a man Holdin understood.

Entering Jill's room, he silently settled into the chair beside her bed. She seemed to be sleeping and he wanted her to rest.

"You're not leaving tonight?" she asked quietly without opening her eyes.

"No. I'll be right here. Sleep, baby."

"Who's watching Drifter?"

"He's safe. My dad is a combat veteran."

"Does he know what to look for?"

"I haven't had a chance to speak with him but security comes naturally to Dad. Stop worrying."

"Call him. Please."

Holdin regarded her silently for a minute. "So it was the second-in-command who was after you?"

"Both him and his boss," Jill confirmed softly.

Holdin pulled his cell phone out of his pocket and dialed. "Dad?" Holdin's voice was calmly clipped. A tone Charles recognized. He'd taught it to Holdin along with the military phrases used in emergency situations. As a combat veteran, Charles had schooled his family on awareness and the fastest way to deal with any threat. Code phrases were part of those lessons.

"Yes?" Charles' answer was brief then he was silent waiting for the code he knew would follow.

"Watch your six. Orange. Red is too late."

"Roger that."

"Tomorrow." Holdin hung up having told his father that he'd be at the hospital overnight and explain tomorrow. "There, little mama lion, your cub is safe as he can be tonight," Holdin assured Jill softly.

"You're sure Charles understands?"

"That was a full-alert conversation. I spoke to him in the most direct way possible and he understood, Jilly-girl. It's a code used in the military that he taught me when I was a kid. I couldn't have been more plain-spoken or urgent just now. The colors indicate the level of danger. Red means the threat is present. Telling him red is too late was a statement indicating professional skill level of the aggressor. Giving him condition orange told him to watch for it. Using colors with universal meaning helps the military communicate situation information quickly, just like it did in this conversation. Okay?"

"Thank you," she murmured seriously as if he were doing her a favor.

"Drifter is my concern too, baby. I simply have more faith in Dad's natural abilities." Holdin lifted her free hand and brought it to his lips for a light kiss.

Jill opened her eyes and a little smile warmed her tone. "You're charming me again, aren't you?"

"Hope so. Mostly I want you to relax. I got this. You can sleep, Jilly-girl. You're not the one on guard duty tonight."

"I know." Her eyes closed again but the smile remained. "Thank you."

"Let's make that the last time you thank me for protecting our family. It gets insulting." Holdin let humor soften his words but he was serious.

Jill's hand tightened on his briefly but she didn't respond. Soon she was asleep.

Ten minutes later an orderly came in. "Dr. Coates said to bring you one of these," the young man explained, and began setting up a cot on the other side of Jill's bed against the wall.

"Hang on." Holdin stopped him. "Put that over here," he directed, pointing to the spot he'd just moved the chair from.

"You'll be in the way," the orderly argued in hushed tones, glancing at Jill who appeared to be sleeping. "The night staff will wake you up every time they come in."

"It's all right. Put it here," Holdin insisted.

Placing his body between her and door was exactly what he intended. It had been nice of Robert to send a cot but guarding her wasn't about Holdin getting a good night's sleep. He wanted to know every time that door opened.

It was a long, uncomfortable night. After the limited amount of sleep he'd had last night, it should have been difficult to remain alert tonight. It wasn't. Partly due to the surface he was supposed to be sleeping on. It was possibly the most uncomfortable bit of construction anyone had ever had the nerve to call a cot.

Holdin did wake up every time a nurse came in to check Jill's temperature and other vitals. The nurse had to stay long enough to update the chart and Holdin never resumed dozing directly after she tromped out. But Jill slept though the night peacefully.

At four-thirty a.m. Coates pushed open the door and strolled into the dimly lit room. The tall doctor stopped at the foot of Holdin's cot and grinned down at him. Holdin's eyes had been open as soon as Robert touched the door. "Go home and get a shower. You look like shit. I can be here for a while."

"You'll stay with her?" Holdin questioned, not moving.

"Yes. I don't start rounds 'til six. Be back by then." Robert picked up Jill's chart, scanning the stats from the previous night. "She's not had a fever. We'll remove the catheter and have her out of bed a little later. Everything looks good."

Holdin stood up slowly. "Thanks for the rack. It kept me awake nicely." He acknowledged the uncomfortable cot with a grimace as he stretched sore muscles.

"Thought you'd appreciate it. Worse than a field bunk at a MASH unit." Robert enjoyed handing out that information as he watched Holdin. "I'm here to help. It was the least I could do." Robert chuckled and put Jill's chart back.

Holdin exited the room, rubbing his back and feeling ancient. He was tired, sore and needed coffee.

He made it to the large estate on the north side of town in record time after a brief call to his father to ensure he made it into the house alive. He was out of the vehicle and opening the door from the garage to the kitchen before he came face-to-face with his father in nothing but boxers, holding a rifle high enough for a head shot. The gun quickly swung down, muzzle to the floor.

Holdin nodded. "Thanks," he grunted as he hurried past toward his room. Charles Powell followed.

"Who's with Jill?" Charles wanted to know before he asked for an explanation.

"Coates is with her. He's aware there's a threat though he doesn't know the details. He's military," Holdin explained as he stripped and turned on the shower hurriedly. "Coates has to do rounds at six. I need to be back before then."

"When the hell are you going to explain this?" Charles demanded over the sound of the shower, standing in the bathroom door.

"As soon as I can." Holdin stepped into the steamed shower cube and started shaving under the warm spray.

"What's going on?" Drifter had appeared beside Charles in the bathroom doorway. His eyes took in the weapon in Charles' hand.

Holdin glanced at the two of them watching him shave through the foggy glass door and grimaced. "Nothing is wrong with your mother," he reassured the boy, "but I'd like some privacy, guys. I'll explain over coffee if the two of you can manage to make some. I'll be there in under ten."

When Holdin walked into the kitchen, he found Drifter fully dressed and sitting at the table eating a bowl of cereal. Holdin's mother and father, both in bathrobes, each had a cup of coffee and a steaming cup was waiting for him on the table.

"Thanks, Mom. I didn't mean to wake everyone up." Holdin sat down and took a grateful sip.

"Start talking," Charles growled. "No one slept anyway."

"What's the problem?" Drifter wanted to know as he glanced around at the serious adult faces.

"There's not much time but here's what I know so far," Holdin stated, looking at his son directly. "Your mother witnessed a crime when she was a girl. That's why she and your grandfather were on the run. One of the men they were running from is still a threat. He's on trial for a murder right now and in federal custody but it'd be bad if he's acquitted. I don't know all the details. Your mom hasn't been in shape to talk about it. What I do know is if this guy figures out she's still alive, no one she cares about is safe and neither is she." Holdin finished the rest of his coffee, the three people in the room waited for him to continue.

Holdin glanced around as he stood up. "That's about it."

"No, it's not." Charles Powell scowled. "You know who and what the man is?"

"I don't have a name. Really. My investigator wouldn't name him over the phone. Said the trial was a big deal though, and it'd be all over the news when the jury came back in. I haven't been watchin' the news lately so that's it."

"Damn," Charles breathed.

"I'm going back with you." Drifter stood and followed Holdin to the garage door.

"You figured it out?" Holdin asked his father over his shoulder as he strode to the SUV. Charles and Carol were following them.

"If it's who I think it is, be worried," Charles replied as Holdin started the Navigator. Drifter strapped in beside him.

"Who?" Both of them asked through the driver's side window.

"Stigzanno. Don of the East Coast supposedly. Get going. We'll be there shortly."

"Damn," Holdin echoed Charles' sentiments as he pulled out of the garage.

"What does it mean?" Drifter scowled and shifted uncomfortably as Holdin passed through the big metal gate at the property perimeter.

Holdin thought for a second and decided Drifter deserved the unvarnished truth. He had to be responsible to watch out for himself and his mother too.

"You know who Darth Vader is?"

"Yeah, really powerful bad guy." Drifter frowned as Holdin pulled onto the main road.

"It's like havin' that guy after your mom if he figures out she's alive," Holdin explained. "Even if the guy is convicted, he's still a powerful enemy. That's why we have to change up a few things in the story we tell people. Think you can handle that?"

"Sure. What are you going to do?" Drifter wanted to know.

Holdin grinned. Drifter expected him to have a plan and that pleased him. It meant the boy accepted it was Holdin's responsibility to protect both him and his mother. Perhaps it was unconscious, but it was still a step in the right direction.

"For right now I'm going to make sure the media does not get a hold of her real identity. If it looks like the guy might be figuring it out, I'm callin' in the Jedi knights. I happen to know them."

Drifter was silent as they negotiated the beginnings of morning traffic. "Why not just call the Jedi now and take care of it? Who are they?"

"Best option is not to draw this guy's attention. Jedi are a last resort." Holdin grinned at Drifter. "I could tell you who they are but then I'd have to light saber you."

Drifter laughed then sobered. "Are you sure they're the Jedi? Not just regular rebels?"

"Yeah. I'm sure," Holdin confirmed confidently. "I've met Obi-Wan. He's friggin' scary. I don't think he'd have regular guys in his crew."

"Do I get to meet the Jedi?"

"If I call them, you'll never know they were here. They'd be shitty Jedi if you could tell. This has to remain just between us, son. The fewer people who know the better. Dr. Coates is with your mother now. He knows to watch out for her but he doesn't know the details. We can't tell him or he'd be in danger too. You understand that. Right? A man has a responsibility to protect his friends too."

"I'm not an idiot. I know that."

Holdin sighed and glanced at his scowling son. "I wasn't insulting you. We have to be very careful and I need you as a partner."

"Then stop treating me like a baby."

"If I were treating you like a baby, I'd have lied."

Drifter hunched his shoulders a bit. "Okay, I get it. We're cool."

"Good. The family is counting on you." Holdin pulled into the hospital parking lot. It was ten 'til six in the morning and few cars were in the guest lot. At the front door he saw several photographers. "One of the things we have to change in our story is your age. People need to believe I met your mother a year later than I did so that makes you thirteen."

"What?! Why can't I be older instead of younger?" Drifter protested in disgust.

"Because then your mom would have been a minor when she had you and everyone in Connersville would have known all about it. They don't so we can't use that story," Holdin explained quickly. "This is important."

"Yeah, yeah. But I'm not going to act like an idiot."

"You don't have to act like anything. Just don't say anything when we go by the reporters."

"What reporters?" Drifter and Holdin were out of the SUV.

Holdin nodded at the front door. "Those guys. They're waiting for us. Sorta put your head down so they can't get a clear picture of your face. We can avoid them when we leave by using a side exit but the doors only open one way so going in has to be past them."

Drifter glanced at Holdin with the ever-present scowl but did exactly as he'd been asked.

When they'd gotten past the reporters and were in the elevator, Drifter worried out loud. "You didn't check if Ms. Carol or Mr. Charles had told anyone about Mom."

"I doubt it. We're not a chatty family," Holdin returned with a similar frown. "I'll ask as soon as they get here though. That's some good thinking, son."

Drifter nodded without looking at Holdin. His response to Holdin's praise was only a shifting of his shoulders as he straightened a bit out of the customary slouch.

Jill was sitting in the chair when they entered her room and Holdin could almost feel the boy beside him radiate joy. Seeing her like this was so much more natural. There was only the IV in her arm. All the other tubes and monitor wires had been removed. She looked like his mother again, not a hospital patient.

"Mom!" Drifter exclaimed before he remembered to be bored. He rushed to her like the boy he was for once.

Robert Coates straightened off the wall where he'd been leaning. "Be careful," he warned in doctor mode, causing Drifter to slow and be careful as he hugged Jill.

"Thanks." Holdin nodded at Coates as Drifter straightened from Jill's arms. Coates raised a brow at Holdin. "Nothing much interesting happened here. I trust your family is well?"

"No problems," Holdin confirmed Robert's question with a smile. "We're a naturally careful bunch."

"Yeah, thanks for lookin' after Mom." Drifter grinned at Robert while echoing Holdin.

Robert smiled and swung an arm around Drifter's shoulders, giving him a quick squeeze. "I have to do rounds now. Make sure your mom gets back in bed soon. She's being stubborn and insisted on waiting for you in the chair."

Drifter glowed as he nodded. "No problem. When will you be back?"

"Not 'til around noon, I hope. If you see me before then, it's because she's developed a problem." Robert released Drifter and was at the door as he turned and looked at Jill. "Be good. If I have to come back early, you'll be in trouble." His tone was softly teasing.

Holdin gritted his teeth as Jill smiled at Robert and waved him out of the room with a saucy "In your dreams, big boy".

As the door closed behind the departing doctor, Holdin rearranged his features to hide the jealous snarl. There was nothing he wanted Jill to know about Robert Coates' dreams. "I believe your doctor just ordered you back to bed, mama lion," Holdin murmured in apparent good humor.

"In a minute." Jill reached for Drifter's hand and smiled up at her tall son. "I'm enjoying seeing that face grin again, brat. Think you could fetch me the cup of water on the bed stand?"

"Sure," Drifter beamed at her, "as soon as you get in the bed, I'll hand it right to ya."

"Oh so that's how it is? Guys all stick together?" Jill pretended to tease as she shifted to stand."

"Come on, Mom. Give it up." Drifter grabbed her elbow to lift her as much as he could. "You know better than to ignore Robert."

Holdin pulled back the covers and was on the other side of the bed to help her in as Drifter steered her to it. He remained silent and let her son do all the talking. Drifter needed to be the center of her attention and Holdin understood that. But he sure wished Drifter's talking didn't have to include Robert Coates as if he were some godlike figure. Holdin swallowed back the sharp remark to that effect.

Robert Coates had saved Jill's life. Tolerating Drifter's hero worship of the man was the least he could do. Holdin even liked the guy personally. The only thing he didn't like about Coates was Jill smiling at him in that soft, teasing way. Even that shouldn't have bothered him. Something was different.

Holdin gave himself a mental shake as he moved back from the bed. Drifter was pulling up the chair and getting Jill that drink of water. The two of them were doing some mock bickering about nonsensical little things. Holdin knew the sharp comments back and forth were about both of them connecting and making sure the other was okay. Drifter wasn't the type of child who'd cling to her for a long time. So Jill got his long-term attention other ways. This was one of them.

Drifter needed his mother's focus. He saw himself as too old to express that in any other way than to tease her.

Jill glanced at Holdin a few times throughout the morning, but she didn't reach for him as Drifter filled her time. After Jill's breakfast, Carol and Charles came in.

Drifter quickly asked if they'd called anyone about Jill's coming back. The older Powells assured him they hadn't and there was a lot of nodding and short sentences as everyone agreed they would discuss the issue later at a more appropriate location. His grandparents offered to take Drifter out to have a bite to eat. Holdin stepped in at that point.

"Thanks, but I'm starved. Drifter and I will grab breakfast." He felt it was time to establish who he was to Drifter as well as Jill. Watching the boy with Coates had shown him how much he was missing if he couldn't earn his son's affection. Perhaps someday they'd find a way to be father and son. Letting everyone else take care of the boy was not helping Holdin move in that direction.

Besides, being near Jill and remaining politely distant was difficult. It felt as if some mysterious wall had suddenly gone up between them. He wasn't sure where it came from, but it most certainly was there. It hadn't been like this before her surgery. Then he'd been perfectly comfortable to express his need to touch her every time they were in a room together. Now he felt a subtle resistance from her. Intangible and eerily silent, the distance was troubling.

Her need to focus on Drifter today was natural. What Holdin didn't understand was the feeling he got that she was defensive about that focus. Course, he was guessing at her emotions. They hadn't spoken much this morning.

Holdin took Drifter to a little Tex-Mex diner full of locals. It was a couple blocks away from the hospital but in a firmly middle-to-lower-class section of town. A few people asked for Holdin's autograph but mostly they left him and the boy alone. Several glanced between the two of them but no one was so impolite as to ask if Drifter were Holdin's son. Not even the few who had asked for a signature.

Holdin knew the owner Benito Montez. A large Hispanic man, who made the best huevos rancheros in the city. Benito ran a small but prosperous business from breakfast through lunch. The service was fast regardless who the person was and the food was outstanding. Holdin and Drifter each received their heaping plate of the spicy breakfast and a tall glass of sweet tea in record time since Benito didn't bother to wait for his waitress to ask what they wanted.

When Holdin and Drifter came through the door, Benito had glanced up from the grill and smiled. Holdin nodded and slid into the booth he usually sat in on Monday mornings. That's when Holdin had come here most of the years he'd been with the team. Monday he could physically afford this type of breakfast. Any other day it'd interfere with practice and he'd had himself on a very strict diet to enhance his abilities.

Breakfast was full of male-speak short sentences and wolfing down food. Deep conversation was a lot to expect of a guy when he was hungry. Especially a fourteen-year-old who could eat enough to feed a small village. Holdin simply wanted to spend time with Drifter. Start making a history with him. He fully understood that it was the little things that built a relationship. The big gestures were the result of all the little ones. It occurred to Holdin that he was jealous of Robert Coates on that score. Coates had a history with Drifter.

During the short drive back to the hospital, Holdin called his housekeeper. Petra and her husband Eduardo lived on his estate in a separate house at the far entrance from the main house. Petra handled Holdin's house and Eduardo took care of the grounds and handyman needs for the large property. There was little need to instruct the busy guardian of his home. Part of the reason she and Eduardo had been with Holdin almost from the day he'd built the place was her take-charge attitude and her husband's relaxed reliability.

Holdin wanted to be sure Jill would be as comfortable as she could be and that there was no question where she'd be sleeping. He briefly told Petra how many would be coming back to the house this afternoon or evening and staying over. He casually made sure she knew they wouldn't need another guestroom prepared. Petra didn't like speaking on the phone, a quirk Holdin appreciated right now. She quickly got the facts and hung up to arrange things to her satisfaction.

Drifter made no comment besides a glance at Holdin. They were already pulling into the hospital parking lot and it didn't seem the two of them had much to say as they repeated the entrance through reporters, just like earlier this morning. Holdin was glad he hadn't made the mistake of repeating the instructions to keep his head down to Drifter. The boy would have probably seen that as treating him like a baby too. It had been a temptation as they got out of the SUV but Holdin had resisted it to see what Drifter would do.

The rest of the morning was as uneventful as it could be in a hospital environment. After the bland lunch she was served, Coates signed off on Jill being released. She was doing fine with no apparent complications. Charles and Carol went back to Holdin's house to wait for them there.

The checkout process seemed long to Holdin. Mostly it was the growing distance that was forming between Jill and him. Hospital staff bustled around them and Drifter was constantly at her side. She was polite and even pleasant to Holdin but there wasn't even a hint of the intimate connection.

It was his natural instinct to stop everything, clear the room and demand to know what was going on. Suppressing that seriously inappropriate reaction, he'd pulled the cloak around him that he'd worn every day she was gone. He appeared comfortable and even pleasant to everyone close by while the man behind the mask looked on with growing impatience.

Their connection had been a pulse beating between them, as much a part of their world as the air they breathed. It had been undeniably present from the day they met so long ago and hadn't seemed to falter before the surgery. It'd not mattered where they were or who was there, Holdin and Jill were intimately aware of each other.

The complex connection was a living thing that bound them into a unit. Intangible and seemingly indestructible, it was the relentless knowledge he'd always had that Jill was in the world. Now there was nothing but dead space and it seemed to be expanding with every moment it existed.

Holdin went through the motions of checking her out, gathering what few possession she'd brought and bringing the Navigator around while Drifter wheeled Jill out. Everything was polite and cheerful. Jill gently protesting that she could move around just fine as Drifter hovered over her throughout the preparations and trip to Holdin's place.

The only hiccup was when they entered the house and took Jill to her room. She immediately realized it was the master bedroom.

Jill was tired and eager to lie down a few minutes but she'd regarded Holdin levelly. "I'm not going to argue with you. I get my own room. I don't care which one it is." Her tone was quite but firm.

"Relax, Jill," Holdin instructed with patient calm as he held the comforter back for her. Drifter was right there and both Charles and Carol were in the hall. "In my house, this is your room." Holdin paused as she simply regarded him and remained standing beside the bed. "Even if it isn't my room," he finished for her. Jill nodded and sat down to take off her shoes.

Drifter's face was very carefully blank as he bent to help Jill with the shoes. Shortly Jill was under the covers and Holdin realized Drifter was not leaving until he did. Man-child was on guard and Holdin repressed a grimace. A boy should *never* have to guard his mother from his father. If there was one thing he needed to get across to both Jill and Drifter, it was that he would die for them before he could be forced to willingly hurt either one. Obviously he'd failed at expressing that.

Holdin and Drifter silently walked across the house after shutting the bedroom door behind them. Holdin felt the caution in Drifter and would bet the hairs on the back of the boy's neck were raised. Jill's son could read the adults in a room with amazing ease. He was a natural at feeling emotional currents and apparently knew they were often separate and sometimes opposite from the words being spoken. Not that the air between Jill and him just now had been that damn difficult to read.

No amount of verbal assurance would affect Drifter's suspicious nature. Taking that route would probably make him more suspicious and cautious. It was a life issue they would just have to live through. Mostly Holdin had to live through it. Earning the boy's trust would take time. Gaining his loyalty was a prize Holdin would like to think he'd have someday, but never at the expense of Drifter's natural instinct to protect Jill.

Right now, protection was uppermost on Holdin's mind. The statement his publicist had released was circulating, but as he'd suspected, it hadn't done a thing to quiet the media who lived off sensationalism. Currently there were at least six wild stories about him and the mystery woman. Drifter was even being referred to as a secret love child. Holdin had used the ridiculous phrase to emphasis how bad the publicity firestorm could be. He hadn't seriously thought someone would use it. He'd been wrong.

Keeping the press at bay was something he was relatively used to, but now it was critical. Even though he had the estate covered with a video system that would warn of intruders, there was nothing defensive about it.

He knew Gray Winston was not in the business of home security. Calling Winston was more about working the bigger safety issues for his family. Holdin wanted to establish contact so if he had to call in a hurry, Winston would know exactly what the problem was and be ready to move on it.

Comparing Winston to Obi-Wan for Drifter had been a rather warm-fuzzy interpretation of the skilled predator Holdin had met. Nothing he'd learned since that original meeting had softened his original assessment. Gray Winston was exactly the type of professional Holdin wanted if push came to shove.

Excusing himself from Drifter and stepping into his office, Holdin made the call to Miami. The call back came within five minutes this time.

"Powell, I've been expecting a call from you," Gray Winston greeted him.

Holdin had to smile. There was something reassuring and downright spooky about that fact. He totally believed Winston had been expecting his call. "I'm in need of some advice and I'm willing to pay any price for it," Holdin stated honestly.

"Right now we're two buddies chatting. Let's keep it that way as long as we can. Tell me what the real problem is and I'll see if I can help," Winston prompted.

At the end of listening to Holdin's basic problem Winston made a recommendation and an offer. "I think you've taken the proper steps so far. Letting the press make things up and ignoring those stories is correct. You're enough of a celebrity for that to fly and now any story about her is suspect.

"I'd recommend you have a friend of mine go over your security and install a few options with some teeth. That way you'll have a bit more protection. However, pulling the trigger on my attention was probably your best bet. I'll hear before you do if your problem puts action on the little lady. If that happens, I'll not have time to contact you before taking care of the annoyance. Do I have your directive to correct the problem and discuss business expenses later?"

"Absolutely."

"I'll give my associate a call then. His name is Samuel Callaway though he's normally referred to as Blaster. He should be in contact by this evening. He's an independent security consultant though I stand behind anything he recommends."

"I'll be expecting a call from Callaway. Thank you, Winston."

Winston chuckled. "Thank me after you meet Blaster. I'll be in touch, Powell. I'm glad you choose to take up my offer. I'd have been concerned if you hadn't." With that obscure farewell, Winston hung up.

Holdin regarded the phone in his hand a moment then gently set it back on its base. Truthfully, he felt better. There was something about Winston that imbued extreme confidence at the same time the man tripped the "chilling bastard" switch.

Chapter Eleven

Jill's arms circled her knees in a tight hug as she watched Holdin jog past outside. The bedroom window seat was partially shielded by bushes halfway up the wide expanse of glass. She was sure he couldn't see her curled onto the corner of it. The track through his North Dallas estate was a mile and a half long. She knew that because she'd heard Holdin and Drifter discussing it one morning at breakfast. Holdin was explaining that it was that long because of all the twists and turns in it, he didn't really have a mile and a half of property this close to the city.

They had been in Holdin's house for three weeks and things were coming to a head. It wasn't the magnificent, sweaty man outside putting pressure on her. No. The need to settle things was hers. Holdin had been unfailingly thoughtful and attentive while remaining at the polite distance she'd set that first night here. She didn't blame him for the distance. Again, the reason for the distance was almost all hers. However, the strange middle ground she currently existed in wasn't a place a girl could live.

It was shadows and ghosts, a murky emotional landscape that couldn't be escaped unless she opened a door to the future. Being brave enough to do that was the trick. If she actually chose the only door she could see right now, she'd be closing the one to the relationship she needed to live. Holdin. He wasn't behind the door she stood in front of. The only place she could see him was in the past.

She had already enrolled Drifter in school and it was time for her to go back to work. Inevitably, it was time to deal with the past and face the future. Holdin had been wonderful. He'd rescued her in every way. That was what he was good at—taking charge. Now she had to deal with her life.

The danger to Drifter and her hadn't gone away entirely, but then, when was anything nicely neat and simple? Stigzanno had been convicted. His case was in appeal but the Feds had not let him out on bond to wait for that process. Nor was he free between the trial and sentencing phase. He was a huge flight risk and the judge had made sure he stayed put. So it wasn't as if he were dead, but nor was he actively looking for her. Coming forward with the information she had about his criminal history wouldn't protect the general public any more than they already were. All that talking would do was focus attention on her. Something it'd be wise to avoid.

Holdin had made a point of his feelings on this. He was completely opposed to her contacting the authorities with her story. It was not needed. He'd been calm, obviously controlling strong emotions when it'd come up around the supper table the evening they'd heard about the conviction. It was Drifter who had asked if Jill should still tell what she'd seen. His thinking had been to get rid of the need for any story besides the truth. Holdin had been very firm in his reasons for not doing that.

Number one, accusing people of an old murder was dangerous. Since Jill had witnessed the man killing someone, that was good reason to believe the guy was willing to do it again. If she didn't have hard evidence in hand, just a visual account that was years old, all she would start was an investigation. Second, this guy was off the street already. He was scheduled for a life stay at a federal facility. No reason to give him something to think about in all that time he'd have to sit around.

Holdin had been adamant about sticking to the altered truth. The only person who minded was Drifter. Since both Jill and Drifter had insisted Drifter was going back to his old school, Holdin had agreed that changing his school records was not required. But he'd only agreed with them on that point in concession for several others. Like they would consent to the protection of having someone with them when they left the property. Whether it was Holdin or Eduardo, they were not to leave alone.

Throughout the last three weeks, the three of them had discussed, laughed and argued as a family. Everything was on the table except the foundation of that family. Holdin, Jill and Drifter were a unit. Jill knew that united family couldn't go on unless Holdin and she came to some decisions about their relationship.

She'd been camping in the master bedroom and so had Holdin. Her suitcase was on the floor with her things neatly stacked in it. She'd refused to take up room in his master bedroom. Even her toiletries didn't remain in his bathroom when she left it. If he refused to give her another room, this was how she'd remain in this one. The discussion had been brief between them. It was only a day after she'd arrived so she'd been lying in bed when it occurred. That's when she discovered she could end any conversation by closing her eyes. Holdin had clamped his lips in a grim line and left.

He didn't sleep in the room with her nor did he move out. He entered without knocking, showered and dressed in the room but even when he was doing that, they didn't interact. Usually he came in to dress early and he tiptoed around as she pretended to be asleep. Jill had encouraged his belief that she never knew he'd been in the room.

The secret pleasure of sitting here watching his hard body glisten in the morning sun as Holdin rounded the property again was one of her favorite activities. She did it every morning since she'd discovered he jogged at six a.m. After the jog, he disappeared into the gym at the back of the house for another hour. Jill had little fear of being discovered ogling the rippling perfection of her own superhero as he glided by outside. Even when he ran, he appeared smooth, fluid. He was such a mouth-watering man. His body moved like silk in the wind. Unbreakably strong and unbearably beautiful.

A few days after she'd been in the house, she'd asked him if he was sure he was retired. Why else would he spend so much time working out? He'd smiled at her and said it was how he handled things. The subject had dropped though her interest in it hadn't.

Now as she watched the sweat roll down his bare chest, she wondered at the man. It seemed he'd become leaner, more ripped since she'd been here. She wouldn't have believed that was possible three weeks ago.

Jill tore herself away from the window and went to dress for the day. When she was showered and clothed, she paused by the nightstand and looked down at the necklace that had lain there for three weeks. Holdin had dropped it on the small table without comment her first evening in the room. Since then, the housekeeper had lifted it to dust several times but it always reappeared exactly where Holdin had left it.

She couldn't bring herself to put it back on. Something didn't seem right about wearing it now. She'd never taken it off until Holdin did it for her the morning of surgery, now she couldn't put it back on. Everything was so much more complicated now. Putting it on would be some sort of statement. She was unsure what it would mean but she knew it would be wrong.

The first time he'd put that necklace around her neck it'd been like a promise for the life they would have had if they'd really been the two free people he had thought they were. Even though she'd known they weren't, at the time she'd never intended to take it off. It had been like wearing a little bit of a dream hanging around her neck. When Holdin had taken it off for her, it felt as if he were taking back that bright dream. She knew that was not what he'd intended but that's how it had felt. Now Jill didn't feel as if she had a right to wear it.

There was no longer any huge emergency. Her life wasn't in immediate danger. Their son was as safe as he could be. As Holdin said, taking a car on the highway was probably more of a risk than the one they lived with from Stigzanno. As long as they didn't draw his attention, there was no real reason to do anything other than carry on with life.

The future was once again stretching before both of them. At the ranch, in the emotional turmoil of uncertainty and fear, they'd come together at exactly the same place they'd left off. She'd needed him so desperately and he'd provided for her as only Holdin could. He'd given her assurance on the basic level she'd craved in order to face death. But she couldn't hold him to those desperate, emotionally charged expectations.

In this new reality, they had lived very different lives and were almost strangers. She couldn't expect him to be the same person he'd been. No one ever was. She wasn't the same girl. Trying to hold him to promises made back then would be a horrible mistake. Except for their connection through Drifter, she had no right to anything from him.

Jill ran a finger along the gold chain as she gazed down at the necklace and smiled sadly. It was still shiny, like those pretend dreams. The simple ornament was exactly like the beautiful, simple expectations it had symbolized. An uncomplicated life. One that was normal. She never really had that gift to give Holdin but it had been nice to dream. Nothing was simple or dreamy in reality.

In reality Holdin was insanely rich and a public figure who was involved in things she felt completely inadequate to be any part of. There were charity organizations, advertising responsibilities and municipal foundations. He was involved in nationwide organizations and local ones. For a retired guy, he was busy as hell. He'd put off a bunch of public appearances and other responsibilities to spend time with her and Drifter. She couldn't expect him to postpone his life anymore. He deserved to get on with it.

Now that he knew she was safe and what the whole story about them was, perhaps he'd finally moved on. If he had, he deserved a woman at his side who could be an asset in his life. Not a simple girl who hated crowds and didn't know how to act when sitting beside another celebrity. She would embarrass him in so many ways if she tried to hold him to those long-ago promises.

Understanding her own limitations was a function of being a grown-up. What was worse was knowing how much she really did love Holdin. In these last three weeks, she'd gotten to know the man he'd become.

Holdin was thoughtful, gentle, understanding, intelligent, humorous and she could go on forever. Those qualities didn't even touch on the fact that he was the type of good-looking that made a grown woman's womb clench in physical appreciation. Almost every woman gasped the first time she saw Holdin in person. Jill knew what elicited that response. It was the woman's surprise at her body's reaction to him.

Being in love with this Holdin was so much more than anything Jill had experienced before. He was overwhelming. Just sitting across the table from him at breakfast sometimes made her panties wet and she'd have to stop looking at him for a while. She was terrified he'd read her blushing features and know exactly what she was feeling. That would be horrible.

Holdin was so honorable. If he ever found out how she felt about him now, he'd insist on keeping those long-ago promises. That would be a new kind of torture. Living with a man she loved more than life and never knowing for sure if he could love her back. He wanted her physically but that wasn't the same. No, it wasn't anything close to the way she felt about the man who'd save her, saved her baby and would selflessly protect both of them the rest of his life. She couldn't let him sacrifice every chance at personal happiness on the altar of her need.

Being in love with Holdin meant letting him go. This time it wasn't only letting him go, but freeing him from his belief that she needed him. He would never look to his own happiness if she didn't find a way to convince him that he didn't need to worry about her anymore. Holdin deserved to be happy. Hell, he deserved to have a princess by his side.

Someone sophisticated who could enjoy his sparkling world and make him happy in it. That princess would never be plain old Jill.

Jill walked out the master apartment's double doors, closing them softly behind her. Holdin's home was a beautiful, mission-style construction with large Spanish tiles on the floor throughout. The open design with its arched stucco walls and spacious rooms was made to provide ventilation and natural relief from the oppressive Texas heat. Holdin had it decorated in traditional Tex-Mex style with more handmade rugs on the walls than on the floors. The house didn't exactly echo but it was easy to hear others moving around in it.

Barefoot, Jill padded from the private wing into the house, passing large arched openings as she went. First was the one to the main entrance with its custom-made carved door, across from it an arch to the formal sitting room that looked like a slice of Texas history. Tasteful antiques and interesting artifacts were scattered around the comfortably elegant space. Next was the family room, not to be confused with the game room that opened off it.

Between the family room and the open-style kitchen was a space big enough for two tables. At the back in a nook created by a large bay window sat a traditional card table. It had eight padded captain's chairs around it. Right between the kitchen and den was a "family" table. It was invitingly rustic and functioned as a multipurpose meeting place with ten chairs.

Nothing about Holdin's home was stuffy. No space felt uncomfortable and yet it was amazingly perfect. Evidence of an interior decorator that probably cost more than Jill made in two years. Just like his life, it appeared simple but the underlying style and sophistication was far above anything Jill had ever seen before.

Even his gym was state-of-the-art, made to appear casual. Jill smiled as she took the orange juice out of the fridge and poured herself a glass. Whoever decorated for him was brilliant at hiding the look of wealth and making it appear normal, even charmingly simple.

Chances were good that the decorator was a "she" who would look right at home in these surroundings. This kind of attention to detail and absolutely perfect taste came with more than a price tag. It came with expectations.

Jill had seen the signs in the master bedroom as well. It was made for two in every way. The two walk-in closets were defiantly his and hers. The one Holdin used was perfectly masculine. The one that was empty reminded Jill of the closet she'd seen in the movie *Princes Diaries 2*. There were drawers for every conceivable thing a woman with everything would need. There was a dressing mirror that had a surround view, even an antique, ladies' dressing settee.

That was not to mention the master bath with two sinks and two of everything a man and woman needed in there. The warm, light browns of the floor tiles were a perfect complement to the navy blue and blushing coral used to accent and enhance the space. There was nothing bachelor about this house. It was meant for two and a family. Holdin had built it long before Jill had returned. Every perfect corner of it whispered to her that he'd built it with someone in mind.

Jill made herself a slice of toast and sat down to gaze out the family room's double sliding doors to the tiled patio and Olympic-size pool out back. There was a guesthouse on the other side of the pool nestled behind concealing shrubs and trees. A private world of its own as well. This was the perfect house, set on the perfect property, made for casual entertaining in understated luxury and style. How could ordinary Jill compete with that?

Poignant sadness settled around her as she crunched on the toast. She didn't feel much like eating but knew she'd have to prove that she had when Holdin came in from his workout. He was always concerned about the little things. Even how much she ate or didn't eat. A perfect caregiver in a perfect environment.

A really annoying irony was, Jill suspected she couldn't even hate "the decorator". That was the name she'd given the ghostly female she felt in every room. The rooms Jill liked best were the ones she felt the decorator's touch most strongly. In the warm, Southwestern kitchen the woman breathed down Jill's neck. When in the front sitting room, with its delightful mix of gracious history and modern casualness, Jill could almost smile with her over the beautiful artifacts. Of course she lounged in that perfect closet and the womanly sophistication of the master bath.

Whoever she was, Jill liked her style. Liked her consideration of Holdin's needs in the sturdy furniture and comfortable arrangements she'd made for his life. That card table was just one example of the woman's thoughtfulness. It was comfortably situated so whoever was gathered there had a clear view of the big-screen TV in the family room. Jill could see Holdin and his buddies gathered there for poker night as they also watched some sports show on the TV. Close enough to the kitchen for snacks but not as if they were in someone's kitchen. The woman was a genius all right. She knew how to live graciously.

Jill heard the interior door to the gym bang and firm footsteps heading in her direction. She closed her eyes and tried to gather composure as the man she loved too much to keep neared. Today Petra, the housekeeper, would not be in. Drifter was off with Carol and Charles doing some school clothes shopping. They had left early to have breakfast first. So it was just Holdin and Jill for the first time since she'd come to his place. Time to set Holdin free.

Jill smiled brightly as Holdin entered the kitchen. His eyes found her in the large love seat immediately. It was a favorite chair of hers. Across the kitchen and eating space separating them, he seemed to reach out and touch her just by entering the room. How did he do that? Every time she saw him, it was as if she were a girl again.

Jill busily crumpled her napkin and stood to put her dish in the sink. She just couldn't meet his gaze right now. He didn't appear to notice as he pulled some items for breakfast out of the fridge.

"How are you feeling?" Holdin asked the same question he asked every morning. The fresh scent of the masculine soap he used in the gym shower wafted around her. He was even slightly damp. His T-shirt clinging to the fascinating muscles as he moved around the kitchen.

Jill was at the sink rinsing her dish, her back to him doing her best to ignore the temptation to turn around and stare at him. "Fine. Great really."

In the interest of not appearing stiff and defensive, a very good reason she assured herself, she turned around to watch him. He'd never let her fix him a meal. Said he'd been a bachelor too long to need a woman's help to eat. Petra had the freezer stacked with roasts and casseroles along with an assortment of breakfast foods. There was hardly any need to make more than a salad for the main meals.

The frozen food tasted homemade. Jill suspected Petra cooked them in her house across the property and had Eduardo bring them up to the main house when no one was home. She'd never caught them at it though. Holdin thought he had a delivery service for them.

Holdin put two breakfast burritos in the microwave. "Sit anyway. It'll make me feel better," he directed her with a smile.

Jill complied. She suspected the conversation she wanted to have would be difficult enough. No reason to fight him on the small stuff. At the large table, she watched him make his plate and bring it over. He sat across from her.

"What are your plans for today?" he asked after he'd swallowed about half the first burrito.

"I thought you and I could talk this morning," Jill told him seriously.

Holdin looked up sharply. Her tone said the talk she wanted was an important one. He put down his utensils and took a sip of coffee. "What's on your mind, Jilly-girl?"

Jill sighed and looked away. Damn, this was hard. "I thought we should discuss Drifter and me moving back to our apartment. I'm fine now. It's time everyone moved on with their normal lives."

Holdin regarded Jill levelly for what felt like several minutes. "Why?" His deep voice was supremely calm as he asked the simple question.

"Ah, well, school starts in about a week and I thought we should settle into our routine. I know you'll be involved with his life but I don't want us to be plopped in the middle of yours forever. I mean…" Jill hesitated as Holdin frowned darkly. "It's just simpler if we are in our own space. You know?"

Jill cursed silently in her mind. She sounded like a hesitant fool. This was no way to convince Holdin that she was completely recovered and didn't need him anymore.

"No, I don't know. It makes absolutely no sense to me," Holdin informed her. "But if you don't like this house, I guess we can move into your place. It'll be a tight fit. Maybe you'll look at some bigger places you do like when you're feeling better?"

Jill cleared her throat and tried to inject firm resolve into her tone. "I'm feeling perfectly fine and I intend to go back to work next week. I'm not asking you to move in there with us, Holdin. This is your house. It's lovely. I love it. But it's not my house. I think we've disrupted your life long enough. You've been wonderful through this whole ordeal. Really wonderful."

"If I've been so wonderful, why are you trying to leave?" Holdin asked directly.

"To give you back your life. I'm not an idiot. I know you're busy and stuff. We'll be happy to see you whenever you can but I don't want to…ah," Jill stuttered and frowned as

Holdin pushed back his chair abruptly, scooped up his plate and strode into the kitchen. There he dumped the remaining food into the sink and flipped on the garbage disposal. After he'd shut the noisy thing off, he rinsed his plate and cleaned up the rest of what he'd taken out for breakfast. Both of them were silent. He was moving in short, jerky motions. It was the first time she'd ever seen him look anything but smooth and coordinated. He didn't slam things but anger radiated off him in the clipped movements.

Finally he stopped and placed his hands on the kitchen counter. His back was to her as he seemed to brace facing the cabinets. "So you want to leave?"

"I think it'd be best," Jill responded quietly.

"Why?" he asked again tightly. "Make me understand, Jill. Why are you always leaving?"

"Holdin, it's not an issue of leaving. I know we said a lot of things before the surgery but that was a high-stress time for both of us. You'd just learned what had really happened to me and that you had a son. I was afraid of everything. Dying being the most urgent because I had no way to control what would happen to Drifter then there was the mob. We touched each other with the remains of a relationship that required closing. You gave me the reassurance I needed to face surgery. I will not trap you with those things. Now it's time to be grown-ups. To face what's best for each other and our son."

Holdin turned around and leaned against the counter. His arms crossed over his chest, emphasizing the broadness of his shoulders as compared with slim hips. His ankles were crossed and in that stance, thick thighs seemed to bulge under worn jeans. He was a statue of what a perfect male should look like. Jill gulped in a deep breath and looked away.

"Trap me? How could you possibly trap me?" he asked in puzzled incredulity.

Jill's hands spread out in frustration. "You know what I mean. I'm the mother of your child. A child you had no idea about for years. You're already trapped. I don't want to make the situation any worse than it is. We need to get along, be some kind of family for Drifter. I'm trying to make this easy for you. Why are you not getting that?"

"Your leaving me is what I don't get," Holdin growled. "I realize you're used to just slipping away but this time you have to explain it to me."

Jill's teeth snapped shut in a rush of anger. "Just slipping away? You're throwing that at me now? You know exactly why I had to leave the first time. And now I am trying to have a civilized conversation with you. I'm not the one throwing around hurtful accusations and being confrontational."

Holdin's scowl darkened as he leaned toward her for emphasis. "I'm not the one running away, Jilly-girl. I can hardly be called confrontational when I'm willing to work though our differences instead of running away from them."

"I'm not running away from anything except maybe the ghost of the woman you had in here decorating. That bitch is annoying as hell."

"Who? What are you taking about?"

"Nothing. Sorry. That wasn't fair," Jill apologized and tried to relax. Her heart was beating in the pounding rhythm of fight or flight. She knew her face was flushed and she had to clap her hands tightly in her lap to keep them from trembling. Voices were being raised at each other but it hadn't gotten to yelling yet. That was sort of shocking since she could never remember Holdin arguing with anyone and certainly not her. Of course she'd never opposed him in the past.

"There's a ghost in the house?" Holdin pressed, frowning. His tone was no longer challenging, but it was still a hard punch of authoritative demand that she explain. "I just built it six years ago and no one's died here. There can't be a ghost."

"I was speaking metaphorically," Jill quickly interjected, not wanting to explain her emotional outburst. "Forget it. Look, I'm not running away. You'll know exactly where we are and what we're doing. It's time for you to have your life back. Time for us to go back to ours." Jill tried to sound calm and reasonable. She hated conflict and this was getting dangerously close to something she knew she couldn't handle.

Disapproval from Holdin, even if it was simply verbal, felt like a slap. He was too important to her. She couldn't let him know how easy it would be for him to steamroll her.

Holdin's lips turned down as he growled, "I would rather know right where you two are because I look at your faces every morning." He continued to study her with an expression that told Jill he was rolling the previous exchange around in his very active brain.

"That's not a realistic living arrangement, Holdin. We will be..." Jill couldn't find the right words to imply the delicate subject of his being a man who had to be used to bringing home women whenever he wanted to. "In the way."

"In the way of what exactly?" Holdin asked in silky tones as one of his eyebrows rose in question.

Jill heard the difference in his voice and felt the hairs on the back of her neck rise. He hadn't physically moved but suddenly he was all different. Gone was the puzzled astonishment. What surrounded him now was an air of watchful predator. Jill shivered just looking at him.

Suddenly she wasn't facing the Holdin who'd been the soul of patient consideration and gentle humor these last three weeks. The man leaning against the kitchen counter bore a striking resemblance to a Bengal tiger. A golden beast whose next move was patently unpredictable and inherently dangerous. He was watching her with the eerie stillness of one who was listening with all his senses. Gauging her responses on more than her words. Power rippled under his skin as he gazed at her, waiting for an answer to his question.

Jill's body clenched as she swallowed hard. "We'll, ah, you know it's impossible to have... I mean if you wanted to... I'm sure there is someone who misses you," Jill finished in a whisper as she watched the cunning hunter push away from the kitchen counter and glide toward her.

"Exactly what are you implying, Jilly-girl? Just come out and ask me, baby. I'll give you a straight answer. I always have," Holdin instructed quietly as he approached her.

Jill resisted the urge to shrink back into the chair as Holdin rounded the end of the table and came at her. What could almost be called a smile just barely marked his grim features as he approached and Jill suddenly felt as if everything were moving in slow motion. Holdin stopped beside her chair and held out his hand.

Jill hesitated taking it as she looked up at him in growing concern. "What I meant was..." she tried to backtrack hurriedly.

"Come with me, Jill," Holdin interrupted her quietly as he waited for her to place her hand in his.

Jill cautiously placed her hand in his and stood. "Where?"

Holdin's hand closed over hers. "We're going to find that ghost who's bothering you and get rid of her. Where do you feel her most?"

"Ah, I didn't mean an actual ghost. It's more like a feeling that there's a woman here who wants to return. Come on, Holdin. She decorated your house. She lives in every room of it. For God's sake, she made herself a palace of her closet in the master bedroom," Jill explained in nervous exasperation as he began slowly leading her back through the house.

Holdin nodded and smiled. "So she's in the master bedroom. Good. We'll start there."

Chapter Twelve

They were at the double doors to the master suite already as Jill frowned and tried to make sense of his actions. The heavy wooden doors clicked shut behind them and Holdin hadn't slowed as he led her through the private sitting room. They walked through the wide arched opening to the sleeping quarters and past the bed to the empty closet.

Holdin flipped on the ceiling's indirect lights and the room was bathed in a soft golden glow. There were brighter lights around the huge mirror and at the dressing table but he left those off. Holdin turned to her and released her hand.

"Strip, Jilly-girl," he commanded softly.

"What?" Jill stumbled back in surprised reaction and he immediately caught her shoulders.

"You heard me. Or would you rather I did it for you?" Holdin's hands were light on her shirt but he squeezed briefly for emphasis.

"I don't think..." Jill glanced around nervously then back up at his calm face. "Really, I didn't mean..."

"Start now or I will." Holdin's voice was calm but the steel at its core was evident. "Blouse first."

Jill blushed as her hands went reflexively to the button on her loose blouse. "Holdin?" she breathed in question as her fingers started reluctantly working the buttons.

"Trust me, Jilly-girl. You want to know who owns this palace and I intend to show you. Now shrug that off and hang it up in on the short bars to your left."

Jill turned away from him quickly and did as he instructed. Then she remained there facing away from him, breathing hard as she gathered her wits. The frantic scramble to untangle her thoughts and figure out why she simply "obeyed" him was interrupted much too soon.

"No, no, baby. You're not stopping to think now." Holdin was right behind her. Calloused fingers pulled the back of her bra away from her skin and deftly unhooked the four little latches. He slid the shoulder straps down her arms that had crossed over her chest. Quickly he flipped up the shoulder latches and pulled the straps out of them, reached around her and yanked the bra out from under her arms.

Jill gasped. His hands had worked the bra clips so quickly that she hadn't had time to react before the garment was gone.

"I see you do want my help," he purred as he pulled open a drawer and dropped the bra into it. Holdin gently gripped her shoulders and turned her around to face him.

Jill's arms were crossed over her chest and her face flushed a deep crimson. He simply stood there looking into her eyes and then he smiled. It was the bone-melting grin that went to her head like vodka. "I was planning to get to it a little later but if you keep asking so sweetly, I'll be happy to cuff your hands behind you now."

"What? Wait! Holdin!" Jill exclaimed as his hands went to the snap of her jeans and flicked it open, sliding down the zipper in the same move. "We're supposed to be talking."

"We will, just as soon as we're done in here," he promised as he shoved jeans and panties down to her knees. "Now grab my shoulder so you can step out." Holdin dropped down on one knee to help her, his hands pushing the jeans down to her bare feet. Jill didn't move and Holdin glanced up at her. He took his time, his eyes mapping every inch on the way up.

"You don't want out of the jeans, Jilly-girl? Excellent, they make a very handy hobble." Holdin remained on one knee as his hand skimmed up the inside of her thigh. Jill reflexively pressed them together but it was too late.

Her action simply trapped his hand on its side, forefinger wedged between the dripping folds of her clenching pussy. She couldn't control her vagina's contractions forcing the wet evidence of her excitement onto his fingers.

"Now that's not very nice, baby. Loosen up those thighs. My little pussy is begging for attention," Holdin commanded, his gaze centered on his hand and the damp curls shielding her sex from view. "Jill, do as you're told," Holdin commanded firmly when she hadn't moved. "You can't lie to me about this so don't try." He leaned into her, breathing in deeply.

"Please, Holdin. You know you can have me anytime you want." Jill was almost sobbing as she finally grasped his shoulders to steady herself as her legs relaxed. "Why are you hurting me this way?"

Holdin's hand turned up to cup her intimately. He looked into her face now inches from his as she gripped his shoulders. There was no longer any attempt to hide from him. "How am I hurting you, Jill?" He gently squeezed the damp mound in his hand and Jill mewed softly before she could speak.

"You're proving what I am for you. My body is yours to play with, you've always known that. This hurts me like nothing else can, Holdin. Making me this, you'll shred my soul and the little pieces will never fit back together again."

Holdin's hazel eyes changed colors. Winter skies' dark promise of a storm boiled in them as his face tightened, his voice dropped down into a snarl. "Are you saying you think I'm making you my whore?"

"What do you call a woman like me?" Jill gasped in despair. "I can't say no to you. There's nothing I wouldn't do for you."

Holdin's hand left her body as he surged to his feet. Jill forgot her ankles were hobbled and tried to step back. Holdin had to grab her shoulders to keep her from falling. His hold was firm as he glared down into her face.

Cold fury rolled over him as he looked at the woman who held his soul. How could she not know his heart was hers? Why did she refuse to see him? And why was she always willing to leave him? The answer was humbling. She didn't love him. She wanted him, loved the edgy sex they indulged in but she couldn't attach deep emotional commitment to it because there wasn't any there for her. The anger dissipated into determination.

If he couldn't have her heart, he'd have her body. There was no damn way he'd let her and Drifter go off to live by themselves. He couldn't protect them from a distance. Even if Stigzanno was in prison, that didn't mean he couldn't reach out. Holdin dared not let her prance her ass off to live somewhere else. Not now, not ever.

So he'd give her what she craved and tie her to him by any means. This was about survival—his. She would be his. If he had to fuck her every hour on the hour, she'd know who she belonged to. Know there was no other place for her but by his side. He'd spent fifteen years hiding the fact that he loved Jill. Doing it with the benefit of fucking her wouldn't be difficult.

His lips actually drew back from his teeth as he answered. "The only label I've ever tried to put on you is wife," he hissed softly. "Yet every time I turn around you're looking for the nearest exit. Perhaps I'll have better luck keeping you as a whore. What the hell, nothing else has worked.

"I brought you in here to prove to you that the only woman you feel in this house is you. I built it for you. Every bit of it, furnishing, design, it all was done for Jill. Every time I saw something I thought you'd like or wished I could share with you, this is where I put it. In this house. It's a damn monument to the life I dreamed we could have together. But apparently you can't wait to get the fuck out. So yeah, if making you my whore is the only way to keep your ass in my bed, believe me, I'm willing to give it a shot."

Jill's mouth had dropped open as he snarled into her face. The enormity of what he was saying couldn't have shocked her more. Not the part about being his whore. She already was that. As soon as he said the words about the house, she'd realize the truth of them. The reason she loved the house was it was exactly what she would have chosen, right down to the drapes. Every inch of it reflected her personality and tastes. No wonder she'd hated the woman she'd assumed decorated it. Hated the thought of that woman living here. It would be like watching someone else live her life.

"Since you're all ready to accommodate, we'll use that sweet little mouth first," Holdin continued as his hands on her shoulders pushed her to her knees. One hand fisted in her hair, being careful to keep away from the side she'd had surgery on. He held her still while the other hand ripped open his jeans with violent, jerking motions. "If I can get your damn mouth full, perhaps you'll listen long enough to learn something," he continued as his long shaft swung out. He let it fall on her face and held her so she couldn't move away.

"That what you want, Jill? Show me how a good whore takes a face-fuck." Both hands gripped her head again. He tilted her and jabbed at her lips with the slick head of his cock. She opened around it and he pushed in roughly. "Look up here. I want to see your eyes to make sure you're listening," he snarled as he began pumping in and out of her mouth.

"This is how a whore receives her instructions. So here it is, Jill. You're mine. I intend to keep you in my bed and in my house. If I have to cuff you to the bed, I will. You will never run away from me again. If you do, I'll find you. When I find you, you'll be brought back here and when we get in this room, I will punish you. Until you can wrap your mind around the fact that I am never letting you go again, consider yourself property."

Holdin pulled his cock out of her mouth. "Stay right there," he commanded darkly as he quickly toed off his shoes and shoved his jeans, shorts and socks off. Grabbing his shirt at the collar behind his head, he ripped it off too. Naked, he grabbed her elbows and hauled Jill to her feet, stepped on her jeans and jerked her up out of them. Crushing her to his chest, he strode over to the section of the closet where a high, oval clothes pole hung from the ceiling. Holdin turned to press Jill's back to the wall.

"Look over my shoulder." He grasped her thighs and yanked them up around his hips, opening her over his cock.

Jill opened her mouth to speak and one of his hands landed on her bare butt with a sharp smack as his hips thrust forward, plunging his engorged shaft deep into her wet body. "No talking unless you're told to," he instructed coldly as his lower body power-fucked her against the wall hard and fast. He was thick and long and every thrust into her was forcing her body to yield to an intruder that hadn't been there in a very long time.

The hard invasion of his cock into her needy cunt almost sent Jill over the edge. The shattering eroticism of his simply taking her because he needed to added such a sharp emotional depth to his domineering fuck that she was half sobbing in air, trying to handle the churning mix of sensation and emotion.

Holdin didn't lie. He hated deception. Every word he'd said to her was true. Understanding that showed her how desperately in love with her he was. His emotions matched hers in every way. This harsh, burningly erotic handling was his only way of expressing the depth he was willing to go to for her. Jill felt joy splinter through her mind in a white-hot explosion. It eclipsed the fierce fuck she was receiving for a few seconds. Then nothing could distract her from enjoying the hell out of being Holdin's whore.

His voice was cold and detached as if he were instructing a slightly dim employee. "As I said, look over my shoulder. This is where you'll hang your formal clothing." He flipped a switch beside her on the wall and the oval rod moved. "These are the controls."

Holdin shut off the controls and supported Jill's weight with his hands gripping her ass and stepped away from the wall. Still buried deep in her, he stalked to rails going up the wall. They were perfectly spaced for blouses and skirts. He lifted her off his cock and away from his body. Putting her feet on the ground, he turned her and placed his hand at the back of her neck. A firm push bent her over the lowest rail.

From behind her, he snarled, "Spread," as his hand landed on her upturned ass before she had a chance to obey him. She realized his intentions as she automatically spread her legs at the double shock. The sharp sting of that slap radiated up her back. Jill clutched the rail on either side of her, presenting herself as commanded.

Hard and fast, his cock thrust into her cunt once more with no preliminary touches. Jill's head jerked up and she sucked in a breath through clenched teeth. In this position, he penetrated her so deeply. Each demanding thrust slamming him into the back of her womb where seldom-stimulated nerves went nuts. Her body convulsed on him in shuddering response that milked him in fierce contractions.

The thick cock pounded into her a few seconds before he started speaking again. "These are for blouses, skirts and pants. The two upper rods can be lowered. I'll show you how sometime when I'm not fucking your brains out." Holdin was breathing hard now, his hips slapping against her with each demanding thrust. Again he stopped abruptly and pulled out of her gushing pussy.

His large hand closed around the back of her neck and he pulled her up off the rod to steer her as if she were a walking doll over to the built-in drawers laddering up one wall. Beside the drawers was a custom-made stepladder to enable a woman's use of the upper tier. "These should be self-explanatory."

Standing behind her, he reached around her to fill both palms with her heavy breasts. Squeezing them roughly, he lifted their weight for a few seconds then went for her nipples.

Hard fingers grasped tender points and pull them away from her body. Twisting as he stretched them. Not giving her too much but enough to send flaming arrows of sensation shooting straight into her contracting pussy. Pain and pleasure. He was the master mixer. His own special brew that he'd taught her body so long ago.

Jill moaned and her upper body bent into his sharp tugging, pushing her bottom back into his crotch. His long, damp cock slid between her ass cheeks easily. Holdin chuckled and pushed forward with his hips in a crude thrust.

"Exactly what I had in mind, my little whore," he growled behind her, and released one breast. His hand went to a dial-lock device above a jewelry drawer. There were three just below center of the column of drawers. "I'd teach you how to open all of these but my whore only has to know this one," he stated harshly.

Bent as she was, when he pulled the drawer open, her nose was directly above the contents. Lined up were dildos, ass plugs, several types of lubricant, a neat row of nipple clamps and there was more. Several things Jill had never seen before and some she had, like the soft leather restraints. All of them neatly arranged in the velvet-lined interior, an almost artfully decadent display. Jill gasped in shocked surprise.

"Don't sound so shocked. Didn't you just accuse me of keeping whores? What self-respecting degenerate wouldn't have these on hand? Pick up a lubricant and the medium dildo. Today it's going to be your ass plunger. My whore is excited about that, right?" he chuckled darkly.

Jill's hand shook as she reached for the dildo and lubricant. It wasn't fear. It was shock at how much she wanted him to take her like this. Just like this. His harsh demands drove the dark pleasure higher. His complete command of her body freed her to be his whore. Oh she loved being Holdin's whore. He took her to this hazy paradise where her body was his instrument and he was playing it like the master conductor he was. Excitement, pain and incomprehensible pleasure, all were his to measure out. He did it in generous excess.

Even as he handled her harshly, bringing them both to the razor edge where pleasure became pain and pain became an obsession, Jill trusted him. Trusted him to walk that edge, let her walk it with him and never allow either of them to fall into the abyss. That sinister place where obsession became deadly, consuming its worshippers as they knelt in surrender. No. He had the power to take her there and he was showing her that, but he would never leave her there.

"I see you're tired," Holdin observed the tremor in her hands and released her breast. His tone held the bitter sting of mockery. Sharper than any lash he could have used, the words bit into her. "Time for my pretty whore to learn why the lovely old lounge chair started its life in a brothel."

His arm around her waist and a fist in her hair to pull her upright again, Holdin turned Jill to face the old-fashioned ladies' chair. It was exquisite. Its short back was a gentle roll of cushioned damask. The arms were also padded and only long enough for a lady from the early West to rest her elbows on it as she swung her legs and long dress up on the undulating cushions. It appeared a genteel piece of furniture from a bygone era.

Jill sucked in a sharp breath at his statement and Holdin continued. "See all that sashing and fringe skirting the thing? They hide so many handy items for holding the whore in position. Ass up has always been a favorite. Come on. Let's see how it works."

Jill hadn't thought he could drive her deeper into the whirling pleasure-pain of this aggressive control. She'd been wrong. The prospect of being bound for his use, openly displayed in every way caught at her like a sharp spinning star of excitement and embarrassment. Her entire body started trembling in anticipation and she had to bite her lip to remain silent.

Holdin stood her behind the chair and sharply pressed her head over the low back and down toward the seat. "Drop your toys and grab the arms." The command was harshly clipped and Jill obeyed immediately.

Her wrists were quickly secured with soft leather straps that came up from beneath the wide padded arms. She was bent over the back of the chair and restrained in two seconds, Jill thought he was done. Not so. He swiftly pulled two straps up from beneath the chair and snapped them around her ankles. The leather straps forced her stance to match the width of the broad sofa chair. Bent and spread, she couldn't move. Her weight was mostly supported by the deep cushioning of the rounded chair back. She wasn't uncomfortable physically but she was totally, helplessly exposed. Immobilized as she'd never been before.

Holdin stepped back to look at the results of imprisoning her. "I can see why every room needed one of these," he growled to cover the almost knee-buckling realization about how they'd gotten to this harshly erotic place where her body gushed in excitement as he forcefully demanded her submission. They were in this place together and there could only be one of two possible explanations for it.

Looking at Jill submitting to this dark passion was almost drugging as he pushed her hard. The woman who wanted to run from him could not have come down this path with him. That frightened, distrustful female should have whirled on him like a wildcat when he ripped her bra out from under her arms. When he'd started taking, not asking.

There were only two reasons strong enough to hold her in this room. One was love and the other was hate. She either loved him enough to trust him, even now. Or she hated him so much she was letting him dig his own grave. Her submission was pushing him as hard as he was pushing her. Maybe harder. Either way they were both in too deep to stop now. His fate was sealed. He would not turn back and they would never be the same from here on out.

Grimly, Holdin walked around the chair to the drawer for the other item he needed.

Jill heard a rip and then he picked up the dildo from under her nose. Craning her head up, she watched him pull a condom over it. Then he grabbed the tube of lubricant.

Behind her again, he didn't bother talking as he laid the dildo on the top of her ass and a hand roughly pulled one of her ass cheeks farther to the side. Suddenly the cold nozzle of the lubricant was jammed against her opening, the small protrusion of its head inserted into her body. He squeezed the chilly grease directly into her opening. Jill gasped and would have strained away if it were possible. It wasn't.

He grunted at her flinch. Removing the lubricant from her ass opening, he picked up the dildo to apply some to it. He slathered her impaler as he enjoyed the view she presented.

"Look at my little whore. Dripping down your leg in excitement already and you're only thinking about this stick up your ass. Damn, I like that in a slut. Right now I'm going to enjoy watching this go in while that juicy pussy weeps for attention."

The hard head of the dildo teased her opening in small circles. "Push back and open for it. You know how, Jill." He held the dildo with light pressure at the tight flower of her back entrance, waiting for her to accept it physically. "If you can't manage to do as told, I'll be happy to encourage you by turning this bottom red. Very pretty to watch a bright red ass accept its fucking," he warned darkly.

Making her physically accept her ass-fucking this way drove Jill deeper into the amazing place Holdin took her. He dragged her darkest desires up and let her enjoy them by commanding her to be exactly what she was. He knew she loved this feeling and knew she felt shame over that. As if it were wrong. Holdin commanding her to participate and bare her desires to his will freed her from the shame and bound her to him on an elemental level. She needed this from him. He never let her down.

Jill's opening relaxed as she pushed back. The head of the dildo slipped inside her and a new level of submission, pleasure and pain rocketed through her. He held it there while she breathed through the initial shock of it forcing her open around it. Then slowly he pressed in, twisting the long tool as it entered her to spread the lubricant he'd injected in her. In unrelenting demand, the plastic phallus drove into her. It stretched her open with a very clear disregard for her comfort, though it never crossed the line into pure pain. As always, Holdin's hand knew exactly where that line was.

Finally seated deep in her bowels, only the very end protruding from her ass, Holdin chuckled again. "Now I'm gonna show you how fun you can be, Jill. If you come without permission, I will stop and spank your pussy. Not your ass. Your pussy. So be a good girl and take it as long as you're told to."

The dildo in her ass started vibrating as Holdin repositioned his cock while crudely holding her labia open so he could shove into her contracting vagina. "Nice," he purred as this time he slowly thrust in and pulled out.

"Vibrating cunt. Very nice. God, you amaze me. Look at your needy ass turned up and stuffed. And you're so wet waiting for your cunt-fuck that you're about to make a puddle on the carpet. Damn, Jill. You do make a fine whore."

The slow friction of his use drove Jill insane as he wallowed in his enjoyment of her tight channel, made even tighter by the thick vibrator filling her rectum. His large cock forced its way in and out of her with relentless demand. Each thrust grated along her pleasure centers with no relief. He was in no hurry.

His previous entries had been rough and fast. Hard banging that brought her to the edge sharply but never let her over it. This slow fuck with the vibrator stimulating both of them was insanity and torture. Pain and pleasure. It was unlike anything Jill had ever experienced in the past.

With each hard intrusion, she plunged deeper into the dangerous world of dark addictions and even darker needs. He took her there with the skill of master. One who knew the way and enjoyed the journey. Her soul trembled and wrapped around the anchor of his strength, clinging to him as if she looked over the sharp rocks of a cliff face. He would hold her above them or she would be lost. There were no other options for her now.

Her entire body shuddered as she battled the rising orgasm with muffled grunts to each thrust in and out of her body. Holdin leaned down over her back so his mouth was close to her ear. "You're close, aren't you? Little whore loves her ass full as a cock fucks this pussy. This time you're going to wait for it like a good slut. I'm going to come in this pretty pussy then in that needy ass. You will not come until I'm ready to use your mouth again. Do you understand? You will not release until you're swallowing semen."

Jill moaned in protest as his teeth closed over her shoulder but she nodded. Holdin's hips picked up speed as he plunged into her. His excitement radiated off him in waves of almost visible sparks. He held her beneath him in what could have been a brutal control. His mouth clamped over her shoulder was a primal declaration of dominance that shot through her. His hands reached around to crush her breasts while he fucked her with increasingly powerful strokes.

The savage energy beneath his skin built with a fury of intensity. She'd known this storm of need and hunger raged in him but he'd barely let her glimpse it before. His iron control always held it at a distance from her as if he were afraid it would hurt her. Not this time. In this moment he was hers as he'd never been before. All of him. He'd given up his control to her as surely as she'd submitted to his will. Jill's heart felt as if it would burst as her body reveled in the greed of her man. He needed her as desperately as she needed him. She'd never known that before.

His teeth released her shoulder as he slammed into her. She could feel his cock swell and his body tighten and then his head went back. A harsh shove buried him deep in her body with fierce power and he roared his release. His hands on her breasts clenched in spasms of pleasure he was unable to control. That sharp pain distracted her enough to keep her from helplessly following him over the edge into ecstasy.

Hot jets of possession painted the walls of her womb as the man marked his woman. Jill was so sensitive as to be aware of every spurt. He'd never taken her to this edge of excitement and not let her over before. For a few dizzying seconds she was afraid feeling his seed deep in her body would be enough to make her lose control.

Holdin lay over her panting for only a few seconds. He released her breasts and flipped open the snaps on the leather cuffs around her wrists as he peeled himself off her back.

"Don't move," he growled in guttural command as he pulled out of her and stepped away from her body. His hands were at her ankles, releasing those straps as well. Jill stood perfectly still and waited for his instructions.

Her body blazed on a shuddering high of erotic sensation and there was nothing she needed more than his next command. Tears dripped off her cheeks as even the slight breeze of the air around her as he moved stimulated her sensitive pussy lips.

Behind her out of her sight, Holdin stumbled back against the wall and stared in awe at her bent form. He'd dreamed of fucking Jill in every way imaginable but nothing prepared him for the reality of losing his mind in her body. Their play had always been harshly controlled on his part. He'd never allowed himself the freedom of fucking her as he wanted to.

Her sweet body was so turned on right now she could hardy stand it. He knew her signs. Reading her level of excitement was one of his best talents. He'd fucked her long and hard, even coming, and her eyes were dilated, her expression dreamy with the intensity of a woman on a sexual high. His precious Jill was having the time of her life. He'd thought she was trying to get away from him. Had she really been pushing him? Trying to get off the pedestal he'd always had her on? He would never have gone this far into his dominant personality with her if he hadn't been desperate.

Right now he was betting the future, his life, on the fact that what held her beneath him was the same emotion that overwhelmed him. If she loved him, this all made perfect sense. If she hated him, she at least loved this. Either way, they were meeting in the most intimate way possible and he'd take what he could get. If this was all he'd ever have with her, it was a damn sight better than most men experienced with their wives. He would do exactly what he'd promised. Keep her any way he had to.

She was his woman, his whore, and she damn well was going to be his wife. Holdin straightened off the wall and strode back to the shuddering, gushing woman he couldn't get enough of and no longer worried that he had to be careful with. Oh he'd always be sure she was safe, but he wasn't going to be cautious about wanting her.

His hand landed on her dripping cunt in a sharp slap, two fingers entering her sticky opening and her body jerked in shock. The other hand on her shoulder, he pulled her up off the back of the chair onto the fingers in her. The heel of his palm kept the vibrating dildo deep in her ass as she now stood trembling in front of him.

Holdin pressed his body up her back, bending to place his lips at her ear as he growled in satisfaction. "Last time I fucked this cunt bareback, I didn't even come in it and you got pregnant. This time I know you had your period last week. So you shouldn't be ovulating but who knows? I don't care."

His free hand reached around to spread over her lower abdomen. Massaging it in firm strokes, he continued. "This belly is mine. I'll fill it with a baby and don't think for a moment I'll worry about discussing it with my whore. You are mine," he hissed.

Jill's head turned and big eyes blinked at him as if she were having a hard time following his reasoning. Holdin smiled grimly as she understood what he was saying and gulped back a gasp. "That's right. I intend to have more children out of you. Right now I'm going to show you how this chair works as a baby maker."

His fingers still buried in her cunt, he felt her respond to his statement about children. Her body had gushed agreement. Perhaps two fingers up her was the best way to discuss anything. Lord knew he wouldn't mind.

Walking her around the chair, he had to pull his fingers out to sit her down. The reclining back bent her body at an angle. Pulling her knees up, he strapped her thighs open with the bands from the short arms. Cunt and ass were tilted up and available. The sharp tilt also trapped his seed in her body, forcing her to let it do its thing.

"See how that works?" He stepped back and took his time looking at her because he knew she was reacting intensely to this position. "Keeps the whore open and fuck holes tilted up. While your mouth is available like this." He swung a leg over the chair, straddling her in the space behind her drawn-up knees. Her mouth lined up with his cock and he shoved into her.

"Good girl," he crooned when she immediately started sucking on the cock buried in her. He didn't move. "Suck it, bitch. I'm going to fuck that ass and we both know how much you love a fat, hard cock. Taste your greedy pussy... That's it, lick it off."

Jill's unrestrained hands grasped his shaft as she sucked him as hard as she could. Her head couldn't move so she tentatively pushed back so see if he'd let her explore him. His hips moved and the hard, veined tool slowly pulled back, allowing her to swirl her tongue around it. Pulling back to present her with the fat head he demanded her attention to it without saying a word. He might know her body but the other side of that was she knew how to drive him over the edge too.

Licking strokes worked his shaft, dragging up over the head to sweep his opening with swirling flicks.

The scent of their sex filled her nostrils as she licked her own taste off him.

"Open your mouth. I want to watch you lick it. Yeah, just like that," he commanded harshly as she did as directed.

Cradling his shaft with both hands, Jill worshipped it with her tongue. Holdin leaned over to clutch the back of the chair as she rubbed his pre-cum over her cheeks, painting her face with him then returning to bathe every inch of him she could reach. One of her hands reached to gently massage his balls while the other firmly pumped the base of the cock she worshipped.

"Enough!" Holdin snapped as he felt the tingling skitter up the back of his legs. She was damn good at this. He pulled out of her mouth and swung off the chair.

Reaching down to stroke his wet cock in her face as he stood beside her, his face was pulled in a grimace that bared his teeth as he looked down at her. "Looks like I'm ready to enjoy me some ass."

Holdin grabbed another condom from the toy drawer and smoothed it down his engorged cock.

Jill watched. Her face glistened with his mark. Her lips were swollen and her nose red. Her widely restrained legs displayed her more harshly than any stirrup table would have and she was a dripping, contracting, shuddering mess. She couldn't have looked more like a fuck toy if she'd tried.

He still had a few adjustments to make though. Holdin grabbed a pair of nipple clamps from the drawer. Jill's eyes widened and her head shook no.

"Oh yes," Holdin snarled in satisfaction. "Whores do not get to say no. Weren't we clear on that earlier?" He was beside her again and without warning, he brought his open palm down on her pussy.

The sharp spank made Jill scream through gritted teeth as stabbing fire shot up her body. Pain wasn't the problem. That touch ignited every tingling cell in her body and she was on the edge just that fast. It would have been too late, but just as she felt the rush, he took hold of both her nipples and harshly pulled out and up.

"Oh no you don't," Holdin snapped as he held her breasts up by the tender tips. "Don't even think about it, whore. You're not coming. Your job is fuck toy. Concentrate on it. These will help." He released her nipples to hold each breast and clamp plastic-coated teeth around her now distended nipples.

Jill gasped in shuddering reaction. Pain burned through her breasts at first and tears streamed down her cheeks. She didn't know if she were crying because of the clamps or because of the near orgasm. Still panting with an open mouth, she watched him caress her breasts for a few seconds as he watched the clamps do their work. "Thank me," he commanded softly as he looked at the clamps.

"What?" Jill gasped in surprise. Her body was on fire, every inch of her begging for his attention and she didn't want to talk. He'd told her not to earlier. Now he wanted something else?

His hard eyes rose to stab into hers. "Thank me for keeping you from coming. My nasty little whore almost came from her pussy spanking and she needs to thank me for helping her." His face was harshly beautiful as he regarded her. Every feature cut and defined, as was his body. A light sheen of sweat coated his perfect body. He stood beside her, looking down at her with arms crossed, legs set in that masculine stance of a male with a massive hard-on, and he was perfect.

"You will know whose property you are, Jill. Thank me for keeping you out of trouble. Or do you want that spanking?" he inquired coldly. "We've never gone in that direction, little cunt. Don't think I won't. Now do as you're told."

"Thank you," Jill breathed shakily.

"More. That was hardly sincere." Holdin reached down and casually turned the knob at the end of the dildo in Jill's ass, shutting it off.

"Thank you for helping me," Jill tried again, and couldn't keep a moan out of her voice as Holdin slowly pulled the big plastic impaler from her. He stripped off the condom, turning it inside out and dropping it on the floor.

"Good enough. Hold this." He handed her the dildo. Holdin knelt on the long chair and positioned himself at her ass, entering her with a hard thrust. Again with no preliminary touches or encouragement. He was simply fucking her ass as if he owned it. He grimaced in pleasure as her tight opening closed around him.

His face now inches from hers as he leaned over her, his eyes opened to look directly into her eyes as he plowed into her. "Damn, that's good," he breathed then continued. "I expect you to use a Fleet from under the sink every time you have a bowel movement. Ass and cunt are mine. I expect them available. You'll use a plug every day for at least two hours. Respond if you understand."

"Yes," Jill breathed. Her mind felt fractured as he fucked her while instructing her on how to make herself available for his use. It was hard and direct. It was shockingly erotic. She was his body and he would have her as he pleased. His words gave her an anchor to cling to as his cock powered in and out of her. He was bigger than the dildo had been and he stretched her to her limits. The burn of her clamped nipples was nothing compared to the fire he so casually disregarded in her well-oiled ass.

"Now turn on the dildo and hold it over your clit."

"Oh God," Jill exclaimed. "I can't—"

"Are you refusing a command?" Holdin interrupted her harshly.

"No. No, but—"

"Then do it," he snapped ruthlessly again.

"But—"

Holdin's hips slammed into her with increasing force as his lips peeled back from his teeth. "Do it now."

Jill turned on the dildo again and slowly reached down to hold the tip over her distended clit. As soon as it touched her, she moaned in excited agony.

"That's right. Feels so good, doesn't it?" Holdin praised her as he took her hard and fast now.

Jill was dazed in a swirling maelstrom of sensation as he continued to murmur to her. His words held her even as they drove her higher.

"Feel how good it is, Jill. Your ass was made for fucking. That sweet cunt begs for it with your witch's scent. I smell you every time I walk into a room. Your wet invitation will never be ignored again, sweet slut. You're mine. My whore, my nasty witch who can't get enough cock in her. My cock, Jilly-girl. Only mine. I will never allow you to feel needy again. Do you understand me?"

Jill was too restrained to thrash but her head rolled back and forth on the chair back as her body absorbed his use. Her brain could hardly register his words but she needed them. His hard, demanding use drove her to a place of such delight and unimaginable pleasure that she was only just able to contain it. He'd stripped her of any responsibility except to receive him. Now she knew what that left her. It left her nothing and everything.

His whore was flying with the stars and he hadn't let her come yet. Jill moaned desperately but couldn't answer him.

Holdin chuckled darkly as he looked down at her. "Not yet. You will not come without permission, woman. You will learn to wait for it. My cunt, my ass, my mouth. When you're clear on that, you get to show me how high you can fly."

He reached between them and pulled the dildo out of her hands, dropping in on the floor. His fingers went directly to her clit. Thumb and forefinger clamped around it and pulled up harshly. Again the spike of pain pulled her back from the edge. Holdin held her there as his cock rammed into her with savage force and then he was bellowing his release. Jerking thrusts slammed her as he came. Still he held her clit, forcing her to feel his orgasm while her pleasure was delayed.

He released her clit and slumped over her as his big body shuddered on the fading currents of the hard orgasm. His head on her shoulder, Holdin gasped in air and growled it out. He seemed to be rumbling in pleasure. Jill had never heard him like this. The image of the Bengal tiger flashed in her mind again. The rough, guttural sound might be what one of those huge cats sounded like when it purred.

She was shaking, sweating profusely and felt as if her entire body were a pincushion with a thousand needles pricking her. Every nerve vibrated in electric excitement. Again, hanging on the edge of ecstasy had taken her to a new level of sensation.

Holdin slowly peeled off her. He flicked the leather straps open and gently stretched each leg down, rubbing her thigh muscles briskly as he did it. Taking her hands, he pulled her off the chair, not letting her lay there for even a minute and recover.

"Time to clean up," he informed her as with her hand securely in his, he left the closet and strode into the master bathroom.

In the bathroom, he pointed at the toilet. "Sit. Pee if you can."

Holdin disposed of the condom from his cock and turned to the shower to flick it on. His tone told her to sit on the toilet. His words said he didn't care if she couldn't pee, that was where she was instructed to be. His complete ownership extended to this room and he was making sure she knew it.

Jill sat on the toilet and studied her toes, unable to even look up. She couldn't pee but several drops of his cum and her juices slid out of her. Her shuddering body calmed as she breathed deeply. What were they doing? What was happening to her?

His fierce demeanor was a side she'd never seen. Her reaction to him like this was a shocking revelation. She'd read novels about domination and submission. Read a lot of them in her lonely hunger these last years. Recognizing herself in the submissive heroines hadn't been difficult, but since she'd never experienced this level of submission, she hadn't realized how much she wanted it.

The events in those novels turned her on, gave her a squirming thrill. But she'd still distanced herself from them by believing it was just a naughty fantasy. Like looking through a peephole into a world she would never visit in person.

Today he'd taken her to the other side of the peephole. She sat trembling on a toilet with his seed dripping out of her. Her body was on fire and it was his harsh, demanding use that had made her that way. She was afraid, afraid of the woman she hadn't known she was. This woman who shuddered with excitement as she watched him across the tiled floor was a stranger. And yet, she'd been deep in Jill's soul for so long.

Jill blushed as he glanced back at her.

"Come. Get in," he commanded as he slid the shower door open.

Jill shyly wiped and followed him into the steamy cubicle. Holdin was standing under the water, letting it stream over him with his eyes closed. Again the beauty of his glistening body struck Jill. Every muscle was distinct under the light fur of his golden body hair. Across his chest the fur became a pelt that narrowed down and darkened to a slender line between the hard ridges of his tight midriff. Below his navel the dark blond curls surrounding his cock and balls seemed an appropriate cushion for those impressive parts.

Jill was so enthralled watching the clear water sluice down his body that she didn't realize his eyes were open, watching her. At her renewed blush his smile was almost tender. Holdin stepped out of the spray.

"Wash me," he instructed quietly. Jill reached for the washcloth. "No, soap your hands."

Jill took the soap and slicked her hands with it. Hard, hot steel met her touch. Soft fur, firm tendons, this was an amazing new torture, she realized. Her body was zinging with unfulfilled need. His forcing her to run her hands over his body only took her right back to sexual desperation. He didn't touch her, simply turned occasionally to accommodate her.

Up to this point he'd done almost all the touching. Restraining her or arranging her as he chose. Commanding her to indulge her senses in this sensual bathing showed her one more way he knew exactly what she needed.

Jill didn't realize she'd started moaning as her lips opened to pant in air. She vibrated on the high wire of erotic indulgence as she obediently caressed every inch of him. Lovingly outlining his magnificent muscles in slow gratification. He decided when she was finished. She'd have stood there for hours petting him.

Under the spray, he pulled her to his chest. As the soap rolled off him, his knuckle slid under her chin to turn her face up. His expression softened into a smile at her unfocused eyes and harsh breathing.

"Mine." His head lowered and his mouth sealed over hers.

The kiss was a gentle invasion and exploration of the damp recesses of her hungry mouth. He wouldn't let her suck on his tongue as she wanted to. Evading her and licking softly, he seduced the insanely willing woman writhing in his arms.

He gently pulled away from her mouth. Large hands caressed her back as Jill moaned in disappointment. "Shhh, baby. It's all right." He stepped out of the spray. "Come. Use your mouth and take what you need."

Jill fell on him like a cat in heat. Her fingers clawed up his sides as her mouth went to his chest. Sucking a flat male nipple into her, her teeth scraped him and Holdin jerked in a gasp. She didn't waste time though. Her lips dragged down his body as she sank to her knees and found what she now wanted more than her next breath.

Long and hard, the glistening cock took up her world. She needed it. Needed to feel it in her. Jill's mouth opened over it and she thrust her head down on it, pushing it into her with force. Holdin's fingers combed through her hair but he didn't restrain her in any way as Jill sucked him in.

This had been the test. Holdin felt euphoria slash through his fear as Jill took him. He knew he'd ruthlessly taken her to subspace and then beyond. He'd pushed as hard as she pushed him. He'd been making damn sure she knew he could take her anywhere she needed to go. Holdin Powell was going to be her only dominant, the only male who could plunge her into need and pull her back out again. He owned the submissive slut in her. His iron fist on that magnificent bitch's collar could not be disputed. Not even by Jill herself.

Holdin gritted his teeth and looked down at his woman. She was shatteringly beautiful. Even though he'd taken her to this place where she needed to do this, be this, it was still almost more than he could bear. More than he could take in. She met him at every turn and matched his needs with a sexual hunger that pushed him higher. Took him to an intensity he hadn't known he could reach. Watching her, feeling her, knowing how deeply she needed to be where she was at this moment squeezed the last bit of his soul from his possession and handed it over to the woman on her knees at his feet.

Her head moved in harsh, deep thrusts, fucking him into her. Her body naturally knelt with legs spread wide in a submissive's position of service. The little spray that reached her around his back made rivulets of water that streamed down her body. Several ended in her crotch and the water petting those sensitive folds were unpredictable fingers of sensation that strummed with decadent results. Her hips started thrusting in time to her long sucking strokes on his cock.

Her fingers gouged into his hard thighs as she groaned over her task. Dark guttural sounds hummed down his shaft to his balls.

Holdin braced his legs and fought to endure the depths she was taking him to. He'd known she'd want this. Driven her to it. Known her body was so sensitive that he dare not touch her in the shower until she'd come. He would never cheat like that and force her to fail. That was not what they were about. But he hadn't expected this level of lust and animal pleasure in her. She was all things hungry and needy. His beautiful Jill.

The amazing creature between his legs drove him to lust much faster than he'd ever thought possible. He'd come twice, he wasn't a kid anymore and here he was fighting the urge to come again. It was every fantasy he'd never dared dream come true at once.

Maybe he'd gone too far in driving her into her submissive soul. She'd kill him at this rate. Holdin squeezed his eyes shut and he tried to think of last year's lineup. Envisioning the defensive line should have cooled him off. They were damn ugly bastards. They all seemed to leer at him while watching his woman. He wiped that thought from his mind.

His hands went to the walls of the shower stall to brace himself as Jill turned up the speed of her sweet mouth bobbing up and down his cock. Have mercy. This woman refused him any and he knew asking for it was useless. But he would not let her have him in two minutes. He had to be more of a man than that. Holdin gritted his teeth and envisioned a room full of reporters. He'd always secretly hated those interviews. Damn it to hell! That was worse. He felt as if they were all busy snapping photos. Not what he wanted at all.

His balls tightened and burned in protest and Holdin gave up. She could suck his soul out his cock. He didn't care anymore. Reaching down abruptly, he released her nipple clamps. Dropping them carelessly on the shower floor as the fire roared over him. As the first jet hit the back of her mouth, Jill swallowed then released him, turned her head up and came with him as his seed painted her face.

The exploding release of the nipple clamps burned from her breasts down to her belly in abandoned waves of fire. Freeing her tender nipples at that moment added too much sensation. Too much heat. Too much pleasure mixed with such decadent pain. And the utter domination of his knowledge of her body was shattering. The casual removal of those controlling devices screamed at her that he knew her body, knew its reactions and most shattering of all, he could send her into orgasm any time he wished. The demonstration of how he owned her was complete as he pumped jets of semen into her mouth and drove her to climax with little more than a casual flick of his fingers. Not even really touching her.

Fire raced through her. Jill's body clenched in shuddering contractions and her mind surrendered to everything he was. Everything she was. His whore, slut, whatever he wanted, because all she wanted was more of everything he'd given her. Much, much more.

Her hands were still clutching his thighs and her nails dug in, creating red crescents as she screamed the release, her hips thrusting in contractions she had no control of.

Above her Holdin snarled fierce expletives as his head sank between his shoulders and he watched himself bathe her with his mark while she howled in release. A release that was her surrender to him, to his hand on her body, her soul, her mind. She'd swallowed his mark, the rest, painting herself with his seed, had been more. So much more. A surrender that shook him in ways he hadn't been prepared for.

The sensual completeness of that moment was almost painful to Holdin. It shouldn't have been possible for her to take more of him than he'd already surrendered to her. But she had. That image she gave him would burn his mind 'til the day he died. There could be no higher perfection, no deeper expression of who they were. What they were.

As soon as he could breathe again, Holdin pried her fingers out of his thighs and sank to his knees in front of her. She collapsed into his body as he reached for her. Both of them clung and panted, eyes closed. Holdin had no idea how long they sat in dazed exhaustion on the shower floor.

Holdin's head came up sharply when he heard Drifter's voice calling from the bedroom. "Hey! Mom? Are you in here?"

"We'll be out in a few minutes," Holdin responded as he opened his eyes and tried to focus.

There was a few seconds of silence then Drifter pressed, "Mom, are you there?"

"Yes. I'll see you in a bit," Jill called back to him. Her voice was breathless but she couldn't help it. A second later they heard the outer door close.

Holdin let out the breath he'd been holding. On his knees, he turned them so Jill sat under the shower spray. Very tenderly his hands ran over her, rinsing away the evidence of their lovemaking. His hands were shaking but there was no hiding it. Nothing remained between them but harsh honestly.

"Can you stand?" he asked softly.

Jill looked up at him and shook her head no.

"It's okay, I got you," he whispered, and placed his hands under her arms, standing and pulling her up with him, flipping off the shower while supporting her draped against him. He lifted her legs over his arm and cradling her like a baby, Holdin stepped out of the shower and carried her to the toilet. He pulled the lid down with his toes and sat her on the covered seat.

In silence he knelt in front of her and dried her with soft touches. She sat unmoving. Quickly wiping himself off, Holdin rose and picked Jill up again. He strode into the bedroom. Very carefully he placed her on the comforter.

Jill sank down on the pillow. She was on her side facing him and watched as he disappeared into his closet and came back wearing shorts and a T-shirt. He picked up her suitcase from the floor and carried it into the other closet. A few seconds later he reappeared with her clothes. He dropped the clothes beside her and sat her up as if she were a porcelain doll.

"What are you doing?" Jill whispered. She couldn't manage a normal tone yet.

Holdin dropped a reverent kiss on her forehead as he pulled her panties up her calves. "I'm dressing my baby. Hush. Can you stand for me?"

Jill stood obediently and he pulled the panties into place, grabbed her shorts and had her step into them and sit again.

"Not your whore?" she questioned as he slid her arms into the bra.

"Always," Holdin confirmed then dragged in a deep breath as he continued. "But also my princess and the mother of my children. The woman I've been in love with since the first time she let me kiss her." Holdin swiftly shifted so he was sitting behind her, straddling her to close the bra. "Hold them up, baby, or we'll never get this on."

His voice was hushed and she thought she heard a hitch in it. Overwhelming emotional confusion finally rushed over her. The enormity of where he'd just taken her, who she'd become. How much she'd wanted to be that woman. Her body still hummed in sexual arousal and she couldn't turn it off. His touch was now gentle and he had her wanting.

Jill hiccupped a sob as she cupped her breasts for him so he could close the bra and adjust the shoulder straps. Tears adorned her cheeks but she didn't make a sound. A tear dropped on the back of Holdin's hand as he pulled the strap tight before slipping on her top. His arms went around her and he pulled her against his chest. Jill gave in to crying softly. She was flying apart in his arms and he was somehow holding her together.

His big hands began to move on her body over the clothes as she shuddered. Leaning back on his chest, his hard legs bracketing her thighs, Jill was surrounded by him, the shower-fresh scent of him, the feel of him. She turned her head to the side, ashamed of what was driving her to tears.

His mouth dipped to her neck and opened over it, gently licking as he started murmuring to her.

"I got you, baby. I know." He kissed down to her shoulder as one of his hands undid her shorts again and slipped inside. Her body jerked in response to the caress down her belly. "Hook your legs over mine, darlin'," he instructed softly. "This is mine and I'll take care of you. Always, honey. You don't have to cry."

Jill's legs lifted over his, spreading her body open to his touch. Following his commands with desperate need, being the woman he'd known she was. His hand slid down into soft curls to brush lightly over the sensitive folds of her sore, needy, wet pussy.

Jill's back arched in electric reaction to that gentle touch as if he'd slammed down on her.

"Yes, baby. That's my good girl," Holdin murmured, encouraging her as his fingers sank between her labia to stroke the tender nerve endings there. "It's okay to need," he continued softly. "The only wrong thing would be if you didn't let me know." His fingers gently glided around her opening, delicately swirling as she moaned and pushed up with her hips. Carefully he coated his fingers with her silky lubricant before drawing them back up her to stroke the damp tips around her clit.

One thick arm was clamped around her waist, holding her firmly against his chest as the other hand petted her into moaning pleasure. She was safe. No matter how she thrashed, he would hold her safe. She had nowhere to go but into the pleasure his knowing fingers demanded of her.

"That's it. Feel how good it is." His lips moved back to her neck, finding the spot where even the lightest lick sent currents of sensation directly to the needy pussy he petted.

Jill panted as his fingers stroked around her clit in increasingly firm circles. Her hips strained up to him and she couldn't think. The muscles on her legs were beginning to burn as the shocks of his unrelenting touch enveloped her. Slick fingers stroked with a hard pressure as he gave her the touch she needed.

"Please," Jill breathed as the need became overwhelming. "Please, I need more."

"Tell me what you need, baby. Anything you want."

Jill gulped in air. What she wanted was so difficult to say. How could she want this? What did that make her? And yet, what was she without it? She turned her head and closed her eyes to whisper in his ear what she needed.

As the words left her mouth, Holdin shuddered. Then a low rumble moved up his chest in acknowledgment of what his woman needed. His perfect little whore.

"My way," he informed her in a low growl as he abruptly lifted her legs off his thighs and swung around to crouch briefly in front of her and drag the shorts and panties off.

"Lie back. No, don't move up on the bed," he directed as he stood.

Jill's torso laid back on the bed, her legs over the edge.

"Pull your knees up and hold them open, Jilly-girl. Present what's mine." His voice rumbled with satisfaction as she did exactly as he told her. Her breathing caught in sharp excitement as she submitted and Holdin felt the dominant within him expand in pride. Pride in her. Or of her. She was so perfectly beautiful in her hunger.

"Look at the pretty pussy." Holdin gazed down at her, freely letting her feel his approval and acceptance of her needs. He wanted her to know it was never wrong to tell him, no matter what she needed.

Jill shook as she gripped her knees, spreading herself on the edge of the bed. The submission he required was a hard emotional push and she craved it. It added to the physical sensations in ways that had become an addiction. Not always easy, but always exciting. He made her be so bold, but it was what she wanted so badly.

"Your cunt looks like it's had a hard fucking, baby," he continued, stroking his stunning submissive verbally. "But now you get what you crave. Look at me, Jilly-girl. I want your eyes on mine."

He was right. The new touch he'd shown her was one she desperately wanted more of. How he made her feel when he did this was the thrill she had to have again. One she needed so badly she'd asked for it. His command to look him in the eyes was almost too much. Reluctantly her eyes lifted to his. She knew he wanted her to accept this part of herself, to see that he wanted it from her, but looking into his eyes as he spanked her pussy because she needed him too was so difficult.

"My pretty whore," he growled as his hand came down on her gushing pussy in a restrained smack. He gave her a light touch with just enough sharp pressure to bring every tingling cell to fiery life. Making her look him in the eye was simply giving her more of what she'd really asked for. This request told him how much she needed as a submissive. Her release was almost totally bound up in feeling safe with him in control as she mixed new sensations. His amazing Jill needed a rough edge to the play for her little body to surrender to him. She craved it.

Jill's body arched into his as the new fire shot up her. Her head jerked but she restrained herself from flinging it back as she moaned. Again his hard hand landed on her sensitive folds and she felt the burn she craved. Pleasure laced with his delicate mix of pain. It was intoxicating. Part of it was the new sensations. Part of it was his complete control of her. In this position, her surrender was absolute.

"Yes, baby, show me," he encouraged her as his hand landed over and over and Jill lost all reason. Though his hand was only landing on her lightly, each touch brought a rush of blood to the surface, increasing her sensitivity every time. The act itself drove her deep into his keeping. He was the master of her pleasure as surely as he was the owner of her soul.

"Come for me," he commanded as Holdin dropped to his knees and it was his mouth that sucked her in. He was painfully gentle yet to her it felt as if he licked her with a burning instrument of delight. Tenderly he sucked her clit into his mouth and Jill exploded into a million pieces.

Hard, gushing contractions bowed her body as sensation swept through her in decadent abandon. Her only concession to the present was her hand over her own mouth to muffle the scream as he took her into oblivion.

Tenderly Holdin drank from the altar that was Jill's body. Light licks were all she could stand as he took her silky taste that was still mixed with his own. At every touch she shuddered and gasped.

She'd awed him again. Shown him what a magnificent submissive she was. Her needs matched his in ways no one should be able to. Precious was too tame a word for her value. He had no words to express the way he needed her. She made him more of a man. A better man. She always had.

Holdin took a last, tender lick, dragging his flattened tongue up swollen pink folds to swirl around her sensitive clit, just to feel her shudder in weak reaction then kissed his way up her soft belly. Gently dragging his mouth over her breasts, kissing each peak. The perfection of his woman, this woman, the woman he'd given his soul to, overwhelmed him again.

The hard warrior who'd spent the last fifteen years fighting for the right to touch her, hold her, would never give her up. It didn't matter what the real reasons were. In reality he'd been earning her as opposed to lying down and giving up. The fortune he'd amassed was in preparation for her. Every battle on the gridiron had been for the right to have this woman. Now that she was in his arms, the reality was so much more. Her passion and intensity shook him to his soul. There was no price he wouldn't pay to keep her and he knew that could be a dangerous thing.

His low voice murmured to her between kisses. "My beautiful princess. My gorgeous baby. Do you know how perfect you are?"

Finally lying beside her, he pulled her panting body into his arms, his head bent to her neck. Jill was sluggish as her arm crept around him. Reverently he continued kissing her neck and shoulders until dragging his lips up to her ear, he nibbled around that perfect shell while whispering to her.

"You make me a better person, Jilly-girl. You could make me the worst person. I'll never let you go, baby. Not willingly. Telling you I love you is not enough. It never was."

When she calmed down, Holdin went to the bathroom to wash his face and hands. Returning with a warm, damp washcloth and a towel over his shoulder, he dropped down in front of her. Her legs hung over the edge of the bed but she'd not moved more than that. Very gently, Holdin wiped her thighs and then pressed the warm cloth over her center. Not stroking because she was too tender to take even that. Giving her a minute, he then dried her and sat back on his heels to pull her shorts and panties up again.

Jill let him move her body as he wished to dress her. The powerful response he'd dragged out of her over and over again had drained her. Lifting her up to sitting again, he pulled her shirt down over her head and gathered her into his arms. Jill's arms crept around his shoulders and she buried her face in his neck.

"Jill?" he questioned softly after a few seconds. Pulling back, he put enough distance between them to look into her eyes. His serious eyes gazing into hers were amazingly green now. The gold flecks in them had receded into bold striations of color. He was the big cat he'd always appeared.

"Our son is out there, waiting to show his mom what he just bought. We have to go but first there are few things I need to say. Can you listen?"

Jill nodded.

Holdin's body tightened as if he braced himself. "First. We both know I can't hold you against your will. You'll have to bring the law to get rid of me though. The reason for the law is that this house and all its assets are in your name. I did that the first night after you came back. So you'll have to evict me. Then I'll be the guy living in a tent just outside the restraining order's perimeter. I can't let you go. I'm not strong enough to live without you. I'm sorry, baby, but one of the many things I need is to protect you, even if it's from a distance.

"I understand if you don't think you can love me enough to marry me right now. But maybe you could hang around a while and see if I grow on you. I'll be honest and tell you I know exactly how long it's going to take to make you my common-law wife. If I can't have you any other way, I'm banking on that."

Jill sighed deeply and the smile on her face was a strange mix of sorrow and peace. Into that moment, just as she opened her mouth to speak, there was a loud pounding on the double doors to the suite.

"Are you guys okay in there?" Drifter demanded.

Holdin glanced in the door's direction. "He's not very patient."

"He's his father's son," Jill explained in softly amused tones.

"He's gonna come in here any second," Holdin predicted.

"Let him. It'll cure him," Jill murmured.

"You haven't answered me," Holdin growled.

"I didn't hear a question."

"Well, I have one answer, baby. This is my answer to you." He reached over to the nightstand and picked up the gold chain laying there.

Jill bit her lip as she watched him straighten it and then drape it around her neck, clasping it on. His hands petted it against her soft skin as he pulled back to look at it.

Her finger reached up to rub the familiar charm, big watery eyes looked into the glowing golden green ones.

"You know what that is? What it always was?" Holdin asked softly.

Jill nodded. "I knew. Why do you think I didn't put it back on?" she chided softly, trying to cover up the tears.

Holdin chuckled. "Because you couldn't, could you, my precious little submissive?"

Jill sucked in a breath, trying not to cry. He had no trouble naming her demons. He'd always known them for what they were.

"Shhhh, don't cry, baby." He gathered her into his chest. "The collar has always been yours."

The outer door opened and Drifter strode through the sitting room. "Are you guys going to answer me?" he demanded, and then stopped short in the bedroom arch. Holdin on his knees holding Jill seemed something of a shock to the boy.

"It's not polite to yell in the house," Jill said calmly as if it were the most obvious explanation.

Holdin released Jill slowly and stood. He immediately reached down and lifted her into his arms. Carrying her across the room, he smiled at Drifter. "You've got some things to show your mother?" And proceeded to leave the bedroom.

Jill's head rested on his broad shoulder and she smiled tiredly at her son.

"Yeah." Drifter stepped back to let them pass.

"Stuff's in the family room?" Holdin asked as he stepped out the door.

"Yeah." Drifter followed them, scowling. "Hey, why are you carrying her? Is something wrong? Is she sick again?"

"Nope. Your mom is tired. I get to carry her when she's tired," Holdin informed him as he entered the family room.

Charles and Carol, already seated on the couch, looked up beaming when they entered. Holdin put Jill down on the love seat and dropped a kiss on her forehead. "Coffee, baby?" he asked.

Jill's smile was gentle and intimate as she looked into his eyes. "Please. That would be nice."

"Feeling tired, dear?" Carol asked cheerily. The twinkle in her eye was telling, even if she hadn't reached over and slipped her hand into Charles' large paw. Charles grunted and pulled his wife closer to fit her under his arm.

Jill smiled and looked pointedly at the pile of bags dumped on the floor at the end of the couch. "I bet you're exhausted." She cocked her chin at the pile. "Looks like you emptied the mall. Weren't you the two people who promised not to spoil the boy?"

"We lied," both Carol and Charles said with placid smiles as if there had never been any doubt that they would lie about that.

Holdin returned and put Jill's coffee cup on the table beside her then lifted her to sit down with Jill tucked under his arm. The love seat was hardly big enough and he mostly had her on his lap. Handing her the coffee, he looked expectantly at Drifter. "So what did these people let you talk them into?"

Drifter was still standing in the doorway watching the four adults. His eyes moving back and forth between the two couples as a dull blush colored his cheeks. He ran a hand down his face and sighed heavily as he now scowled at them with a long-suffering look of persecution on his face. The smile behind that expression was barely concealed.

"Do all y'all people hang on each other all the time?" he wanted to know as he strolled in to lean against the entertainment console. "Coz I'm gonna need a hell of a lot more stuff to distract me if I can't turn around without being grossed out."

"Right." Holdin nodded sagely. "Didn't work for me at your age. Good luck with that argument."

Charles shook his head and added, "As I recall, you thought a Corvette was the only thing that would repair your shocked sensibilities after that one time you walked in on us in the kitchen."

Carol and Drifter gasped. Jill spit coffee in shock.

"Get your mom a paper towel," Holdin instructed Drifter as he rescued the coffee cup from Jill's clutches. She was now shaking with laugher and in danger of spilling the rest of it.

Drifter quickly brought several paper towels. "Damn, that's harsh." He handed one to Holdin and used the other to dab up the tile floor in front of the love seat. "You walked in on the deed and no one thought you were damaged for life?"

Holdin grinned and patted the coffee off Jill's hands. "I thought the Corvette was a starting place for negotiations to repair my shredded sensibilities. I'd have settled for a Mustang. Dad said I'd be okay and it wouldn't hurt for me to learn a thing or two."

"What!" Carol turned to Charles and smacked his shoulder. "You said that to my baby? Beast! I thought you were going to explain things to him."

Charles shrugged and drawled. "What was to explain? If he couldn't figure what was going on, I'd have had to put him down, for God's sake."

Drifter took the damp paper towels, crumpled them into a ball and pitched them into the sink, making the distance in a perfect, arcing shot. Then he narrowed his eyes at the couple on the love seat. "Make you a deal," he said darkly, "you guys stay in your suite and I'll never open the damn door. I can't see these things."

Holdin nodded gravely and said more seriously, "This is how it is, son. Do we need to discuss it?"

Jill bit her lip as she glanced between Holdin and Drifter.

Drifter shoved his hands into his pockets but he didn't look away from Holdin's gaze. "Long as she's happy and you're the only one bleeding, I'm fine, I guess."

"Bleeding?" Jill asked in alarm, glancing at Holdin.

Holdin adjusted Jill's legs over his lap to better hide the pink crescents marking his thighs. "Yeah, that's the plan."

Jill's big eyes stared at the bit of Holden's thigh she could see. "Oh my God." She gulped and blushed scarlet.

"I'd appreciate it if you didn't embarrass your mother by mentioning it every time she marks me. Seems to wig her out," Holdin told his son seriously.

"I see. Kinda interesting," Drifter commented as he eyed the new shade of red his mother had turned and directed the real question to Holdin. "You'd better have the correct plan in mind."

"All she has to do is say yes," Holdin confirmed.

"Good," Drifter acknowledged then dropped into an overstuffed chair as he looked at Jill and grinned again. "Don't be in a hurry. As I said before, you have options."

Jill gave up being embarrassed about the blush. It was apparently way too late. However, she wasn't going to be pressured into blurting something this important out in front of a crowd. "I believe you have some things to show me? Remember, I get to say what's offensive to adults on a T-shirt. You're a very poor judge of that. Time to show me every shirt you bought."

"Yeah, yeah, I didn't get anything that's gonna turn your hair green. I was shopping with my grandparents, ya know." Drifter grimaced but it was obviously playful as he glanced at his grandparents and continued. "Ms. Carol has a fetish for pastels and Mr. Charles is too chicken to tell her what that looks like on a guy."

"Hey! Who the hell is chicken?" Charles defended himself. "I was letting you fight your own battles, boy. A man has gotta learn how to stand up for himself. Especially in a mall. Things can get ugly in there and ya gotta learn survival skills."

"Right," Drifter snorted. "Which skills were you showin' me? Duck and cover?"

The conversation flowed in dry humor and light combat around the room. It was natural, comfortable. Holdin was almost relaxed when Jill's hand reached up to his hand resting lightly on her shoulder and threaded her fingers though his. She squeezed gently and leaned back under his arm. Holdin was afraid to breathe. As the discussion heated between Drifter and his grandparents on some item that no one was taking credit for, her face turned up to his.

Holdin looked into the large brown eyes and she smiled. It was the soft, intimate smile that sank into him. Their gazes held for long seconds as the connection between them glowed and burned.

"Have mercy, woman. Say yes," Holdin commanded in a whisper.

"I refused mercy a long time ago," she answered softly. "And my answer was yes then too."

Epilogue

Jill and Holdin stood in the doorway of their Dallas home and watched the limo glide away.

"Damn. He doesn't even like the chick that much and he's taking her to prom in a limo," Holdin snarled in disgust as their son's ride disappeared. "I would have given my left arm to take you anywhere in a limo."

"He's growing up in a different world than ours was," Jill commented softly.

Four and a half months pregnant was the best time, she'd decided. Since she was short, she was showing already but it wasn't difficult to move around yet. Her husband and son seemed to think she'd suddenly developed spun glass for limbs and waited on her hand and foot. There was only one problem with that. A very intimate problem.

No one spanked pussy on a glass lady, much less fucked her like the whore she loved being. That part sucked. It wasn't as if she hadn't tried. Seducing Holdin was sinfully easy, but of course he was always in control. So they ended up making long, gentle love. Fantastic, tender, amazing sessions where Holdin melted her like chocolate in the summer sun. And still she craved the other side of that coin. Oh yes, even being physically satisfied didn't take away those naughty cravings.

Tonight they were home alone for once. Jill didn't want to be a bitch about the candles and bubble bath seduction she was expecting. But damn, what she wouldn't give for even short session with her fierce Dom.

Turning from the door, she trailed slowly back into the family room. Holdin followed her with his hands in his pockets and seemed pensive about something. She glanced at him curiously, continued walking into the kitchen and went to the fridge for a cool glass of milk. She didn't dare get the cola she really wanted. Not with the "food warden" right behind her. Holdin monitored her every breath, it seemed. She didn't mind, unless it meant she couldn't have a few measly sips of cola. Drifter slipped her a sip out of his straw sometimes. At least she could count on him for a fix.

"I'll be right back," Holdin said quietly. He turned and disappeared toward the bedroom.

Jill sighed. Here came the candles and bubble bath. There wouldn't even be champagne, she pouted morosely to herself.

Holdin reappeared shortly. Jill was sitting in the love seat. She smiled as he entered. Holdin didn't return the smile. He walked over to her and picked her up.

"What?" Jill asked in surprise as he turned and strode from the room.

"Hush" was all Holdin said as he strode back through the house into their private apartment.

Jill smiled. This was kind of nice, being picked up and taken. Holdin carried her through their sitting room in to the bedroom. There he stopped in the middle of the floor and looked down at her.

"What do you want, baby?" he asked quietly.

Jill regarded his beautiful face and smiled softly. "I don't need anything you haven't already given me."

Holdin's jaw clenched as he looked down at her. Jill's smile faded in mild puzzlement at that. He wasn't smiling. He hadn't since the door closed on Drifter, she realized.

He set her feet down on the carpet and stepped back. His arms folded across his chest and feet were braced wide as he regarded her grimly. Jill glanced around. There weren't any candles. Looking back at Holdin made her shiver. His face was harshly stern as he regarded her and seemed to be waiting for something. Heat flickered in the pit of her stomach.

"Tell me what's in your heart." Holdin repeated softly.

"I'm, um...love you," Jill floundered, trying to find what he wanted.

"I'm well aware of that. What else are you?"

Jill shrugged and spread her hands in a helpless gesture to express her confusion. "I don't know. I don't understand what you want."

"Tonight we're going to take care of your confusion. When I ask you what you are, you will have one answer of which you're very sure, Jill."

Jill swallowed and felt a tremble start low in her belly. His snarling tone told her there'd be no bubble bath to go along with the lack of candles. The Holdin who stood before her was someone she hadn't seen in months. Her dominant.

"Strip. Do it fast. I'm not in the mood to wait," he snapped. "Maybe you'll be able to come up with the correct answer when you're as you should be."

Jill bit her lip and moved to hurriedly peel off her shirt and jeans. Her bra dropped to the floor next and she was reaching for her panties when he stopped her. "Enough. Leave them," he barked. "Come." He gripped her upper arm and marched her toward the door to his closet.

Jill glanced at the door to her closet in confusion. They'd named hers "the bordello" but they hadn't played in there in months. She'd never stepped into his closet.

Holdin walked her into the room that was just as large as the one Jill used. It was neat and as elaborately appointed but for a man. She looked around searching whatever it was he'd brought her in here for. Holdin walked them to the back wall. She was standing in front of the full-length mirror looking at the reflection they made.

Her body, bare except for the silk panties below a rounded tummy. Her breasts were heavy and her complexion pale next to the tall man in black jeans and T-shirt behind her. Even his hand circling her upper arm appeared dark as he held her in the harsh light before the mirror. Jill blushed and looked down. The image was too embarrassing. Her soft curves were enhanced with her pregnancy and, well...she didn't want to look.

"Look," he commanded behind her.

Jill's eyes jerked up to the mirror. "Much better," Holdin approved softly but his grim features hadn't changed. "Your closet has some interesting additions from a bordello that was run by one of the finest madams in Texas," he drawled silkily in her ear. "However, mine has a few additions from a much less respectable establishment." Holdin's foot moved to a small rise in the carpet just to her right. He tapped it lightly and the mirror slid to the side revealing a black curtain in front of her. She couldn't see into the room beyond it, though she could feel the surprising space.

Holdin let go of her arm. "You go in there of your own free will." His voice was soft in her ear as he continued. "But if you step in there, Jilly-girl, you will never have a problem remembering you're my whore."

Jill shivered as she stood with her nose to a black curtain and heard a promise that could only be taken as an erotic threat. His large hand glazed lightly over her silk-covered bottom as he stood behind her.

"What's it going to be?" he pressed softly, his lips bent to her ear. "Are you going to run away again, Jilly?"

The air from behind the curtain was slightly chilled. There were several light scents on it that raised goose bumps up her arms. Jill's body clenched as she felt her nipples tighten and the damp heat between her legs began to burn. She breathed in deeply and recognized just a whiff of recently oiled leather and there was a lemon spice of floor cleaner. Her hands fisted at her sides for a moment. Then she reached up and pulled aside the curtain to step into Holdin's room.

Directly behind her, as soon as they crossed the threshold, Holdin's hand closed around the back of her neck, halting her. "Take a good look," he commanded in her ear. "Because most of your time in here will be spent wearing this." From a small table beside the door, Holdin picked up a black leather object.

Jill couldn't tear her eyes away from gazing around the room to look at what was in his hand. But considering what was in the room, she had no doubt it was a hood. There was almost no furniture to speak of. In the center of the room a single, harshly bright light shown down on what looked like an elaborate leather contraption hanging from a series of hooks and roll locks above it.

The single, directed light source plunged the rest of the room into shadows. But she could see that the walls were covered with an artful display of amazing items. There were paddles, crops, spreader bars and an intimidating number of other things she couldn't even begin to name. There was a rough wooden table that looked as if it'd been a large butcher block at one time. On it rested an assortment of toys and lubricants. Against one wall was a deep utility sink. Beside it a drain in the floor under a showerhead on a hose. Some distance from that on the same wall sat a toilet.

Behind the leather contraption, hanging from the ceiling was a doorframe set into the concrete floor. There was no door in its opening. Just the frame made of thick posts looming in the shadows. Off to the side in front of the sink she could see what looked vaguely like a weight lifter's bench and there was a strange-looking sawhorse beside it. She got the impression of an easy chair on another wall.

He only gave her a few seconds to gaze around before his hand tightened on her neck and he was walking them to the center of the room. The concrete floor was cold to her bare feet.

"You'd better have used the item I left on the sink for you this afternoon," he said softly as she came to a halt where he directed. "You'll be sorry later if you haven't."

He was referring to the double-size Fleet enema that had been sitting by her bathroom sink after lunch. Jill opened her mouth to answer but he stopped her. "That wasn't a question. You will not speak unless asked a direct question," he continued in harsh command. "Knees." His hand on her neck pushed her down, her knees connected with the cool concrete. Holdin stood in front of her, the large bulge in his jeans at her nose.

"You will not move unless given permission. And now," he held up the leather hood and smiled down at her, "we see how this fits." He swiftly pulled it over her head, jerking it down as the tight leather closed over her to her nose. Her eyes were completely covered. The bottom of the hood was open but pulled around under her chin and buckled in the back into a stiff choker with a metal loop at the front. It cut off her sight and most of her hearing while leaving her mouth available.

Jill shuddered as it closed over her. She'd never worn such a thing. She'd read about them, seen pictures, but the reality of feeling one close over her head was shockingly restricting. She couldn't see. It was difficult to move her head with the stiff collar around her neck.

"Don't move," he directed, and she could faintly hear him moving around. Locked in the darkness, she was straining to hear him. Focused on the sound of his breathing as he took his time doing something.

Abruptly his hands closed over both sides of her head. "Open," he commanded. The warm head of his cock rested on her lips. Jill's mouth opened and he pushed into her. Holding her, he went immediately to a harsh rhythm, using her mouth. Then he stopped but didn't withdraw his cock. "Suck," he snarled.

Jill's head moved to slide him in and out on her own but his hands tightened on her. "I said suck it, bitch. If I wanted to fuck your face, I'd do it. Your job is to follow instructions. That's one you've earned for later." Holdin's deep voice was speaking softly, a sure indication of restrained emotions that ran fast and hard well below the surface.

"As I've said before, when your mouth is full is when you listen best. Now suck dick and listen. You stepped through this door of your own free will. Now you will spend tonight where you belong. At the end of the night, when I ask you what you are, you'll have no trouble figuring out what to say.

"There are a few lessons you have yet to grasp and I'm tired of hoping you'll figure them out. So now you get to learn them my way. For one, when you're commanded to suck, do it as well as you can, not this lazy crap. That's two you've earned for later."

Jill had been so consumed with what he'd been saying, she'd almost forgotten the cock stretching her mouth. His harsh reminder along with the ominous counting brought her back to the thick, hard rod in her mouth. It pulsed as she drew on it. She didn't dare move her head so all she could do was nurse on what he gave her.

Kneeling on the hard concrete sucking his cock, she found she was almost dizzy with the wash of emotions. This was her dominant. But not like she'd known him before. Harshly commanding, his strict requirements shot through her needy body with blazing spikes of fear and pleasure.

Holdin watched her cheeks hollow as she pulled on his cock with noisy suckles. His lids were lazy as he gazed at the bare-breasted whore at the end of his dick. He smiled to himself. Grasping her head again, he pressed into her mouth. "Relax your throat. You'll learn how to take this properly. Breathe through your nose." He pressed into her relentlessly. Her neck stiffened in refusal.

"That's three for later," he told her silkily. "I feel you stiffen in refusal again, I'm going to count it as two instead of one. Take it, bitch. I want my cock down your throat and I will fuck you that way. Try again...ah, that's it. There."

He was finally pressed into her, past the back of her mouth and into her contracting throat. Her hands were fisted at her sides and he frowned down at them. Not very submissive as she took cock.

"Hands behind your back," he snapped.

Jill's arms swung behind her to clasp hands behind her back. The movement straightened her posture and suddenly the effort to hold the cock forced down her throat was easier. She couldn't stop making guttural sounds around the thick impaler.

Holdin chuckled. "You are a loud one, aren't you?" Her throat was contracting in strong spasms though he knew she was breathing normally. The milking she was giving him tightened his balls. He didn't try to hold back. Coming down her throat had been his intention. Doing it relatively quickly would be best for both of them. He'd have more time to play with her and she'd be very clear this face-fuck was for him. Not her. A good way to start with the needy whore on his cock.

"Very nice," he approved harshly as his body jerked in shallow thrusts. The tightening of tendons came quickly. Just looking at her taking it deep and hard, a hood covering her eyes and her breasts trembling below his balls did it for him. Grunting with male urgency, he welcomed the flash fire of release. It swept over him and he pumped his seed down her.

Then he held her there as he enjoyed the damp warmth of her opening. His cock began to soften and he still hadn't pulled out of her. She held him, her lips closed around the base of him, her nose pressed into pubic hair. Even semi-soft he remained deep in her, forcing her throat open.

At last he slowly pulled out. "Lick it clean."

Jill's tongue swept over his retreating cock, quickly trying to obey. Dropping out of her mouth, his soft cock dragged over her chin. Holdin grasped her elbows and stood her up.

"Stay," he directed.

Jill was trembling and he smiled. Time to see how hot the little slut was from her face-fuck. If he knew her, there would be a huge wet spot on the panties. She would wish she could hide it from him. His little whore still blushed like a schoolgirl when he found her wet and needy. He'd realized his submissive loved being found out. She loved being made to acknowledge it even more. It made her gush every time when he directed her to take off the panties and hold up the wet spot for inspection.

"Step out of those panties. Show me the wet spot," he directed.

Jill quickly pulled the panties down, her head remained stiffly straight up because of the collared hood. She fumbled when trying to figure how to hold up her wet spot when she couldn't see it.

"Use your cheek to find it. Rub the silk until you come to it," Holdin snarled in some impatience. Letting her know he'd have thought she should figure that out.

What little of her face he could see blushed deeply as she rubbed her panties on her face. It wasn't that difficult. When she held them up, most of the silk was damp.

"My greedy little whore loved her face-fuck," Holdin mused softly as her shaking hands held the telling silk up. "So wet you couldn't find a dry spot. We'll see if we can do something for that needy cunt." Dry amusement rippled in his tone. Holdin took her elbow and led her across the floor.

Jill had no idea where they were going. His demanding use of her mouth had consumed her and now she was disorientated as he walked her somewhere. They stopped. Holdin let go of her but she didn't move.

There were several sounds as metal clicked into place on something. Every snick of a pin slipping into a slot on whatever they were standing beside was a hard pull on her womb. Excitement and fear created a buzz so intense her womb contracted with each click. Warm streams of need snaked down her inner thighs as she stood and waited.

His hands landed on her waist from behind. He lifted her easily. "Bend your knees back. Try to put your heels on the back of your thighs and spread," he instructed.

Jill attempted to follow his instructions while he dangled her in midair. He grunted and slid her onto a firm, padded surface that supported her from her pelvic bone up. But the board was tilted down sharply, raising her ass. Her knees slid into padded stirrups on either side of the board. She was basically kneeling with head down, ass up. The padding was comfortable but the cool leather bands being secured around her body were disturbing.

A thick band just above each knee bound her kneeling legs to the stirrups. One around her waist secured her to the tilted table, pulling her body in an arch. There were handlebars attached to the post below the padded board her head rested on, her hands naturally grasped them. He didn't bother with restraining her hands. In this position, securing them was not required. She couldn't reach behind her. Her body was completely available, spread and restrained.

"Remember," he murmured darkly. "Not a word unless asked a direct question." Then he was gone. His hands left her body and the hood muffled most sounds. If he'd moved away from her, she had no way of knowing where he was or what he was doing.

Lying there, secured in a kneeling position with her ass jutting up and her legs pulled wide, Jill had never felt more vulnerable. More exposed and completely helpless. She couldn't hear him. The restraint around her waist allowed a small amount of movement and she couldn't stop her bottom wiggling in agitation. With each second that ticked by, the excitement and anticipation mounted in her mind. The burn from her exposed pussy grew to what she thought was unbearable.

Then to her left she heard water running. It was the shower? What?

Warm spray hit her squarely on cunt and ass. Jill jerked in surprise.

"Be still." His hand landed on her butt with a hard snap. Harder than he'd ever touched her before. Jill froze.

"Good. Now hold still."

The water shut off and then she felt him rubbing something into the curls surrounding her sex. Jill sucked in a gasp. She knew what was coming now. He was shaving her. In this position, in this room with the handy spray shower, it'd be quite easy. The prospect of being even more naked shook her mentally.

They'd talked about it but somehow never gotten around to it. His doing it now was pure possession. He would see all of her. He'd told her before that being shaved would make her more sensitive. That was probably the reason she'd not been in a hurry to do it. Being more sensitive to his touch seemed impossible. She'd known he wanted her to. There was no longer a choice. He would have her exposed and completely receptive to his use.

The razor started around her opening, swiftly scraping up her labia. When they were naked, two fingers spread them and he rid her of the hair between. Rinsing the razor often, he continued with the clinical shave, carefully swooping around the top of her slit. His fingers pulled and prodded, stretching her for the razor with efficient ease.

Done a few minutes later, he rinsed her then rubbed another cream over her now naked folds. His fingers coated every surface and crevice, dipping inside her cunt for several firm thrusts. His fingers left her for a second then returned to smooth the cream around the crinkled opening of her ass. Her body clenched in surprise. The coating on her cunt had begun to warm, sinking into newly shaved skin with a slightly uncomfortable tingle.

Now he was rubbing it on her ass and she couldn't help the tightening of her sphincter. His index finger tapped her ass in demand. Jill gulped in air to prepare herself but she didn't move fast enough. His other hand landed on her with another stinging slap.

"That's four and five," his deep voice rumbled above her. "Push back and open ass."

Jill squeezed her eyes shut beneath the hood and relaxed for him. Two fingers, not one, plunged into her. The slippery cream was swirled around her interior as his hand on her stinging cheek pulled her open even more. The fingers in her ass fucked in and out for what felt like several minutes. Then there were three in her. The intrusion was steady, a firm demand on her orifice, opening her to stretch around him as he injected even more of the cream into her.

The flesh of her shaved pussy was now tingling and hot. Inside and out. It didn't burn, it was just uncomfortably warm and felt like champagne bubbles were popping on it. Jill was gasping and moaning as he screwed the wicked cream deep into her ass.

Then his fingers were gone. Water ran in the sink and she could hear him washing his hands. At her side again, he loosened the strap around her waist one notch and then nothing. No sound, no touch.

The fire in her cunt and ass built. Moaning in frustration, Jill realized the loosened strap allowed her to squirm. Ass and cunt high in the air, she couldn't control the need. Seeking some relief from the fire he'd smoothed over her, her body helplessly wriggled in an effort to bring her legs together to rub the engorged folds. She needed to be rubbed so bad.

In the complete darkness of the hood, her ass and cunt on fire and demanding relief, she didn't realize it when low growls erupted from her lips as her exposed bottom moved in desperate demand for some attention. Then the light aroma of one of Holdin's expensive cigars wafted past her nose.

Jill thought her head would explode as she realized he was sitting somewhere watching her writhe in need, smoking a cigar. Totally naked to his view, every inch of her open, he was enjoying his handiwork. Her head thrashed as she whipped it around trying to find where he was. Her lips pulled back from her teeth in a grimace of deep rage and need. Almost ready to forget his command of silence her mouth opened.

He spoke into that moment. "Is there something you need, little whore?" his quiet question made her gasp in reaction.

About to tell him what an ass he was, along with a load of other things, he stopped her again. "Before you answer, remember, you have five coming already. Careful you don't add to that total." His voice was not near. He was some distance away.

Jill's head was turned to him, her teeth clenched as she breathed hard through the need.

"Be a good whore and ask nicely. You might get what you want."

In hard gasping words, she said very slowly, "Please let me off this thing."

"Certainly" was his smooth reply. "But think carefully. If you get off it, I will not assist you. Is that really what you want?"

"Yessss," she hissed at him.

His hands were undoing the straps on her legs, in a few seconds she was free and he gently helped her up off the tilted table.

Jill couldn't stand still. Her hand went immediately to her burning pussy to rub it, regardless of how she looked spreading her legs for her hands.

"You weren't given permission!" he snapped, pulling her hands away, holding them by the elbows. "That's six. Ask for what you need."

Jill froze, trying to work out what he wanted from her. She needed relief and she needed it now. In the dark interior of her hooded world, the needs of her body were magnified. He'd told her he wouldn't assist her, whatever that meant. She didn't care. She needed a touch now! "May I please touch myself," she asked shakily.

He pulled her a short distance away before answering. "Certainly. Here, lay down on this." Her feet touched the edge of a blanket. Holdin was helping her down. Jill found her bottom on the blanket. "You may do as you please as long as your legs are open," he told her softly. "Close them and you will be restrained in the proper position."

Jill gasped in reaction to the rub of the blanket on tender skin. Her body reclined back to lift needy genitals off it with straining legs. Both hands went to the fire, rubbing over drenched folds but it wasn't enough. Sobbing in relief, two fingers sank into her constricting channel. The relief was so intense her knees clenched together on her trapped hand.

"I told you what would happen," he commented quietly above her.

Hard hands grasped her legs. She couldn't bring herself to take her fingers out of her needy pussy so there was no resistance as soft straps were closed around her thigh just above the knee of one leg. The other was jerked open and restrained the same way at the end of the bar between them. The bar was pulled up, bringing her knees up somewhere above her breasts. There was a click at the ring on her choker, and another above her.

She couldn't pull her legs down. The bar was connected by a short leash to her hood. Her body was slightly bent, knees above her, spread wide. Her weight rested on her back. The blanket was hardly any covering for the concrete floor.

The shock of the hard bar ensuring her legs remained open rocked her, spiraling her into a dark place of growing excitement. How could his command of her body be even greater? Even more disturbing was how quickly that concern evaporated as her free hands moved over herself. In this position she could reach both screaming cunt and burning ass. Slick with her own juices, two slim fingers disappeared in her ass. Two from the other hand pumped in and out of her cunt and Jill moaned in snarling pleasure at the touch she gave herself.

Whatever it was he'd spread on her, it was a low fire that exploded to the touch. It created need and hunger. At least she thought it did. It drove her to do things. Made her do things.

She knew he was somewhere watching. She'd never done such a thing in her life. Somehow the hood closed her into her own world. It didn't matter. Even though she could smell his cigar, hear him shift nearby, she couldn't stop. Her busy hands rubbed and plunged into hungry openings.

Grunting in pleasure, her fingers drove her up the peak she craved so bad.

"Remember. Ask for what you need." His low voice broke into her dark, private world.

Jill's fingers slowed and she panted hard, trying to gain some control. Coming without permission was something she'd never dreamed of doing. Never. The harsh demand of her body was clamoring at her.

The cream he'd smoothed on her didn't burn anymore. Now it was all her. She'd stimulated herself deep into hedonistic desire. And he'd watched. Suddenly she could feel his eyes on her and another rush of depraved pleasure washed through her. He'd watched. He'd even restrained her so there was no obstacle to his view as her hands stroked and fingered both her cunt and ass.

At no time had he hid the fact that he watched. He'd been very deliberate about preparing her to give him this show. She couldn't escape the fact that she'd known and loved it. Every minute of her self-gratification she'd known he watched her.

Heat rolled up her body. Its sharp flames burned through the bite of embarrassment 'til there was only a faint remnant of it. She'd known he was there. Every single second she'd known it. He'd watched her. He knew her. He'd given her this.

"Please, may I come?" she gasped in a strangled whisper.

"What are you?" he asked softly.

"Your whore."

"Then you may come if you use the dildo beside you," he answered smoothly. "It's a double. Shove it in both holes. It'll be easier for you."

Jill could barely reach her ass, the promises of deep, satisfying penetration, even if he watched, brought a grateful moan. Her hand searched the blanket beside her and found the dildo. Her fingers explored it briefly. It was thick, one side fatter than the other. Both equally long. The middle was softer to bend and fit in any set of orifices. Turning it quickly, she had no trouble choosing where to put the thicker end.

Her legs restrained up, both hands available to press the fatter head into her ass, the other into cunt. It sank into her and Jill's head arched back, pulling her knees higher in the air. It felt so good, so damn good. But it was difficult to pull and push it. She tried so hard but the resistance of her body slowed the motion she needed. Sobbing she strained and couldn't quite reach the pressure and strength to push her over the edge.

"Ask for what you need," he said quietly again.

Gasping in frustrated sobs, Jill's hooded head turned to his voice. "Please, please help me. Fuck me hard."

"Are you asking me to use the dildo on you?"

"Yes!"

"Certainly, but this might be more comfortable for you." He deftly lifted and rolled her so she rested on her knees. The bar and its leash held her in a tight crouch but it was much more comfortable.

"Lift. Ask for it," he instructed.

In this position Jill could straighten her legs and raise her ass. Asking physically and verbally for the fuck. "Please, fuck me," she sobbed.

The complete submission of raising her ass and cunt, asking him to use the toys protruding from them took her to a new high of submission. His eyes on her, his hand ramming the thick dildo into her was what she needed. He was the only one who could give her this. Her body was dying for it. Her mind overwhelmed with the place he'd taken her to.

"Good girl," he crooned, and then he gripped the center of the dildo and used it on her like the fuck toy she was. Hard and fast he powered it in and out. Her body sucked it in eagerly, pressing back on it with each thrust. The cream that only had heated for about ten minutes lubricated both her orifices and allowed the thick ends of the dildo to ram her ruthlessly.

Her body climbed back to desperation fast and hard. Then his hand landed on her ass in time with each thrust. It was too much. She screamed unimaginable pleasure. His amazing mix of pleasure and pain reached a new level. His ownership drove her with each sharp spank. Jill came in shattering waves. Her mouth open in a gasping howl as he pounded her through it.

Abruptly he stopped. Both the fucking and the spanking. She was done but he'd never just stopped like that before. He pulled the dildo from her body and unsnapped the spreader bar from her legs. Jill fell to the side, gasping. Holdin pulled her legs down, rubbing calves and thighs briskly, making sure the circulation was good as he turned her on her back and removed the bar and leash.

Last, he unbuckled the hood and pulled it off her. Jill lay unmoving on the blanket with her eyes closed. After the deep dark of the hood, she didn't really want to open her eyes. Amazingly she acknowledged that she didn't want the hood off. It had been her private world. A safe place where she could do outrageous things.

Off to the side she could hear the water running in the sink again. Turning her head slowly she opened her eyes a slit and watched him wash the dildo. Then set it in the sink drainboard as he washed his hands. Without turning around he spoke. "Come here. Wash your hands."

Jill rose to her feet. It wasn't as difficult as she thought it might be. The concrete was cold again as she stepped off the blanket and went to the sink. He handed her the soap and stepped back as she washed.

Leaning against the drainboard, he watched her. Jill kept her head down, concentrating on her task. When she was done, hands dried, she stood there staring at them.

"Good girl," he approved. "Waiting for instruction. You're learning."

She hadn't consciously been doing that. But it was true. That's exactly what she'd done.

"Come here." He held out his arms. Jill almost tripped rushing into them. She sobbed in gulping gasps of air as his big body wrapped around her. "Shhhhh, baby, shhhhh," he crooned, and lifted her into his arms, carrying her to a large leather chair. He sat with her cuddled in his lap and began rocking them both on the smooth gliders. Jill wept in sobbing reaction, clinging to him with arms wrapped tightly around his neck. Holdin petted her back and bottom tenderly as she shook with emotion.

"I'm so proud of you, baby," he praised her softly. "Such a beautiful, sweet whore. My pretty little cunt." His tender tone mingled with the words of ownership arrowed into her heart. All of those things were true. For him she was all of these things. And she found she was proud of it too.

The emotional storm eased and she lay in his arms panting lightly. Naked while he held her fully clothed and she didn't care. He was the strength she needed. The safe place to bring her desires.

Her tears dried and as she lay on his chest her hand shyly stroked up and down the center of it.

"Do you know why we came here tonight?" he asked her. "Look up here, baby. Let me see your eyes and we'll talk about it."

Jill pulled back to look at him. For some reason she blushed. It wasn't her nakedness or even what he'd watched her do. It was how clearly he looked into her soul.

"Please tell me," she asked softly, remembering his instructions to ask for what she needed.

"It's because you were running away from me again," he told her seriously. "You wanted something and refused to tell me. Choosing to hide it from me. You wanted your dominant. Your husband knew it and I kept waiting for you to ask me. Tell me. I've waited so damn long for you, Jilly-girl. Stop making me wait."

Jill bit her lip in shame. He was right. Tonight he'd given her everything she needed and more. Taken her and yet, she'd gone exactly were she wanted to go. He'd drawn the starving whore out of her soul and showed her how much he wanted her just like that. Just as she wanted to be. The only thing that had ever come between them had been her inability to be honest with that whore. To trust him with her. Handing over ownership of that needy woman to the man who made her "needy" seemed so simple. It wasn't.

Jill swallowed hard. She'd disappointed him and herself. He knew her. He knew her soul and he'd known her needs even when she didn't have the nerve to face them.

"After tonight do you think there is anything I don't want to see about you? Can you possibly think there is something you need to hide? Something I don't want to help you with?" he asked seriously.

"No."

Holdin's hand came up from her back to cradle her head in his palm. "I love you so much," he whispered as he drew her mouth to his. The kiss was deep as she opened to him. He let her head fall back in the surrender she needed while still supporting her. Lifting his lips off her, he smiled softly.

Looking directly into her eyes, his free hand smoothed over her rounded belly, down to the bare, tender skin below it. "Spread, my wayward little whore," he growled into her lips. "Time for the pussy spanks you've earned tonight."

Jill gasped, her eyes lighting in a new fire as she understood his intentions. Her legs shifted over the arm of the chair, spreading as wide as she could manage. Her body arched up into his palm.

Holdin's fingers drifted lightly down over bare, sensitive folds as he looked into the future in her eyes. Her face flushed crimson in a blush she apparently would never outgrow. Gently he stroked her eager pussy, bringing her body to humming excitement. "So beautiful," he whispered, kissing down her neck. "So fucking beautiful."

Even as she blushed, her hips pressed up into his touch. His naughty little witch strained to spread herself open for him, drawing her legs wider. She became decadent greed under his hand.

Coming back to her mouth, he covered it as his hand rose and landed in a gentle smack. His hand remained holding her stinging folds, applying pressure as his head lifted from her lips.

"Open your eyes. Look at me," he demanded softly. "That's my good girl. Whose cunt is this?"

Jill was panting harshly as her eyes lifted to his. Looking him in the eye made her even more naked to him. Loving this was so shattering, and he knew she wanted to hide that little piece of herself from him. He wouldn't allow it.

"Your cunt," Jill whispered.

His hand rose again to deliver the stinging pleasure. "Mine," he breathed as she jerked in wicked bliss. His finger stroked lightly over sensitized folds as he continued. "What has my cunt learned?"

"No hiding."

Her reward was another sharp spank, followed by knowing fingers swirling around her contracting opening. Teasing but not dipping into her hungry channel.

Jill longed for the dark safety of that hood now. He'd taught her that too. She couldn't keep her hips from undulating for him, begging him with her body. His beautiful face smiled as his hand rose again. "What do you get when you hide?" His hand landed in an explosion of sensation.

Jill wailed as her body jerked. The intensity of his voice and touch drawing her so fully into the moment that his stroking fingers felt like branding irons moving over her.

"Nothing," she gasped. "Hiding means the nothingness again."

"Yessss, for both of us," he agreed as the dizzying pleasure of sharp smacks to engorged folds came in quick succession now. His lips dove down to her open mouth. Jill screamed into his mouth and came again on the last smack. Convulsing in his arms, he folded her into his chest while she shuddered. His grip was almost desperate. Her need and his were one and always had been. She could take them both to hell or heaven. It would always be her choice. He needed her to know that. Understand they both paid a price.

Panting heavily from the short but hard orgasm, she buried her face in his neck. He was so intensely powerful to her. Larger than life in ways that forever amazed her. She'd been ashamed of how much she needed him. And he knew. He always knew.

Now she was ashamed of not trusting him. Not being strong enough to know that her needs were his. He'd waited so patiently for her. Denying his feelings so she could grow up in hers. Waiting for her to stop being afraid of who she was.

The erotic spanking coupled with his complete control was exactly what she craved. That was why she loved the stimulation so much, she realized. It took her over the edge every time. The combination of exploding sensation and his absolute commitment to her as he gave her the freedom to surrender her soul into his keeping. He could hurt her so badly but he didn't. That dangerous edge of submission to Holdin was her addiction. His voice broke into her hazy glide back to reality.

"I have something for you. I want you to remember tonight," he murmured into her bent head. "Every time you look in the mirror I want to you remember this night and know it's yours any time. Who we are right now is always true. No matter what else we do outside the doors of our bedroom. Now sit up straight."

Holdin picked her up and turned her to face him. Holding her above his lap, he instructed her to drape her legs over the arms of the chair.

When he'd finished, she was sitting on his knees facing him, her body spread in submissive exposure. It felt so much more decadent now that he'd shaved her. Jill shivered in shy excitement as he gazed at her. It was like feeling power burn over her body and her head dipped down to avoid the intensity of it.

"Hands behind your back. Look at me. See how perfect you are to me," he said as his eyes moved down over her breasts and down her body. "Good girl," he praised when her back straightened and arched for him.

Reaching beside him to the short table there, he picked up a case. Flipping it open, he pulled out a sparkling gold chain. The links were sturdy like one saw on men's bracelets though not thick and masculine. It was a delicate chain of glowing gold with a small padlock at one end.

Jill gasped. Her eyes wide as she looked at the very obvious collar. Putting that around her neck would make this part of their relationship very public. Something he'd never hinted at doing before. A chain with a lock like that could not be mistaken for anything else.

Holdin smiled as he held it and watched her. She didn't shrink back. "That's my brave little whore. Stand up please," he approved.

Deep within, his hardened warrior melted for her again. She was magnificent. He knew what she thought he'd do and she was facing him bravely. Submitting her entire self into his keeping and he thought he might explode with pride in her. There was nothing he'd love more than to proclaim to the world what an amazing woman she was. But the world wasn't ready to see what he had. No. He'd never place his precious Jill in an uncomfortable situation. Her trust in him, even now, was unfathomable. Living up to it would take a lifetime.

Jill slid off his lap to stand in front of him.

"Give me your right foot and hold on to my shoulder," he instructed.

Jill's foot in his lap, Holdin snapped the anklet around her and clicked the pretty lock. On her ankle, it was a beautiful piece of jewelry. The only thing hinting at what it really signified was the lock securing it on her.

Jill stared at it in wonder. The rich gold glowed against her skin. The little lock looked lovely against the glow of her skin. Placing it on her ankle was so perfect. Looking up into his eyes, she smiled in shy amazement.

"Thank you."

Holdin pulled her back into his arms, hugging her fiercely. "Baby, I know you thought that was a new collar. There's no need for that between us. You are as free as your heart wants to be. The choice is always yours." He breathed in deeply as he told her what she knew. "All I want is to remind you that those feet need to come to me, Jilly-girl. My heart is the only place you bring a problem. No matter what it is."

Also by Gail Faulkner

೫

eBooks:
Ask For It
Darius
Full Ride
Into His Keeping
Jamie's Cherub
Romeo
Slip Knot
Stealing Carmen
Wanna Play

Print Books:
Hurts So Good
Knot Tonight
Jamie's Cherb
Slip Knot

About the Author

෨

Hello everyone. If you're reading this, I hope it means you've enjoyed reading one of my books. If you have some other opinion of them, feel free to lie to me anyway. I hereby absolve you from all possible guilt and consequences for flagrant, adjective, saturated lying to the author.

I'm a chronic fantasizer. Every good romance novel ended too soon. After awhile, I started making up stories when I had a few minutes to while away. So now, instead of sitting around with a blank look on my face, I've taken to writing them down.

Because of my father's job, we moved every three years in my early life. My first memories are of Bermuda, and then we were in several African countries. It was a wonderful childhood. I gained a rich cultural background in the world community, but never learned to spell. As an adult, I avoided writing at all costs, embarrassed over my limitations.

But the writer will not stay silent forever. She broke out, and insisted on learning the mystical world of grammar and spelling. Haven't mastered all of it yet, but they let me write for you anyway. Bless every editor on the planet. They give dreamers a place to send fantasies and save us the embarrassment of owning our shortcomings.

Gail Faulkner welcomes comments from readers. You can find her website and email address on her author bio page at www.ellorascave.com.

Tell Us What You Think

We appreciate hearing reader opinions about our books. You can email us at Comments@EllorasCave.com.

Why an electronic book?

We live in the Information Age — an exciting time in the history of human civilization, in which technology rules supreme and continues to progress in leaps and bounds every minute of every day. For a multitude of reasons, more and more avid literary fans are opting to purchase e-books instead of paper books. The question from those not yet initiated into the world of electronic reading is simply: *Why?*

1. *Price.* An electronic title at Ellora's Cave Publishing and Cerridwen Press runs anywhere from 40% to 75% less than the cover price of the exact same title in paperback format. Why? Basic mathematics and cost. It is less expensive to publish an e-book (no paper and printing, no warehousing and shipping) than it is to publish a paperback, so the savings are passed along to the consumer.

2. *Space.* Running out of room in your house for your books? That is one worry you will never have with electronic books. For a low one-time cost, you can purchase a handheld device specifically designed for e-reading. Many e-readers have large, convenient screens for viewing. Better yet, hundreds of titles can be stored within your new library — on a single microchip. There are a variety of e-readers from different manufacturers. You can also read e-books on your PC or laptop computer. (Please note that Ellora's Cave does not endorse any specific brands.

You can check our websites at www.elloracave.com or www.cerridwenpress.com for information we make available to new consumers.)

3. *Mobility.* Because your new e-library consists of only a microchip within a small, easily transportable e-reader, your entire cache of books can be taken with you wherever you go.
4. *Personal Viewing Preferences.* Are the words you are currently reading too small? Too large? Too… ANNOYING? Paperback books cannot be modified according to personal preferences, but e-books can.
5. *Instant Gratification.* Is it the middle of the night and all the bookstores near you are closed? Are you tired of waiting days, sometimes weeks, for bookstores to ship the novels you bought? Ellora's Cave Publishing sells instantaneous downloads twenty-four hours a day, seven days a week, every day of the year. Our webstore is never closed. Our e-book delivery system is 100% automated, meaning your order is filled as soon as you pay for it.

Those are a few of the top reasons why electronic books are replacing paperbacks for many avid readers.

As always, Ellora's Cave and Cerridwen Press welcome your questions and comments. We invite you to email us at Comments@ellorascave.com or write to us directly at Ellora's Cave Publishing Inc., 1056 Home Avenue, Akron, OH 44310-3502.

Discover for yourself why readers can't get enough of the multiple award-winning publisher

Ellora's Cave.

Whether you prefer e-books or paperbacks,

be sure to visit EC on the web at
www.ellorascave.com

for an erotic reading experience that will leave you breathless.

Made in the USA
Lexington, KY
10 August 2011